SINCERELY, GRACE

THE KNOCKNASHEE STORY

BOOK 4

JEAN GRAINGER

CHAPTER 1

KNOCKNASHEE, CO KERRY, IRELAND

NOVEMBER 1941

Grace McKenna sat contentedly as the wind and rain off the ocean buffeted the house, causing the windows to rattle and the front door to creak. It was a feature of life on the Dingle Peninsula, and nobody ever truly won against the wind; draught excluders and heavy curtains could only do so much. The storm had been raging since early afternoon, but the old fishermen said it would blow itself out before midnight, and they knew far more than the weatherman who used to be on the wireless from Dublin.

That man was silent now. The government had put a stop to his forecast once the Emergency began two years ago, just in case the Germans were tuning in to Irish radio. Not that it would have done Hitler any good if they were; the man's predictions were always wildly wrong. The only way to properly tell the weather on the Dingle

Peninsula was to heed what the old fishermen had to say as they sat mending their nets of an evening.

The weather was the reason two German spies had come ashore in Dingle last year with all sorts of meteorological equipment. They didn't get away with it. The local publican saw sand on the shoes of the first man and noticed something about his accent was off, so he got him drunk on whiskey until the guards turned up. The second German kept his transmitter buried on the beach and did get off a few messages, but he was picked up after two days. Strangers stood out here in the rural west of Ireland; nobody could do anything without getting noticed straight away.

For instance, there wasn't a soul in Knocknashee who didn't know Charlie McKenna's new wife, Dymphna, was expecting, even though she had told nobody, only made the mistake of looking at baby clothes in Peggy Donnelly's drapery shop and mentioning she'd asked Mary O'Hare for a remedy for a sick stomach.

Grace was so happy for her friend, but she'd also felt a twinge of envy at first. Her new 'mother-in-law', as she laughingly called Dymphna these days, would be forty next year, while Grace was still only twenty-one, and they'd been married the same length of time, three months, Dymphna to Charlie and Grace to Charlie's son, Declan.

But her jealousy had subsided because, if her calculations were correct, she was three days late, so it looked like having polio as a child hadn't ruined her chances of having a baby after all, despite that horrible comment from Canon Rafferty about her 'ill health' precluding her from her duty to God.

She hoped with all her heart that she was about to prove that horrible priest wrong. She was in such a hurry to fill this home with the happy voices of children. For a long time after her parents died and her sister, Agnes, ruled the roost, this house was cold and austere. But now it was back as she remembered it as a little girl, warm and cosy and welcoming to all.

Smiling at the thought, Grace put aside the letter she was writing and reached across from her armchair to turn the wireless up; there was a lovely programme of songs on, and she enjoyed having it playing in the background as the weather raged outside. The fire crackled merrily in the sitting room grate, and her young husband sat in the armchair on the opposite side of the hearth, reading a Dickens novel, his long legs stretched out towards the warmth. The light of the flames played across his fine-boned face, lending his high cheekbones a faint flush, and he looked so well and healthy.

She felt a rush of love for him. His tall frame had filled out, and even without the help of the firelight, he was so much less pale than when he'd returned from the reformatory four years ago. Twelve years of his life he had spent in Letterfrack – his mother dead, his baby sister sent to be adopted – taken from his father as a six-year-old boy because the canon deemed Charlie McKenna, then a humble labourer, unfit to cope as a single father. At last, after everything the priests did to him in the reformatory, the cold and fear and endless beatings, Declan had come home. His father, now the village postman, had minded him until he was strong, physically and mentally, and then Declan had fallen in love with Grace, and she with him of course, and at long last, he was safe and happy.

Grace watched him as he read, slowly turning the pages of *Great Expectations*. She loved the serious face he made when he was concentrating, whether on a novel or on one of his construction projects, or as a teacher gently explaining something to the senior children in her school, giving them the impression that there was all the time in the world.

He would make a wonderful father. She hadn't said anything to him about her missing period yet. She would leave it another two weeks maybe, to be safe…

Sensing her gaze, Declan glanced up with a smile of his own, using his finger to keep his place in the book. 'Am I in trouble?' His indigo-blue eyes twinkled at her as he raised his dark eyebrows under a mop of dark-brown silky hair.

'No why?'

'Because you were staring at me the way you do if one of the children is doing something they shouldn't.'

'No, you're on your best behaviour, Mr McKenna. Just keep it up and I'll give you a gold star.' She winked.

'I'd prefer a different reward.' He winked.

She chuckled. 'Well, we'll see...'

'Seriously, though, is there something on your mind?'

How well he knew her. 'Oh, nothing,' she said airily, and cast around for something interesting to say to stop herself blurting out about the possibility of her being pregnant. 'Tilly was here this morning while you were out with Paudie and Kate at the beach.'

Paudie and Kate were Dymphna's children from her first marriage to Tommy O'Connell. Poor Tommy had taken his own life, and Dymphna was devastated, but she had learnt to live and love again and Charlie and she were a perfect pair. Declan and his father had taken her children down to the strand to see the Barnacle geese, newly arrived from Greenland for the winter. Though the real reason was to give Dymphna time to rest as she was expecting a baby. Nine-year-old Paudie and seven-year-old Kate weren't difficult children but she was exhausted. Paudie was a sweet boy and incredibly clever, with a face that would melt the hardest of hearts, green eyes with amber flecks, dark auburn hair and a serious expression, although when he smiled, it lit up a room.

When he got interested in a topic, he needed to know every single thing about it. At the moment it was migratory birds, and everyone in Knocknashee, from Bríd Butler in the sweetshop to Nancy O'Flaherty in the post office, had become much more knowledgeable about the flight patterns and laying habits of all of the different types on the peninsula.

Paudie was such a sweet little lad, nobody thought him a know-it-all; they just accepted his cleverness and loved him for it. Hilariously his best friend was Teddy Lonergan, who couldn't give two hoots about school and only wanted to be farming all day, every day. As was often the way of friendships, it couldn't be explained but worked perfectly.

'The damp makes Tilly's mam's rheumatism so much worse,' Grace added. 'Poor Mary is really struggling now Dymphna has the morning sickness and can't go up to mind baby Odile while Tilly is out in the fields. And the farmhouse is up in a heap again – they've even lost that lovely photo of Alfie and Constance. Tilly's been searching everywhere, but the clutter has got really bad. Everything disappears, especially now Odile is nearly two and toddling around. Tilly's getting panicky about it all because Eloise is coming for Christmas and she wants to have the place nice.'

'Ah, Eloise is easy-going enough, and I'm sure she'll muck in and help clean,' said Declan lightly, going back to his book. 'And Odile loves her.'

'I know she does.' Grace sighed. 'And her French is coming on so well.'

Grace struggled to like Tilly's new friend. Tilly and Grace had been best friends since baby infants, so it hurt to feel she was playing second fiddle to a Jean Harlow lookalike from the Swiss Alps, a language teacher who spoke fluent English, French, German and Italian, who was an amazing amateur photographer and brilliant at the piano and who could climb the local cliffs like a mountain goat.

Eloise had won over everyone in the village, even the bad-tempered cobbler Pádraig O Sé, to whom she'd presented a pair of traditional Swiss dancing shoes with silver buckles because he was so fascinated by the stitching on hers. The only person who didn't think Eloise was marvellous was the canon, and that only made everyone else like her even more. Grace wished the Swiss woman could have just one fault, but it seemed she couldn't put a foot wrong.

Grace knew she shouldn't be a dog in the manger. She spent so much time with Declan now, and she didn't begrudge Tilly the companionship of Eloise. It was just...

She went back to her letter, resting the sheet of thick cream paper on the encyclopaedia of Irish seabirds she'd been reading earlier in an attempt to keep up with Paudie's endless questions. The letter was to Richard, who had written to her a week ago, sending news of the war from London. Everything about the Emergency was censored in the Irish press, so it had been fascinating to hear his eyewitness account.

She was glad they were corresponding properly again, as friends.

He'd written her such a cold, short letter after she'd told him about her engagement to Declan. And then for a wedding present, he'd sent that very expensive set of Victorian silver cake forks and a cake server nestled in a leather box on royal-blue velvet. As if she was someone snooty like his ex-girlfriend Miranda and not a girl from a simple village in the west of Ireland, with no use for fancy cake servers – if indeed there was any cake, which there hardly was these days thanks to the rationing. Dymphna, when she felt well enough to bake, was doing her best with lard instead of butter, but it wasn't the same.

It must have been the stress of the Blitz that made Richard act so out of character, because now that it ended, thank God, he'd gone back to being his warm, chatty, good-natured self, though no less busy in his job as the Capital's London war correspondent. He and his friend, the photographer Jacob Nunez, worked around the clock, and their New York editor's voracious appetite for copy and pictures prompted Richard's sister, Sarah, to also send in stories now for the women's column. She worked with a female photographer called Pippa Wills, the girl Richard had pulled from a burning house and who now seemed to have moved in with the three Americans.

'SHE SOUNDS LIKE A NICE GIRL. I hope that turns into something,' Declan had commented when she'd told him about Pippa. Her husband never asked to see her letters, but she always read them to him anyway; she felt it was important for Declan to know she kept no secrets. And besides, Richard's letters were very entertaining.

She even read some extracts to the children in school, and they made a game out of finding Americanisms.

Most of the children spoke English, if a little haltingly and very reluctantly, and they didn't enjoy learning it, preferring their own native language, so anything to make it seem a bit more fun was a good thing. Associating the language with America, instead of England, was in its favour too. Memories were tenacious, and the English language, the accent, everything about it caused a visceral reaction in a population brutalised by their nearest neighbour for centuries.

Picking up her fountain pen, a gift from the Warringtons, Grace scanned what she'd written to Richard so far, using her usual lilac ink. She'd talked about the school, and how the canon had got bored trying to catch the children out on their catechism; they were too quick and clever for him, so he barely bothered coming into the class any more. And she'd mentioned that there was a new housekeeper at the priest's house, a meek older lady called Mrs Coughlan.

Now she added that Tilly had still heard nothing from her brother, Alfie, and his fiancée, Constance; Grace called them 'A' and 'C' because they were fighting for the French resistance and no one knew who was reading these letters. Then she wrote a bit about the awful weather, though when she stopped to listen, she realised the wind had died down and the rain was only tapping lightly on the window now. The old fishermen were right – the storm was fading.

What else should she say? Something about Pippa perhaps. Richard had not said as much, but like Declan, Grace suspected it might 'turn into something'. And she hoped it would, of course. She sucked the end of the pen, then wrote, *I'm delighted your editor is paying Sarah and your friend Pippa to write and take photos for the* Capital. *I wish it hadn't taken a war for people to realise what women can do given half a chance.*

She sucked her pen again, thinking she should cross out the last sentence, because it seemed very callous, like she thought the war was a good thing...

A loud knock on the door interrupted her thoughts.

'Who can be calling at this time of night?' Declan said as he laid his book down and went out into the hall.

Grace heard muffled voices, and then Declan reappeared with his father, Charlie, damp and windswept, looking stern. Immediately she feared for the baby. Charlie was so excited to be a father again. It would be a tragedy if Dymphna lost the child.

'What's wrong?' she asked anxiously, looking from one to the other of them.

'A lifeboat is after being pulled ashore,' Declan told her. 'English merchant seamen, two dead, three alive just about. Their ship was hit by a U-boat about half a mile out.'

'Oh God…' Though she was relieved it wasn't bad news about the baby, her heart sank. There had been several attacks on cargo ships in Irish waters since the war started. Technically the U-boats were not meant to violate Irish neutrality, and that included territorial waters, but Hitler cared nothing for those kinds of laws.

'Dr Ryan has taken the three survivors to hospital in his car,' added Charlie, unbuttoning the collar of his coat in the warmth of the sitting room. 'They said there's five bodies in the water, all dead they think, but two other lifeboats too. Those men are still alive, but their own boat was drifting without oars and they lost visual contact a few hours ago as the sun set.'

'Oh that's awful.' She knew now what was coming, and her stomach tightened.

'So we're getting a crew of local men together to take out their *naomhógs*.' *Naomhóg*, or 'little saint', was the Kerry name for a *currach*, the traditional west-of-Ireland fishing boat, ideal for the shallow coves and choppy waters. 'The more eyes we can have out there, the better the chance of finding them. The chances are slim, but you never know.'

'Will you come out with me, Da?' Declan had dragged his oilskin jacket on over his shirt and sweater and was ready to go.

Charlie didn't have his own *currach*, but Declan had one he had built himself with the help of Seán O'Connor. The local undertaker had made the sturdy frame, his coffin-making skills coming in handy, and Declan had covered the hull in cow hides, then slathered them inside and out with tar. And he'd fitted an outboard motor, something few fishermen had ever seen. He'd got it from a shipyard in Cork, and it had worked for a bit but then gave up. Declan stripped it down and repaired it even fashioning some spare parts himself out of brass. His was the only *currach* with a motor; all the others were still propelled by oars. He'd even found some strong oak to use as a stern board to attach it to.

'No, you've only room for Seán and John O'Shea. John can't row since he hurt his shoulder, but he knows the coves better than anyone. I'll go in with Oliver Daly's grandsons – there's two of them in it, so they have room for one more.' Charlie buttoned up his collar again and headed down the hall to the front door. 'I'm just going to let Dymphna know we're both going.'

'I'll join you outside in a minute, Da.'

'Right, I'll make some sandwiches and a flask of tea, and I'll bring it to the pier.' Now that she was alone with Declan, Grace hitched up her skirt and put her calliper back on; she'd removed it earlier to be more comfortable. She loved that she didn't have to be shy about her crippled leg in front of her husband; he seemed to genuinely worship every part of her. Only that evening he had helped her with her exercises after she'd had her hot bath. She blushed now to think what that had nearly turned into...

Declan gently helped her with the straps and fitting the steel into her shoe. 'I can wait and take the sandwiches with me, save you going out in the rain.'

'Not at all, I'm grand. The rain is easing off now. You go down and get organised. I'll see you below.' She hugged him and sent him on his way. Alone in the kitchen, she cut bread and some leftover bacon from their dinner and made up some sandwiches. She wrapped them, along with some currant bread, in waxed paper, made a big flask of tea and put it all in a wicker basket.

In the hall she dragged on her mackintosh and tied it tightly at her waist, then pulled her hat right down over her curly copper hair, nearly covering her round green eyes and turned-up nose. She couldn't wear wellington boots because of her calliper, so she'd just have to stuff her blue leather shoes with newspaper when she got back and set them by the fire, where hopefully they'd dry out by morning.

Within five minutes she was making her way with the basket to the harbour, where the fishermen pulled their *naomhógs* up onto the shore. The wind was still quite strong, and she was tiny, less than five foot tall and as light as a feather – that's what Declan said every time he lifted her up into his arms – and a sudden gust hurried her along the street and round the corner down to the sea, where the waves were splashing high against the narrow slip.

At the pier everyone pitched in, hauling rope and loading first-aid boxes and flasks of hot tea and baskets of sandwiches the women had prepared into the boats; every available vessel in the town was employed. An emergency at sea was something the town was used to, and everyone seemed determined to help, glad now the wind was dying down, though the waves were still high.

Declan and Charlie stood on the pier, discussing with Oliver Daly – who at eighty-four was far too old to join the search but still the best head for the currents out there – which boat should go in which direction. Grace knew that Declan would be intending to go the furthest. His own *naomhóg* was rocking by the slip, tied to a bollard; John O'Shea, who was Janie's uncle as well as Mikey's father, was already aboard and eager to go, and Seán O'Connor was climbing in.

'Declan,' Grace called. He looked around, said something to his father and Oliver, then came towards her. 'Be careful, won't you?' she begged him softly as she handed him his sandwiches. 'I'm worried. When Mammy and Daddy…' She remembered with a shudder the day her parents were lost. The local men searched so long for them. And that had been in daylight, in perfect weather. It had been just one of those terrible unexpected squalls that sometimes struck the coast off the west of Ireland.

He wrapped his arms around her, not caring that it wasn't done in rural Ireland to show public affection to your wife, and cradled her head to his chest, her face against the wet oilskin. 'I'll be fine. Sure we all know this coast like the back of our hands. We probably haven't much hope of finding them, but we'll try anyway.' He pulled back slightly so he could look into her face. 'Please God, we'll find the other poor men, but either way, I'll see you in a few hours.'

'I'll be awake and waiting for you.' She smiled and reached up to kiss him. 'I love you.'

'And that fact, Mrs Grace McKenna, is a source of constant astonishment and delight to me.' He winked at her in that way that made her heart melt. 'I love you too. You mean more to me than anything.'

She felt a sudden urge to tell him about being three days late. That there might be another person now for him to love more than anything. But just then Charlie came striding over. 'Gracie, will you go up to Dymphna and keep her company and make sure she doesn't worry too much, and reassure Paudie and Kate if they wake up and don't let them wear my poor wife out with questions.'

'Of course I will, Charlie.' It always touched Grace how affectionate and gentle Charlie was towards Dymphna and her children. They'd all had a very hard time in their lives, so it was lovely to see them so happy together.

'Declan, we're ready, come on let you!' Seán O'Connor and John O'Shea were shouting for her husband, and Declan dropped a last quick kiss on Grace's head and ran.

All around, farmers and fishermen readied their oars. Dotted on the pier, holding lanterns, were the wives of the men going out, and as the men rowed away, there was nothing left for the women to do but stand along the shore and watch. As the boats disappeared into the dark, the splash of oars faded and only Declan's motor could be heard, *chug-chugging* softly until that too was gone. The rain was soft and the breeze light as the women stood, watching and waiting.

Grace heard Nancy O'Flaherty begin the hymn, and soon all the voices of the women of Knocknashee joined in unison in the hymn of the ocean, begging the Virgin Mary to look over their men this night.

Hail, Queen of Heaven, the Ocean Star,
guide of the wanderer here below.
Thrown on life's surge, we claim thy care,
save us from peril and from woe.
Mother of Christ, Star of the Sea,
pray for the wanderer, pray for me.
O gentle chaste and spotless maid,
we sinners make our prayers through thee.
Remind thy Son, that He has paid
the price of our iniquity.

Virgin most pure, Star of the Sea,
pray for the sinner, pray for me.
And while to Him, who reigns above,
in Godhead one, in persons three,
the source of life, of grace, of love,
homage we pay on bended knee.
Do, thou, bright Queen, Star of the Sea,
pray for thy children, pray for me.

Grace felt a sudden longing for Father Iggy. If he was still in Knocknashee, he would have been down here with them at the pier, offering them comfort and friendship. He would have blessed the boats and the men. He'd have opened the church to let people light a candle or say a special prayer to beg for their safe return. But of Canon Rafferty, there was no sign. Not that anyone wanted him, but still. He wouldn't dream of coming out in this filthy weather.

CHAPTER 2

The hours dragged on, each feeling as long as a day.

Grace and Dymphna drank tea – weak because of the rationing – as the fire burnt in the range. Conversations began but fell away on their lips. Mostly they just sat as the wind died to a whisper, though the persistent rain still pattered on the window.

An hour before dawn, Tilly O'Hare appeared, letting herself in the back door of the postman's kitchen. She had ridden her horse, Rua, a sorrel gelding with a silky mane and tail, down from the farm on the hill, leaving her mother to mind Odile if the little girl woke up.

'I knew you'd be here when I didn't find you home,' she said to Grace, hugging her and then Dymphna, who was pale with morning sickness, not made better by being awake all night worrying. 'Tomás Kinneally next door came to tell me about the men going out. Do you want me to go down to the pier and see what's going on?'

'No, let you stay here with Dymphna and I'll go. The sun will be coming up soon, and the tide has turned, so it should be bringing the men home.' Grace tried to sound cheerful and confident. And why wouldn't she be confident? All the fishermen knew this coast well. It was only because of what had happened to her parents that she felt so nervous, and there was no logic in that.

Dymphna got to her feet, determined. 'I'll come with you.'

'But I promised Charlie to mind you?'

'I'll tell him you couldn't stop me! I am your mother-in-law after all.' She grinned as Grace and Tilly laughed. 'And it will feel good to have something to do, not just be sitting here staring at the wall. Let's make a few more sandwiches and a flask of tea to bring down – they'll be hungry and cold when they get home.'

'Oh, but the children…' Grace glanced towards the stairs of the little one-up, one-down postman's cottage. Declan had built a sleeping loft above Charlie's bedroom for himself when he came home from the reformatory, but now that he and Grace were married and lived in her parents' house beside the school, it was perfect for Paudie and Kate.

'Tilly, will you stay behind to feed the children when they get up?' asked Dymphna. 'There's porridge in the press. Tell them I'm going down to meet Da.'

Charlie had never tried to take the place of the children's father, but Paudie and Kate had asked if they could call Charlie 'Da', the same as their new baby brother or sister was going to do. And they already looked at Declan as their big brother, Grace knew, because she'd heard Kate boasting to her friends in the junior class about being related to Mr McKenna who taught the seniors.

Tilly was pleased to be useful. 'I will, of course, and I have some of Daisy's nice creamy milk to go with it – it's outside the back door keeping cool.' Daisy was Tilly's Jersey cow, who ate thick, rich grass on a corner of the land Tilly had reclaimed from the bog.

'Thanks, Tilly. They can walk over to school themselves,' said Grace, beginning to butter bread.

'School?' Dymphna sounded surprised. 'Surely you won't open the school today? Declan will be too exhausted to teach?'

'But the canon will have something to say about me closing up without permission from the patron, so Janie will have to mind the juniors while I take the older class.'

Tilly frowned. 'You haven't slept a wink either, Grace.'

'That's true, but I don't suppose telling Canon Rafferty that will make any difference to...' Grace bit back a nasty word for the priest. She was reluctant to speak badly of a man of the cloth; it was a dangerous thing to do, especially when you were the headmistress of the village school. Nobody would be spying on her, at least she hoped not, but in Knocknashee, neighbours wandered in and out of each other's houses all the time.

'The auld *divil*,' finished Tilly under her breath.

Dymphna crossed herself. She also hated the canon, who'd had Father Iggy banished to the poorest, roughest area in Cork for blessing poor Tommy's grave, but like Grace, she knew it was safer not to say it. 'I suppose you're right, Grace. We all have to keep on going despite the emergency. And now you've said it, I'll ask Nancy to get Fiachra to do Charlie's post round as well as his own. Charlie will probably grumble I'm making an old man of him, but he's not got his full strength back since he had the shingles last year, so he'll need his rest when the tide brings them home.'

The rain had stopped and pale-yellow light crept over the horizon as the two women walked slowly down to the harbour, each carrying a small basket of supplies and leaning a little on each other. Grace's leg was aching with tiredness, and Dymphna was weak with the morning sickness, even though she pretended not to be.

John O'Shea's wife, Catherine, was there already, standing on the edge of the pier, wrapped up in her threadbare shawl, looking out across the grey sea. Seán O'Connor's snobby wife, Margaret, was beside her, a thin wiry woman with a slight dowager's hump, a head-scarf tied under her chin and wearing a good woollen coat. As the wife of the village publican and undertaker, she would normally consider herself a cut above poor Catherine O'Shea, a poor farmer's wife with fourteen children and barely two pennies to rub together, but this morning she seemed to have made an exception.

'Hello, Mrs O'Shea, Mrs O'Connor.' Grace greeted them with a friendly smile. They were all in this together.

Catherine glanced at Grace unhappily but said nothing as Margaret whispered in her ear. Declan had warned Grace that Margaret O'Connor thought the outboard motor very dangerous and was always trying to persuade her husband Sean against going out in the boat, even though he'd helped build it himself, because she was convinced it would catch on fire or something. It looked like she was frightening Catherine with the same story.

The other wives were arriving in a steady trickle, and a ripple of excitement flowed through the younger ones, who were holding their babies in their arms. 'They're coming, they're coming…' But it was only a pod of dolphins leaping and dancing far off in the early light.

Then another dark shape came over the horizon. At least ten boats had gone out, so the wait to have them all back could be a long one. As the boats drew near, Grace could make out lacy wings of water, a shower of silver drops in the morning sun, as the men rowed for shore on the incoming tide, their oars rising and dipping in the dawn.

Oliver Daly's boat was the first to the slip, rowed by Charlie and Oliver's two strapping grandsons, and Dymphna rushed with a cry of joy to embrace her husband as he climbed ashore, stiff and cold while the younger bucks bounded out. But Grace's heart sank, because although Charlie looked glad to see his wife, he was also clearly distressed. She hung back, afraid to ask, while Margaret O'Connor and Catherine O'Shea rushed forwards.

'Where are Seán and John and Declan?' snapped Margaret O'Connor, who looked more ready to be angry than upset. Catherine was a gentle little woman shrivelled by years of poverty and childbirth, but Margaret had a hard look; it was she who counted the money in the O'Connor household and made sure her husband never buried anyone for nothing, not even the families that didn't have it, nor slipped a penniless farmer a free pint, not unless half a dozen eggs were placed on the counter in return.

Charlie shuddered and looked ill. 'They're behind, I'm sure. We found the other two lifeboats, capsized, God rest them, and no sign of the other men. The empty boats were found drifting off An Fear Marbh.'

'Oh, the lifeboats…' Grace swallowed, guilty to feel relieved. So it was the English sailors who had her father-in-law so upset; they were lost forever. An Fear Marbh, translated as 'the dead man', was a nickname of Inis Tuaisceart, the most northerly of the six Blasket Islands. An Fear Marbh resembled a man lying on his back, his hands on his chest. Her parents had been returning home from the school on Great Blasket when they drowned all those years ago, and so the islands off the coast, though beautiful, always filled her with dread. 'So you have given up the search?'

Some other boats were arriving now, pulling up alongside the pier. Wet, tired, cold men clambered out and were hugged by smiling wives and ushered away for a breakfast of fresh-baked soda bread and boiled eggs and pints of tea. There were five or six boats still unaccounted for, and one or two black silhouettes against the horizon. Grace strained to see the only boat without oars and to hear the soft chugging of its engine and as she did the heavens opened once more.

Charlie put his strong, sinewy arm around her shivering shoulders and addressed all four of the women around him with a reassuring smile. 'Declan, John and Seán had another cannister of petrol, so we decided they could do one more circle of the island, for fear there were any survivors in one of the caves or something.'

The undertaker's wife turned to him, furious. 'Charlie, how could you let my Seán and Catherine's John risk their lives like that? Sure everyone knows the waters around those islands are treacherous even on a calm day, and the sea is still high after the storm. If anything happens to our husbands, while you were safely looking after yourself in Oliver Daly's boat, I'll be holding someone responsible.'

Charlie looked astonished. 'Mrs O'Connor, isn't my son out there as well? 'Twas the men's own decision.'

'To go in a boat with an engine that could catch on fire any moment?' sobbed Catherine O'Shea, clinging to Margaret.

'Mrs O'Shea, please don't worry yourself about that. Declan knows exactly what he's at, and he wouldn't take such a risk with anyone's life. I wouldn't allow him to risk his own either, he's my only son –'

'That's not true, Charlie,' snapped Margaret O'Connor. 'You have another baby on the way now, and as for Declan, he can afford to be reckless because he has no children of his own to care for, and probably never will.'

'Mrs O'Connor!' Grace felt sick with shock. Dymphna grabbed her hand and pressed it.

'Well, I'm sorry, but it's true.' Though the undertaker's wife didn't look or sound sorry at all. 'Everyone knows you will never have any children, Grace. Didn't the canon say it was impossible with the polio? But Catherine here has fourteen mouths to feed, and I have six, all boys. And a young man like Declan, brought up in a reformatory, he shouldn't have been fiddling with things he knows nothing about. No good will come of him taking a notion that the way the men rowed boats for as long as anyone can remember wasn't good enough for him. Sure he's probably as careless with his own life as your own husband was, Dymphna, when he walked out into the sea.'

Poor gentle Catherine gasped, scared and ashamed, as Dymphna stood stoically. 'Margaret, you shouldn't say such things.'

Charlie was only half listening, his gaze trained on the horizon.

Grace tried to tell herself it was only fear that made Margaret O'Connor say such a cruel thing. She longed to shout back at her how wrong she was, that at that very moment, a tiny baby was growing in her and as soon as her husband got home from the sea, she would tell him, even if it was too soon. For years she'd dreaded that she would grow up to be a spinster with no family of her own in a cold and lonely house – that's what her sister, Agnes, had always told her would happen – but it was no longer true. She was a wife, a much-loved wife, and this baby in her womb was going to be the first of many.

But before she could open her mouth, a deafening roll of thunder crashed across the sea from the direction of the islands, and the next moment, a terrible scream went up among the women further down the pier as a pillar of fire rose from the horizon towards the sky.

'Oh, good God.' Charlie spun around and limped back down the slip towards the *naomhóg*, where young Ambrose Cotter was already pushing Oliver's boat to the water's edge, along with the Daly boys. 'Ambrose, get away and let me in there.'

'Charlie, for the love of God, would you have a bit of sense! You don't know what you're going to find, and besides, you're exhausted and will only slow Liam and Dathai down. We need to get out there before the strong currents wash everything away as far as America.' Ambrose was short and stocky and, like most men around Knocknashee, both a fisherman and a farmer.

'I'm as fit as you are, and it might be my son out there!' roared Charlie. 'Let me in!'

'It might be nothing to do with them at all.' Dymphna tried to soothe him. 'If the English ship was carrying explosives, it might have been –'

'Let the strong young men go, Charlie McKenna!' screeched Margaret O'Connor, beating her fist on Charlie's back as Catherine clung to the undertaker's wife with terror in her eyes. 'Encouraging that delinquent son of yours in his prideful ideas of motors and the like, and now look what's happened!'

'Please don't say that, Margaret,' sobbed Catherine O'Shea. 'We don't know what –'

'Don't go without me, Liam, Dathai!' Charlie shrugged off the bitter woman and tried to grab the rope, but Oliver Daly approached then, placing his hand on Charlie's shoulder and leading him back up the pier away from the water.

'Ambrose is right, Charlie. Leave them to it. This is for the *garsúns* to do. 'Twill be some very hard rowing now the tide has turned, and with this southwesterly blowing, they'll have their work cut out. My boys and young Cotter are fine, strong men. They have it in them, and you'll only be in the way.' He led Charlie back. 'And as Dymphna says, it could be anything. It doesn't mean anyone is hurt. But let the lads get out there as fast as they can to put everyone's mind at rest. The swell is strong out there, Charlie. I'm sure the other men not back yet are grand, probably sheltering in one of the coves on the islands. Be patient, there's a good man. We'll just have to pray they'll be safe.'

Dymphna joined Oliver and her husband then, and Grace couldn't hear what she said to Charlie, but she could guess. After a few minutes, the postman's shoulders slumped in defeat. Dymphna placed her basket of sandwiches in the hull of Oliver Daly's *naomhóg*, then took the other basket from Grace's numb hand and added that to the supplies.

Several other men from the gathered crowd ran forward to push the boat out on the water, then stood in silence as the strong young fishermen rowed out into the frothing, foaming surf. The increasing rain meant there was very poor visibility, so within a few short minutes, they were swallowed up in the fog and the spray.

'Come on, Charlie, let's go home and wait.' Dymphna took one of her husband's arms and Grace the other, and together they walked him away from the treacherous sea. 'I'm sure Ambrose and the lads will find out what's happened, but Declan and all of the others will be safe. They'll be sheltering in a cove somewhere.'

'I pray so.' Charlie's voice sounded mechanical. Grace squeezed his arm, unable to say anything at all, her heart full of unnamed fears. *What on earth was that explosion?* Of course it wasn't the outboard motor – Declan had explained to her why Margaret O'Connor was completely wrong about the chance of that blowing up. But then, what was it? Surely the Germans hadn't fired a torpedo at a little rowboat?

Nancy O'Flaherty was at the school gate. 'I hope I'm doing the right thing, but I'll be sending back home any child who comes, Grace. Most people will know not to come anyway, but some of the ones from further out won't have heard yet. But you can't be in the classroom today. There are a few boats not back yet, and everyone is too worried to concentrate on anything else. And Charlie, we won't bother with the post at all today. The whole village will understand.'

Nancy didn't need to explain why things had changed, why it was no longer necessary to deliver the post and why not even the canon would expect the school to be opened.

In Charlie's house, Tilly had Kate and Paudie up and dressed, each finishing a bowl of porridge. Without asking, she put out three more bowls and served them out, honey and the top of the milk on each. 'Let the children see you eating,' she whispered as Grace pushed the bowl away.

It was strange, but once she took a mouthful of the warm, soothing, sweet porridge, she found she was hungry after all. And of course what Dymphna had said was true. The explosion was probably nothing to do with any of the *naomhógs*. It was all the talk about outboard motors and Margaret O'Connor's hysteria that had got under her skin... Obviously it wasn't true. God wouldn't let that happen to her, to have the sea take her parents and then take Declan. It wasn't possible. That would be too cruel.

CHAPTER 3

'I've run your bath,' Tilly said quietly as Grace sat in the armchair by the fire. 'It will help your leg.'

Grace didn't answer. Her leg hurt, but she was used to it. And compared to the other pain, it was nothing.

'Come on, Grace, I'll help you.'

She allowed herself to be steered by Tilly towards the bath house Declan had built for her, and where he'd installed her water heater and her bath.

Since the news broke last night, people had come and gone – Nancy O'Flaherty, Biddy O'Donoghue bringing some ham, Tomás Kinneally, so many more. Tilly's friend Eloise was catching the train down from Dublin to express her sadness. It was all a blur. But mercifully now the house was quiet. Tilly must have sensed she didn't want anyone else, so Eloise hugged her, said how much she admired Declan and left with Mary O'Hare and Odile.

Sergeant Keane was the last person to visit. He had the job of telling them the news.

He thought it was a naval mine, floating and ready to detonate if a ship so much as touched it. There would be no bodies. Declan and the others might have thought the mine was some debris from the lifeboats and decided to investigate.

They were out there now, trying to recover all they could, but it didn't matter. Declan was dead. Catherine O'Shea was a widow, and someone else would have to take over as undertaker in Knocknashee because poor Seán O'Connor, who had buried the people of this place since he was a boy by his father's side, was now at the bottom of the sea.

The town was in shock and mourning. The sea had taken its fair share of people from the locality. It was bountiful and fed their families, but it could be cruel too. It had taken her parents, and now it was to be Declan's grave as well.

Charlie and she were both cold and numb. They should have been a comfort to one another, but they had nothing to offer anyone. Charlie kept going out to see if he could find Declan's body; a futile exercise, but nothing would dissuade him. She knew from the time her parents drowned that this numbness was temporary; she recognised it. She didn't cry or rail or scream or react at all really. She was frozen. It felt horribly familiar. The unbearable pain would come later.

Hugh and Lizzie Warrington had come, coaxing her to eat, trying to reach her, but it was as if she were underwater. She could hear them and see them, but they were indistinct and distant. They were needed at the hospital so stayed overnight but then went back to Cork. She was touched by their kindness, but nobody could help her now.

She allowed Tilly to help her undress, and she lowered herself into the water. The air outside was cold but the water was warm, and she felt the familiar release of pain from her leg. Tilly said she'd be back in twenty minutes.

She ran a film of Declan in her mind over and over. His laugh, his crinkly eyes, the face he made when he was concentrating on one of his projects, his gentle way with the children in school, explaining something to them, giving them the impression that there was all the time in the world. Then her mind wandered to the nights in the sitting room, the fire glowing in the hearth, she in his arms as he kissed her and told her how he loved her, how beautiful she was, how he never could have imagined such joy. And as soon as the glow of those happy memories faded, her mind went to when he told her about his life in Letterfrack, what the priests there did to him, the cold and fear. She couldn't bear it. Sweet Declan, whipped from his father as a little boy, his mother dead, his little sister vanished. And then after enduring that awful experience in Letterfrack, he came home and they fell in love. At long last he was safe, content and doing what he loved.

He was funny and kind and gentle. He wrote once a month to his sister, Lily Maheady, in Rockaway Beach, New York, though she wasn't aware of the connection yet. And now she would never know him as her big brother. And Charlie, who almost went mad in his grief at the loss of his wife and children but managed to cobble together a life for himself out of such unspeakable loss, had his son restored to him just a few short years ago. How cruel life was, how awful, that the sea would take his son away from him again. How could he bear it?

The gentle knock on the bath house door cut through her thoughts. Tilly was back and had brought Grace's nightdress and dressing gown and slippers. She helped her dress and brought her into the kitchen.

'You have a visitor,' Tilly said gently. 'He's in the sitting room.'

'I don't want to see anyone, Tilly. Can't you…' She couldn't take any more sympathies.

Tilly led her out to the hall and into the sitting room. 'It'll be all right, Grace, trust me.'

But before she could reply, she saw Father Iggy, his thick glasses, his round face, and he stood as she entered the cosy room. The wireless was playing and the fire glowed. It wasn't the done thing for priests to be physically affectionate, but he opened his arms to her and she allowed herself to be enveloped in a hug. He wasn't much taller than she was, but she drew strength from his presence.

'I'm so sorry, Grace. What a terrible, terrible thing…'

She was glad he didn't go on with God's plan or how the good were taken young. She knew people meant well, but she'd had to listen to a lot of that and she'd have to bite her tongue if Father Iggy started that nonsense. She felt so angry, that was the truth. She'd discovered it in the bath. Her silence wasn't grief, or sadness or loss; it was white-hot fury.

This God, who was supposed to love her, had taken her parents, then her sister, Agnes. He'd given her polio, and now he'd taken Declan. She had no interest in anyone talking about God.

But this was different. Father Iggy might be God's representative on earth, but he was her friend.

Tilly withdrew, leaving them alone. The priest released her and placed his hands on her shoulders, his large eyes searching hers through his thick glasses.

'Talk to me, Grace,' he said quietly.

She opened her mouth, but no sound came out. She couldn't speak; it was like something was stuck in her windpipe. She swallowed and tried again, and when the words came, they arrived in a whispered torrent.

'I hate God, Father Iggy, I hate him so much. How could he do this? Have we all not had enough sorrow? Have we all not endured enough?' It was like she couldn't stop the words coming. 'How dare he do this to me? How dare he take Declan? He's not a kind God who loves us – that's a load of rubbish. If he exists at all, and I really don't think he does, then he's a mean, vengeful, cruel God and I want nothing to do with him, nothing at all.' The words became rasping sobs that scratched her throat raw.

He led her to the sofa and sat down beside her, leaning towards her, his voice gentle. 'I don't blame you one bit. 'Tis a very, very hard blow, and I'm not going to say any of the things that people say to make themselves feel better to you.'

'Thanks.' She managed a small smile.

'I think when people go on with "ah, they had a good innings" or "only the good die young", well, really what they're saying is "I don't want to be uncomfortable, I don't want to acknowledge your pain because I wouldn't know what to do with it, and I'm afraid I'll say the wrong thing, and me being comfortable is more important than you being able to say how you feel."'

Grace looked at him. His light-blue eyes were kind and wise.

'So you can tell me how you really feel, and I won't say things to make you stop or old platitudes or anything. It might not help, but it might. And getting things off your chest is always good.'

She inhaled, steadying herself. 'It's all so unfair. Poor Declan. He was just a happy little boy, and then his mammy died and his little sister was stolen and he was sent to a place that no child should ever have been sent to. They did terrible things to him, Father, terrible, so terrible I can't even say it.'

He nodded but didn't interrupt, his eyes mirroring her pain.

'And then God took my parents, and they were wonderful. Everyone loved them. I tried not to be angry or bitter or complaining, but then I got polio, and Agnes was so mean to me, and I took care of her anyway, and when she died, I found out about the canon and what an awful person he is. And I probably shouldn't say it about a priest, but he was evil, the things he made her do. And I know it wasn't all his fault, but she was just a girl and he was a grown man, and he led her on, made her think there was something between them, and he works for God. And then Declan said he loved me, like really loved me, like a man would love a woman, and I never thought in a million years that could happen to me because of my leg and everything. But Declan didn't care about that. He just loved me as I am, and I loved him too. We went to America, we found his little sister, and she's a happy girl with a nice family, so he was so relieved about it, and finally – finally – he had some joy in his life, for the first time since he was a child. He'd endured so much, we both did really. But we got married and then he was taken away from me. And I hate God… I HATE HIM!'

She screamed 'I hate him' over and over till her voice was coming in raw raspy howls and she had no more strength.

Father Iggy let her rage. He didn't try to soothe her or stop her or contradict anything she said. Eventually she stopped, breathless with the exertion of it all.

He gave her a handkerchief from his pocket and poured her a cup of tea from the brown earthenware pot Tilly must have made while she was in the bath, the one her mother had poured thousands of cups from. He added milk and a spoon of sugar.

'I don't take –' she began.

'You need a bit of sugar.' He smiled.

She accepted the cup with trembling hands and sipped. 'I'm sorry. I didn't mean to rage at you.'

'You weren't raging at me, you were raging at God, and you're entitled to.'

'But that's a terrible thing, to say you hate God.'

He shrugged. 'Yerra, God is able for it, and you won't be the first nor the last who roars at him, I'm sure. You're hurt and heartbroken and life has dealt you a hard blow on top of many others, so you feel how you feel.'

She looked at him. He had a softly spoken manner, almost shy. A long moment of silence sat between them. 'Why does he let these things happen, Father? He's supposed to love us?'

'I don't know, is the truth, but will I tell you what I think?' he said eventually.

She nodded. She would love some explanation of why life had been so cruel.

'I think we see this life from our point of view only. And when someone we love dies, we feel terrible because we'll miss them, we want them back, here, with us.' He poured himself a cup of tea now as well. 'But I believe that this precious life we're living might actually be hell, or if not hell, certainly something close to it. This life, with its wars and loss and grief and pain, is hard. Look around the world now, innocent people being bombed and killed and treated terribly. We have some bright points of course, but nobody gets through this life unscathed. Pain seems to be part of the experience of life. I don't know why, but it is. But I believe that one day, each and every one of us will get to leave here and go home to heaven, and there we'll be with the people we love once more, but this time there will be no pain, no suffering, no wars, no goodbyes ever again. Maybe all of this will make sense then, why we had to endure so much.'

'Are you sure?'

He considered the question. 'I suppose I should say that yes, I'm completely sure, no doubts in my mind, but that would be a lie. I might be a priest, but I'm a frail human being, the same as everyone. So I'll say that I definitely hope so. I do think that there is a better world awaiting us – I've seen evidence of it, or what I believe is evidence of it. But I do know this for absolute certainty.'

He sipped his tea.

'What?'

'That I'd rather live this life believing that we are going home, that God is merciful and loves us and wants the best for us, even if that seems hard to understand sometimes. Like mothers and fathers have to get their children to take medicine and go to the dentist and eat vegetables and all the rest, because it's for their good, but the child doesn't see it like that. Maybe this is God being our parent, doing things for our own good, but we can't see why.'

He sighed then, 'I don't know, Grace, maybe it's all nonsense and there's nothing after we die, but if I have a choice to live as a believer or not, then I'll pick being a believer.'

'I can't bear the idea of him in bits at the bottom of the sea. We don't even have a body to bury.' The hot tears slid down her face again.

His chubby face was filled with compassion, and she knew she meant more to him than as just another former parishioner. 'Where Declan and Seán and John are now, they have no need of their bodies, and all we'd be doing with them is putting them in a box in the ground. The body is just a shell, Grace. It's nothing without the spirit, and I believe their spirits are gone to God.'

'I can't accept he's gone, that I'll never see him again.'

'You will, though, some day, when your turn comes. And until then I think you'll feel him around you. You'll find yourself talking to him, and if you ask him something, he'll answer you. He's in your heart, Grace, and death can't end that – nothing can. The people we love don't ever leave us, not really.'

She nodded, wanting to believe him and feeling comforted by his words. 'What will we do? How do we have a funeral without a body?'

'We'll have a memorial Mass, we'll say prayers for the repose of their souls, we'll comfort each other, and we'll let the community of Knocknashee do what they are very good at – minding their own.'

'Will he let you say the Mass?' she asked, knowing Father Iggy would understand exactly what she meant. He'd never said a bad word against the canon, but she knew how he felt all the same.

'I'll concelebrate it with Canon Rafferty and Father Lehane. We'll all say it.'

'THANKS, Father Iggy. I…I really appreciate you coming.' She forced a smile. 'But I mustn't keep you.'

'Grace, I'd like to think that we're friends. So when I heard, I had to come.'

'We are friends, and I'm grateful.'

He stood then and put on his hat and coat. 'I'll see you tomorrow at the Mass, but now try to get some sleep.'

She walked him to the door, knowing he had to face Catherine O'Shea and her children and Seán O'Connor's family too. As she waved him off into the dark, cold night, she wondered at how priests did it.

Tilly reappeared as she shut the front door. 'You look very pale, Grace. I think you should go to bed – you must be shattered. Come on, let's go.'

As Tilly helped her into bed, Grace noticed a look cross her friend's face as she slipped her dressing gown off her shoulders. She saw it then, the stain of bright-red blood on her nightie.

'Don't worry, Grace, I'll get you a nightie and some clean knickers and a belt and pad – where would they be?' Tilly was at her chest of drawers.

'First drawer on the right,' Grace said weakly. So that was it, her last hope that something of Declan McKenna remained for her in this world. She wasn't pregnant.

CHAPTER 4

Grace had changed into clean clothes and Tilly was gathering the soiled ones when there was another knock on the door. Grace couldn't bring herself to tell her friend how her last hope was dashed; she just wanted to be on her own.

'I'll go down, and I'll say you're gone to bed,' Tilly whispered, knowing Grace couldn't bear any more visitors today. She went downstairs, leaving Grace's bedroom door ajar.

Grace climbed between her sheets in the bed she'd shared with Declan, and she held the eiderdown to her nose – did it still smell of him? Of course not. She dragged herself out of bed again, opened the chest of drawers and took out a jumper of Declan's. It did have that faintly salty smell of him, combined with soap and oil. She brought it back to bed and snuggled down once more, foetal position, the jumper clutched to her face.

She heard Tilly answer the door, then the distinctive voice of Sergeant Keane. She got up and went to the landing. He might have some news – maybe Declan's body had been washed up after all.

But as she turned the corner, she saw Tilly and the sergeant in quiet conversation. Tilly looked upset.

Grace went down to join them. 'Sergeant? What is it?'

'Nothing, Grace, nothing for you to worry about. I just need to have a word with Tilly here.'

'With Tilly? Why?' she asked.

'They've arrested Eloise in Dublin, Grace,' Tilly said, clearly upset and confused. 'Some mad nonsense about German spies. They think Eloise had something to do with the U-boat, or the mine that killed Declan, and they want to talk to me now too.'

'Tilly, they say she's been to Germany, they know she has, and they know she was taking photographs of the coastline around here,' the sergeant said quietly.

'Eloise has never been to Germany, I know she hasn't,' Tilly said, and Grace's heart sank. That was a lie. Tilly had told her that Eloise had been so many places, even to Germany several times, so why was her friend trying to protect Eloise? Could Eloise actually be a spy? Grace's head swam.

'And I asked her to take the photographs for me – she was going to put them in an album for me.' Tilly was a terrible liar, and she blushed to the roots of her hair.

Eloise had been taking pictures for her own collection; she'd told Grace she wanted to get the same spots in all the different seasons. Why was Tilly lying? Did she know something? Grace's brain was struggling to focus.

'I'm sorry Tilly, I'm only doing what I'm told. The detectives above in Dublin came down today to investigate, and they seemed to think that Eloise might have something to do with it. I don't know, they got a tipoff from someone, I think, but they didn't give me the details. I was just told to take you in for questioning.'

'But Eloise is Swiss, not German…' Tilly said.

'Best you come with me now, and the detectives will explain everything tomorrow, I'm sure.'

'Can't she go to the garda station in the morning?' Grace asked.

Sergeant Keane shook his head. 'My orders are to bring her in now, Grace. I'm sorry.'

He looked genuinely contrite, and Grace knew he no more thought Tilly a German spy than she did. But this was coming from authority beyond a local garda sergeant. Still, the niggling feeling persisted. If Tilly was innocent, why did she lie?

Tilly, though shocked, was anxious to reassure her friend. 'It's all right, Grace. I didn't do anything wrong, and neither did Eloise. I'll be fine. Please tell Mama and look after Odile for me, all right?'

Grace stood, helpless, as the sergeant led Tilly away.

* * *

The memorial Mass had been an ordeal. She, Margaret O'Connor and Catherine O'Shea sat in the front pew as the town filed past to pay their respects and sympathise with their loss, each woman knowing that it could just as easily have been her husband or son. Behind them sat the O'Connor and O'Shea families, but Grace had no family, and that day of all days, it was abundantly clear. Tilly, who would certainly have sat beside her, was in custody, which in the normal course of events would have her distracted with worry. But in her current numb state, it was just one more problem to face alone.

Father Iggy did his best, but in the face of unspeakable tragedy in a small community, there were no words that could heal the wounds. Part of her just didn't believe it. Declan's body wasn't found, no part of his boat was found, and surely there would have been something? And wouldn't she feel it if he was just gone?

There were no afters as would be normal for a funeral. Usually people would go back to the pub afterwards, but since one of the victims was the local publican, and because there was nothing available to give people a feed, it was decided just to have the Mass and leave it at that.

Recent days had passed Grace by. Detectives from Dublin had been there, she remembered that much, and the Warringtons, and everyone fussed around her while she longed just to go to bed and be left alone. But when she was by herself, she panicked and needed company. It seemed there was no way for her to bear this loss. It was all surreal. Declan just could not be dead. She still expected him to walk in the door.

Sergeant Keane knocked on the door two days after the Mass. The guard was gentle in nature, but he was six foot three and must have been seventeen stone of muscle. He'd played rugby as a younger man and was nicknamed the 'armoured car'. Only a fool would tackle him.

'Good morning, Sergeant,' she said as brightly as she could. Maybe he was coming to tell her Declan had been found safe and well.

'Can I come in, Grace?' he asked.

'Of course…' She stood aside. He had always been kind and gentle to her, and she'd taken extra care with his daughter Mairead, who Agnes had dismissed as slow. Grace knew the girl was very bright orally but found reading and writing difficult. Sergeant Keane and his wife always went out of their way to tell her how much they appreciated her help.

His bulk seemed to fill the hallway. 'We found a bit of Declan's outboard, Grace…' he said quietly. 'Washed up out by Ballyferriter.'

'But that doesn't mean…' she began, twisting the wedding ring and diamond engagement ring on her finger. She'd started doing it subconsciously since hearing the news.

'Grace, listen to me. I know this is very hard to accept, but Declan is dead. There's no way he could have survived. Every other boat is accounted for, and those sea mines are terrible things – they blow everything sky-high. There would be nothing left. We're lucky to have found the bit of the engine…'

'Maybe it was a different one…'

'No, love, it's his. The name of the manufacturer was on it, Charlie identified it as Declan's, and besides, nobody else around here has one.' He was trying to make her accept it while also being gentle.

'But he might have been captured or…' Grace knew she was grasping at straws.

The policeman shook his head. 'It was a U-boat, Grace. They won't come up to the surface, it's too risky, and we'd have seen them if they did. Our waters are being closely watched, even if we don't notice it. And besides, why would the Germans want three fishermen from a neutral country?' He paused, allowing her to realise the logic of what he said.

'They wouldn't, I suppose,' she said quietly, finally accepting the truth of what he was telling her. She felt a pang of pity for him; his was a hard job.

He left her then.

She could go over to Charlie's – she knew she was always welcome there – but he was mired in his own grief and it felt wrong to lean on him, so she managed on her own. She must have slept and ate in the days that followed. There were several times people called, and she either didn't answer or she didn't invite them in. She needed to be alone.

Father Iggy had sent a young woman from Cork, the daughter of a friend who was a teacher; the school she'd been in had closed when it amalgamated with a larger one, so she was seeking employment. The priest had asked Grace if she would like him to arrange for the young woman to come for a few weeks, until Grace felt able to go back to work. She'd agreed, and Miss Rose Brennan had arrived. Nancy O'Flaherty was renting her a room in her house, and between Rose and Janie, who was bravely going on after the loss of her uncle, John O'Shea, they were keeping it all going. She would have to fill Declan's position as well, but she couldn't think about that yet.

A week after the Mass, wanting some air, she put the trap on Ned and headed for the farm. Ned *clip-clopped* along the road, his shoes clicking against the ice-cold ground. She was wrapped up, but the cold was razor-sharp and it was spitting rain.

She wanted to see Mary.

At night Grace was tormented by the idea that Eloise was the reason Declan was dead and that somehow Tilly was covering it up. When dawn arrived, she knew it was crazy, that Tilly would never knowingly help a German spy, but in the small hours, her mind ran amok and went to thoughts so dark and frightening, she often got up and sat in the sitting room rather than risk falling asleep again.

Mary was in the farmhouse kitchen when she arrived, along with

Odile, who sat at the table with some bread and jam. Mary was coping with Odile alone since Tilly had been taken away by Sergeant Keane.

As she approached, Grace could hear Mary telling Odile the story of Cú Chulainn. The little girl squealed as Mary told her how the boy who became the most famous warrior of Irish mythology pucked the *sliotar* into the dog's mouth. Grace pushed the cottage door open, and Odile turned, her face breaking into a grin, showing off her tiny white teeth. Her hair was dark and beginning to curl, and her brown eyes were unusual in these parts. Grace wondered if her parents would recognise her now. Her poor father would never see her again, but perhaps her mother would. She prayed she would. Richard did say he was going to keep in touch with Didier Georges, the Frenchman who was in London who knew Alfie, to see if there was any more news, so that was something to tell Mary.

'Gacey! Gacey!' Odile called, delighted to see her.

'Hello, *a leanbh*.' She went to the child and gave her a cuddle. It seemed like Odile got bigger every time she saw her.

'How are you, Grace?' Mary asked, her normally gruff manner belying a deep compassion for Grace's loss.

'I'm all right, Mary. Well, *cúiseach,* but you know…'

'I do, *a pheata,* I do surely.' She sighed and stood up from the range she was filling with turf. Her rheumatism was terrible in the winter, and Grace could see she was in pain. On the kitchen table were three loaves of soda bread and a dozen scones. Mary supplied the shop in Knocknashee.

'Have you heard anything more from the sergeant?' Grace asked.

'He was here this morning. Tilly was moved up to Dublin, and Eloise is there already. They're both in the women's prison.' Mary sat down wearily, and Grace joined her at the table.

'It's rubbish about Tilly. I mean to say… How can they think… I don't know about Eloise –'

'The photograph of Alfie and Constance is gone. 'Twas on the dresser there, and it's gone, Grace.'

'What? Who took it?' Grace knew it was missing but assumed it had been swallowed up in the mess. Neither Tilly nor her mother were careful housekeepers so for things to go missing wasn't unusual. She was surprised to hear Mary infer someone had stolen it. Why would they?

'I don't know, Eloise maybe? It's hard to believe, but if the guards above in Dublin are right and she was working for the Germans, then she'd have known from us what Alfie is up to, and maybe she told them where he was or who he was or… I don't know…' Mary's voice cracked with the stress of it all.

Odile dropped her crust with jam and squealed in indignation. The floor was filthy – Mary wasn't able to clean, and Dymphna, who came to care for Odile and keep the farmhouse tidy, hadn't been out since Declan's death – so Grace cut more bread and buttered it, handing it to the child.

'*Subh*,' she demanded, and Grace did as she was bid, slathering it with blackberry jam.

'What if she's told the Nazis about him and now they know where to find him?' The old woman's face was suffused with terror.

'I really don't think she would have, but what do we know? I'll write to Richard, have him speak to this man he knows, a Frenchman who knows Alfie. He'll surely be able to get word to him to lay low.' Grace had no idea if Richard could do that, or if Didier had any way of reaching Alfie, but if it comforted Mary, it was enough. 'Richard's contact said he was fine last time he saw him and keeping well out of trouble, so please God that's still the case.'

'Please God, but knowing my Alfie, staying away from trouble isn't what he's good at, and if they have information about him…'

Grace tried to reassure her. 'Even if Eloise did give them a photograph, what good is that to them? She can't have told them where he is because we don't know, and he's survived this far – he's well able.'

'I pray so.'

'They'll both be fine, Tilly and Alfie.'

'And you? How are you doing?' Mary asked.

Tears pricked Grace's eyes; she couldn't help it. She shook her head. 'Not good.'

Mary inhaled and then exhaled loudly. Odile was finished with her bread, and Mary lifted her and put her on the settle for a rest, tucking her in with a blanket and an old doll of Tilly's.

The sound of a car outside startled Grace. The two women went to the window to see Sergeant Keane getting out of the canon's car, the priest himself driving.

The two men entered Mary's house, the sergeant looking awkward but the canon full of his own importance as usual. He muttered a cursory greeting. 'I won't beat about the bush, Mrs O'Hare. I understand your daughter, Matilda, is now in police custody for some involvement with a spy ring, and given the situation' – he glanced around at the dirty farmhouse and wrinkled his nose – 'it will be best for that child to be somewhere she can be cared for properly. I'll take her now, so gather her things if you please.'

'You'll do no such thing. She's perfectly fine here –' Mary began.

The canon wrinkled his nose and looked around the messy room. 'Clearly that's not the case. You are an old woman with rheumatism, and keeping a clean house is beyond you. The best interests of the child should be foremost in your thoughts, but obviously not. If you are going to be obstinate, I will go to the courts, but it would be easier on everyone if you do the right thing now, less upsetting for the child as well...'

Grace felt a surge of rage. How dare he? 'Her name is Odile, Canon, Odile O'Hare, and what you propose is absolutely not happening. Mrs O'Hare is her grandmother, this is her home, and she is staying here where she belongs.' Grace didn't know where the strength to speak to the canon like this was coming from – maybe it was grief, or outrage at how he'd done this exact thing to Charlie when he took Declan and Siobhán – but she felt no fear. To hell with him and his consequences and threats.

'We've not been able to help much on account of recent events, but Dymphna will be back to help soon – she just didn't want to leave Charlie in the early days of losing his beloved son, especially as it was so soon after he got him back from where he was sent when he was only an innocent little boy.' She glared at the canon, her meaning unequivocal.

'Grace is right. You'll take this child over my dead body.' Mary picked Odile up off the settle, the commotion was upsetting the child, and held her so tightly that she cried. 'She's my Alfie's little girl, and she belongs with us.'

The sergeant, who Grace knew had been press-ganged into this by the canon, spoke up then. 'Right so, I think Mrs O'Hare is clear – she doesn't want the baby looked after by anyone else, is that correct?' He made eyes at Grace and Mary to play along.

'Absolutely not. We'll take care of Odile, and Dymphna will be back tomorrow, so there's no need whatsoever.' Mary stood her ground, Odile in her arms, her eyes glittering with determination and resentment. Even the canon knew he wouldn't win in a fight against Mary O'Hare so he said nothing.

'Very well then.' The sergeant sounded relieved. 'The canon just wanted to offer... But if you're sure ye can manage, we'll be on our way, unless there's anything else?'

The canon was fuming, Grace could see, but he would not down-face her. She knew too much, and he wouldn't risk it. Thank God she was here; if it had been just Mary, he might have got what he wanted.

'There was a picture in a frame up on the mantel there, of Alfie and his wife, Constance, and 'tis gone, Sergeant,' Mary said. 'I've searched high up and low down and there's no trace. I'm afraid if someone was... Well, I'm just worried.'

The sergeant nodded. 'I'll mention it to the detectives, Mary, don't worry. Now, we'll let ye to it.'

The men left, and the women watched the car drive away. ''Tis the hand of God you were here, Grace.'

Grace fought the tears, but they came anyway. 'Why is it all so hard, Mary? Declan, now Tilly, and worry about Alfie and Odile...and her poor father dead. And if it ever gets out that she's not Alfie's child...well, the canon would have a field day with that.'

'It won't get out. 'Tis only us few that know the truth, and we'll not breathe a word. Eloise thought she was Alfie's, so she couldn't say anything if she was a German. 'Tis only you and me and Tilly who know the real story.'

'I know. I just…I don't see how things can ever be right again. I feel so broken, so empty inside…'

'You are, of course, but you're brave as a lion, Grace McKenna. 'Tisn't everyone could face down that auld snake the way you just did. I'm proud of you.'

'I don't feel brave,' Grace said wearily.

'I know you don't, which is why it's even more remarkable. You and my Tilly are strong women. I don't know what that Eloise was about – she seemed like a nice girl to me, but we'll have to wait and see – but I know my daughter, Grace, and she's no German spy. They'll figure that out soon enough. Now move over there beside the fire, where your leg will be warm. You probably don't feel like hearing a story now, but I'll tell it to you all the same.'

Grace remembered sitting on this exact rocking chair at the O'Hares' as a small girl, when her parents were still alive and Mary was a sprightly young woman, before arthritis bent her bones. Mary would tell Tilly and Grace stories as she made bread or peeled potatoes, and they ate bread and jam and drank glasses of creamy milk straight from the churn. Then as teenage girls, trying to navigate being adults – Mary had stories for that too. And while the stories in and of themselves were entertaining – Mary wove a tale like a spider wove a web – they always taught her something too. A story, here in this big, untidy, warm home where she'd always been welcome, was just what she wanted.

CHAPTER 5

'There was a very rich man, long, long ago...' Mary began as she eased herself with a groan and a wince of pain onto the settle, lying the dozing Odile back down to rest.

After stoking the fire, which sent turf sparks flying up the huge chimney, Grace sat in the rocking chair and pulled a crocheted rug over her knees.

'And this very rich man had everything he could ever want – gold and jewels, a fine castle, horses and servants galore – but he wasn't happy. Every night when he went to sleep, it bothered him. Why wasn't he happy? It bothered him so much that it made him sick.'

Odile, half asleep, crept onto Mary's lap and snuggled up to her, her thumb in her mouth. Mary stroked the child's head as she settled down to sleep, lowering her voice so as not to disturb her. 'He got sicker and sicker and weaker and weaker, so his servants, who were fond of him, called for the druid, a very wise, very old man, and the druid said to him, "There's only one cure for what ails you."

'"What is that?" asked the man sadly.

'"You need to go out into the world, leave your big castle with your feather bed and your fine food and go like a beggar into the world. When you're far from home and all your comforts, then I want you to find a ring, but not just any ring – it's a special one that can make a sad man happy and a happy man sad. Once you find that, your health will be restored. And don't come back till you find it."

'"How will I know I've found it?" the rich man asked the druid.

'"You'll know," was all the druid said.'

Grace allowed the words to wash over her, and somehow the heat of the fire and the sound of Mary's voice soothed her battered soul.

'So the rich man did as he was told. He took off his fine clothes and his warm cloak, and he dressed in beggar's clothes and set off to go far from his own place and his own kin. He went to every silversmith and goldsmith in all of Ireland. He said that he could pay, despite appearances, if they could just give him a ring that would make a sad man happy and a happy man sad. But nobody knew what he was talking about.'

The clock ticked on the dresser, and no other sound could be heard except Mary's voice and the wind off the sea.

'They offered him beautiful rings, with fine engraving and precious stones, but the man knew they were not what he needed. He walked the length of the whole country, up mountains and down valleys, reaching the ocean in the north, south, east and west, but to no avail.

'Defeated, the rich man turned for home. There was nowhere left to look. Three miles from his castle, he saw a blacksmith's forge, and in there was a blacksmith, hammering shoes for horses. It was his last chance, so he went in.

'"Would you have a ring that would make a sad man happy and a happy man sad?" he asked the blacksmith wearily.'

Odile stirred but didn't wake, and Mary soothed her by rubbing her small back. Grace thought of how she would like to be small again, the cares of the adult world far away. Mary smiled down at the child and went on with her story.

'The blacksmith looked at him for a long time and then slowly nodded. He took a small piece of iron and fashioned it into a ring, burnishing it in the flame, and then he plunged it into cold water. Then the man watched as the blacksmith set about carving something into the inside of the ring with his tools, working quietly, his head bowed.

'When he was finished, he spat on the ring and polished it off his britches, which were filthy. Then he handed the small iron band to the rich man.

'"How much do I owe you?" the rich man asked.

'"Nothing," said the blacksmith with a smile.

'The rich man thanked him and took the ring, deciding to give him all the business of shoeing his horses in the future. He knew that this was the ring he needed, though he couldn't say how he knew it. He walked out of the forge and sat on the wall outside, intrigued as to what the inscription might be. As he read, he felt the sadness that had dogged him lift, and he knew that he'd found the ring that makes a sad man happy and a happy man sad.'

Grace's gaze was now glued to Mary as she weaved her tale.

'So he went back to his castle and greeted everyone with a smile and a wave. That night the druid came to the feast they had to welcome the master home. He glanced down at the man's hand, saw the iron ring there, and said, "You found it, I see?"

'The rich man nodded. "I did."

'"And you know now what will make a sad man happy and a happy man sad?" the druid asked.

'"I do," replied the rich man.

'The druid poured a cup of mead for himself and another for the rich man. He didn't need to see the inscription – he simply raised a toast.' Mary fixed Grace with an intense look, and Grace knew this story was not just to soothe her – it was a lesson.

Mary went on, her voice strong and sure. 'As their goblets clinked, the men said in unison, "This too shall pass."'

Tears slipped down Grace's cheeks. The words hung in the air, and she knew that no matter what happened, they would be all right.

CHAPTER 6

Three weeks later Grace took the bus to Cork and the train from there to Dublin. It had taken most of a day of travelling; the train relied on turf since coal was in such short supply, and it was nowhere near as efficient. She was bone-weary. She'd stayed in a boarding house off Mountjoy Square, where she'd slept very badly, and this morning she planned to see Tilly.

Sergeant Keane had helped secure a visitor's pass, and Grace was on one hand longing to see her friend, but it still haunted her that Tilly had lied. Mary and everyone in Knocknashee were awaiting her report.

The imposing Mountjoy Female Prison intimidated her, but she had the necessary paperwork and was ushered through the gate. Led by a female warden who said nothing, Grace was brought into the prison, which smelled of human bodies and overcooked vegetables, and then to a small bare room where she was told to wait. It was painted a dun colour and empty but for a battered table and two chairs. Sergeant Keane had warned her that because Tilly was being held without charge under some special act brought in because of the Emergency, she was kept separate from other prisoners and so Grace would not meet her in the visitors' room with the other inmates and their families. Under this new act, it seemed the government was answerable to nobody and people could be held indefinitely without any explanation.

After what felt like a long wait, Grace heard footsteps. Then the door opened and Tilly came in, followed by another warden. She was wearing prison clothes consisting of a grey dress and black shoes and stockings, but she looked well enough.

'Sit. Ye have twenty minutes,' the warden said, and left the room.

'Are you all right, Tilly?' Grace asked, and her friend nodded.

'How about you? Are you coping?'

Grace tried to smile. 'I'm all right. Your mam and Odile are managing. I was up with her the other day.'

'Good. I think I won't be held much longer. They've asked me around a million questions…but I don't know what they want me to say. Eloise did nothing wrong, I'm totally sure of it…' Tilly paused, and a look crossed her face. 'What?' she asked.

'Nothing.' Grace knew she was an unconvincing liar.

'Grace Fitzgerald, I've known you since Seanie Keohane laughed at your drawing of a rabbit in baby infants, so don't bother lying. What's wrong?'

'Well, I just think maybe we should… I'm not saying Eloise did anything wrong, but the truth is we don't know, do we? It's not like you've known her since baby infants. She's only been around for a short time and –'

'I don't believe I'm hearing this.' Tilly's jaw clenched, the jut of her chin defiant. Grace could sense her indignation. 'Grace, I do know. I know her. She would never –'

'You don't know her, Tilly! How could you really know her in that short space of time? You know what she wants you to know.'

'What? Did you come up here to say this to me?' Grace had never seen her friend so upset. 'I thought you were coming to see me! It's been so horrible in here all on my own, and I was so looking forward to seeing you, and now you only want to tell me I've been a blind fool, is that it?'

'Of course it isn't. I'm just saying that we –'

'Don't know. You said.' Tilly's words dropped like stones. Grace had seen this in her friend before, the shutdown, the belligerence – never directed at her before, but she knew her friend.

'I don't want to fight, Til. But I…well…' Though they were out of anyone's earshot and were speaking in rapid Irish that she doubted very much the warden could understand, she whispered, 'You lied to Sergeant Keane, saying Eloise was never in Germany, but we both know she was – she said she was. I heard her say it that she'd been there many times…'

'On holidays with her family,' Tilly hissed.

'All right, that's as may be, but why lie?'

'To protect her of course.' Tilly was sullen now. Her arms folded across her chest, refusing to make eye contact with Grace.

'But why would she need protecting if she did nothing wrong?' Grace knew she was pushing the point, but she had to try to stop Tilly incriminating herself further for a woman they barely knew.

'Oh, Grace, you're so naive. I didn't –'

It stung that Tilly called her naive when she was the one being sensible. Suddenly the rage, the sheer red-hot fury bubbled up inside her. It was an unfamiliar sensation, but it had been happening on and off since Declan died. Without her control, the words gushed out in a torrent. 'I'm naive? Me? I'm the innocent fool, am I? Not from where I'm standing, Tilly, and not from where anyone else is standing either. You're the one being blind! You are so dazzled by her, she can do no wrong at all. She could do anything, and you'd find some excuse to forgive her. Tilly, you're the one who needs to wake up, not me. Declan, Seán and John are dead because someone is helping the bloody Nazis, and it sure isn't me or anyone else from Knocknashee, and you won't for one second consider a random woman who just turns up out of the blue from Switzerland – or so she says – could have something to do with it?'

'So you're blaming both of us? Is that it? Eloise and I are responsible? I loved Declan too, you know.' Tilly's eyes glittered with unshed tears. This was not how Grace had wanted the visit to go, but she was so upset herself and now this. 'And you think I'd shield someone who could hurt him? I thought you knew me, Grace. Of all the people in this world, I was sure you knew me, but clearly I was wrong.'

'I don't know this version of you, that's for sure. It's best I go.' Grace stood, and without a backwards glance at her oldest and dearest friend, she left.

CHAPTER 7

LONDON, ENGLAND

6 DECEMBER 1941

Richard stood soaked to the skin and absolutely exhausted. Kirky, hungry for anything he could send pressed him for more and more copy. The appetite for news about the war, and in particular the impact on the civilian population, grew ever more voracious as the likelihood of America becoming more involved in the war grew every day. Lord Halifax had recently visited Detroit and had eggs and tomatoes pelted at him by American isolationist women. The debate about whether the United States should have troops on the ground was heating up, and all eyes were on Britain and the British.

The egg-soaked peer was quoted in the press as saying, 'How fortunate you Americans are. We in Britain only get one egg a week and are very glad of it.' Which caused a huge outpouring of support for Britain and Lord Halifax. Kirky wanted more of that, more of the British attitude about the USA's involvement, so Richard had gone out and tried to engage people on the subject, on the streets and in the cafés, but the weather was horrible today, bitterly cold, sleet and rain alternating, and nobody wanted to talk to him about America or the war that felt unending or anything else. It was a little more than two weeks to Christmas, and London was doing its best to be festive, though the city and its inhabitants were punch-drunk and shattered.

Nonetheless, as their indomitable spirit shone through, they decorated their homes and tried to get gifts for each other to make it a cheerful occasion, despite the deprivations. Sarah had had their father ship over a big box of small toys to distribute to the refugee kids, and she'd given two dolls and a toy army truck to the mother who lived next door. Her husband was in the Air Force, and they had two little girls and a boy of six. She looked like she'd been given diamonds and confided to Sarah that she'd been awake at night wondering how she was going to explain to the children that Father Christmas couldn't come this year, and now she didn't have to.

While all around was deprivation, destruction and loss of every kind imaginable, Richard was happy here and felt he was doing some good, because it was imperative that America enter the war fully. Britain had been so strong for so long, standing alone, but it needed help and that help had to come from his country. Part of him couldn't wait for that little runt Hitler to see the might of the United States military, to feel their wrath. He might not be such a bully then, because the only thing bullies understood was someone bigger and stronger meting out the kind of punishment they'd inflicted on others. He toned his personal opinion down in his stories as he didn't want to seem inflammatory, but there could be no doubt about his feelings on the matter to anyone reading his articles. If he influenced even one person away from isolationism, then he'd consider that a personal victory.

But this evening, as he trudged up the steps of the Tube station, his wet socks squelching in his shoes, his overcoat soaked through, he did wish he could transport himself back to Savannah, just for a day or two, to a family Christmas with a glittering tree and gifts wrapped beneath. They always had turkey at Thanksgiving, so Christmas was usually roast beef, with green bean casserole and mashed potatoes, followed by Southern bread pudding. His mouth watered at the memory. The food in wartime Britain left a lot to be desired, but even prewar food couldn't hold a candle to real Southern cooking, he was sure.

He, Sarah, Jacob and Pippa had gone out to the Savoy to celebrate Thanksgiving, and Jacob was forbidden to complain about the price. They each said what they were thankful for, and the conversation was jubilant and fun-filled. Sarah was grateful for her new American stockings, unheard of here since the war; Jacob was grateful for the carton of Lucky Strikes his uncle had sent from New York; Richard said he was grateful for the windows in the new flat that didn't let in draughts like the old place did; and Pippa had smiled and met his gaze and said she was grateful that she didn't burn to death in a fire and that a handsome American hero had pulled her out. They'd eaten their fill and drank a bit too much, and it was a wonderful night.

The feeling of being full was one he'd not had in a long time. There was just about enough food day to day – Pippa saw to that – and it was nutritious, lots of vegetables, a tiny amount of meat and fat and almost no sugar, but it was monotonous and often tasteless, despite her best efforts. Both girls had decided that he and Jacob should wash up and they'd cook, considering neither of the men could boil an egg. Sarah couldn't cook either – she'd been reared on the assumption that she would have staff – but Pippa had taught her and they did their best.

He hoped it might be fish and chips tonight rather than the potato-peel pie Sarah had made last week, which was so disgusting, he had to pretend he was too tired to eat it. Lord Woolton, the Minister of Food, was always coming up with recipes, one more vile than the next as far as Richard was concerned.

He was hungry and cold and in need of a bath, but he had to go back out later – Sarah had lined up an interview with a bunch of Russians who had found their way to London. The uneasy alliance of Britain, the United States and Russia was critical to the success of the Allies, so he would need to make sure the tone was one of cordial refuge. It wasn't hard to sell Britain as an ally to the American public, but old Uncle Joe in Moscow was a whole other ball of wax.

He hadn't been joking when he said he was grateful for non-leaking windows. The mews house in Marylebone was much better than their old flat, though the heating was temperamental at best so they had to layer their clothing. There was no way to dry clothes, and so the place looked like a laundry most of the time, with damp or soaking garments draped everywhere.

He and Pippa shared one room, Sarah and Jacob the other. It was hardly a great love story; they'd just sort of kissed that one night, then slept together and then kept on going. He and Pippa never really discussed their relationship, and she was at great pains to say they were fine as they were, that neither of them had a parent breathing down their necks, horrified at the premarital sleeping arrangements. She was right, but he went to the trouble to make her feel special. She knew he was faithful to her; he wasn't the kind of man who had girls all over the place. Any time he tried to bring it up, that they should at least have 'an understanding', as they said over here, she shushed him with kisses, saying that they were fine as they were and no need to do anything until the war was over at least.

'There's a letter for you,' Pippa called from the tiny kitchenette as she mashed potatoes. 'The old landlady forwarded it to here. From Grace.' Richard had told her all about his relationship with Grace, so he wasn't hiding anything, but he noticed Pippa rarely mentioned her.

'Thanks.' He kissed her cheek. Whatever she was making actually smelled delicious. She was a much better cook than Sarah. She had some herbs growing in pots on the windowsill and added them to everything to give their meals a bit more flavour.

'Cor, you're drenched. Go and change. I finally got some stuff dry today – they're in your wardrobe.' She helped him off with his coat. 'And amazingly there's some hot water, lord knows for how long, so there's time to have a bath before dinner if you like? Jacob and Sarah said the Russians are done in, they just need to sleep, so they asked could you meet them tomorrow instead? The lovebirds are going to the pictures, so it's just us for dinner.'

Relief flooded his body. He didn't have to go out again. He could stay here, in this cosy flat for once, have a warm bath, a change into dry clothes and a nice dinner with Pippa. Bliss. 'What's on the menu? Eye of newt in a crocodile sauce?' He laughed. He found the names of British food hilarious; it was as if they were trying to make things sound unappetising on purpose. Pigs in blankets, toad in the hole, bangers and mash, spotted dick, fat rascal, jam roly-poly... He had been sure she was making it all up, but it seemed she wasn't.

'No, smarty-pants, it's bubble and squeak tonight actually, with tinned pears for dessert.' She tried to hide it but he knew she was hurt. She was normally so bubbly, now she seemed dejected. 'I waited in a queue for an hour and half to get a bit of bacon, but the butcher sold out by the time I got to the top, so no meat for us tonight.'

He thought of the juicy steaks and hamburgers, hotdogs and pork-chops he took for granted back home and wondered if he would ever be so blasé again about food. He'd written to his father and asked for some treats and decorations from home for Christmas, so that box would arrive shortly. Arthur would have instructed his secretary, Lynette, to spare no expense. To be fair, his father was most forthcoming with anything they asked for, and he always wrote saying 'Mother sends her love', which everyone knew was a lie. Richard was looking forward to seeing Pippa's face at the sight of a big box of American candy and cookies and Christmas decorations.

'I'm sure it will be delicious.'

'I hope so. Looks like you've had a long day.' She hung his sodden coat on the back of the door. None of the furniture here matched anything; it was cobbled together from leftovers found in junk shops, as far as he could see. But tonight the heating was working, so it was warm and comfortable. They had a sofa and two armchairs either side of a gas fire, a wireless and a small round dining room table with four chairs. There was a hideous orange rug on the floor, and the curtains might once have been green but were now so faded, it was hard to tell.

She was undressing him now, peeling first his sweater and then his shirt off him. As he stood there bare-chested, he drew her into his arms. She felt warm and smelled of rosewater and gravy.

'I love coming home to you,' he said, with a sigh of contentment.

It was true, but they didn't really use endearments as such. She teased him, she kissed him, she slept in his bed, she led the household on the domestic front – she was much better equipped for self-sufficiency than the rest of them – but how they felt about each other wasn't really verbalised.

She grinned. 'That's your grumbling tummy talking.'

'I mean it, Pippa, I really do. And I know you don't want to talk about it...'

'I like it too. But you know, I can move on whenever. I'm all right now, and I don't want to be –'

'A burden, I know. You keep saying that. But you're not. Pippa, you're my girlfriend and we live together, so please stop saying you're only passing through, OK?'

'Oh, I am, am I?' She laughed.

'Aren't you?' he asked seriously.

She looked pensive for a moment. 'I suppose so, but I'm not your responsibility, Richard. I know you feel like you can't abandon me, but I'm not a kitten you found. I was in a bad way back then, granted, but I'm all right now.'

'I don't think I rescued you... Well, maybe I did spring you from the awful pig farm and pull you out of a burning house.' He chuckled. 'But those are the lengths a Yank has to go to to get a girl over here.'

'Oh yeah, 'cause us English girls aren't dazzled by you lot even a bit.' She raised an eyebrow. 'My mate Joanie at work says her brother and his mates hate the Yanks 'cause the girls have no time for English blokes no more, not exotic enough.'

'It's the attraction of novelty. Americans are just as annoying as Englishmen, I can assure you.' Richard chuckled. 'Maybe even worse.'

'Oh, you don't need to tell me that. Don't matter what nationality you lot are, us girls still wind up pickin' socks off the floor.'

'I pick up my own socks!' he exclaimed indignantly.

'Sometimes,' she said raising a sceptical eyebrow. They both knew the truth. 'But any ideas on how they get from the laundry basket back in the drawer clean and dry?'

'Magic?' he suggested with a cheeky grin.

She swatted him on the bottom, and he wrapped his arms around her tighter, feeling a surge of affection for her. She was so brave. Pippa was a girl with no home, no living relative who worked all the hours God sent in a munitions factory, as well as took care of him and the others, and she never complained.

'I think you're amazing, truly,' he said.

'Nah, I'm just like everyone else. What choice do we have? Curl up and die or just keep calm and carry on.'

'It must be hard, though, having no family left,' he probed. She didn't often talk about her situation.

'Me and loads of others.' She was circumspect as usual as she gazed out of the window. It was dark outside, and he could see her face reflected in the glass. She looked so lonely.

'How old were you when your mom died?' he asked gently.

'Eight.'

'Do you have many memories of her?'

Pippa turned then from the stove where she began mashing potatoes and nodded. 'Some.'

'I bet she was amazing. I know her daughter is.'

She shrugged. 'Nah, not amazing, she was just my mum. But she was lovely.'

'And your dad?' Richard realised he'd never really spoken to her about this before.

She nodded. 'All right, most of the time. He served in the last war, came back shellshocked and deaf in one ear, so he was a drinker. A lot of men who came back were, but he was all right. Not violent or nothin', just a bit...I don't know... I don't remember him much. He was knocked down one night, drunk he was, never saw the car, just the year before my mum.'

'That's awful. I'm so sorry. What were your folks' names?' he asked gently.

'My mum was Philippa, after her father, my grandpa Phil, and I'm named after her.' She gave a weak smile. 'Dad was Gareth. When I was small, he used to say he was descended from one of the Knights of the

Round Table, one of them was Sir Gareth, with King Arthur, y'know, and all of that?'

He nodded with a smile.

'I told the teacher that once in school, and the class all laughed at me. I was only five, but I never said it to no one after that.'

Richard felt that familiar urge to protect her, to never have her feel outside or alone again. 'That's really hard.'

'I'll be fine. You don't need to always look after me.'

'Would that be so awful?'

She waited for a moment, and just when he thought she was going to return to the cooking, she said, 'Not awful, but not right either. Go and have a bath. Dinner will be in twenty minutes, and don't forget your letter.' She took it from the mantelpiece and handed it to him. The silence between them spoke volumes.

CHAPTER 8

He went to the bathroom and stripped off his sodden trousers, underwear and socks. His watch had stopped; it must have got water in it, he was that wet. He sank into the bath gratefully. He would have loved a hot shower, or a bath that covered his shoulders, but the regulation five inches would have to do, and at least it was hot for once.

He lay back, looking at Grace's letter and feeling a myriad of emotions. He was longing to hear from her but dreading reading about her and Declan. Seeing her familiar writing on the envelope and the stamps with the harp on them made him ache.

He'd write tonight, a cheery note wishing Mr and Mrs McKenna a happy first Christmas. He'd tell her about him and Pippa; it was high time she knew. He felt guilty that he had not mentioned their relationship to her before.

He reached over to the sink where the letter was propped and took it. He unsealed the flap and extracted the single sheet of paper and began to read. It was short.

Dear Richard,

I can't believe I'm actually writing these words. I've been staring at the blank sheet of paper for ten minutes, willing myself to commit them to paper.

Declan died.

He went out on a boat with two other local men to try to rescue some survivors of a U-boat attack, and they came on a naval mine – it's a kind of floating bomb – and when they approached, it detonated. They were all killed instantly.

I wish I could tell you how I feel. Pour it all out onto the page like I did all that long time ago when I wrote to you about Agnes. But I can't. It's stuck in my chest somewhere. I can't talk about it or feel anything but rage.

As well as that, Tilly has been arrested and is in prison in Dublin. Another thing I'm writing but can't quite believe. It seems the gardaí believe that her friend Eloise is not a Swiss teacher but an agent working for the Germans and was only befriending Tilly so she could photograph the west coast without suspicion. Of course Tilly knows nothing about that, she's entirely innocent, but she has been taken for questioning because of her and Eloise's close friendship. I don't know what to believe about Eloise.

The reason I'm telling you this really, though, is we think that if it's true and they're right about her, then Alfie might be in even more danger than previously. There was a photograph on Mary O'Hare's mantelpiece of Alfie and Constance – Jacob gave it to her when you visited Knocknashee – and now it's gone. Mary is so worried that Eloise might have somehow given it to the Germans and that they know who Alfie is and what he's doing, and now, if this is true, they have a photo of him into the bargain. I told Mary I'd ask if you could tell the contact you have in London and ask him if he can get a message to Alfie to lay low.

As I'm writing these words, I know it sounds ridiculous, but it's all true.

I want to run away, Richard, away from Knocknashee, away from school, away from the sea that has taken so much from me, away from being me.

Sincerely,

Grace

He folded the letter and got out of the bath. She never ended her letters with 'sincerely'. It sounded odd to him, strangely formal, but then the whole letter sounded stilted. *The poor girl.* His heart went out to her.

Dinner would have to wait. He would do as she'd asked right away; it was the least he could do. And if this Eloise person was working for the Germans, then that was bad news for Alfie. Alfie O'Hare was not the kind of man to shy away from danger. Richard would go and find Didier, who would either be at the *Daily Worker* offices or in the pub down the street. He had a room there.

Richard wanted to write to her, and he wanted to have something reassuring to say. He could do nothing about the shocking news of Declan. *Poor Grace.* He could hear her pain in every word. He needed to be on his own to think about what Grace had told him.

He dressed in dry clothes, borrowed Jacob's dry overcoat and went into the kitchen, where Pippa was setting the table. 'I need to go out. I'm sorry, but I have to do it now. Grace's husband has been killed and… Look, it's a long story, but I need to meet someone and get a message to France. It's complicated, but I'll be back as quick as I can.'

A flash of something crossed her face. Fear? Disappointment?

'Of course, that's awful. Poor Grace. I'll eat and leave yours on a plate – you can heat it up when you get back.' She didn't ask him what could possibly be so urgent to take him out into such filthy weather, and he didn't explain.

The rain was relentless, landing with such force on the sidewalk, it bounced back up, soaking walkers twice. He pulled his hat down, water streaming steadily off the brim, and within minutes he was as wet as he'd been earlier.

As he walked to the bus stop and caught the bus to the offices of the *Daily Worker*, he was oblivious to the discomfort; the contents of Grace's letter swirled in his mind. Declan McKenna was dead? He remembered briefly meeting him in person that time he'd gone to Knocknashee, and even though he always knew Declan was a rival for Grace's affections, he'd found him to be a charming, decent guy. He remembered being jealous of his looks – Declan had that real Celtic look, deep-blue eyes, chiselled cheekbones, a strong jaw, lean and delicate looking. No wonder all the girls liked him. Beside Declan's delicate fine features and physique, Richard had felt like a bear. That was Grace's type – slight, handsome, beautiful almost, deep and cerebral. The opposite of him. Grace said Declan could have had anyone, and Richard believed her. It was hard to imagine he was just gone.

He was relieved to find his feelings were those of profound regret and pity for Grace; he would have horrified himself if he'd been happy or relieved or glad that Grace was free once more. He tested the thought. *No.* He wasn't happy. Of course not. He didn't want Grace to marry Declan, but he definitely didn't want him dead.

The bus crawled through the blacked-out streets, taking forever. He eventually arrived at the *Daily Worker*; the office was open but unmanned. He ventured up the metal stairs to find a young woman with short mousy-brown hair wiping something off her hands with a dirty rag. The building was an industrial one, all iron girders and red brick, and smelled of ink and oil.

'Can I help you?' she asked, her belligerence at having the inner sanctum intruded upon belying a fear that he was up to no good. She peered at him through thick spectacles. She wore a brown cardigan, brown moleskin trousers and working boots.

'I was just looking for Didier Georges?' Richard said calmly. 'I'm Richard Lewis from the *Capital* newspaper in New York?' He showed her his press pass.

She glanced at it and handed it back. 'Didier isn't here, and he won't be back for a week or so at least,' she said, still not convinced.

Richard remembered how Didi said he was going to Scotland to speak at the Communist Party meeting there. 'Oh, right, he mentioned he was going – I just forgot. Can I leave a note for him?'

'I suppose, but as I said, I won't see him…'

Richard scribbled a note from the journal he always kept in his pocket, along with the stub of a pencil. *Didi, our mutual friend in Paris in new danger. Urge to lie low if you can. RL*

He handed the note to the girl unfolded; he was happy for her to read it.

She took it, scanned it and nodded. 'If I see him…' she said, her tone doubtful.

'Thanks, it's important,' he said, knowing she would deliver it, and went back down the stairs.

CHAPTER 9

As he trudged back – it was as fast to walk as take the bus that smelled of diesel and unwashed bodies – the weather worsening if anything, he mulled it all over. Grace needed him. He wanted to go to her that minute, but that was impossible. This was terrible. Less than half an hour ago, he was telling Pippa he wanted to take care of her. What on earth was he thinking? He was sleeping with Pippa, but admittedly they had made no commitment to each other, nothing like that. But still. And anyway, just because Declan was dead, it didn't mean anything had changed. He could hardly write and tell Grace what he should have said last year. He would have to keep his feelings to himself and be the friend she needed now.

A terrible guilt washed over him as he walked. The traders and shops were closing up for the evening, but he spotted a jeweller's shop open up ahead. He stopped outside, scanning he trays of rings, necklaces, bracelets and earrings on their velvet trays.

Noticing him window shopping, the shopkeeper opened the door and ushered him in. He thought he might buy something for Pippa, who had almost nothing in terms of possessions; what little she'd had was lost in the fire at her aunt's house.

The very polished and groomed middle-aged lady who'd opened the door smiled. 'Can I help you, sir?'

'I'm looking for a present for my girlfriend.'

'Best be prepared,' she tinkled, the sound vaguely incongruous coming from someone of her years. She reminded him of his mother's friends, desperately trying to dam the tide of age with expensive clothes and cosmetics. 'What are you thinking?'

'Earrings maybe?' A tray of pearls caught his eye and remembered Pippa admiring Sarah's pearls one time. 'Pearls, I think.'

He registered the gleam in her eye as she took in his expensive clothes and shoes, though Jacob's coat was shabby. Commission was small to non-existent these days, as luxuries such as these were far beyond the reach of most people, many of whom were hanging on by their fingernails.

She took out the tray and extracted a pair of earrings, placing them on her palm with a flourish. 'We have these beautiful Akoya pearls, on a fourteen-carat-gold post, with this stunning ornate filigree setting. It's a most luxurious piece of jewellery, something to pass on through generations, and the pearls themselves are light crema with rose overtone.'

They are beautiful, he thought.

'Your young lady will be thrilled.'

He wondered if she would be. The last time he'd bought her jewellery, it was a ring in an antique shop in Plymouth to make it look as if they were married. It was an antique gold ring, but to this day, Pippa thought it was cheap brass. There would be no way to pass these over as cheap, though; they were luminescent and really lovely. He could imagine them on her creamy skin.

'I'll take them.' He could see the woman's astonishment that he hadn't asked the price.

'They are eleven pounds, is that all right?' she asked, trying to contain her glee.

'Fine. Can you gift-wrap them for me please?' He took the cash from his wallet.

'Certainly, sir, certainly.' She scurried off to find some paper and ribbon as he admired the other things in the shop.

* * *

HE CAME BACK into their house as Pippa was washing up at the sink, his plate covered with another on top of a saucepan, ready to be reheated.

'You're back then.' She smiled weakly as he took off Jacob's soaking coat and hung it beside his own.

He nodded. 'I'll just go and change, again.' He kissed her cheek briefly and left the room. Standing in their bedroom, he put the earrings in his sock drawer, right at the back, stripped and dressed again quickly, throwing his wet clothes in the basket. She was right – he didn't have any part in how they got from there to clean and dry and back in his closet. It wasn't right; he was using her. And no matter what she said, it was wrong.

When he went back out to the kitchen, she'd reheated his meal and had placed a knife and fork beside the steaming plate. He sat down to eat the potatoes and cabbage fried together and bizarrely called bubble and squeak.

'I wasn't sure if you were coming back...' she said quietly.

'Of course I'd come back,' he said between mouthfuls. A pregnant pause. 'Poor Declan, Grace's husband – he was blown up by a naval mine.'

'That's horrible! Poor chap. At least it was quick, I suppose.'

'I guess.' He took another bite.

'Maybe you should go over there, to see her.'

He didn't reply.

'You can travel with your press pass, can't you?'

'I could, but...' He wasn't sure where to go with this.

'Go to her. You know you want to.'

He could hear the resignation in her voice. This was what was stopping her from committing to him; he'd always known it deep down. She'd asked him before about Grace – apparently he'd called out her name in his sleep – and he'd explained they were pen pals. But he knew she didn't believe that was all there was to it.

'No, it's not like that. We're not… She's married, or was…' He sighed. 'It's not like that,' he repeated lamely.

A long pause. Then Pippa put her mug down. 'So explain it to me – what is it like?' She looked up at him then, her eyes raking his face for a clue as to the nature of this relationship.

'She's my friend.'

'And her bloke, was he a friend of yours too?'

'Through her, I knew of him more than knew him, but I met him once as well.'

She forced a smile. He knew her well enough by now to know when she was faking it. 'Well, she's a lucky girl to have such a good pal as you, and I should know. You seem to have a knack for saving damsels in distress. Richard the Lionheart, that's what we should start calling you.'

'Pippa, I…' He faltered.

'You don't owe me anything, Richard, that's what I keep telling you. You go to Ireland, see your friend, and it's high time I stood on me own two feet again anyway. High time. And I'll always be grateful.'

'Pippa, I –'

'You're a smashing bloke,' she cut across him, 'Richard, truly, one of the best people I know, and you've been ever so kind. But I know that this Grace is more than a friend. You can say what you like, but she is. And I might not have much, but I don't deserve to play second fiddle to anyone, so I'm going to let you go with an open heart. So do it, Richard, go to her and tell her how you feel…' Tears shone in her eyes, and Richard could see what this was costing her to say.

She stood and his gaze met hers. He knew he admired her, that she was so brave and gutsy, and she could make him laugh so hard, and she was beautiful, responsive and kind. What was he doing? Pining for a girl across the sea, a girl whose heart was broken because the man she loved was gone, while this wonderful girl cried tears because she loved him. She didn't need to say it, and he wasn't being arrogant to assume it; she loved him. She was here, in front of him, available and wonderful. This was stupid. Utterly stupid and pathetic. Grace wanted his friendship, and he would offer it to her as he always did, but it was time he got on with his own life, for once and for all.

He stood as well and placed his hands on Pippa's shoulders. 'I'm not going to Ireland. I'll write and tell her how sad I am that she's had this terrible blow. She and Declan were madly in love, so I can't imagine her pain, but I don't need to go there to say that to her. I'll put it in a letter, because where I should be is right here, in London, with you.'

'But you love her...' Pippa said, and the pain was so obvious, it was palpable.

He shook his head. 'Not the way I love you,' he said as he put his arms around her. 'I promise.'

They stood, wrapped around each other as long seconds ticked past. Then she spoke,

'You mean it? 'Cause I know I'm tough, but I can't let you in if you're going to break my heart, Richard Lewis.'

'I'm not going to break your heart,' he murmured, meaning it.

He remembered the earrings and went down to their bedroom, reappearing moments later bearing the small box. She gazed at it, then up at him, and her face was a mask of confusion.

'Richard...I...' She swallowed, and her eyes shone with tears. She opened the small box and saw the little pearls. She tried to hide it, but he saw it then – she thought it was going to be a ring. He cursed himself. Why could he never get it right?

'A Christmas present,' he managed. 'I... Did you think it was a ring?'

She shook her head, no words coming. He knew he was babbling now, trying to take the sting out of this situation. 'Because I already got you a ring, the one I bought when we went off from the pig farm. I let you believe it was brass but it's not – it's gold.'

'Good to know. Thanks, Richard. And these are lovely.' She sounded choked, and as she turned to the sink, he knew she was crying. He felt like a complete heel.

CHAPTER 10

The following morning, he woke to find everyone gone, including Pippa. Someone, Sarah probably, had left a copy of the *Washington Post* on the table.

Things were heating up at home even more than before. The isolationists were in the minority, but boy were they loud in their condemnation of the United States getting involved over here. But Richard's stories of refugees and British people alike gave folks back home a glimpse of what despotism unchecked looked like, and the American public sure didn't want that.

He thought he would go for a cup of decent coffee and see what was going on. It would cost him, but the Ritz had nice coffee and he felt like treating himself. He could go to the Savoy, but he would run into too many people he knew there; besides, the band there played all day and night sometimes, and he wasn't in the mood to hear the 'Chattanooga Choo Choo' forty times. The newspaper world was a hive of gossip and rumours and he normally tuned in to it all, but he needed to compose a letter to Grace so he needed some peace and quiet.

As he entered the hotel, he ran into Dan Rutherford, a junior staffer on some rag based in the Midwest.

'Hey, Richard, you heard the latest?' Rutherford was fizzing with excitement.

'No?' Richard found Rutherford insufferable. He was the son of some minor politician, and to hear him, you would think he was FDR's closest confidante.

'We printed this morning, Rainbow-5, the top-secret war plan. Shows that Roosevelt had no intention of ever honouring the pledge of last year that no Americans would fight in a foreign war. The isolationists are going crazy, saying they're being proved right.' Rutherford cackled delightedly.

This was just a game to people like him; he was too dumb to realise that leaking secret documents was risking the safety of the entire nation.

'Oh, right. Look, I'm meeting someone, so I gotta go.' He walked away. It was rude, but he didn't care.

There was a lot of rumbling in the United Press office about Japan, and though some Americans thought it was nonsense, he wasn't at all sure. The meeting a few weeks ago in DC between Cordell Hull, secretary of state, and the Japanese ambassador did not end well. The Japanese were demanding that America withdraw from China, lift all sanctions directed against Japan and put the brakes on all American naval buildup in the Pacific. Roosevelt wasn't going to do that, and the Japanese didn't sound like they were in the mood to negotiate. If the Japanese did make a strike, it was probably going to be in Borneo or the Philippines, or maybe French Indochina, where they were apparently building up troops, much to the fury of FDR. And if they did, it would open up a whole new theatre of war at a critical juncture for this one. Stalin was pushing the Germans back, and while things were not yet turning in the Allied favour, it was looking increasingly like that was a possibility. If Stalin was successful, the Allies needed to consolidate, not get involved in Asia as well.

Bob Nakamura, a Japanese American from the *Boston Globe*, had told him the day before yesterday that the Japanese press was saying there was no hope of a compromise between them and the United

States. But it could just be fighting talk with nothing behind it; nobody was really sure.

He sat in a corner seat at the upstairs bar of the Ritz and ordered coffee. The downstairs bar was apparently the place for homosexuals to socialise, at least that was what he'd heard. The Albanian royal family lived here for a year, complete with their entourage, and all the aristocracy used it as their hub. But it wasn't racy enough for newspapermen – usually they preferred the Savoy or the Berkeley – so he hoped he could get some peace. He'd write to Grace, and then he wanted to spend some time on his novel. His progress was slow, but he enjoyed working on it immensely when he did get time. It was about a wealthy family scandal and was set in Savannah in the 1920s, full of intrigue and double-dealing. He knew his mother would blow her top if it ever got published – too many people were recognisable – but he didn't care. Life had expanded for him beyond the genteel streets of Savannah, Georgia, and he could never see himself living there now.

He sipped the real coffee and sighed contentedly. He missed coffee more than anything else, he thought.

He still felt dreadful about how things had gone with Pippa last night. He'd put his arm around her in bed, but she pretended to be asleep. He'd really hurt her, and he hated himself for it. He'd have to make it right, but his mind was in such a spin right now. *One thing at a time.*

He took out his writing pad and fountain pen and began. *Dear Grace...*

What to say? Everything he thought of sounded trite. He had to tell her about Pippa – he should have said something ages ago – but this wasn't the appropriate time, was it?

He could write of trying to get a message to Didi; that could be the second page. But writing the first bit was harder. Eventually he did what he always did, he wrote from the heart.

Dear Grace,

I don't even know what to say; everything seems trite and meaningless. This English language of ours has its limitations, but I'll do my best.

I couldn't believe it when I read your letter telling of that terrible, terrible night that Declan died. I still can't believe it. He was a young man like myself, with his whole life ahead of him. He had so much to offer the world, and what I knew of him, through you and by meeting him in person briefly when we came to Knocknashee, he was a man worthy of all the praise heaped on him. Even going so far as to risk his life to save strangers—he was amazing. My most heartfelt condolences, Grace. I can't imagine what pain you must be in. I know you loved him, and he you, and you should have enjoyed a long and happy life together in idyllic Knocknashee. But that was not meant to be, and for that I'm so very sorry.

He meant every word. If he could wave a magic wand and bring Declan back, he would. The image of Grace in pain hurt him. Then, unbidden, came the familiar thought he fought back. Grace was single. Declan was gone. *Stop it.* He ordered his imagination to show some respect. She was his friend, she was heartbroken, and all he could do was daydream about how he might now have a chance? Though he didn't. He knew that. He'd told her how he felt before she and Declan were an item, and she didn't reply. No answer *was* an answer, as Sarah pointed out. Besides, his world and hers were so far apart, not just geographically but in every way...how would it work? *STOP!* He shook his head to dismiss these awful thoughts and kept writing. What kind of a monster imagined such things when hearing such tragic news?

This war is so greedy and cares nothing for those left behind. I sometimes fear I'm becoming inured to war and loss and death and bloodshed; the Blitz here had that effect. So many people lost their loved ones. It's become commonplace to hear "My son, my wife, my child was killed by a bomb." But Ireland is neutral; it's supposed to be safe. The Germans are indiscriminate killers. They care nothing for civilian versus military deaths. Clearly they don't respect neutrality, and that is why they must be beaten, at any cost. I had no real emotion about this war before now, but seeing the waste, the human misery caused daily, would melt the heart of stone.

So as I go about my business and try in my miniscule way to make a difference, I will do so from now on with Declan McKenna in mind. He should not be dead. He should be alive and inventing things and making my best friend happy.

He paused. She *was* his best friend. He was telling the truth about that. The love of his life too, but his friend first and foremost.

I am not sure about God and all of that. I was raised Episcopalian, as I told you, but it never really stuck. My parents were churchgoers because it was what you did rather than out of any profound sense of faith. But I know you are a true believer, and so I hope and even pray that Declan is in heaven and watching over you always.

Things are heating up on the Japanese side of things, so everyone is watching and waiting. There have been several German U-boat attacks along the East Coast too. Facing the Japs on one side and the Germans on the other isn't a position the United States will tolerate, so I won't be surprised if it's off to war we go very soon, once again.

The British have done well, amazingly so, standing up to Hitler alone, but that little Kraut with his stupid mustache and horrible voice had better be shaking in his boots now. If he's not, I think he will be soon. He has poked the wrong bear, and if he thinks the valiant RAF and the French and everyone else that's fighting back, covertly or overtly, were a lot to contend with, he won't know what hit him when the might of the US military comes down upon him. So while the loss of Declan is something you will never forgive or forget, know this, Grace—they will pay, and pay dearly, for what they've done. I believe now that, along with our allies, the United States of America will see to that.

Forgive me if this is insensitive, especially now, but I wanted you to know, I've also asked my father to write to you if he gets notification of my death. I gave him your address. But I hope you never get a letter from Arthur Lewis.

So I'll sign off now. Sarah and Jacob and I are working around the clock to file copy, and Kirky is voracious for more. I'm in the middle of making a glossary of words GIs will need to know. We speak the same language—sort of.

I'll enclose my informal glossary as it might make you smile. If you're not in a smiling mood, throw it in the fire.

He looked up as an older aristocratic-looking British woman in a fur coat and hat stood by his table. 'Are you an American?' she asked archly.

'Eh...yes, ma'am, I am,' he replied, annoyed at being interrupted but too polite to show it.

'The chap at the bar said you were, and a journalist.' She indicated the young bartender who had served his coffee.

'Can I help you, ma'am?' he asked, secretly cursing the bartender and his big mouth.

'Yes. Do you think Roosevelt will send us soldiers?' Something about the directness of the question made Richard want to be honest.

'Well, ma'am, I think he wants to, and personally, I think we should, but a lot of folks back in the US feel that this has nothing to do with them, and after the last time...it's hard to tell.'

She sniffed and went to leave but then turned back to face him. 'We'll win with or without your lot, but it would certainly speed things up.'

He nodded. 'I agree. If Herr Hitler has to face the might of the combined United States and British military on one side and Stalin on the other, that sure would bring about a happy ending to this war.'

'Yes, well, if you have any influence, please use it.'

'Yes, ma'am, I sure will.' He smiled and stood as she walked away regally.

He finished his letter, not mentioning Pippa; he'd do it next time. Poor Grace didn't need to hear about his romantic life.

He paid and asked for a receipt. Kirky was happy to pay his expenses, but he demanded receipts. No receipt, no reimbursement.

He decided to go to the Associated Press offices for the evening. The day was slipping away, and he needed to write up his latest copy for Kirky, and it was a good place to hear first what was happening politically. His niche was knowing about the events on the international stage and then reporting on how they impacted ordinary people, connecting politics to repercussions in daily life. He would also have to track Jacob and Sarah down to interview the Russians, but he could do that tonight.

The AP office was a hive of activity as usual, *clack-clacking* typewriters, a fug of cigarette smoke, the constant hum of conversation. He found an empty office upstairs and set to work. He had several pieces that needed polishing, and he was working on a selection of essays about transport and communications and the difficulties people faced transferring information to each other when the normal routes were closed due to fear of espionage. As darkness fell, he kept working and even managed to write a bit of his novel. He'd never told anyone he was writing fiction – he felt a bit silly in the current climate – but it was enjoyable, and even if it never saw the light of day, it was a pleasant way to pass the time. Sarah and Jacob would know where to find him if they needed him, and Pippa was doing a double shift at the munitions factory, so he used the time and enjoyed the unusual solitude. The offices got quieter as the evening wore on. The lure of the hotel bars and the nightclubs of Soho beat the typewriter every day, so he knew there would only be a handful of cub reporters left in the building. He checked his watch; he'd forgotten it had stopped when he'd been soaked yesterday. He'd have to take it apart and see if it could be fixed.

Deciding there was no time like the present, he did just that, and to his delight, after an hour it was ticking happily again. He went to the hallway to check the time on the large grandfather clock there and saw to his dismay it was almost nine. Time to go home for certain.

'Mr Lewis,' the doorman said to him as he left, 'there's a telegram just arrived for you, and it's marked very urgent.'

'Thank you, Ernie.' Ernie served as unofficial secretary to the newspapermen who used the offices on and off. Richard noticed he wasn't the only one getting a telegram; several more envelopes were perched on Ernie's desk.

He took the small card from its buff envelope. It was from Kirky.

Lewis/Nunez. Drop everything. Japs attacked Pearl Harbor, Hawaii. USA at war. Make contact immediately. Get out of GB and head to Singapore ASAP. Don't care how. Sarah and freelance photographer to remain reporting from London.

The blood rushed to his brain. He tried to focus. He looked up at

Ernie. 'Is this true?' Ernie obviously knew the contents of the telegram.

'I believe it is, sir. Would you like to come and listen to my wireless? There will be a news bulletin any minute, I would imagine.'

Richard nodded and followed Ernie to his small glass office inside the door of the building. Soon they were joined by two or three others who'd just heard the news as well. The crackle of the BBC filled the small dusty cubicle.

Japan has launched a surprise attack on the American naval base at Pearl Harbor, Hawaii, and has declared war on Britain and the United States. US President Franklin D Roosevelt has mobilised all of his forces and is poised to declare war on Japan...

Richard dashed out of the offices and ran all the way home, his heart pounding tightly in his chest as he arrived. Sarah, Jacob and Pippa were at the table eating toast and tea.

He quickly told them about Kirky's telegram, and Jacob switched on the temperamental old wireless. Richard saw the gleam of satisfaction in his eyes; this was what he wanted. Sarah looked terrified. At the end of the bulletin, he took the letter to Grace from his pocket, added a note onto the end telling her he was going and went downstairs to the mailbox on the street

When he returned a few minutes later, he went to pack. Pippa leant on the doorjamb. 'Are you going tonight?' Her voice quivered.

He nodded as he threw some clothes and his portable typewriter in his leather carryall. 'Everyone will want to get out. We'll head to Southampton and get passage from there, a troop ship or something, I don't know...'

'Richard, I'm sorry I was strange about the earrings last night. They are beautiful and I'm ever so grateful...'

He stopped what he was doing and moved towards her, leading her to the bed. 'I could wait until tomorrow. We could go to the registry office, get married?'

She smiled. 'Don't be daft.'

'I'm not being daft, as you say. If you are my wife, you're a de facto

American citizen. If this country gets invaded, then at least our embassy has to offer you protection. You'd be safe.'

'I'm English, Richard, and I want to stay that way, dead or alive. So thanks but no thanks.' She gave a small sad laugh. 'Besides, I think I might hold out for a slightly more romantic proposal if it's all the same to you.'

He wished she would not be so stubborn, but he understood her too. This little country had withstood so much, been so brave in the face of unspeakable horror, she wasn't going to change coats now. But whatever happened next, and it was impossible to tell, this new phase of war was only just beginning.

CHAPTER 11

KNOCKNASHEE

JANUARY 1942

Sitting in Charlie's house, Grace forced herself to focus on what Paudie was saying to her, something about a mare and a donkey having a baby. He loved to share with her the things he learnt from his extensive reading, and normally she was interested, but these days her mind seemed to be covered in a wet dark blanket of grief and she found concentrating on anything hard.

Christmas had been a miserable affair, neither she nor Charlie able to be jolly for the sake of it. There was nothing to give as a gift, and even the little home-made tokens were thin on the ground this year. The Christmas dinner was a chicken with some spuds and carrots and a turnip, no plum pudding due to the lack of dried fruit, and Dymphna had made a kind of trifle with a thin cake base, a tin of peaches and some cream, but by nobody's standards was it a feast. Dymphna and Charlie tried to fill stockings for the children – Grace had donated a few pencils and a notebook to the cause – but all in all, everyone was glad for it to be over.

'Grace, so which is it?' Paudie asked.

'Sorry, Paudie, I...' She shut her eyes and inhaled. 'What was the question?'

Kate looked up from the floor, where she was colouring in a picture.

Paudie showed her a picture in an encyclopaedia. 'Which is it? If the mammy is a mare and the daddy is a donkey, is it a mule or a jennet?'

'A mule,' she answered automatically, not caring if she was right or not.

'Are you sure, Grace?' He looked worried. He was a stickler for facts.

'I'm sure...' She left him to his reading as the sounds of retching came down the stairs of the McKennas' small cottage. Odile O'Hare was sleeping peacefully in her cot upstairs, and Grace prayed the sound of poor Dymphna throwing up wouldn't wake her. Normally, she was told, nausea subsided after the first few months of pregnancy, but poor Dymphna seemed to have it all through. Would she have felt sick like that if she'd actually been pregnant, Grace wondered. The thought was like a stab of pain, and she dismissed it. She couldn't think about it.

Charlie, like her, was in a fog of grief over the death of his son, but the impending arrival of a new baby was taking the edge off the pain for him. She was glad and didn't begrudge him the bit of comfort. She wished she had something nice to focus on, but she couldn't find anything. Declan was dead. That was all.

So much wasted potential. He'd had a whole life to look forward to. But there was nothing left of Declan McKenna in the world now. And it felt cold without him.

People tried to help, take her mind off it, but she didn't want to be distracted or to hear about God's will or how the good die young. She just wanted him back. Week after weary week, she would get up, often in the early hours, and just sit in the window, looking up at the stars that twinkled over the Atlantic. Was he there? Was he in heaven? Could he see her? Did he know how much it hurt her to lose him? She tried talking to him, asking him to give her some indication that he was there and all right. But she got nothing. She had no sense of him, and the loss was a huge gaping chasm of confusion and pain.

Paudie was talking again, now the topic was desks, another of his fascinations.

Charlie had found an old desk with lockable drawers in the attic of the cottage, and he and Paudie were doing it up so the boy could do his reading and research on it. They were excited to discover a secret drawer, opened by pressing a knot in the wood. Paudie had to research it, so he wrote to Lizzie to ask her if she could find a book in the library in Cork on old furniture, and of course she'd sent it. 'Grace, do you know that secret drawers and secret opening mechanisms were very common and my book shows where to look for them. They hid levers in knots of wood or where one piece joined another, to keep valuables safe.'

Grace was trying to tune him out, but he was insistent when telling you something so she had to pay attention. For children, life just went on. She was tired despite sleeping a lot and needed to get away from Paudie and his endless chat about old furniture.

Mercifully his mother called him upstairs and he left her alone. She was so fond of him but at the moment she just wasn't able for his endless chatter. She found the company exhausting and had avoided the neighbours in as much as was possible in Knocknashee.

To her astonishment Margaret O'Connor, who'd been so horrible to her the night Declan died, had asked her for a word as she crossed the road to Charlie's earlier.

'I wanted to say I'm sorry, Grace,' Margaret said, looking genuinely contrite. 'I've been thinking about what I said to you, and it was very wrong and unfair of me. I was just distraught over Seán, but I had no right to say what I did, so I'm sorry.'

'Oh, Mrs O'Connor, please don't give it another thought. We were all so worried. We've all said things in the heat of the moment.' Grace forgave her immediately.

'Well, that's very gracious of you. 'Tisn't everyone would be…'

'Please, it's forgotten.'

Grace was pulled back to the present. Margaret O'Connor was right. People did say things in the heat of the moment. She was so sorry for how she'd spoken to Tilly. She'd write tonight and apologise, try to put that right at least. She'd been seething since the meeting, but life was too short and she and Tilly needed each other now like they never had before. She'd swallow her pride and apologise.

'I drew a picture of us all,' Kate said shyly, giving it to Grace. It was a colourful drawing of Dymphna, Charlie, Paudie, Kate and Grace. 'And I drew Declan up in heaven with the angels,' she added, showing her the winged Declan in the corner of the drawing with a big smile on his face.

'It's lovely, pet, really lovely.' Grace tried to infuse her voice with some enthusiasm.

'You can have it for your wall, to see Declan whenever you want.'

The tears pricked her eyes then, and she couldn't help but let them fall. Kate gave her a hug and found a slightly crumpled but basically clean handkerchief stuffed up her sleeve, offering it to Grace. They were used to tears.

'Charlie said he'd bring us butter nuggets from Bríd's because we peeled the spuds and laid the table for the dinner last night – Mammy was too sick.'

'Then if he said it, he will.' Even if he had no ration coupon, Grace knew Bríd wouldn't refuse Charlie a few sweets for the children under the circumstances. Charlie had taken Paudie and Kate to his heart as if they were his own, and they loved him.

'Is Tilly coming home soon?' Paudie asked then, looking up from his book. 'I want to show her this bit about Edwardian desks, they had a special lever under the drawer…'

Grace shook herself. This wasn't right, all this wallowing. All over the world, people were losing their loved ones and were just getting on with it. Richard had said in his letter how he met bereaved people every single day. It was how life was, and she had to toughen up. He'd added a note to his last letter as soon as the Japanese attacked Pearl Harbor, saying he was being sent to report on the situation in Asia, and she'd not heard anything since. She would like to know he was all right but didn't dare write to Sarah in case it upset Pippa. Richard hadn't mentioned her in the letter, but she was sure they were more than friends.

He'd said he was going to Singapore. She'd looked on the big map Father Iggy had bought for the school, much to the displeasure of the canon, to see if it was anywhere near where Maurice was in the Philippines. The Philippines was a protectorate or something of the United States so had been invaded by the Japanese as well. She worried for her brother. She'd sent a telegram, asking for news that he was well, but had heard nothing back. The whole world was at war now. It was hard not to wonder if any of them would survive another year.

She forced a smile and put her hand on Paudie's thin shoulder. She felt him relax as Dymphna came down the stairs.

'Are you feeling better Mammy?' the little boy was concerned.

'Much better love. Now show me this book on the desks you got, it sounds very interesting.' She winked at Grace as she passed her.

'Will I check Odile?' Kate asked, not wishing to have her brother take all of Grace's attention.

Kate's idea of checking on the baby was waking her up, and Grace wanted her to sleep for another while. She was almost two years old and a bundle of fun, but now that she was walking, she was into everything, and you needed to have eyes in the back of your head for her.

Mary was doing her best up at the farm, but her rheumatism was terrible and her mobility was not up to running after a toddler. Aware of the canon's threat to remove Odile from Mary's care, Dymphna took her to her house most days. But poor Dymphna was so ill now, Grace was stepping in as much as she could.

As Dymphna examined the book with Paudie, ashen-faced and

exhausted, there was a knock at the door. Charlie was out on his afternoon round and wouldn't be home until after six.

'I'll get it,' Grace said. 'You sit down there by the fire.'

Dymphna did as she was bid, and her children clambered around her. Grace limped to the front door. Her steel calliper was digging in. She needed to get to Cork to have Dr Warrington order her a new one, but she couldn't face it. The last time she'd been there was with Declan, around the time of their wedding, and she knew it would just be too hard to go back so soon, no matter how much the Warringtons coaxed her to visit.

Nancy O'Flaherty, the postmistress, was at the door.

'Hello, Nancy.' Grace was surprised to see her. She wasn't a usual visitor, but everyone saw her all the time because she ran the post office.

'Grace, I'm glad I've caught you, *a stór*. Let me in, for the love of God, for fear I'd be spotted.'

Nancy stepped into the small hallway, and Grace stood aside. 'Is everything all right, Nancy? Is Charlie all right?' Grace felt the panic rise up in her.

'Everything is grand, lovie, don't be worrying, but I do need to talk to you.'

'Come through.' Grace led the postmistress down the passageway into the back kitchen, bypassing the sitting room where Dymphna sat with her children.

'Grace, you know I shouldn't be doing this, and I wouldn't normally stick my beak into things, but I couldn't in all conscience stay quiet. You have to know.'

'Know what, Nancy?' She was worried now.

'Your man above' – Grace knew she meant the canon, as nobody else elicited such scorn from the normally kind Nancy – 'is after summoning that long string of misery Francis Sheehan back to replace poor Declan.'

Grace was aghast. There had been a substitute teacher found by Father Iggy when Declan died, but she got a permanent job in Limerick and took it, so Grace was trying to manage with just herself and Janie O'Shea, the monitor. She had intended to try to find someone else but now, if Nancy was right the canon had stepped in unbidden.

Agnes had hired Francis Sheehan to replace Grace when they'd had a massive falling out, and he was a tyrant. The children were scared stiff of him, and he was very enthusiastic with the strap. Grace was able to confront the canon with his wrongdoing once Agnes died, and she made one of the terms of her silence the removal of that fiend from her school. How dare the canon rehire him? The high-handedness of it. She was the headmistress – she was at least entitled to a say, if not the final word.

She could not countenance Francis Sheehan being the other teacher in her school. She wouldn't.

'How do you know?' she asked.

'He sent a telegram, thanking the canon for the offer and saying he would gladly take it up after Easter.' For Nancy to reveal the contents of a telegram meant for someone else was a big thing. She was a decent, kind person of impeccable morals, so this would have taken some soul-searching. Grace was grateful that she had, though.

'I will not have that man here, Nancy, I just won't.' Grace exhaled through her nose, her pulse thumping. She'd rarely felt such fury.

'I'd like to think you can stop him, Grace love, but you know what that one is like – he'll do his own thing and thinks he's the lord and master over us all.'

'Well, leave him to me, Nancy, and don't worry, I won't say how I heard it in case you're worried. I met a woman on my teacher training course from Wicklow who knew him – he was teaching up there, last I heard, God love the children of Wicklow – so I'll say I heard it from her.'

Nancy nodded. She would be in a lot of trouble if it was discovered she was gossiping. 'What will you do?' she asked.

'I don't know yet, but I'll do something. That man has caused enough hurt and pain to the people of this place. He won't inflict that monster on us – I won't have it.'

Nancy smiled. 'You're a sweet little thing, Grace Fitzgerald, but I wouldn't like to be on the wrong side of you.'

Nobody ever called her Mrs McKenna. She and Declan had only been married a matter of weeks when he died, and besides, she was Miss Fitz to the children and their families, so changing her name at the time seemed unnecessary. She wished she had now, though.

'Thank you for telling me, Nancy. I know it wasn't done lightly, but you did the right thing.' Grace showed her out.

Nancy then grabbed her elbow. 'Hold on, I just thought of something.'

'Go on. Any ideas, Nancy, I'm all ears.' Grace's mind was racing. She would not allow this, no matter how heartbroken she was, she would fight back. How dare he?.

'That Mrs Worth – you remember Douglas Worth, used to live in the big old place out the Dingle road? His parents, Mr and Mrs Worth, lived there?'

Grace had no idea where this was going. Nancy assumed everyone knew everyone for six generations, and Grace often found herself lying and saying she knew people when she didn't.

'Ah, you do. Douglas would be one age to your Maurice, I think. He went to school in England on account of them being Protestants, and he never came back, but the parents used to visit him and his wife in Liverpool.'

Still at a loss as to what this had to do with Francis Sheehan, Grace knew she'd have to be patient; Nancy would get to it in her own time.

'They both died, and the place went to rack and ruin. Terrible pity, 'twas a lovely house. She had green fingers, old Mrs Worth, God be good to her. I often thought her blooms were wasted on the altar of the Protestant church, with only a handful of a congregation to see them, but that's the way of it, I suppose...'

'And how could she be of help to us?' Grace urged gently.

'Oh yes, she's a teacher...well, a headmistress actually, over in

Liverpool – the young Mrs Worth – and she and her daughters were bombed out of it, the craythurs, so they're living up in that draughty old place now. She might be glad of a job... But the canon would never allow it.' Her face fell as she realized this. 'Sure she'd be Protestant too...'

A spark of hope lit in Grace. 'But she is a teacher? You're sure?'

'Oh, I am, she called into the post office the other week to tell me she was there and to ask if there was a local handyman she could employ to fix the old place up a bit. She told me then that her school was bombed as well as the house, and her husband is in the Air Force.' Nancy shook her head. ''Tis a pity. I thought we had something, but he'll never go for that, not in a million years.' She looked as sad as Grace had felt a few minutes ago. 'Anyway, enough about him. How are you doing, *a stór*?'

'Ah, I'm grand, just keeping going, you know?' Grace forced a smile.

''Tis a very hard blow you're after getting, Grace. Poor Charlie is fierce upset too, but he has Dymphna and the children and the new baby now to look forward to...' She stopped, clearly thinking this line of thought wasn't helpful. 'It's just very hard, and I want you to know I see it.'

'Thanks, Nancy. It's hard, but what can you do only keep going?' Grace sighed.

'When my Ned died, God be good to his gentle soul, I had the girls, I know, but losing your person, where you are their number one and they are yours, no matter how good other relationships are, nothing ever is the same again.'

Grace had never heard Nancy talk about her late husband so emotionally before. He'd been dead for years – Grace barely remembered him – but in the postmistress now, she could see a kindred spirit; she understood.

'I was thinking I might go to Cork for the Easter holidays, but only if Tilly is home. Mary needs me here and poor Dymphna is so sick. But sometimes I just want to go somewhere, where his memory isn't on every corner. This morning I was buttering my toast, and the knife was one Declan sharpened for me. He said my knives were so blunt, they wouldn't even cut butter, so he sharpened them and then gave me dire warnings not to cut myself. Of course I did exactly that the first day, cut my thumb, and he was so upset, he took that one off and blunted it a bit. I just took it out of the drawer and the tears came... It's like that, isn't it? The smallest thing...'

'I haven't cooked a turnip since Ned died. He hated the smell of them boiling, but I used to make them for myself and the girls and he'd have to pick bits of turnip out of the stew, but he never complained. So now I never get them.' Grace could hear the pain there, as if he'd only died last week, not twenty years ago.

Maybe that was how life would be for her now, forever changed.

* * *

THAT EVENING, as she was mounting the stairs to go to bed, she had barely placed her good foot on the step when she started and let out an audible gasp as the knocker hit the brass plate on the front door. The sound reverberated around the tiled hallway. Who on earth would be calling at this hour of the night?

'Grace, open up for God's sake, I need the toilet!'

She couldn't believe it. She limped as fast as her leg would allow to the door. 'Tilly!' she exclaimed, thrilled to see her friend. She'd been worrying constantly about the big fight and wondering if things would ever again be the same.

'I need your privy, Grace. We're seconds from me watering the plants outside.' Tilly stormed past her up the stairs to the bathroom.

Grace waited, astounded and delighted as she heard the flush and then the loud banging of the pipes as Tilly washed her hands before bolting back downstairs again. Were things going to be all right between them?

'Hello, Grace.' Tilly smiled uncertainly. 'Are we all right?'

Grace nodded and put her arms out wide.

'Good. I was scared after... Well, look, let's get the hugging out of the way,' she said, mock weary. It was a running joke that Grace was the more emotional of the two of them and Tilly was tough as old boots.

'Come here.' Grace squeezed her, hardly able to believe she was home at last. She and Tilly were friends for too long to let a fight get between them. Grace was still not convinced Eloise was innocent, but she knew for certain that Tilly was. The rest could be left to the authorities.

'Right, tea?' Tilly asked as Grace released her.

'Not only tea, but Pádraig O Sé gave me a bottle of poitín if you fancy a drop?'

'Oh, that's the way of it, is it? I turn my back for five minutes and you're on the booze?' Tilly grinned as they went back to the warm kitchen. 'You'll be below in O'Connor's picking fights next, and Dr Ryan will spend as much time patching you up as he does Neilus Collins and those mad brothers of his.' She laughed, then motioned to Grace to sit. 'One of them was on the bus, could hardly see out of a black eye he had. What a shower of eejits they are, battering each other night and day.'

She insisted on making the tea and opened the tin to find half a madeira cake.

'God, is this all there is, Grace' She wrinkled her nose, used to a better class of confection in her friend's house.

'With the ration, 'twas the best Dymphna could do,' Grace said with a sigh. It was as if the fight had never happened.

Tilly sighed. 'Well, needs must, but I won't say I wasn't dreaming of a big slice of apple tart or a chunk of gingerbread with sultanas...'

'Was the food desperate in jail?' Grace asked, dying to hear all about everything.

'It was, but that was the least of my troubles...' Tilly poured the tea and pulled a chair up at the table. 'I'm so sorry, Grace, for how things went when you came to visit – I was just so stressed. Can you forgive me?'

'I'm sorry too, Tilly. I was demented over Declan. I should never have spoken to you like that. I don't think Eloise is guilty, but even if she had something to do with it, then she is the one responsible, not you. Declan wouldn't blame you and neither do I, so please, let's just try to get on with things and let it all go, shall we?'

'I was so scared you wouldn't...' Tilly's voice broke.

'Ah, Tilly, we're friends for years and years. One little bust-up isn't going to change that.' Grace held her hand.

'I know, but...I... You get a lot of time to think in jail...'

'You're home now. Nobody here blames you for what happened, Tilly, I promise you that.'

'Do you not like Eloise, Grace? Like not because of Declan or anything but just...' Tilly's gaze was downcast, and her shoulders sloped. Tilly was so rarely crestfallen, it was awful to see her beaten down somehow.

'I do... Well...' She sighed. 'I just am a bit jealous of her, I suppose. You're my best friend, and I...I don't want to lose you, and I feel I could never compete...'

Tilly looked directly at Grace then and swallowed.

'What?' Grace asked. 'What is it, Til?'

'I...' Her friend swallowed again and gazed at her hands. 'You'll always be my best friend, that position isn't available.' She gave a small smile. 'But I... Eloise and I...we're not like friends... Well, we are, but not...' Tilly flushed dark red then, and Grace wondered what on earth she wanted to say.

'Tell me, Tilly. Whatever it is, just tell me.' Grace leaned closer.

'Do you know what a lesbian is, Grace?'

Grace flushed now. She did. She'd read about them, women who were attracted to other women in the way most people were attracted to the opposite sex. All she could do was nod.

'Well, that's what Eloise and I are. We' – her voice was husky with emotion – 'we love each other.'

In that instant Grace was transported back to the railing of a ship, sailing from Ireland to New York, with Declan. He'd mentioned something about Tilly having no interest in men. 'Declan knew,' she said, almost to herself. It was a statement, not a question.

Tilly nodded, the tears that had pooled on her lower lids flowing down her face now. 'He was the only one I could talk to. He knew and didn't judge me or try to talk me out of it. I loved him too, Grace, so much. I could never have been involved in anything that could hurt him.'

'I know you couldn't...' She held onto her friend's hand while trying to process this news.

'Are you disgusted? Shocked?' Tilly seemed smaller than Grace had ever seen her. Tilly was always the lion, she the lamb, but now her friend looked so diminished somehow.

'No. I'm sorry I didn't know sooner – I wish you'd have said. But I'm not disgusted. I'll be honest and say I don't really understand it, but I know you don't like men, not that way anyway, so liking women is... It probably makes more sense to you...' Grace hoped she wasn't offending or insulting her, but she was floundering here.

'But you don't...well, you don't mind?' Tilly winced.

'Of course I don't mind. Why would I mind?'

'Well, just that people think it's wrong...unnatural...' Tilly's voice was barely audible now.

'Well, I don't. I don't know what I think, because this is all news to me, but I don't think you're unnatural or bad or anything like that.'

'Didn't you suspect? Remember when Richard's sister sent me that book, *The Well of Loneliness?*'

GRACE DID REMEMBER.

'Well, that was about women like me, and like Eloise...'

Grace laughed then. 'Either I'm the most innocent creature to ever be put in shoes or I'm blind as a bat, but I genuinely had no idea. Everyone else seems to have caught on way before me.'

'I always thought you did know but weren't saying...'

'I love you and you're my best friend. Nothing you could ever do would be wrong for me. I understand a bit better now why you're so sure Eloise is innocent. If someone accused Declan of something, I know I could say with complete certainty that he was innocent because...well, I knew him, better than anyone. And if you say that about Eloise, I believe you.'

'So everything is all right with us?'

'Everything is fine.'

CHAPTER 12

Once Tilly finally left, Grace was wide awake, so she decided to take a bath. How often Declan had joked that he'd deliberately chosen a huge bath – it had begun life as a cattle trough – so that when they were married, he could join her. That had never happened. They'd never had the chance. Like so many other things they'd never got to do and now never would.

She forced herself to carry on. After her bath, she sat down to mark the exercise books for her classes. She taught both the juniors and the seniors together now with Janie's help, but the workload was taking its toll on her. Between all the work in school and the sheer grief of losing Declan, she was wiped out. At least having Tilly home meant the work of caring for Odile was back with her.

Once she'd had a cursory glance at the work and stamped them all with the ink stamp of a beaver giving a thumbs up that Richard had sent, she allowed herself to think about what Nancy had told her.

Over her dead body was that horrible man, Francis Sheehan, coming back to teach in Knocknashee. She remembered how Sergeant Keane's daughter, Mairead, who was a very bright girl but struggled to read and write, and with whom Grace had worked a lot one to one over the years, had been badly beaten by him last time he was here. The sergeant took him to task, but Grace wasn't sure how much he could do. The teacher was master in his own kingdom, and with the full backing of the canon, well, it was difficult.

The canon was high-handed enough to think he could just fire her like that, but she was in no form to put up with him. Every instinct she possessed told her to go up there, confront him with all she knew about him, how he'd lied and cheated to get Agnes to spend money on him, how he'd taken advantage of a young girl who had her head turned by an older man who had taken a vow of chastity, how he'd sold babies to couples in America. She knew all of this to be true, but she had no evidence. Declan had heard the story in New York too, but he was gone. He was a powerful canon, not even just a priest, and he was the chairman of the school. Ultimately he could throw her out, give her the sack so she would have to tread carefully. It was a while yet to Easter, so she had some time, but she would have to find a way to outmanoeuvre him.

She did her exercises alone, trying not to remember the nights when Declan would help her and how it often turned into lovemaking, and went to bed, unable to sleep, the thoughts whirring relentlessly around in her head.

The running of the school single-handedly was too much for her. If only Father Iggy was still here. The children loved him, but he'd been moved to allow that other snake back to the parish. If only Mrs Worth wasn't Protestant.

She tossed and turned, her worries piling on top of each other as sleep eluded her. As well as the school situation, she remembered how the canon had been sniffing around last year, wondering if there was proof that Odile was Alfie's daughter. They'd said that of course she was, but in fact she was no relation of his at all, and the fear that the canon would somehow find that out was one of her many worries. To add to it, she dreaded hearing bad news about Richard.

She couldn't picture him in Singapore, and it had made her worry too for her brother, Maurice, in the Philippines.

Sleep eluded her, so she opened the biscuit tin, the one Charlie had given her when Richard's first letter arrived, which was now almost full of correspondence.

She selected Richard's last letter.

His letter after hearing of Declan's death was one of her favourites. It was beginning to tear on the creases, she'd read it so often; she thought she might try to put some gum on it tomorrow or something to stop it disintegrating altogether. After sitting down and lighting the gas lamp, she allowed her heart to be soothed by the words.

The sympathy, the love, shone from the pages. He called her his best friend, said he wished he could bring Declan back. His words were like a salve to her raw pain. Then the note that he was going to Singapore. He'd obviously written the letter before getting the news of the Japanese attack in Pearl Harbor.

He'd sent a separate sheet explaining that a drug store was a chemist's shop, a subway was the Tube, stout was black beer, a faucet was a tap, the trunk of a car was the boot, and how Friday week meant the Friday after next Friday.

She'd made a lesson out of it in school, and the children had great fun speaking American. They had confused their parents by referring to sidewalks for footpaths and trash cans for bins. As she taught them, it made him feel not so far away.

CHAPTER 13

RAFFLES HOTEL, SINGAPORE

16 FEBRUARY 1942

'Get out of here now, that's an order.' Lieutenant Bixby from Fort Lauderdale, Florida, was not in the mood for a debate, and Richard knew he and Jacob had stayed too long as it was. All women and children had been evacuated already, but Jacob was determined to document everything. Richard thanked God Kirky had only sent him and Jacob – Sarah and Pippa were still in London.

'Take a ration pack, and remember with the toilet paper, rub it between your hands to soften it, one wipe up, one down and one to polish, behind enemy lines use leaves or they'll find you.'

They took a pack each, knowing that every minute of delay increased their chances of being taken prisoner. The chaos of the normally clean and well-run city was evident in every corner as they made for the quayside amid droves of people, all with the same idea.

They'd heard on the grapevine that the first wave of Japanese arrived to the city mostly by bicycle. The generals followed by car and were expecting to surrender to General Percival and were astonished to discover he was surrendering to them instead. Their confusion was short lived though, as they took control of the city with lightning speed.

THEY APPROACHED a man standing beside a boat bound for Sumatra. It was laden down. The ancient tub, once a fishing smack, was heavy in the water at Keppel Harbour, amid all other manner of vessels. They parted with an extortionate number of US dollars for passage, and as they boarded, the ship cast off, and they sailed away from the ruins of what was once a spectacular city.

They found a patch on the deck to lie down; they'd not slept for days and both were wiped out. All over the boat were families, mothers clutching fractious babies, old people, some Europeans, a handful of Americans, servicemen of all stripes and in various states of health, all united in their traumatised state by what they'd witnessed.

Miraculously they got to Sumatra, arriving to Medan on the east coast to find it deserted. An officer of the British Army who'd travelled with them said it was just a matter of time before Sumatra too fell to the Japanese so getting off that island should be a priority. He was going south to try to reunite with his company and then make for Java.

'You're Americans, so I'd try to get north, to Banda Aceh – try to get picked up there,' he suggested.

No further instructions, no food or water, just the knowledge that it was a matter of time before this jungle island too fell to the Japanese, and being taken prisoner was inevitable if they didn't get off the island.

Richard felt that since he and Jacob were able-bodied, maybe they should stay and help the old people and the women, but Jacob said their duty was to get the story out; America needed to know what had happened, what the Japanese were capable of, the unimaginable cruelty for the sake of cruelty. Richard both admired and found frustration with Jacob's single-minded approach to the work. He was right – now more than ever the American people needed to understand the adversary they faced, and he and Jacob were placed to do just that – but walking past women laden down with crying babies or elderly people who were so lost and alone tore at his heart. There were servicemen of all ranks milling around, all desperate to do the same thing – get south to Palembang where the Allied resistance was gathering – and Jacob said they could help the civilians, but that was not their job.

They had a compass and the ration packs and not much else. Their departure from Singapore meant that even Richard's precious portable typewriter had to be left behind.

'I guess we head north, keep the ocean on our right?' Jacob said as the British officer walked away from them. Others from their boat were seeking lodging in the city of Medan, but Richard agreed – wasting no time was going to be their best chance of survival. Once the Japanese arrived, it would be swift and brutal. This large island was mainly agricultural. He'd met a Sumatran guy in Singapore, and he'd told him a bit about his home. Rubber, coffee, tea, hemp – those crops had been the most sought-after by the Dutch East India Company, and the entire island was a provider of those commodities. They had little by way of defence. Not that it would matter; the Japanese were going from strength to strength, so resistance would be futile even if they had a way to resist.

They went to a market and managed to get two canteens to carry water, some bread and cheese and a big bag of some kind of nuts. The trader, a young Indonesian, no more than sixteen, had no interest in US dollars but greedily eyed the wristwatch Richard wore. Richard had received the watch for his twenty-first birthday.

'Malcolm Campbell, yeah?' The grinning boy pretended he was driving a car.

'Yeah, Rolex Oyster.' Richard glanced at Jacob. The ostentatious watch had been something Jacob had rolled his eyes at when it arrived, and Richard supressed a grin – they were glad of it now.

They haggled and also got two packs of cigarettes, two mosquito nets and one rain slicker, clearly second-hand but it was the best they could do. Richard parted with the watch, and they set off.

'Before you say anything, yes, I'm glad we had the flashy watch, is that enough for you?' Jacob said.

'That's all I needed to hear.' Richard nudged his friend.

'OK, let's try to save our hides and get to this Banda Aceh. I hope there's some kind of transportation here.'

The kid at the stall had said that it would take at least a week to get north on foot, but Richard hoped they might be able to get some kind of transportation. However, the US dollars that had opened so many doors in Singapore seemed worthless here, and they had nothing else to use as payment.

'The Japs will go south first to get the oil refineries and airfields down by Palembang,' Jacob remarked as they walked on the unpaved road. The humidity was brutal, and the sun beat down mercilessly, the air heavy with the odours of rotting food, diesel and something sweet that they couldn't place. 'They'll need those to fuel their conquest of Java and the rest of the archipelago, so at least that's in our favour, but I don't think we have much time.'

'The KNIL are placed all over the island. Maybe there's a company in Banda Aceh that can get us out.'

'Maybe, though they're more interested in saving their investments than American newspapermen, but we'll see.'

The Royal Netherlands East Indies Army had placed seven companies around Sumatra, and though they would most likely be no match for the Japanese, at least it was something.

They skirted villages and small settlements on the coast. It was impossible to know who to trust, and the Japanese sent scout groups ahead of invading armies, so apprehension was always a risk. The locals were kind, but if they helped any allied servicemen then they faced terrible repercussions from the Japanese. They offered food and water if they could, but Richard and Jacob always made sure to set up camp far from any houses. They stuck to the edge of the jungle where they could; it was safer if they needed to take cover.

They had got into a routine of picking fruit as they went, and as they prepared to make camp on the fourth day, they ate the remains of the bread, had some green bananas that made Richard's stomach ache but were better than nothing and drank the remains of their canteens of water. Richard peeled off his socks and saw his foot blisters were getting worse. Infection was a real risk, and with nothing to treat themselves should the infection take hold, they were very careful not to allow blisters to fester. Jacob said they always had the option of applying maggots, he'd heard of some British officer whose life had been saved by his batman applying maggots to an infected wound, but Richard was hoping that wouldn't be necessary. Instead, despite the stinging pain, they tried each day to soak their feet in the saltwater. It hurt like all hell, but it was the best thing to do.

Venturing to the shore was risky. The chances of being seen were higher when exposed and not protected by the jungle, but the breeze was so welcome and the sea refreshingly cool after long hours of trudging. They'd seen orangutans and snakes and so many damned bugs of various colours, all intent on chewing on them, that sometimes Richard found himself wondering if just lying down and seeing what happened might be best. But Jacob drove them on. They had no idea how far from Banda Aceh they were, but they thought they were at least headed in the right direction.

'What date is it, do you think?' Richard winced when the saltwater touched the blisters. Jacob had a nasty bite on his neck – God alone knew what had bit him – and it was swelling and oozing.

'Not sure. The twenty-seventh or twenty-eighth of February maybe?'

Jacob walked into the sea. He was stripped down to his underwear and was going to get under. Richard noticed Jacob's back was a mass of welts and swollen patches from insect bites too. Luckily he wasn't as tasty to the little critters as Jacob seemed to be.

'I think we need to move inland soon,' Jacob said. 'We're adding distance staying by the coast. It's actually northwest we need to be headed, not due north.'

'I think you're right, but it will make progress slower.' Richard waded in to his waist. It was such a treat at the end of a long hot day's walking to submerge himself in water, even if it made his blisters sting.

They swam and floated on their backs, allowing the warm sea water to soothe their aching muscles. They would sleep for a bit as the sun set and then start walking again. The spectacular sunset over the Strait of Malacca, the majestic oranges and pinks, was so breathtaking one could, just for that brief moment, believe that the world was a beautiful place. It made him think of the sunsets off the west coast of Ireland.

Grace. As he swam through the warm water, his and Jacob's clothes in a pile on the sand the only sign of life, his thoughts went to her. She would be worried by now certainly. He'd received a letter from her when he was in Singapore, telling him how worried she was about her brother in the Philippines. He'd made some enquiries with a commandant who worked directly under Lieutenant General Percival, commander of Singapore, and none of the news was good. The Philippines had fallen, and if watching what happened in Singapore was an indication, then he didn't like Maurice's chances. He had intended to write to Grace, but the departure was so rapid, in the end he never got to. It felt like a long time since he'd seen her, and Ireland and Knocknashee seemed more like something he'd dreamt up rather than real.

He floated on his back, allowing the saltwater to swish around his ears. They would have to get out and rest very soon, but he was enjoying the much-needed respite.

The shots sounded strange, and it took a few seconds for him to register them. They didn't hit him, but they pinged off the crystal-clear water just feet from his head. He turned, treading water, and faced the beach. Jacob was ten or fifteen feet away, and they both registered the danger at the same time: soldiers of the Imperial Japanese Army. Richard felt sick. There was no doubt. They had seen them in Singapore, their khaki shirts and pants, the pants bound to the knee with khaki tape, the high-domed steel helmets with the star and the red rectangle patches on their collars. The two of them, bearing a weapon each, had yellow bars on their collars, indicating their low rank. If the situation was different, he and Jacob might have tried to take them down – there were only two of them from what he could see – but they were twenty yards from shore and in their underwear. The beach was long and narrow and utterly deserted. If they made a run for it, they would undoubtedly be shot. There was no cover anywhere, and the Japanese soldiers were between them and the safety of the jungle. There was nothing to do but surrender.

With Japanese Arisaka rifles trained on them, they began to walk out of the water, hands in the air. Was this how it ended? Shot in his underwear in a warm sea so far from home, Grace on his mind? She'd never know that she had been his last thought.

CHAPTER 14

KNOCKNASHEE

MARCH 1942

Grace was at the board explaining to the class some of the nautical terms that were in everyday use. It was another trick up her sleeve to get them interested in learning English. For too many of her pupils, there would not be enough work in their homeplace and they would have to go further afield, and while their native language had such a place in their hearts, it was of no use on the streets of Dublin, London or New York.

She wrote *let the cat out of the bag, a chip on your shoulder, toe the line.* 'So who can tell me what letting the cat out of the bag means?'

All hands shot up. She selected Ellen Murphy.

'It means to be *beal scaoilte*.'

'In English please, Ellen,' Grace admonished.

Several hands fluttered in the air.

'It means to say something that you don't mean to say and then to get in trouble for it,' Ellen answered haltingly.

'Well done, excellent! And where does it come from?' She scanned the enthusiastic faces. 'Paudie, can you tell us?'

Paudie O'Connell knew, of course. She'd never once asked him a question he didn't know the answer to.

'The discipline on ships was entirely in the gift of the captain, and while some crimes like mutiny or insubordination were punishable by death, lesser crimes like drunkenness or using foul language would be punished by flogging,' he said in perfect English. 'The whip was called the cat o' nine tails – it was a whip with nine cords and a knot tied in each one – and a sailor was usually given twelve lashes. The lash was kept in a red bag so it wouldn't show bloodstains, and so to take the cat out of the bag meant something bad was going to happen.'

Grace grimaced. 'That would be horrible, wouldn't it? Those poor men.'

'And a lot of them were press-ganged, forced to join the navy, and so they didn't even choose it.'

The other children liked Paudie enormously. They knew he was brighter than they were, but he wasn't arrogant or showy, and they found him as interesting as Grace did. He'd learnt everything about the technicalities of naval development, from the oar-propelled galleons to modern battleships, from the school encyclopaedias. They'd all been enjoying lots of reading time from the new books since the canon was away for several weeks now and the risk of him arriving and discovering them reading and not learning catechism was gone. Nobody knew where he was – or cared for that matter.

After the conversation with Nancy, Grace had bumped into Father Lehane coming out of the parochial house. He always blushed puce whenever she or any female spoke directly to him. The poor man was a pity with the shyness, but he was a kind and gentle priest and people were fond of him. Especially as they knew he did all of the hard work of the parish while the snake sat on his backside doing nothing.

'You're busy, Father.' She'd smiled at him as he arranged to baptise four babies over one weekend and tried to fit in a meeting with the Sodality of the Blessed Virgin Mary.

'Indeed, Miss Fitzgerald…' He flushed and looked at his shoes. 'Can I help you?'

'Oh, not at all, Father Lehane. I was just going to set up a time for either yourself or the canon to come to the school to arrange the Corpus Christi procession.' She was bluffing. Corpus Christi wasn't for ages, but she was digging for information.

'Oh, I'll do my best, Miss Fitzgerald, but Canon Rafferty is away for the next three weeks at least, so I'm on my own. But if it's urgent…'

'Not a bit of it, Father, don't worry your head. Sure we've ages yet.' She took her leave with a cheery smile. 'God bless, Father.'

She could go ahead with the plan she'd mulled over for weeks.

'Paudie, can you come up here and explain about the other phrases too? Now, everyone, Paudie is the teacher for the next few minutes, so everyone must listen carefully. And if you are all very good and quiet, then I'll let you out five minutes early at playtime, is that a deal?'

They giggled. Hearing Richard ask often if things were a 'deal' had crept into her vocabulary, and now all the children said it.

They agreed enthusiastically as Paudie, delighted with his captive audience, explained in great detail about how if a person was to steal from a shipyard a piece, or a chip, of wood bigger than what you could hold in your hand, you were in breach of the terms of your employment. But because oak was so expensive, shipwrights often took big pieces out on their shoulders – hence, to have a chip on your shoulder.

Grace tore a sheet out of a writing pad and scribbled a quick note, folded it in two and placed it in an envelope. She then took the note and went outside, and to her relief, she spotted Charlie on his bike, just leaving the post office. She called to him and beckoned him over. 'Can you do me a favour, Charlie?'

He smiled. 'I will if I can.'

'Could you drop this note to Mrs Worth, you know, the English lady who lives out the Dingle road? She just arrived back a couple of months ago from England.'

'I will of course,' he said, taking the note. ''Tis no harm to have people in that house again. She has a few kids with her too, and she always seems very nice when I call. Old Major Worth is dead thirty years, I'd say, but Mrs Worth, his mother, lived up to about five years ago. Mrs Coleman, God be good to her, used to go into her, look after her and that. Douglas hardly ever came back, but she used to visit him for long periods.'

'Did you ever know him, the son Douglas?'

Charlie nodded. 'I did. He was Protestant of course, so they didn't mix much with us, and he was sent to boarding school and then went to England, but what I knew of him, he was all right. Why?'

'I just had an idea.'

'Really?'

'It might not work but it's worth a try. I need a teacher, and she's more than qualified. I was thinking of asking her to come and work here. What do you think?'

'That's genius, Gracie, well done. I think she'd be ideal, and she could use the money, I'd say. Things are rough enough up at that place.'

Grace thought for a moment. 'I heard she was bombed out of Liverpool, and I suppose this was the only place she had to go to, but I'd say that place is damp and draughty, nobody living there for years.'

'It would need a fair bit of money spending on it right enough, God love them. I'll go that way this afternoon, no problem at all.' Charlie took her note and put it in the breast pocket of his postman's tunic.

'How's Dymphna today?' Grace asked, trying not to wince.

He shook his head. 'Desperate altogether. The poor creature is miserable. Dr Ryan was in with her this morning, but...' His brow furrowed and he took off his postman's hat, running his hand over his head. 'He says it's normal, the baby is fine and she'll be fine, but I hate seeing her so low.' He fixed her with a gaze then. 'Are you holding up OK, Gracie?' he asked gently. ''Tis a lot you've had on your plate.'

She wished she could tell him her biggest concern, which was that fiend Francis Sheehan being landed in on top of them again. But she couldn't, because to do so would be to betray Nancy's confidence. Hopefully her idea would pay off, though.

'I'm all right. Some days are harder than others, and I just miss him so much…' She swallowed. This was not the place to dissolve into tears.

'I know, *a chroi*, I do too. And just because me and Dymphna are married and expecting a baby doesn't mean I miss Declan any less.'

She nodded.

'Any word from Richard?' Charlie knew there wasn't; he would have delivered any letters she got.

'He was sent to Singapore after Pearl Harbor to report from there, so he wrote saying not to worry if I didn't hear from him, but I am starting to worry now. It's been a long time.'

'I'm sure he's fine. Communications from that part of the world are very patchy. You know the McNamaras out Coiscéim?'

'I do. Their daughter is a nun in Malaya, isn't she?'

'That's right. They've not heard a thing for months, and she's a great one for writing, so it's that nothing is getting through,' Charlie reassured her.

Grace sighed. 'I suppose they don't want to waste precious space on ships with letters.'

'That's it. I heard the Americans are even suggesting that their men write letters and then they take a photograph of the letter and send the film back to America and get it printed there, imagine that?' Charlie shook his head incredulously.

'This whole world is going mad,' she said, exhaling. 'Anyway, I better go. Your stepson is currently teaching the whole gang about nautical language in common use.' She laughed.

'He's something else, isn't he?' Charlie said proudly.

'He really is. We'll have to find a way to send him to the university when the time comes. He's so clever – things just come easily to him.'

'Declan was like him when he was a *garsún*, so bright and sure, all his inventions and everything. He would have done amazing things if he'd got the chance...' The sadness in his voice at the lost years with his son touched Grace's already broken heart.

'At least we got him back, Charlie, and he got to meet Siobhán and be reunited with you...'

'And he married the girl he loved with all his heart. But it's a cruel thing, and for you too, to lose your parents and your husband to the sea...' They stood gazing out at the calm sparking Atlantic, looking so innocent and innocuous. But they both knew the ocean was a great benefactor but also took with impunity. Nobody was immune.

'Look, we'll not bring him back with tears anyway, and if he were here, he'd be hunting me into the classroom and you on your round.' She smiled and patted his shoulder. Charlie was as close to a father to her as could be, and she loved him dearly.

CHAPTER 15

Grace was eating her breakfast. Mercifully it was a Saturday, so she could relax, and Dymphna seemed to have turned a corner all of a sudden and was feeling brighter and able to mind Odile and take care of Mary up at the O'Hare farm, allowing Tilly to catch up on all the farm work that was neglected while she was in prison, though the baby was well advanced now and Dymphna had a fine big bump.

This morning Grace had an appointment with Mrs Worth, who had written to her as soon as she got the note Grace had sent with Charlie. It was an odd thing, Grace thought. Most people would just call in, but Mrs Worth seemed very proper in how she conducted herself.

The day she'd arrived with several boxes of books, weeks ago, ones her daughters were finished with and those that had been in the Worth house, Grace had been teaching and had not had time to do more than thank her for her generosity, and that was the first and last time she'd met her.

There had been no word from either the canon or Francis Sheehan, but Grace knew the canon's plan was to spring the teacher on her as a fait accompli the first morning back after the Easter holidays. But

Grace had plans to outmanoeuvre him. It was a gamble, but it was the best idea she could come up with, and no matter what, Mrs Worth would have to be an improvement on the alternative. She'd said she would call at ten o'clock, so any minute now.

THE KNOCK on the door signalled her arrival, and Grace showed her into the sitting room. Mrs Worth was in her late forties, fifty maybe, Grace judged, and looked sensible if a little careworn. She was a solidly built woman dressed in a brown dress and a cream jacket, with a beige felt hat on her head and sensible walking shoes. She wore a little powder and a slight touch of lipstick. There was something imminently trustworthy about her.

'Thank you so much for agreeing to come to see me, Mrs Worth. Can I get you a cup of tea?' Grace said warmly.

'Not at all, Miss Fitzgerald. Thank you, but I've not long ago finished breakfast.' She sounded English but northern more than London; her vowels were broad, but her enunciation was clear. Grace liked the sound of her sing-song Liverpool accent; she wasn't as posh as Grace had expected her to be.

'Please, have a seat.' Grace offered her the wingback leather chair, cracking on the seams, beside the empty fireplace that she'd now filled with tory tops she'd stored from the winter. If Agnes were still alive, the chair would have been thrown out – she didn't like anything to look worn or old – but Grace felt differently. She liked the shabby, well-loved look of her home. It showed it was a place people lived and not a showpiece to impress God only knew who. Nobody around here had any real money, so there was no point in having airs and graces, but Agnes seemed to have them all the same. Grace had added colourful knitted throws and cushions, artwork the children in school had given her as presents and little knick-knacks their mother had loved but Agnes had stored in the attic because they were 'only clutter'. It was undoubtedly a bit less tidy but much more homely.

The weather was warming up and the days stretching. Grace hated the winter evenings now that Declan was gone; the night seemed to go on forever when the sun set at four thirty. The arrival of spring, cheery daffodils peeking their heads up and lambs in the fields heralding bright days, always cheered her up. The stinging cold being gone meant there was no need to have the range going in the kitchen as well as the fire in the sitting room. Fuel was in such short supply nowadays, it was nice to be able to manage with less. She would not light her fire again until the late autumn, and the tory tops were cheerier than an empty grate.

'Thank you for coming, Mrs Worth. You must be wondering why I asked you here?' Grace smiled and the woman returned it, though clearly she had no idea the purpose of the visit.

'Well, it was very nice to hear from you. I don't know many people here – well, nobody actually so…' She gave a small smile.

'Oh, you will, don't worry. Right, I'll get to the point. I heard you were a teacher, and we are in need of one, so I asked you here to see if you would be interested in joining the staff of the school.'

The woman seemed nonplussed. 'I…ah… Well, I…I wasn't aware there was a position…'

Grace steadied herself to say the words. She could not cry in front of this woman; she'd think Grace was unhinged and probably run for the door. 'Well, there is. My late husband, Declan McKenna, was the other teacher, but he was killed last November when a sea mine exploded as he tried to rescue some marooned crew off the coast.' She blurted it and quickly moved on. 'And so I need some help. I'm currently teaching both the junior and senior children together, but it's a lot. I know you were a headmistress in England, and I thought you might be interested in the job?'

Mrs Worth paused, and Grace wondered if she'd got this all wrong. Then the woman beamed, a warm, bright smile that lit up her whole face. 'I would dearly love the job, Miss…Mrs Fitzgerald, and my deepest condolences on the loss of your poor husband. That was a terrible thing to happen.'

Grace accepted her condolences with a thin smile; she could not talk about Declan now.

Maybe the woman sensed that, as she went on. 'But I don't know any Irish, and the children here learn through Irish, don't they?'

Grace inwardly heaved a sigh of relief. If that was the only impediment, she would be fine.

'Yes, they do, but I speak Irish all day long and so do the children, and I'm actively trying to improve their English actually. For obvious reasons they are often not keen, but you teaching completely through English would be no harm, and I'm sure if you were around them for a few weeks, you'd pick up plenty of Irish anyway.'

To Grace's surprise Mrs Worth now looked like she might be the one to cry. 'Well, I will be entirely honest with you, Mrs Fitzgerald –'

Grace stopped her. 'Please call me Grace, everyone does. The children call me Miss Fitz because that was my maiden name. If I'm a Mrs anything, it's Mrs McKenna, but I had barely any time to get used to that, so just Grace is fine.'

'Thank you, and I'm Eleanor. I don't know what to say, except thank you very, very much. We lost our home and the school I worked in last May. We stayed with my sister in Manchester for a while, but her house was full to begin with and then her husband was invalided out – he was at Dunkirk, lucky to come back alive – and she didn't need us as well. My husband is in the forces, so myself and my daughters came to the only other home we had, Douglas's parents' house here.'

'I'm sorry to hear about that. I can't imagine. It's such a horrendous war and it feels never-ending.'

Eleanor nodded. 'It's just things. Others have lost loved ones, and that puts things in perspective, but I was beginning to despair about what we would do. The girls can't come to school here because they have no Irish, so I'm teaching them myself, but they miss their friends and their school. We've lost everything except the clothes on our backs. And my late parents-in-law's house, Heather and Roland's, is badly in need of some care, but we're not exactly skilled in that regard and we have no money to pay anyone. The roof leaks and the windows rattle, but anyway, all that to say, I would be so grateful for a job, and I'd do anything you need of me.'

'Wonderful.' Grace smiled. 'You would be paid the going rate depending on your experience. How long have you been teaching?'

'Ah, since I was nineteen. I've taught all ages, from reception to school leavers, and I was headmistress of a girls' school in Liverpool with six hundred pupils for the last eleven years.'

'This will be a bit of a demotion for you then,' Grace replied apologetically.

'Not in the slightest. I love teaching, and frankly I was beginning to panic about how we'd manage, so I'm very grateful and relieved.'

'Well now, there's only one tiny hitch...' Something about her made Grace confide in her, knowing instinctively the woman wouldn't repeat what she'd heard. She went on to explain the situation regarding the canon and Francis Sheehan.

'So my idea would be to get you registered and hired as quickly as possible. As headmistress I can appoint staff, though technically they need to be ratified by the board. But the canon is away at the moment, and so I'm going to use the excuse that he wasn't here and we needed someone. I've all the paperwork ready, and I'll send it to the Department of Education once we fill out your details, qualifications, experience and so on.'

'Well, if you're happy to go ahead, I certainly am. I've met him, by the way,' Eleanor said as she scanned the forms Grace had handed her. 'He won't like that I'm not Catholic.'

'No, he won't, but he won't like anything about your employment, so leave that to me. Now about your daughters, how old are they?'

'Joanne is eleven, Libby's nine, and Olivia is twelve.'

'Well, if they are happy to pick it up as they go along, they'd be most welcome to come here too. The children here are nice, and I'm sure they'll make friends. The language might be a barrier for a while but not for long.'

'Are you sure? Won't that draw more wrath from the canon?'

'Probably.' Grace sighed. 'He's a formidable enemy, to be honest, and never underestimate him or what he can do, but he is not without his Achilles heel either.'

Eleanor nodded and didn't enquire further. 'He stopped Joanne coming out of the grocer's a few days after we arrived and asked who she was, what she was doing in Knocknashee and why she was here. She said he kind of interrogated her.'

'That sounds like him all right.' Grace had told Eleanor only the bare bones of what she needed to know, but something gave Grace the impression that Eleanor Worth would be more than a match for the canon if it came to it. 'When could you start?' she asked.

'Monday if you want me to?' Eleanor said as she filled in the various parts of the application form.

'Well, that would be just marvellous. I might give you the senior class. We have about forty children there aged between eight and fourteen, and we have a monitor as well, Janie O'Shea. She's excellent, so between the three of us, we'll get along wonderfully.'

Eleanor handed her back the filled-out form. 'I hope so, Grace, and please, anything you need me to do, just say the word. The only thing I won't do is slap children. I never have and I never will.'

Grace laughed. 'A woman after my own heart. My parents were the teachers here before me and my late sister, and they were not believers in corporal punishment either, but the man the canon has lined up to come here is an enthusiastic user of the strap, one of the many reasons I don't want him. The children are happy in this school. They don't fear anyone, and they learn in a positive environment.' Grace could feel the tension leave her body. 'Of course, rare as it is, bad behaviour does get punished, usually on a Saturday morning where they have to do jobs like sweeping the yard or cleaning the classrooms, but it's used very sparingly.'

'It sounds perfect. I'll have to try to brush up on the Irish curriculum over the weekend now, in case I'm completely flummoxed on the first day.'

'Don't worry, it will come back to you. I'll give you the books we're using and show you how far we've come this year. Now will you have that tea? To celebrate?'

'I'd love it, thank you.'

Grace limped to the kitchen and Eleanor followed. For the next hour they chatted about polio, Eleanor's late mother-in-law, Heather

Worth, and about her daughters and how much they missed their father.

They talked on and on, and Grace found herself telling her new friend all about Tilly and Odile and Declan and Charlie and Dymphna, and Eleanor told her about her husband, Douglas, who was an engineer with the Liverpool Council before the war but was now an officer with the King's Regiment, currently in Gibraltar.

'Are you worried about him?' Grace asked.

Eleanor exhaled. 'Not worried exactly. He's a very clever chap and well able to take care of himself. But I wish this bloody war was over and they could all come home. It's such a shock to be here truthfully. Everyone at home – back in Liverpool, I mean – is so absorbed by it all. Everyone has people serving. It was rare to meet someone who hadn't lost loved ones either in the fighting or in the bombing. Everything is in short supply – my daughters can't get over the food that's available here. But it feels somehow…I don't know, like a bit of a betrayal to leave.'

She blushed and hastened to explain. 'I'm sorry. You probably think I should feel more patriotic about Ireland, but Douglas left here as a boy, and I've lived in Liverpool all my life…'

'You don't need to apologise to me. Of course I understand. You're English, so I can see how it would be a wrench to leave, but you had no choice. And I'm sure your husband would rather you and the girls were safe here than remain in England and risk your lives.'

'It was he who suggested we come here. I wasn't keen originally, and even since we got here, I've had moments of despair that we've made a terrible mistake. The girls miss their friends and cousins, and they feel very out of place here. The house is fairly dilapidated – we've been trying to patch it up a little, but…'

'Well, one thing at a time. Let's get you started and earning some money, and you never know – some of the local men might be willing to give you a hand to secure the house over the summer so that it won't be too cold for winter. Once you get to know people here, they're very nice.'

Eleanor hesitated.

'What is it?' Grace asked.

'I... Well, I've told my girls to be careful when they speak to people. The English are not welcome here, and I know why of course, and I know people have long memories, but they are just little girls and I'd hate them to be discriminated against.'

Grace thought for a moment. It would be easy to dismiss the woman's fears and assure her that there was no possibility of anything like that, but she would be lying. The Crown Forces sent to quell the Irish rebellion in the form of the Black and Tans and the Auxiliaries in this part of Ireland were brutal, and it all happened only twenty years ago so very much in living memory.

'Look, Eleanor, what I'd say is this. Your husband is Irish, and that makes your girls Irish too. Yes, they have a different accent and grew up over there, but that just makes you like so many others who emigrated for whatever reason. I'd have them tell people that their daddy was born and raised here and all they are doing is coming home. It might not be strictly true, but it will ease the transition. Anyway, don't worry. Once you're more involved in the community, everyone will know you and the girls and it will be all right, I promise.'

'You're a godsend, Grace, I mean it. I prayed last night for something to happen. The girls were in bed and the house felt so lonely and cold, and we're here without Douglas, and we can't go back – there's nothing to go back to. But I prayed for something, I didn't really know what, and then this happened.'

'Well, Eleanor, I need you as much as you need me, so it's a great blessing for us both.'

As Grace gave her some schoolbooks she was using with the senior class and showed her out, she hoped that the application was processed quickly and before Canon Rafferty got back from wherever he was, because one thing was for certain – once he found out she'd outsmarted him, he would be furious.

CHAPTER 16

CEYLON, SOUTH ASIA

MARCH 1942

The middle-aged lieutenant commander seemed to think their appearance funny, or at least his broad beam and hearty chuckle suggested that. Richard recognised the fellow Southerner by his accent. One of the Carolinas most likely. He was a navy man to his fingertips, not a military-compliant hair astray and his jaw freshly shaved. He looked like an advertisement in a recruitment poster, the picture of American manhood. Richard dreaded to think what he and Jacob looked like.

'You boys sure look like you could use some feeding up, but before that, how 'bout y'all take a shower and have a shave and I'll have the barber sent down to cut all that hair. We can't have you scaring the ladies when we get you back to civilisation now, can we?'

Richard didn't care. The last few weeks had been hell, and several times he was sure they wouldn't make it. He would write their story in due course, but for now all he wanted to do was sleep, eat and sleep more.

'You boys are lucky we just dropped troops and cargo here in Ceylon, so y'all get a cabin to yourselves. This was built as a cruise liner, not a troop ship, but just like us, life for her sure ain't turning out the way we thought.'

His accent was soothing and there was something of home about it, but Richard had hardly spoken to anyone in weeks so found himself reluctant to reply.

'So, where you boys from?'

'Savannah, Georgia, sir,' Richard managed.

'No kiddin'? I'm from Raleigh.'

Richard smiled. 'I thought I recognised the accent.'

'You both from Savannah?' the officer asked.

Jacob nodded, offering his hand. 'Jacob Nunez, nice to meet you.'

'Welcome aboard, boys. Now y'all can get cleaned up, get yourselves some chow, and then you look like you could use some shuteye.' They followed him down a metal stairway to a row of cabins. He opened one with two freshly made bunks. 'Locker room down that way.' He pointed to the end of the passageway.

'Thank you, sir, that would be great,' Richard said.

'No problem. I'm sure you got a helluva tale to tell, but it can wait.' He nodded and went to take his leave, but then he turned back. 'Those Japs are gonna rue the day they took us on, that's for darn sure.'

Jacob and Richard lost no time in taking a long, warm shower and washing their hair. The US Navy had kindly supplied a wash kit each, with a comb, a cake of soap, some toilet paper and a razor, and once they'd scrubbed the jungle and the dirt of the journey off themselves, they felt a bit more human.

A young cadet was sent to cut their hair, which he did wordlessly and with absolute precision. Richard marvelled at the clumps of blond hair on the floor of the locker room. Once the lad was finished, Richard added some Brylcreem and combed it back. Without the week's worth of beard and filthy hair, he looked more like that boy who'd left Savannah, at least on the outside. On the inside he would never again be that boy. He'd seen too much.

'Well, that's an improvement,' the commander said jovially as they appeared in the mess hall.

'I'm much obliged to you, sir. That shower was badly needed,' Richard said as he and Jacob sat down, accompanied by the lieutenant commander and a few other officers, all desperate to hear about their adventures. The meal in front of them, fried chicken, beans and potatoes, was the most food they'd seen in weeks.

'So you boys got out of Singapore, huh?' the lieutenant asked.

'Just about.'

'I heard that was some mess.'

'Churchill was right when he said the administration in Singapore failed,' Jacob said, after swallowing a mouthful of food. 'But they were so sure that the troops in Malaya would hold the island, all their defences were seaward, but the Japs just crushed the entire peninsula in about fifty days. Singapore was a sitting duck.'

'Percival was told not to surrender under any circumstances,' Richard added, 'even when the naval base was under heavy artillery fire day and night.'

'And was it just British troops trying to defend the island?' the naval officer asked, fascinated. Richard noticed the fresh uniforms and the baby faces of the navy men gathering around them now. They were yet to be bloodied, and the whole thing was just a game of toy soldiers to them. He envied their innocence.

'No, there were British, Aussies, Indians, some Malay battalions too, around seventy or eighty thousand between them all, but they were worn out from retreating and defeat. It wasn't pretty.' Richard returned to his meal.

'Sounds to me like they all screwed up, because they were sure the Japs would come from the north and they landed on the west instead.' A fresh-faced ensign who looked no older than eighteen blushed as his commanding officer looked at him.

Jacob took pity on him. 'That's right, they did. And just the Australians were there. The British and Indians were on the north side. To top it all, the Japs cut the phone lines so there couldn't be a coordinated response.'

'And where were you guys?' the lieutenant asked.

'Singapore city, reporting for the *Capital* newspaper in New York.' Richard helped himself to more chicken. 'We knew things were going badly for the Allies, but the sheer speed of the Japanese advance shook everyone. They'd destroyed all communications channels, and so once they cut the water off to the city, it was just a matter of time.' Richard took a swig from the bottle of beer he'd been handed. It wasn't that cold, but it was like nectar.

Jacob took up the story. 'The Malays fought so hard – they all did. The Aussies took a terrible hammering and the Indians were almost left surrounded, but Opium Hill, to the southwest of Singapore City, was held for two days by the Malays. They inflicted such heavy losses on the Japs that when they finally took the hill, they hung the Malay commander Adnan bin Saidi by his feet and bayoneted him to death.'

Some of the men paled at the graphic description of how vindictive the enemy was. Recalling those last days on that bastion of the British Empire in the Far East was horrifying.

'Those sons of bit –' another young ensign burst out, but a glance from his commanding officer stopped him.

Richard said, 'Be under no illusion, the Japanese are spiteful and violent. I've never seen brutality like it, and that's the truth.'

A silence fell over the gathered group as the men who had yet to see a day's combat allowed the words to sink in. Not so long ago, he and Jacob had been just like these naive young men, but not any more.

'Go on,' the lieutenant said.

Jacob said, 'We had gone to report from the Alexandra Hospital, where almost a thousand men were being treated. The hospital was entirely undefended, and when a lieutenant came out waving a white flag of surrender, he was bayonetted to death. The Japanese then went on a rampage, killing doctors and patients alike before marching survivors to a building a quarter of a mile away, nailing the doors shut and forcing them to remain there in insufferable heat without ventilation or water. The following day they came back and killed another hundred people just because they could. We stayed as long as we dared, but then we managed to flee to Sumatra on Valentine's Day along with other refugees. We've brought reports and pictures that will shock Americans when they are presented on the pages of the *Capital*.'

'Churchill sent backup, though, right?' a young ensign asked, his eyes wide.

Jacob nodded as he accepted another bottle of beer. 'Sure did. Just in time for them to surrender too. Total waste of resources. It was a mess. And now the Allies have no foothold in the region, so it's not looking good.'

The lieutenant commander sensed that this was not the patriotic talk that he'd hoped for, so he quickly dismissed the men with hearty exclamations of how the Japs hadn't considered the US of A in their calculations, and how they wouldn't be long turning this around.

Richard and Jacob exchanged a glance. It was exactly this kind of bravado and underestimating of the Japanese that had allowed Singapore to fall so quickly. Manila had fallen in January, with the Americans having to pull back to Bataan and eventually withdraw from the Philippines completely. The Battle of the Java Sea had been a wipeout too, so while America was a formidable army undoubtedly, so were the Japanese. But they kept their thoughts to themselves, glad to be on this ship and looking forward to a long sleep.

'So you boys got from Sumatra to Ceylon OK?' the lieutenant asked.

'Not really. We were on foot from Medan trying to get to Banda Aceh when we were captured by a pair of Japanese scouts,' Richard said, then drained his beer bottle.

'No kiddin'? And how'd you get out of that?'

'We were in the sea, trying to cool off and letting the saltwater disinfect blisters and bites and cuts, when they showed up on the beach, marched us off the beach at gunpoint, in our underwear.'

'They had no camp, so they chained us together, marched us north, luckily the direction we were headed anyway,' Jacob explained. 'But they held our clothes, so we got badly sunburned, and we had very little food or water. There was an air raid and they ran for cover, so we managed to escape.' Jacob's tone left no room for further questioning, and the captain seemed to sense it.

'Good on you, boys,' he said, and Richard could hear the empathy in his voice. He knew what a toll this had taken on them. 'So how'd y'all get to Ceylon?'

'A hot and humid trip for ten days across the sea to Ceylon on a ship loaded with bombs that stank of gasoline. Water was severely rationed. We had bread twice, but other than that, it was white rice for breakfast, lunch and dinner. But we made it.'

The explanation they gave included nothing of the time spent in the jungles of Sumatra, how despite the incredible beauty, they were some of the hardest of his life. The heat, the hunger, the bone-weariness, the constant terror of being caught, then being captured…

'You sure did. I'm proud of you boys, and I'm sure your parents back home will be mighty glad to hear you are all right. Well done.' He patted each of them on the shoulder in a fatherly way, and Richard longed for his own father, who Richard knew would understand. Maybe he would tell him some day. 'Now you need some rest. Sleep as long as you want – we got a long voyage ahead of us.'

The commander didn't mention the obvious fact that they were sailing through very dangerous waters and were by no means out of trouble yet.

A few minutes later, in their cabin, as Richard fell asleep, leaving the lights of Colombo behind, he hoped the British had learnt their lesson and that the hastily scrambled British fleet could hold the Japanese back from India, because if India fell, well, it was probably all over.

He dreamt of Grace, and of Pippa, and in his dream they were sisters and he was with both of them, living in his house on St Simons, but somehow the house was in Ireland and Esme was there taking care of them all.

CHAPTER 17

LONDON

Richard had thought he would never again step on dry land, and he was pleased to see the heavily fortified Portsmouth come into view. The journey had been long, but they'd made it. The ship from Ceylon, the *USS Maya*, had taken some fire once they were through the Suez Canal, but considering everything, the voyage was remarkably uneventful. It was in peacetime a journey of around a month, but it had taken them longer because of drop-offs and collections of weapons, supplies and men. Once they disembarked, the *Maya* would make the treacherous journey across the Atlantic, braving the U-boats, to restock and do it all again.

He and Jacob said their goodbyes to the crew who had become friends, and while they were far less the baby-faced boys they had been when they first met, Richard feared worse was yet to come.

'Y'all take care now.' The lieutenant commander shook their hands as they disembarked. 'Maybe I'll catch you for a beer in the Crystal Beer Parlor when this circus is over?'

'It would be our pleasure,' Jacob replied. 'Thank you, sir. We owe you our lives.'

They caught the train, another long, arduous trip, standing all the way, to London Victoria and from there to Sarah and Pippa's new flat in Kensington. They'd had to move again because of a rodent infestation. The sewers were in disarray after the Blitz, and rats were everywhere. Sarah had written when they were in Singapore to say they'd moved in the absence of a man to defend them from the furry invaders. Richard and Jacob had laughed at that; they were a pair of formidable women, but furry scurrying things were too much for them.

'I can't wait to see Sarah,' Jacob said wistfully as they were shunted into a siding for the fifth time. Every muscle and tendon in Richard's body ached, and he longed for a bath and a night in a proper bed.

'Hmm, me too. Pippa, I mean, not Sarah,' Richard joked.

Jacob sighed and rested his head against the wall, shutting his eyes in exhaustion.

'Imagine if she'd come?' Richard asked, his eyes also shut, as they were crushed side by side. It had rained heavily all day, and everything and everyone on the train smelled of damp.

Jacob shook his head. 'I'm so glad she didn't. Kirky was right to take her on, though, keep the London end of things going. I wonder how it all went?'

It was true Sarah was a fine writer, and she had dug out some really interesting stories when all three of them worked together, so Kirky's mandate that the two boys go to Singapore and Sarah stay, find herself a freelance photographer because Pippa was working all the hours God sent in the munitions factory, and keep sending copy from London was a good one.

'I think we have enough for a feature on the whole Singapore thing,' Richard said. 'When we add in all the eyewitness testimony we managed to get, I remembered most of it, we have to rely on syndicated photos, Jacob had no camera, but it's going to be pretty explosive.'

Richard had used the long weeks at sea to write a series of articles on the war in the Far East. He'd file them once they were back in London.

'It had better be. It cost Kirky enough, and you know how he is about the bang for the buck.'

'Not to mention the fact that we almost died,' Richard added with a chuckle.

'That would be a secondary concern,' Jacob answered, quoting their salty old editor's reply when they had said reporting from the streets during a bombing raid was too dangerous and illegal, as the risk of being killed was too high.

'He knew Singapore could be risky. I think he was actually looking out for Sarah,' Richard conceded. 'But we're dispensable, it would appear.'

'And don't you forget it.' Jacob did an impersonation of the tough New Yorker.

Bone-weary and cold, they knocked on the door. Sarah opened it and threw herself into Jacob's arms, squealing. She hugged Richard too and told him Pippa was on the night shift. He and Jacob just wanted to go to bed, so he promised he'd tell her and Pippa everything in the morning. Part of him was relieved when he went into their bedroom to find a stack of letters on the nightstand. Esme, Mrs McHale, a few from Grace, two from his father, one from Nathan. Tired as he was, he read one from Grace, telling him all about life in Knocknashee and her battles with the canon.

The other letters he left until the morning, he was too exhausted to focus on them, now he just had to sleep.

CHAPTER 18

KNOCKNASHEE

Grace waited to read Richard's letter until she had marked her copybooks, had her dinner and her bath and did her exercises. It had been a long day. Gus Walsh, a chubby little ten-year-old who was an only child and much adored by his parents, was bullying the younger children and was well able to pack a punch if the humour took him. He'd picked on the wrong child today when he stole little Aoife O'Farrell's lunch and gave her a dig into the stomach into the bargain; the cosseted Gus didn't reckon on her brother Jamsie, a solid wall of fourteen-year-old muscle. Using the same methods of punishment that Gus meted out regularly, Jamsie gave him a good thumping. Gus ran home crying, and before Grace knew it, Eily Walsh, Gus's fussy mother, was down at the school with her precious son, who was dramatically moaning and holding his belly.

'A big fourteen-year-old attacking an innocent little boy!' screeched Eily, attracting the attention of every child in the yard. This would be the dinner conversation in every house in Knocknashee tonight.

Grace was trying to calm everything down when Con O'Farrell, Aoife and Jamsie's father, arrived, chuckling to himself as he walked towards the howling Gus and the outraged Eily. Someone must have told him.

'Ara, would you cop on, you big soft clown.' Con laughed and pulled Gus to his feet. 'A day's work is what you need, and a bit of exercise to run all that fat off you. You've an eejit made of that child, Eily, stuffing him with cake – he's ruined. And 'tis lucky my Jamsie didn't really let fly or he'd be up with Dr Ryan instead of moaning here like a fella in the pictures.' Con dismissed the Walshes' complaints out of hand.

Eily went puce and reared up like a lioness. 'Get your big muck savage paws off my child, Con O'Farrell, or I'll –'

'You'll what?' Con laughed again. 'You'll send poor Willy down to me, will you? That man of yours is so henpecked, he couldn't say boo to a goose. You've a pure solid fool made of that child, Eily, and he can be a right nasty piece of work too, I'm telling you. And 'tis some hiding he'll get one of these days if he doesn't mend his ways, you mark my words, and his mama won't be around to stick up for him.'

This was hardly a conciliatory sentiment, so Grace decided the best thing to do was separate both families. Both Gus and Jamsie were sentenced to a morning's weeding in the school garden. Eily opened her mouth to object, but fearing yet more ridicule from Con, she let it go. Jamsie, well used to hard work, would consider it a break, easier than thinning turnips or ploughing a field, but for Gus who only ever lifted cutlery to stuff his face with more food, it would be torture. Honestly, sometimes she felt like Solomon.

Eleanor was a godsend, and nothing short of it. Her years of being a headmistress were evident from the first day. She was kind and gentle and an excellent teacher, but she took no nonsense either. The ideal combination.

Grace still smiled at the memory of the canon arriving back from wherever he'd been to find Eleanor installed, teaching and on the payroll. He told Grace to dismiss her, that Grace had no authority to engage a member of staff without his permission, but she contradicted him, saying he wasn't there, they needed a teacher and Mrs Worth was eminently qualified.

'She's not even a Catholic,' the canon hissed.

'She's Anglican and a good God-fearing woman. She attends church in St James's in Dingle each Sunday, and she teaches the children their catechism just as well as any Catholic would. She's far more qualified or experienced than we could ever hope to attract to Knocknashee, so we are very grateful to have her.'

Grace was as defiant as she dared to be. She kept her voice neutral – he was very quick to dismiss any female complaints as 'women's histrionics' – but she was firm. If he dismissed her, he would find it hard to explain to the authorities, because the school needed a teacher and Grace had provided one.

'You had no right…' he said, failing to hide his fury.

'But you were gone, Canon. I asked Father Lehane where you were, but he didn't know, just that you were gone for three weeks at least. And since the lady Father Iggy sent had to go back to her home place because she got a permanent job, I was left with no choice.'

'She is not a person' – he said the word 'person' like he was saying 'criminal' – 'suitable for our parish, and I'm surprised at you for being so naive as to think she is.'

'But she's a very good teacher, Canon, and the children love her.'

'My good woman, what on earth has that to do with anything? This just shows how foolish you are. What children need is a firm hand, a man who has authority and can keep discipline, not two soft, silly women with feather heads who have no idea how to run a school.' His eyes glittered dangerously.

Mercifully at that exact moment, Eleanor had her class reciting their times tables, their voices in perfect unison drifting out on the spring air.

'They are learning fine, Canon, I promise you that,' she said. 'The *cigire* from the Department of Education was very complimentary about her classroom management and her teaching skills.'

'Was he indeed?' he spat. 'Well, I'll be the judge of that.'

To sack a woman of her experience who was universally liked was not easy, even for him. Grace asked Nancy to make sure people made their opinions on the new Mrs Worth known to the canon, and Nancy had done more than that. She discussed often and loudly in the post office how wonderful it was that the children had to speak English to the new mistress, something that could only be for their good given there was so little work and so few opportunities in their locality. Emigration was a fact of life for communities like theirs, and while no parent liked the idea of losing their sons or daughters to another country, if it had to happen, they wanted them to be equipped, and fluent English was the primary way to do that.

The canon was outmanoeuvred. He was fuming, but the fact that he didn't defy her and sack Eleanor and install Francis Sheehan anyway let her know that for all his bluster and arrogance, he wasn't confident of his position with regard to how much she knew. She'd confronted him about his dealings with Agnes, and he might suspect she knew about Siobhán McKenna, and she was certain he had no idea she'd found out about Kit Gallagher and him selling other babies, but if he was sure of his ground, he would just have overruled her and he didn't.

This was useful information, but she knew not to misjudge him all the same. She wasn't going to pick fights with him for no reason, or publicly defy him, but she would hold her position on this. She could feel Declan's hand on her shoulder. *Well done, Grace.*

The war felt never-ending. Sergeant Keane kept them updated about Eloise with what he knew, which he admitted wasn't much. It was a Dublin operation, and they felt no compunction to keep the local guard informed. Grace assumed it was an ongoing problem in Ireland, dealing with potential spies; Ireland was ideally located so close to the unprotected west coast of the United Kingdom.

There was a story going around Dingle that a German spy came ashore two years ago and asked for the time of the train to Tralee, but since it was fourteen years since a passenger train had run on the line, he was immediately arrested. Another one came off a U-boat, they said, and got so drunk in a local pub that when the two plain-clothes detectives followed him onto the Dublin train, they were able to ascertain fairly easily he wasn't who he said he was.

Strangers stood out here, and though Eloise was exotic for Knocknashee, she was Swiss, not German at all, and while it would stretch credibility to imagine that sweet woman was working for the Nazis, it could be true. But if it was, Tilly, Grace was sure, knew nothing about it.

Because of the Emergency, they were invoking special powers of arrest, and apparently there was no obligation on the part of the authorities to tell anyone anything. Marion O'Hare's husband, Colm, had been wonderful; he'd got Eloise a solicitor, and the solicitor was confident she wouldn't be held much longer and assured them she was in good spirits.

Grace made a cup of tea and ate the heel of the bread with a scrape of butter. She had run out of the jam they made with the blackberries last autumn, so there was nothing else to spread on it. She felt like she was hungry all the time now. She could boil a few potatoes, but without butter or milk to mash into them, they weren't that appetising. She'd manage with just the tea and bread. Tea was rationed now, as was sugar, butter, petrol and chocolate, so were clothes and shoes, but while people missed those things, they were used to being self-sufficient out here on the peninsula and so they managed. Grace had taken to reusing her tea leaves in an effort to stretch the ration. Sometimes it was only coloured water, and she longed for a nice strong cup, but she could cope. Some shopkeeper up the country was fined for selling the mould off the turf as tea leaves, so people were up to all sorts of tricks and the black market was flourishing. Tom O'Donoghue of the grocer's was known to have a nice little side trade out the back door for people who were a bit unscrupulous, but Grace made a point of making do and putting up with the lack of treats.

It was not a warm evening. The spring this year had been chilly, and there was an easterly wind that was biting cold despite it being almost summer. The little robin that was a regular visitor to her kitchen window gazed in, its tiny black eyes unmoving. 'Mammy, if that's you, will you try to look after Richard and Jacob and Sarah and Father Iggy...' The list of her friends she worried for was getting longer. She pulled on a thick cardigan that was hanging on the back of a kitchen chair, one she'd knit from several of Agnes's old jumpers she'd ripped out. She stoked the range and threw in a few sods of turf before she settled down with her letter.

CHAPTER 19

She extracted the fat letter from the envelope. There was a newspaper in there too, which she set aside for now.

Dear Grace,

I'm finally able to write after my mammoth journey back to England from Singapore. I can't believe it's May already. Please note the new address on the top of this letter—Sarah and Pippa moved to a new apartment (Pippa calls it a flat) while we were gone because of a mouse! They said it was several rats, but I suspect one mouse was enough to send them squealing like mice themselves. It's fine anyway—nice and bright and in a good location.

Grace wondered what the sleeping arrangements were. She knew Jacob and Sarah lived as man and wife, which was shocking to her, but she supposed things were different for them. But were Richard and Pippa? She found it painful to think about so carried on reading.

I got your letters. I'm so relieved Tilly is home again. What an ordeal for her.

The fall of Singapore was terrible to witness. I won't go into the details, but I've enclosed the four-page feature Kirky ran based on my writing and Jacob's photographs. It doesn't make for easy reading, and I don't think, awful as the images are in the piece, it actually captures the true horror of watching the island be subjugated by the Japanese. They make the Germans look decent, and that's saying something.

The journey back was arduous and at times terrifying—several times I was sure we were goners—but somehow we made it to Ceylon, and from there by ship back to England, and here we are.

It's great to be back, even if I'm no longer the exotic soul I once was. London is swarming with Yanks now. "Overpaid, overfed, oversexed, and over here" is the phrase used to describe my fellow countrymen, but it's all in good fun. The British are grateful and glad to see American troops, and so am I. Neither Japan nor Germany is going to give up, and it's going to take a hell of a lot more than what this country has got to defeat them.

The British are terrified Roosevelt will pull troops from Europe to fight the Japanese, so they are bending over backwards to make the GIs feel welcome, and I'm writing lots of warm, fuzzy stories about how well liked us Yanks are over here. It's all true too—they are genuinely grateful for us. I just hope we can finish the job now, as Churchill says.

Coming back through the Suez Canal, we were struck by how critical it is that this narrow waterway that links Europe to Asia remains in Allied hands. If the Germans can cut off British supplies from her empire and connect with the Japanese in Asia, well...I don't like to speculate.

Meanwhile back here, Sarah is very busy with the refugees. She volunteers as a translator but inevitably gets drawn into their stories, and on more than one occasion, I've woken up to some stranger on our couch. She's got a much softer heart than she would like anyone to believe.

She is working directly for Kirky too, so two of the Lewis offspring are journalists now. My father telegrammed every day that I was in the Far East —driving Sarah mad—to find out if she'd heard from me. Nothing from my mother unsurprisingly. My father says Mother is asking about us when he writes, but we all know that's not true.

Savannah feels like it exists in another lifetime. It's hard to describe, but it's somehow unreal. London is more like home now. Pippa even teases me when I use Cockney phrases. She was born within the sound of Bow Bells, a church in London—that's how a Cockney is defined—and half the time I have no idea what she's saying. They use words that rhyme with the word they intend rather than the actual word, like plates of meat for feet, or dog and bone for phone. It's all very confusing, I can tell you.

She's working in a munitions factory, which she likes. They work very long hours and the pay isn't great, but there's a great sense of camaraderie there and they sing songs while they work. Given that she's lost almost everyone close to her over the years, I think she appreciates the sense of connection there more than another person might.

She's even volunteered to host a GI, which kind of had us groaning, I must admit. Not because we don't want to help, but we talk to people all day and it feels like an intrusion to have strangers in our home. But Pippa got mad at us and so now we're doing it. She's completely right of course.

When a US serviceman gets leave, where is he supposed to go? He can't go home, and only a handful have relatives or friends over here, so the Red Cross has set up this kind of hosting volunteer program, and British people, though they have almost nothing, are lining up to take the poor lonely GIs in. So we've applied to take some kid from the USA for his furlough and show him around. How well he's gonna take to having three fellow Yanks to greet him and only one native is anyone's guess, but Pippa insisted. (They call us all Yanks because they don't understand the distinction between Northerners and Southerners. My father uses the word Yankee to describe everything he thinks is ridiculous, lazy, or immoral, and if anyone ever called him a Yankee, he'd be horrified, but our hosts don't get it and it doesn't matter anyway, so we're all Yanks.)

For now it's back to reporting as usual. The arrival of American troops in Europe has created a renewed interest in stories from here, and I'm going to spend the next few weeks talking to GIs and getting their take on everything.

So tell me how you are? And don't feel you have to sugar-coat it and say you are fine and all of that. You can tell me the truth, always. I have never lost anyone as close to me as you were to Declan, so I can't promise any great wisdom, but I can offer a listening ear.

I can't wait to get a long letter from you. It feels like forever since I was there, or even heard from you, so write back as soon as you can and tell me all about Knocknashee.

How is Odile? I don't know if Didier is still in London, but now that I'm back, I'll try to find out to see if he has any update on her mother or aunt, and of course on Alfie. I assume Mrs. O'Hare has heard nothing? I know it's so distressing to be in the dark, but please tell them that no news is not necessarily bad news—so little is coming out of Nazi-occupied territory.

I came home to a letter and a package of American treats from Mrs. McHale, remember her? She's the lady who works at the parochial house at St. Patrick's Cathedral in New York, the one who helped me find Father Dempsey. Well, she found out my address from my father—she said she loves finding things out, so she wasn't joking—and she wrote, hoping I was staying safe. She sent me some Hershey's chocolate and a box of Tootsie Rolls. Sarah, Jacob, and I had a feast, but Pippa declared them disgusting. She's got no taste, that girl!

It was very sweet of Mrs. McHale, though. She said she had nobody in the forces to write to and so she was adopting me as her boy overseas. I wrote back, and so now we are in correspondence. I think my connection to Dingle is my main selling point, so I told her about visiting Knocknashee and how beautiful it was. She loved hearing all about it and of course about you. She assumed you were my girl, and I had to explain you weren't, and she was a little heartbroken, I think—in her head she imagined being invited to a wedding in West Kerry!

I sent her a photo of me and Pippa taken down on the pier in Brighton. Pippa took us all down there to experience a British seaside. It was an experience all right—the train got shunted into a siding for three hours on the way back. But Mrs. McHale didn't comment on her at all, so no response is still a response, I guess! I won't tell Pippa—ha, ha!

So that's it for now from me—I've gone on long enough.

Please write to me as soon as you can and make it a long one. I'm so looking forward to it.

Richard

Grace folded the four sheets of thin blue paper carefully. So Pippa was definitely his girl and probably in his bed. She'd known it all along really, but he'd never confirmed it. Not that he had now either, but she thought it was inferred. Why shouldn't he have a girlfriend? He was handsome and wealthy and had an interesting job – no wonder Pippa liked him. And she sounded nice from all he'd said about her.

Grace forced down the acidic jealousy that threatened to overtake her. Richard was her friend. She'd had Declan, and he was perfectly entitled to find someone too. Of course he was. She wished him well.

She opened the large double-page spread of the broadsheet newspaper. 'The Fall of Singapore' was the headline, and there were Richard's and Jacob's names. She felt a surge of pride, though she always felt silly acknowledging how proud she was of him; it wasn't like she had any right to be.

She read his account, harrowing, detailed, colourful and concise. His command of English was wonderful; he could paint such vivid pictures with his words. And though the subject was awful, reading his report, she felt she was right there. The images too were poignant: a mother fleeing with her baby, the child facing the camera, its big eyes confused; the crowds of refugees crushing to board a ship; a building near a hospital that sick people were marched into and sealed inside with no water; a doctor trying to tend to someone while bleeding himself. Richard was right – it made for excruciating reading.

She would write to him tomorrow, but now she needed to sleep.

She dragged herself up. The steel calliper rested on the armchair, and she decided she wouldn't bother putting it back on, that she could make it up the stairs. She quenched the gas lamp. Because it was clearing up outside, the drizzle of earlier blown away by the wind, it was quite bright still. They were still a full six weeks to the solstice, when daylight went from 4 a.m. to 10 p.m., but she smiled at the thought of warmer days. The cold played havoc with her bad leg. And she loved to swim in the sea, loved the sense of freedom she got being weightless in the water. It often struck her, when the sun came out and the people of the parish took a dip, that the sea, like death, was a leveller. Dressed only in swimming clothes – rich, poor, happy, sad, sick – everyone was the same, just bobbing around in the salty ocean. She loved how it made her feel, head and shoulders out of the water, her wasted, twisted leg invisible.

The oil lamp in the hall was on, and she turned the dial to quench that too, taking a moment to allow her eyes to adjust to the dim light before making her way to the bottom stair.

CHAPTER 20

LONDON

Richard sat beside Pippa as Pathé News showed a newsreel round-up of the progress of the war so far. She'd convinced him to go to *Pardon My Sarong*, starring Nan Wynn from West Virginia. It wasn't really the kind of film he enjoyed, but he'd been so busy of late, reporting on American troops arriving in Great Britain, he'd hardly seen her, and while she never complained, Sarah had urged him to make a bit of a fuss over her. Sarah was right of course. Pippa was such a great girl, so kind and funny, and she never made demands, unlike when he was dating Miranda, who had endless requirements, so the least he could do was see the picture of her choice.

The instantly recognisable voice of Bob Danvers-Walker of Pathé News, who told the news stories as if they too were blockbuster films, filled the cinema.

'Major General R.P. Hartle, commander of United States services in Northern Ireland, is overjoyed to be here. In RAF news, twenty-five bombing raids have been completed from Trondheim in Norway to

Genoa in Italy. Meanwhile in the Far East, battles rage as our soldiers and those of the combined Allied forces do daily battle with the Japanese.'

Pippa reached over and held his hand as the images of Japanese prisoners of war being held by American troops in the trenches of Bataan appeared on screen. She knew he still had nightmares about the things he'd seen there.

'The United States Navy has, this week alone, sunk eight Japanese warships, while a Norwegian plane saw off a Nazi bomber over Northern Ireland.' Danvers-Walker spoke with ill-concealed delight at the way the Nazi forces were bleeding on the Eastern Front.

Richard sat in the dark, Pippa's hand in his, as the audience was regaled with the changes Stateside too, and he felt somehow relieved that British people saw it wasn't all sunshine and roses over there while they endured ever deeper deprivations and loss.

'The iconic city of New York is now to be blacked out at night to prevent U-boat attacks, and the United States government has plans to black out ten thousand towns and cities, seeing how successful blackout measures have been here at home.' The skyline of New York disappeared, replaced by a familiar Nazi figure who elicited boos from the audience.

'Reinhard Heydrich, second-in-command of the dreaded Gestapo, was assassinated and died of his injuries on the fourth of June in Prague. His death will be an enormous blow to the Nazi war machine.' This was met with an actual cheer, and Richard wondered if people had become so desensitised to death and destruction that it had descended into a game of theirs versus ours.

'Good riddance,' Pippa said with a grin, and he smiled back.

'There is good news from the African campaign also, as Rommel has failed on his second attempt to capture Tobruk.'

Richard remembered seeing for himself the narrow Suez Canal and realising how important not just Tobruk was, as the only deep-water port in the region, but also how holding it was vital for Alexandria and the Suez too.

As Danvers-Walker wound up the report by telling them of how the Iroquois had declared war on the Nazis, Pippa whispered, 'Are they red Indians?'

'American Indians, yes. They see themselves as a separate nation, independent of the United States,' he whispered back.

'Did you know any?' she asked.

He smiled. British people had no concept of how big the United States really was. She had asked him if he saw Hollywood stars when he was at home, before he explained that Savannah was as far from Hollywood as London was from Moscow.

He shook his head. 'There used to be Cherokee and others in the South, where I'm from, but the government forced them to the Midwest in the mid…' But he stopped as a matronly pair of women shot them a disapproving glare for whispering, muttering something derogatory about loudmouthed Yanks.

Tell me later, she mouthed.

Once the movie started, Richard leant over to the two women and offered them his bag of candy. Initially suspicious, they then accepted and grinned as they popped a candy each into their mouths, whispering their thanks. Candy was a dim and distant memory for most Londoners.

'Claey's lemon drops, all the way from South Bend, Indiana, USA,' he whispered to the women, with a wink at Pippa. They had the grace to look embarrassed about their earlier anti-American sentiments.

The film was funny, Abbott and Costello's antics on boats and on a deserted tropical island giving the audience a much-needed laugh. Richard found himself wondering if Grace had seen it. She didn't often go to the movies. There was a movie theatre in Dingle, but it was a long six miles back to Knocknashee and the busses were infrequent, even more so now that gas was in short supply. Pippa was enjoying it, he could see, and she guffawed with laughter at the witty script. They shared the bag of candy his father had sent in a parcel, or at least his secretary had. The simplest thing, a little piece of candy, could brighten a day when a population had been deprived of any treats for as long as the British had. He was constantly in awe of their good humour. Any touch of grumpiness he was quick to forgive and hoped his fellow countrymen would be the same.

He'd interviewed several GIs in the past weeks and had reiterated to them the information from their commanding officers on how to behave in Britain. It was critical to the success of the war that the British and Americans pulled together. From photos in the paper of Churchill and FDR looking cosy to articles about how happy the British were to have the Americans fully onboard, both sides were making a concerted effort to present a united front.

The fresh-faced American GIs who had flooded Britain were open and friendly for the most part and had been warned about being overly familiar or asking too many questions. British people were reserved and unfailingly polite, but it wasn't the done thing to ask probing questions of strangers. The US forces had even produced a handbook that covered topics such as how reserved the British were but also how tough, how they'd endured so much already and yet remained stoic and uncowed. The booklet explained the rules of cricket and soccer and gave tips on how to converse on the subject.

He'd taken a booklet home to show Pippa, who found it hilarious. It told GIs to be friendly but polite and not to be overly affectionate, that the British didn't go big on public displays of affection. She'd cast aside the booklet then and said she would show him exactly how the British showed affection, and he'd been more than enthusiastic in his response. He knew his parents would be horrified if they knew both he and Sarah were sleeping with people they were not married to, and sometimes he felt a bit of a cad, but he had offered to marry Pippa before he left for Singapore in case he was captured or killed – then at least she'd be entitled to the protection of the United States as his wife – but she'd refused, just joked that she'd hold out for a more romantic proposal if he didn't mind, and it had not come up since he'd been back. They were answerable to nobody, and as Pippa said often, 'We could all be dead tomorrow, so let's just live.'

They'd had two GIs for dinner last week. Sarah had met them someplace and brought them home, and Pippa cooked a pie made with cauliflower, bacon and cheese. It was surprisingly tasty, though she admitted she'd used the full ration of cheese and two ounces of bacon. She seasoned it with mustard and horseradish, and it actually was really delicious. She'd applied for an allotment and was given one in Kensington Gardens of all places, and as a result, there was no shortage in their household of potatoes, parsnips and carrots. The level of industry in that girl never ceased to astound him, and she spent all her time off digging and weeding and reading books from the library on how to grow food.

She'd teased the two six-foot GIs from Rhode Island about the booklet, warning them not to eat too much if they were invited to a meal in a home because people had so little and there was plenty of food in the mess.

'Don't you boys go eatin' us out of house and home now. We heard what you're like,' she warned, mock stern, and then cracked her huge grin. 'I'm only having a laugh with you boys. We've got an allotment, see, so we got plenty. Not much meat or sugar, mind you, and precious little marg, but we manage, and what we have, we share.' They had relaxed and taken a second helping once she assured them they were fine for food.

Do I want to marry Pippa? he wondered as he glanced sidelong at her profile. She had that peaches-and-cream colouring synonymous with English girls, and her skin burnt in the sun – she would turn lobster red if exposed to a Georgia summer. Her strawberry-blond hair was wavy and cut to her jaw, and her kind hazel eyes were round and generally danced with merriment. For a person who had lost so much, she was unfailingly upbeat and cheerful, and she could make him weep with laughter. She had such a funny turn of phrase and a unique perspective on the world that she was the kind of person who lit up a room. Could he picture her in Savannah? Going to his parents' house for lunch on Sundays, meeting Miranda and Algernon Smythe at the yacht club, dancing at the King and Prince on St Simons? Could she sit on the porch and be waited on by Esme? He couldn't see it somehow. Whereas he could easily imagine a life there with Grace.

Stop. He pulled up the mental stop sign, a device he employed whenever she popped into his mind. Grace didn't want him. He'd poured his heart out in that letter when he came back from Knocknashee, and in it, he'd told her they need never mention it again if she was going to reject him, and that's precisely what happened. Or she never got it. Either way, it was done now and there was no going back. The letter, if she'd received it, must have embarrassed her, and she probably hated hearing that he had romantic feelings for her. He deeply regretted putting their friendship at risk like that, but she'd been a perfect lady and did as he asked – she never again referred to it, and they'd carried on writing in a friendly way. He would never risk rocking that boat again.

And besides, she'd married Declan McKenna. She'd had a choice and she picked him. And no matter how hard that was to accept, it was the truth. The fact that Declan had died – and Richard held nothing but sadness in his heart for him and for Grace about that awful tragedy – was neither here nor there. She'd had a choice and she picked someone else. She wouldn't want him as a consolation prize, and if he was honest with himself, he didn't want to be that either. To know the woman he adored was only with him because the one she really wanted was dead would kill him too in the end. No, this was better.

Pippa was wonderful, loyal and kind, and maybe they would marry and he would stay over here? He liked it here. People were less concerned with the trappings of wealth here, or at least they were in wartime anyway. Pippa had snorted when he'd said that to her, that people here were far less snobby than at home.

'England, less snobby? Are you havin' a laugh? Every bit of the class structure that exists all over the bloomin' world comes from here, with "our lord" this and "viscount" that. It might not look like it now, I'll grant you, but that's just 'cause bombs don't care who they fall on, prince or pauper. But once this is all over and we win, it will be business as usual, you mark my words.'

In all the time he'd been here, and despite staggering evidence to the contrary, for him Dunkirk being the worst, followed closely by the fall of Singapore, he had never met a British person who wasn't completely convinced they would win the war. Some commentators viewed it as a remarkable bit of political chicanery on the part of Winston Churchill, while others truly believed it was the inevitable outcome, but either way, the people of this small island that stood alone for so long would not be broken nor shaken in their belief of victory, that was for sure.

CHAPTER 21

When the film was over, they emerged onto Piccadilly Circus, and Richard suggested they go for a drink. He wasn't a big drinker, but he'd had terrible nightmares since coming back to London and found a drink or two before bed helped him to sleep.

'Sure, will we go up to the West End?' she asked, linking his arm.

'Do you mind if we don't? I was thinking of swinging by the Union Tavern – it's near King's Cross station. We could take the Tube?'

She looked perplexed, her brow furrowed. 'I don't mind, but why are we going all the way there?'

'I'll tell you on the way,' he said, leading her down into the station at Piccadilly Circus. The Tube was quiet, and he sat beside her and explained that he'd met Didier Georges there before and that the man behind the bar seemed to know him. He'd told her before all about Odile and the Dreyfuses, so she knew he was personally involved.

'So you want to go and find him? Is that it?' she asked.

'Well, I just want to see if he knows if Didi is still in London. He'd come here to lay low once he'd escaped from the Gestapo, but since he's the only link we have to Alfie and through him to Odile's mother and aunt, I'd like to get an update if I can. Her family in Ireland, her aunt Tilly and her grandmother Mary, are really worried, and they've been through a lot, so if I could find something out to reassure them, it would be good.'

'Of course. Poor little mite. She was lucky, though, that you were able to take her to Ireland. At least she has someone and she's being looked after.'

Richard was reminded again of how tough this woman was, alone in the world. 'She should be speaking French and instead she speaks Irish. It's funny the twists and turns life takes, isn't it?'

'That's the truth.' She snuggled up to him, resting her head on his shoulder. 'Do you think she's still alive, Odile's mum?'

Richard sighed. 'Well, her father is definitely dead, but Bernadette escaped and she's resourceful, so maybe? Someone thought they might have seen her in Lyon, on the Swiss border, but I don't know. If she'd managed to get out, you would think she'd make contact, though to be fair, she doesn't know where Odile is. Alfie just sort of gave her to us last minute, and their place in Paris is no longer theirs, I assume. Didi said the Germans have taken over people's apartments who fled, so even if she was in a position to make contact, it would be difficult for her to find a way to do that. Presuming Alfie and Constance are still together, she might manage to track her sister down through the network of saboteurs, but the O'Hares have heard nothing either, so it's not looking good.'

'Maybe she's in hiding?' Pippa suggested.

'Could be. Let's hope so.'

'I hope so too. A kid needs her mum.'

They arrived at the stop and alighted the train, climbing up the steps. No Londoner who lived through the Blitz would ever see the Tube the same way again. It had been their saviour when Hitler's bombs rained down night after night.

They walked down the street and had to sidestep an altercation of some sort between two American soldiers. A big white GI with an accent Richard recognised as either Tennessee or Louisiana was telling a Black GI he couldn't come into the bar.

'Boy, y'all got your own bars to go to. Just 'cause we ain't at home don't mean nothin'. Same rules apply, so beat it.' The white man shoved the other soldier in the chest, almost sending him flying. The push knocked the hat off the Black man's head, and it landed in a puddle. Richard stepped forward.

'All OK here, boys?' he asked, slipping deeper into his Georgian drawl.

'Just fine.' The white GI's breath stank of beer and cigarettes, and Richard could tell he was very drunk. Occasionally there was a bit of nastiness like this. Just last week a chip shop in Devon had been instructed by the local commanding officer of the US base down there that he was to serve fish and chips to coloured servicemen on Tuesdays and Thursdays only; the remaining days were to be for white personnel exclusively. The chip shop owner refused point-blank, and it had led to a right hullaballoo, as Pippa called it.

The Black GI knew better than to challenge him.

Pippa picked up the wet hat and tried to dry it off with her coat sleeve. She handed it with an apologetic smile to the soldier.

'All right then, maybe might be best to get back inside – it sure is cold out here, huh?' Richard jollied the drunk man along. He was dangerous, Richard could sense it, so diffusing the situation was the best he could do. He gently led the GI back inside the bar to where a group of infantry men were drinking and slipped back out to join Pippa.

'I was to meet a girl in there,' the other soldier said to Pippa as he replaced his wet hat on his head.

'I'll go in and fetch her out for you, no bother – what's her name?'

'Thank you, ma'am, much obliged to ya. Her name is Maureen Lipton.'

'No trouble. What does she look like?'

'Slim, tall, with blond hair and a gap in her front teeth,' he said with a grin.

'Two ticks, I'll be back.' Pippa slipped into the packed pub, and true to her word, three minutes later, as Richard made small talk with the GI from Texas, she reappeared with a girl in tow. The pair seemed happy to be reunited, so Richard and Pippa let them to it.

'Seems so stupid to me,' Pippa said in frustration. 'We're all on the same side, men, women, Black, white. Why can't we all be at least friendly to each other?'

'It's a long story,' Richard said as they arrived at an old Edwardian pub on a corner. Inside there seemed to be some kind of celebration going on; a wiry man in a flat cap was belting out songs on a piano, and people were gathered around it singing.

Pippa asked him for a gin and lemon, and he went to the bar while she found a seat. The bartender was the same burly man as before, muscle-bound, with a flame-red beard and a bald head; Richard assumed he was the proprietor. He waited patiently for his turn to be served. When the man got to him, he showed no sign of recognition.

'A beer and a gin and lemon please?' he called. For as long as he lived, he would never get used to the room-temperature dark-brown soupy beer the English loved. Beer was meant to be cold and crisp and thirst-quenching, not like a wet blanket over your head. But it was all there was here, so he'd had to get used to it. But some day he'd sit in a booth at the Crystal Beer Parlor in Savannah and drink a cold, fizzy, pale-gold beer, and he would appreciate American beer in a way he never had before.

There was a lull in ordering as the man at the piano launched into a rousing version of the George Formby comedic and slightly risqué song 'I Did What I Could with My Gas Mask'. Everyone was joining in and laughing.

Richard used his chance. 'Have you seen Didier Georges recently?' he asked, concealing his nerves. This was clearly not a man you messed with.

'Who, mate?' He looked confused.

'Didier Georges, a Frenchman – I was in here with him a few months ago.' Richard didn't believe for a second the man didn't know who he was talking about.

'You a Yank?'

Richard nodded. 'A journalist for the *Capital*.' He took out his card and handed it to the man. 'But I know Didier on a personal level. We have some mutual friends in Paris.'

The man examined the card, turned it over and then handed it back to Richard. 'I can give him a message if he comes in?'

It was the best he was going to get; this man wasn't going to just hand over information like that. 'Thanks.' Richard scribbled the telephone number of the flat on the back of the card. 'Can you ask him to call me? He'll know what it's about.'

'If I see him.' The man shrugged and put the card beside the till.

Richard had no doubt that the man would see Didier if Didier was still in London. It had been the same when he went to find him at the communist newspaper office. Even though Britain wasn't occupied, people were very cagey, so he expected it. Most likely Didi had no news, but Richard would like to be able to tell Grace he'd checked at least. And of course Mary and Tilly O'Hare too, he added in his head, aware of his real motivation. He walked over to join Pippa, who was now up at the piano with the crowd, and handed her the gin as she sang along to some old Cockney ballad he didn't know.

He was glad of the hustle and bustle in the pub; it gave him time to think. Pippa was singing her heart out. She loved to sing and had a lovely voice. He found himself wondering if Grace could sing. Mentally he berated himself. Was this to be his life now? Every thought that entered his head leading to him wondering if Grace could do it, if Grace would like it, what Grace thought about it? It was ridiculous and pathetic, and he knew he should just pull himself together. Here beside him was a beautiful girl, who he really liked, who was crazy about him, he knew, even though she was jokey about it, and who he could be happy with. If only Grace Fitzgerald would leave his mind. But that was the trouble – he didn't want Grace Fitzgerald out of his thoughts or his heart or his life. That was the very last thing on earth he wanted.

Lost in his reverie, it took a few seconds to realise Pippa was singing solo now. Her gravelly voice always surprised people – she looked like she would have a sweet soprano, not a deep and sultry alto – but it was mesmerising. Her version of the Vera Lynn song 'I'll Be Seeing You' caused the hum of conversation to hush. As she got to the chorus, a young man in uniform danced slowly with a girl who was clinging to him and crying. People around were visibly moved.

'I'll be seeing you in every lovely summer's day, in everything that's light and gay. I'll always think of you that way. I'll find you in the morning sun, and when the night is new, I'll be looking at the moon, but I'll be seeing you.'

The crowd joined in sweetly as she sang the last chorus a second time. The song finished to rapturous applause and several eyes being wiped. This war really was taking such a heavy toll on these people. Though he lived with them, it wasn't his partner or sibling or best friend going off to war, so while he could imagine, he was acutely aware that he didn't know what it felt like. But these people did. Pippa did.

He put his arms around her and kissed her head. 'That was beautiful. You have an amazing voice – you should be on stage.'

Normally she'd have some self-deprecating quip as a rejoinder, but not now. She beamed up at him, a tear in her eye. He led her away from the crowd to a booth as her tears began to flow in earnest. In all the time he'd known her, he'd never seen her cry. She had plenty to cry about, but she was a tough cookie.

'Is it the song?' he asked, unsure of what to say.

'Was your mum and dad nice to you, growin' up, I mean?' she asked, and he was a bit taken aback by the question.

'I don't know if nice is the word. My mother is kind of cold, and my father worked a lot so we didn't see him much, but he was OK, I guess. But we had a lot of opportunities, and we lived in a nice house, went to good schools…'

'Did they say nice things to you, though, praise you and that?' she persisted.

Richard thought for a moment. 'No, they didn't. I don't ever remember them saying that I did something well. My brother, Nathan, is a genius, so he aced all the exams, and Sarah is pretty, so they used to dress her up and say she was beautiful, but I don't remember… I guess I wasn't that smart or a girl so…' He shrugged. 'No, they didn't.'

'My mum loved to hear me. She and I would sing all the time – she loved the old music hall numbers. She used to take me to Brighton Pier when I was little. We'd save up and have a day out on the train, and go and hear the performers down there, get fish and chips for our tea, and then we'd learn the songs and do duets when we were around the house.'

Richard took her hand and gave her his handkerchief to dry her eyes.

'And when she died, I wanted to sing at the funeral, but my aunt wouldn't let me, said it was unseemly. Better to get a professional person – it would sound nicer. And she told me not to sing, so I stopped, for years...' She took a sip of her gin, then turned to him. 'You saying I had a nice voice is the first time anyone's said that to me since my mum died.'

Richard held her face in his hands, her warm hazel eyes still brimming with tears of loss for her mother. He used his thumbs to wipe them and then kissed her lips. 'Pippa Wills, you have a beautiful voice, you sound mesmerising, you have everyone here under your spell, including me, and if your mom is anywhere, she was watching you here tonight, bursting with pride at her daughter's voice of an angel, but also with pride at what a great young woman she's grown into.'

He raised his pint then and clinked off hers. 'To Philippa, and her beautiful, talented, kind, funny, generous daughter. I'm sure you didn't want to leave her, but she's a tough cookie' – Pippa smiled at that – 'and now she's got me to take care of her.' Richard gazed at her, and their eyes met, an unspoken conversation happening between them.

A gentle cough from behind them interrupted the moment, and Richard turned. 'Didi! Good to see you.' He stood and shook the Frenchman's hand and introduced him to Pippa. The bartender appeared with a glass of cognac for Didi and another round for him and Pippa, waving payment away.

'I wasn't sure you'd still be here.'

Didi shrugged and sighed in that uniquely Gallic way. 'I want to get back to France, but the powers that be over here seem to think my expertise is better put to use training agents here who are to be dropped behind enemy lines.' Even though there was nobody near them, he kept his voice low.

'I'd imagine that's very true. Your expert first-hand experience in dealing with the Nazis would be invaluable.' Richard took a sip of his pint. 'Any news of Alfie?'

'Not of him, but just this week, an agent we got out, a wireless operator and so highly valuable' – Richard tried not to wince at Didi's cold description of a human being as merely an asset to be protected – 'she met a woman as part of an escape line called Bernadette who was French. But beyond that, apart from a potential fleeting sighting in Lyon that I told you about before, there has been nothing. That might have been anyone. And people don't use their real names, so it was probably not her. The meeting took place somewhere near the Swiss Alps, but the agent had been sick with fever and couldn't remember much else. The woman she described, as best as she could remember, was thin and in her fifties, which didn't sound like Bernadette at all, but the war means there is nobody left plump any more, and living under occupation ages a person in a way no other type of living does. She did say she had a child, but again...lots of women are mothers.'

'And Alfie or Constance?'

'Nothing. Nobody has heard from him for over a year. But that doesn't necessarily mean he's dead. He could well be living under an alias – in fact, it would be the only way he could live now that he is known to the Germans.'

'So he hasn't popped up in any of the resistance groups you're in contact with?' Richard asked.

The Frenchman smiled at the question. 'People are living with the Boche breathing down their necks – they tend not to announce their subversive intentions, Richard. The only way this can work is if people are kept in the dark as much as possible. It's not like an army of saboteurs are working together and they are all friends. It's more like tiny groups, or more often individuals operating alone and praying they don't get caught. So Alfie might well be alive and we would not know it, or equally he could be dead or captured. It's impossible to tell. Usually though, if they get one of ours, they can't help but crow about it, and Alfie would be a high-profile catch, so if he was dead or captured, generally we'd hear about it. Not always, but often, so...' That Gallic shrug again.

Didi drained his cognac and stood. '*Bon chance,* my friend. Keep up the good work. I see your articles sometimes – it's important work you are doing. Take care.' And without another word, he shook Richard's hand and slipped out the door.

They finished their drinks and made the weary journey home, not talking much, each lost in their own thoughts. As they entered the apartment, Pippa opened their bedroom door, but Richard made for the living room and his writing pad and pen.

'Aren't you coming to bed?' Pippa asked. 'It's late.'

'I will soon. I just want to write –'

'To Grace,' she finished for him, leaving the kitchen before he could reply.

CHAPTER 22

KNOCKNASHEE

Grace read Richard's letter about meeting Didi and decided to go up to the farm after school and tell the O'Hares what it said. It wasn't much, but a possible sighting of Bernadette was a thread of hope to cling to, as was the information that no news about Alfie and Constance was not necessarily bad news.

The day was bright and sunny, and the children were outside drawing flowers when Tilly arrived, fizzing with excitement. Grace normally didn't have visitors when she was working, so at first, she feared it was bad news. But Tilly looked fit to burst with excitement.

The children were getting their summer holidays next week, and excitement was palpable. The sun was splitting the rocks, and they, like all Irish people, believed there were a finite number of warm days in any given year. She could sense their impatience at wasting in school a single one of the days they could be at the beach.

She made a decision. It was five past two, and school didn't finish until three o'clock, but everyone walked home, and besides, a lot of pupils were absent because they were saving hay or shearing sheep.

She motioned to Tilly to wait and went into Eleanor's classroom. The former headmistress was reading to her students – even though they were big boys and girls, they still loved being read to – and everyone in the Knocknashee senior class was right now aboard the *Hispaniola*, with Captain Flint's treasure map, keeping a close eye on Long John Silver, willing Jim Hawkins on and hoping that Captain Smollett could save the *Hispaniola* from mutiny.

They didn't even look up when she entered, crossed to Eleanor and whispered in her ear. The teacher nodded and smiled, closing the book. 'More tomorrow, boy and girls,' she said, to audible groans of disappointment – it was coming to a good bit.

'Do you want to stay?' Grace asked, and they turned to her in confusion. 'Or would you rather go for a swim?'

A few glanced at the clock, wondering if she'd made a mistake, while others nudged them not to point it out. If Miss Fitz let them out an hour early, then woe betide the child who alerted her to the error.

They didn't need to be asked twice, and within three minutes, the entire school was empty of children, the whooping and cheering ringing in the adults' ears as the children escaped.

Joanne, Libby and Olivia stood, unsure of what to do. Grace had watched closely the other children's reactions to these English girls while assiduously seeming to ignore it all.

'An bhfuil fonn snaimhe oiribh?' Janie O'Shea asked the three girls. Despite the protestation at first that they didn't speak Irish, the Worth girls had slowly learnt to communicate, if not fluently, then enough to understand most of what was said. They had yet to actually speak Irish, but Grace had no doubt it would come.

Janie made a swimming gesture, and the three girls turned to their mother.

'May we go?' Libby asked.

'You don't have any swimming costumes,' Eleanor said, bemused.

'Oh, all the children here swim in their clothes,' Grace said with a laugh. 'They dry out on the way home.'

Eleanor looked at her three daughters, two brunettes and one redhead, all petite. They were dressed in cotton summer dresses that would dry easily.

'Well, if you want to, I suppose. It will be freezing, you do know that, despite the sunny day.'

'We don't mind,' Libby answered excitedly, delighted to be in the gang.

'*Aghaidh linn*,' Janie said, and the girls happily followed.

'They're finding their feet,' Grace remarked as they tripped out after Janie.

Eleanor nodded, but there was a sadness there Grace wasn't used to seeing. 'Is everything all right?' she asked.

Eleanor sighed and nodded again. 'Yes, I... It's hard, Douglas being away. He's missing them growing up. They'll be up and gone before we know it, and he'll have missed it all.' A tear slid down her cheek.

'Oh, Eleanor, it must be so hard...'

Eleanor extracted a handkerchief from her sleeve and wiped her tears. 'Ignore me, Grace. I'm a bit of a mess these days. It's his birthday today, so we'd normally have a cake. It just all feels... I think it must be the change.' She lowered her voice. Such matters were rarely, if ever, discussed. Grace had had a conversation with Lizzie about it a while back, when they were in a café in Cork and the older woman suddenly started sweating profusely though the room wasn't particularly hot, and Lizzie had explained about hot flushes and insomnia and very erratic moods that were part and parcel of being a woman.

Grace knew Tilly was waiting for her, but she didn't want to abandon Eleanor either. 'Can you just hold on here for a few minutes for me?' she asked.

Eleanor nodded. 'Of course. I'm going to prepare the vocabulary test for tomorrow anyway.'

'Right, I'll be back in ten minutes,' Grace said, and left her, closing the door. Tilly was in her classroom, but once Grace appeared, she ran towards her.

'Guess who's coming?' Tilly asked, her eyes shining.

'Clark Gable?' Grace guessed with a laugh. 'Laurel and Hardy? Rommel?'

'No, you eejit! Eloise! She's been released without charge. She wrote to me – it's all in the letter. She was innocent, and they finally believed her. The photographs she took were just for herself, and she never stole the one of Alfie and Constance from Mam's. She hadn't a clue what that was about. But knowing our house, it will be found in a drawer or a box or something. They did everything – asked her about a thousand questions, contacted her local police station back in Switzerland and everything. Hard to believe it, but they did. They searched her flat in Dublin around fifty times and found nothing. According to her solicitor, none of the German community in Dublin had ever heard of her. Imagine – they know there are Germans living in Dublin loyal to bloody Hitler and they just let them there. I can't think why they don't round them all up and throw them in jail. They did it to me and Eloise on far less evidence, no evidence at all, in fact.' The words came out in a torrent, expressing the relief, the jubilation at seeing her friend again.

'When is she coming?' Grace asked.

'I'm not sure yet, she has some things to sort out in Dublin but the director of her language school has been very sympathetic and understanding and kept her job open for her, but the replacement is going to see out the term at this stage. I invited her to come as soon as she can, so hopefully she will.'

This was good news Grace knew, but a niggling doubt wouldn't leave her.

'What? Is that not a good idea?' Tilly looked uncharacteristically unsure of herself.

'No...no, it's not that. But if Eloise didn't take the photo of Alfie and Constance from your mother's mantelpiece, and Sergeant Keane said the detectives got a tipoff that Eloise was taking pictures and behaving suspiciously, then who was behind that?' Though Grace was happy for Tilly, she was still torn. Something strange had happened that had had tragic consequences, and they were all just expected to forget about it? She didn't really think Eloise was guilty, but she didn't think it was nothing either.

Tilly shrugged. 'Who knows? Maybe nobody. Maybe that awful

thing happened and they looked for the foreigner, and Eloise is Swiss and had a camera, so they put two and two together and came up with five.'

'Look, the main thing is the nightmare is over now anyway, and she's coming back here. You must be so looking forward to seeing her.'

Tilly blushed slightly, Grace could see how her best friend was very much in love.

'I am. But I'm worried people will think…'

Grace wasn't sure what Tilly was more nervous of, the local people suspecting Eloise was a spy despite being released without charge, or them suspecting there was something more to her and Tilly's friendship. 'People won't think anything, Tilly, they really won't. Everyone liked her when she was here. And besides, she's been investigated and if they found nothing…'

'And what if they question why she's back here?' The usually confident Tilly looked vulnerable, and Grace felt a wave of affection for her. She couldn't understand why Tilly was interested in women in that way but it was just part of who she was. Grace loved her and it didn't matter a jot to her.

'Why shouldn't she? Tourists come here all the time. Sure look around – it's one of the most magically beautiful places on God's earth. Of course she wants to come here. Aren't we inundated with people coming to see this place? Eloise is just another one, and she happens to be a friend of ours into the bargain, that's all there is to it.'

Tilly seemed to relax. 'Right, you're right, I know. I'm just nervous, I suppose, and excited and I…I better go. I promised Mam I'd go to Biddy's for baking powder and into Carroll's for a bag of bones for soup. I used my sweet ration already, so poor Odile will have to do without her lollipop.'

'Hold on.' Grace went to her locked teacher supply cupboard. One of the school supply salesmen, Derry Boyle, had been so happy with her big order of paints and pencils for next year, he'd given her a small box of jelly babies. She doled them out to the children for good work, and since sweets of any kind were a rare treat before the Emergency and were almost a distant memory now, she had to keep them under lock and key. She opened it, took out three sweets and wrapped them in a bit of waxed paper.

'Ah, thanks, Grace. She looks up at me when I come in, her face full of hope. I hate when I don't have some little thing for her.'

'You're welcome. Now, I was going to come up this evening – I got a letter from Richard.' She filled Tilly in on the scant information from Didi, but even that seemed to bring a tiny bit of relief.

'I'll tell Mam. I'm sure it will make her feel a bit better.'

'I have to go, Tilly,' she said, showing her friend out. 'Poor Eleanor is very low in herself today. It's her husband's birthday and she's not seen him in such a long time, so I'm going to bring her back to the house for a cuppa and a bit of currant cake. Dymphna made it yesterday – she sweetened it with some of your honey because sugar can't be got for love nor money.'

'I'm sick to death of this bloody war,' Tilly grumbled.

Grace knew how she felt; everyone was the same. It was dragging on and on, and everything was scarce. It was really sucking the joy out of life.

'You know, in Dublin I passed a shop selling wedding cakes, and I was fascinated as to how they could be selling such elaborate cakes with everything on the ration. But the woman also looking in the window outside told me that you can rent an iced box for a photo – that's what people are doing – to say they had a cake, but if the hotel managed a bit of jelly and cream after the wedding breakfast, that would have to do. I know we have it too down here, but it's much worse in the cities and big towns.'

'I know. At least Kay in the Wooden Spoon still has a few cakes. Poor Lizzie and Hugh are struggling at the hospital to give the children enough nutrition – it's so important for healing – but they don't have a vegetable patch or a flock of hens or even the milk of a cow. They're totally relying on shops and the ration.' Grace stood in the schoolyard, as the breeze made it seem cool. 'Even if they have coupons, often the shops just don't have the supplies.'

'Are you going to visit them once the school breaks up for the holidays?' Tilly asked. Grace had mentioned that she might if Dymphna was feeling better and Tilly was home to take care of Odile again.

'I think I will. It's been ages since I've seen them.'

'Well, give me a few days' notice and I'll make up a box of stuff for them, spuds and carrots and honey and a few other bits and bobs.'

'You're very good.' Grace smiled and hugged her friend. As she watched Tilly walk up the street towards the butcher, she prayed this was the end of her friend's problems.

Back in the other classroom, Grace could hear Eleanor explaining how she was collating pictures of famous buildings, which the children would use to identify aspects of architecture. People would have been surprised to know that the children of Knocknashee could tell the difference between a doric, a Corinthian and an Egyptian column, but they could. Last week it was columns, and next week they would learn about eras of architecture, Romanesque to Victorian. Most of the children in Knocknashee would not progress beyond this schoolroom, and she and Eleanor were determined they would leave with as broad an education as it was possible to give them.

She smiled as she saw the drawings the children had done based on a postcard she'd bought of the Brooklyn Museum when she visited New York. She'd shown them how the neoclassical style was inspired by Greek and Roman architecture.

New York. Had she really been there? Sometimes she wondered if she'd dreamt it. Herself and Declan crossing the sea, visiting the Maheady family, Declan finally meeting his sister, Siobhán, now called Lily, and swimming with her family in Rockaway Beach. A fleeting smile passed her lips as she thought of Brendan McGinty, the big, handsome red-haired New York policeman who asked her to stay. She wished him well and hoped he'd found a more suitable girl. She would always remember him fondly; he was her first kiss. She'd spent most of her life believing what Agnes told her, that she would never find someone to love, the polio precluding her from having a chance at marriage, but Declan McKenna and Brendan McGinty had both thought otherwise.

Declan. That wave of almost blinding grief, a pain so sharp it took her breath away, threatened to engulf her. Sometimes she allowed it to. She had no fight left by the end of the day, and she would let her pain wash over her, reducing her to tears. But now she needed to support Eleanor. She shook off the memory of Declan and took a deep breath.

I'm so proud of you, Grace. She could hear his voice in her mind, and she sometimes wondered if she was making it up to comfort herself, but she didn't think so. When she was alone at night, looking up at the stars, wondering where he was, if he was anywhere, she heard his voice. *I'm right here. Sure where else would I be?*

CHAPTER 23

Everyone else was getting on with things – Tilly with Eloise, Charlie with the ever-growing Dymphna, Eleanor with her daughters and counting the days when she and Douglas would be reunited. Everyone had a future with someone they loved. And although Grace knew she might too sometime far in the future, it didn't feel much like it at the moment.

Would she ever love again? She had no idea. Declan wasn't the man she had envisaged marrying, if she was honest with herself, even if she couldn't say those words aloud to another living soul. When she'd imagined her happy ever after, it wasn't Declan in her imaginings. But that mental image was so hard to allow into her mind, she instantly dismissed it. Declan died as her husband, and she'd married him because she loved him, that was never in doubt. But was there another man who she might have harboured wild notions of? Yes, there was. But she could never allow her thoughts to go to him. She refused to even consider it. And besides, he was with someone, and he'd never even hinted he had such feelings for her. She felt so disloyal to Declan.

Forcing the thought from her mind, she pushed open Eleanor's door.

As she guessed she would be, the teacher was at her desk, putting papers together for the class tomorrow.

'Don't worry about me, Grace, I'm fine. Sorry for being a bit of an old misery earlier,' Eleanor said as she stuck pictures to the pages.

'No, please, I'm glad you could tell me. I'm sorry I had to go, but Tilly was so excited, Eloise has been released without charge.'

'I'm glad it all worked out. Everyone is so jumpy, and it's not half as bad here as it is back in England. Everyone there is living on their nerves.'

'I can imagine. Will we go over to the house, have a cup of tea while the girls have their swim?'

'I'm all right, Grace. I'm sure you have plenty to do...' Eleanor was hesitant, she would never impose on someone's time.

'Not at all. I'm dying for a cuppa, and I'm half afraid if I stay here, Eily Walsh will be down on top of me again. I saw the Dineen brothers having words with Gus in the playground earlier. Once again young Mr Walsh has picked the wrong adversary if he went after one of the Dineens. Their father was a champion wrestler years ago, and they are not a family to be trifled with. They'll batter him, and I'll have to referee that too...'

Eleanor laughed. 'Poor Gus will need to mend his ways, because his mummy won't always be there to rush to his aid.'

'True. I should have intervened, I suppose, but maybe a bit of natural justice is what he needs. He pulled Sinead O'Loughlin's hair this morning and made her cry, and she hadn't looked sideways at him. And poor Katherine O'Donovan was mortified because he pulled up her dress in front of all the boys. Maybe getting a few hidings himself, a taste of his own medicine, is what's called for, but you never heard me say that.' Grace chuckled as they left the schoolroom and went outside. The fishing boats on the bay looked like something from a child's picture book on this sunny day. Seabirds circled loudly overhead, gulls and fulmars, guillemots and razorbills.

Pádraig O Sé was outside his cobbler's shop, stretching. Grace waved at him, and he gave a small nod of recognition.

'I took Joanne's shoes in to have them soled and heeled – I think they'll fit Libby for the winter – and he asked me if anything less than a war would have dragged me back to where my husband came from because clearly looking after his elderly parents wasn't enough of a draw?'

Eleanor sounded aghast at the audacity of the man, but Grace laughed. 'You're a true local of Knocknashee so, Eleanor – he saves his best insults for the natives.'

'We brought Douglas's parents over to visit us in Liverpool twice a year, but with the school and Douglas being away so much with his job, we didn't get much opportunity to travel. Also my mother lived with us until she died and she was an invalid, so there was nobody to mind her if I left.'

'You have no reason to justify yourself to anyone, Eleanor, least of all Pádraig O Sé. He'd fight with his fingernails, that one,' Grace assured her. 'Just ignore him, we all do.'

'I'd hate people here to think we abandoned Douglas's parents, though. That wasn't something we would ever do.' She sounded so sad.

Grace pushed open her front door and allowed Eleanor to go inside. 'Nobody thinks that. Sure didn't Nancy O'Flaherty tell you how much your parents-in-law enjoyed getting letters and parcels from you?'

'She did,' Eleanor admitted.

'There you go,' Grace filled the kettle and rattled the turf in the range, throwing some small dry sticks and a few more sods of turf in to boil the kettle. The fire sparked and flamed immediately.

'I didn't know them but Charlie often told me how they would come home after visiting you and be full of stories about Liverpool and the great time they had. You and your husband did the best you could. You know it and they knew it, so let Pádraig O Sé dream up whatever he likes. He'd drive you daft, so he would. He told Tilly the other day that he'd heard she outfoxed the guards above in Dublin. She's innocent, totally and completely, but he's making out like she's guilty but somehow wriggled out of it. And you should hear him on the subject of my sister, Agnes. When she died, the best he could come up with was "at least you'll get a bit of peace now".' Grace laughed and Eleanor smiled.

'I'll take him with a pinch of salt in that case.'

'Exactly. Now, how are you feeling, rude cobblers aside?'

'All right, just a bit lonely, I suppose…'

'I'm sure you are. Have you siblings?' Grace asked gently.

Eleanor nodded. 'I've a brother, but he and I… Well, he didn't approve of me marrying an Irishman, so we're not close. And I'd another sister, but she died of the Spanish flu in 1919. Joan, she was lovely and only twenty-four. She'd just qualified as a nurse.'

'Oh, I'm sorry. Is Joanne named after her?'

'She is.' Eleanor took a seat at the table. 'She's the one who looks most like Joan too.'

'And where does your brother live?'

Eleanor shrugged. 'I don't know. Last time I saw William was our father's funeral. He refused to speak to me or Douglas. He was in the army and served over here, you see, during the troubles – he was living in Leeds, I think. But as I said, I've not heard anything for years.'

She didn't need to explain further. The War of Independence from 1919 to 1921, when the British finally agreed to negotiate after eight hundred years of occupation, was a bloody war of attrition. Nobody on either side was left unscathed. The Crown Forces were terrified to remain in the smaller barracks dotted around the country for fear of IRA attacks, and the Irish were ruthless. From the Irish perspective, it needed to be done – nothing less would work to rid the country of the oppressors – but Grace was sure it was a very tough posting if you were an English soldier. No wonder he hated the Irish.

'Families aren't always easy. I'm sure you've heard stories about my sister, Agnes, by now?' Grace said as she made a pot of tea, adding a heaped spoon of tea leaves, though she was almost at the end of her ration and there were four days left before she could get more. Eleanor saw her and raised an eyebrow.

'I'd rather have one decent cup and forgo another than drink watery stuff all the time,' Grace said, by way of explanation.

Eleanor agreed, choosing not to comment on Agnes. Of course

she'd heard what a tyrant Agnes was, but clearly she'd decided she wouldn't hurt Grace by repeating it. 'I'm the same. I think of all the things on the ration, I miss tea the most. I miss sugar and butter too, and God knows we all could use a bit more soap, I'm using soot to brush my teeth, but half an ounce of tea, honestly, it's miserable.'

'Have you heard this? One of the children sang it for me yesterday,' Grace said, then sang, 'Bless them all, bless them all, God bless the men of the Dáil. Bless de Valera and Seán MacEntee, for giving us brown bread and a half ounce of tea. Oh, they blame poor old Churchill on all. You can't kid the men of the Dáil. They're bringing starvation to this little nation. Thank God for St Vincent de Paul.'

Eleanor laughed. The Irish parody of George Formby's 'Bless 'Em All' was doing the rounds.

'I never heard that version – trust the Irish to put a funny slant on it anyway,' Eleanor said affectionately. Grace knew that despite her loneliness, Eleanor was happy here. Charlie and a few others had gone over to the Worths' house to fix up the worst of the leaks and draughts, and the girls were settling in well to life in Knocknashee. They'd even taken part in the May procession to the grotto beside the church in devotion to Our Lady. Grace had been unsure if it was all right, but Eleanor didn't mind and the girls loved putting on their best dresses and scattering flower petals with their friends. They could sing the hymn to Our Lady, 'A Mhuire Mháthair' as well as any Irish child now.

'Dymphna says she misses currants or raisins, and Tilly says she would love more paraffin, and Charlie misses his cigarettes, but I've a desperate sweet tooth so I miss the sweets, I have to say.' Grace sighed, then sipped her tea. 'But we do have this.' She opened the tin and showed Eleanor the currant bread.

'Oh lovely…' Eleanor beamed at the prospect.

She cut two slices, and while it would have been nicer with butter, that wasn't an option. Both women bit happily into it.

'We fare better here than over the water, though. At least we have milk and eggs, and even an odd rasher if we're lucky. And most people grow a bit of veg. Over in England they don't even have those things,'

Eleanor said, pouring herself a cup of the strong black tea and adding a drop of milk. She sipped it with a sigh of happiness.

'I have a friend in London.' Grace blushed. Somehow the mention of Richard always made her feel a bit silly. 'He's American, so his family sends him parcels, but he's always saying how he admires the British so much for the resilience they're showing in the face of terrible bombing and being half starved.'

Eleanor sighed and nodded. 'The Blitz was the worst. Every night going to bed, I would kiss my girls and pray to God that this wasn't the night they hit our house. When the school was hit, I was devastated but glad it was empty. But then our house was flattened. Again, I was just grateful we were out – we had gone to the shelter. It's funny how in situations like that, you always go to thinking about how it could have been worse.' She took another sip of tea, and Grace thought it was helping her to talk.

'I had a collection of china ornaments I'd gathered over the years. Some were my mum's, some belonged to Heather, Douglas's mother, and others we got if we ever went on a holiday. I had a shepherdess I bought on our honeymoon – Douglas used to joke she looked like his Uncle Bernard. And I had a few the children bought me as gifts. They were so precious to me, every one told a story…and our photographs and books and all our memories really… But they're gone now.' She exhaled ruefully. 'But my children are alive, my husband is alive I hope, and I'm here, so that's all that matters really.'

'When did you last hear from Douglas?' Grace asked, sipping her own tea and picking up the last crumbs of the currant bread with her finger.

'Not since the start of May, almost two months ago, and it's not like him…'

'Well, Charlie says all communications are up in a heap, so no news is not bad news. The army knows you're here, don't they?'

Eleanor nodded.

'If they had bad news, they'd send a telegram, so if you've heard nothing, then I'm sure he's all right.'

'Bad news does travel fast, I suppose,' Eleanor said with a stoic smile. 'I just miss him. He's such a lovely father to our girls, always playing with them and doing pranks and showing them things. They're missing out and so is he, and all because some horrible little ferret of a man in Germany has decided to rain down unspeakable horror on everyone in Europe. It's so bloody unfair.'

'It is,' Grace agreed.

'Oh, Grace, I'm sorry. Here I am ranting about my husband when you lost yours. I should be more sensitive…'

'No, don't be silly. Nobody has a monopoly on grief or sadness in this whole mess. My friend's girlfriend, Pippa, has lost everything and everyone – she's all alone in the world but for Richard. And Odile's family in France are missing – we don't know if they're alive or dead. So nobody is worse or better than anyone else. We all have our crosses to bear.'

'Well, it sounds like you've had more than your fair share, but still you smile and get on with things. I shall take a leaf from your book, Miss Fitz – best foot forward,' Eleanor said, with renewed energy.

'Well, I don't know if my feet are the best ones to emulate…' Grace said with a giggle, waggling her callipered leg.

Eleanor flushed red but Grace just laughed. 'If I didn't laugh, I'd cry, Eleanor. Don't worry about it.'

CHAPTER 24

LONDON

Richard was only half listening to Jacob as he ranted. He knew why his friend was frustrated, but what was the point of yelling at him?

'You think you have problems?' Sarah replied, her feet thrown across one arm of the lumpy armchair, her head hanging over the other arm. 'One of the WAVES was telling me about a colonel in Denver, Colorado, who called all the women together before they were shipped here and basically told them that no "capricious or petulant feminine behaviour will be tolerated", that this was no tea party.'

Jacob fumed. 'I'm not saying everyone has to put up with things they don't like, but honestly, if Kirky sends us on one more of these cute, sweet stories, I'll quit.'

Richard was in the process of typing up an article on the types of entertainment available to US troops over here, starting with radio programmes they might enjoy, and then going on to explain how British families were ready and willing to host lonely soldiers for a meal or even a few days of leave. The article also assured anxious

American mothers back home that mail would be delivered every day to the troops via special army post offices.

'He wants me to take pictures of the entrants for the poetry competition in the paper.' Jacob was fit to explode. 'I'm a damned war correspondent! I don't care about some guy from Indiana who can come up with six words that rhyme with mom.'

'At least you get treated as an equal. I think you two should do a piece about the discrimination women face every day, see how Kirky and the mothers of America like that. Did you know that women in the navy have to buy their own underwear? They supply it for the guys, but girls have to buy their own.'

Richard knew his sister was trying to wind Jacob up even more; she made a sport of it.

Jacob sighed. 'Oh, Sarah, don't be stupid. You know perfectly well what I want to do.'

'Oh, I do. You want to take off for France, or better still Germany, and be in the thick of it and probably get a bullet in your dumb skull for your trouble. Not content with nearly being killed in the jungle, you're both hell-bent on doing it all again. I hear the screams and the nightmares, so don't tell me, either of you, that you weren't scared half to death out there, because I know you were.'

'What's he getting a bullet for this time?' Pippa asked as she let herself into the flat. She'd been in the munitions factory on a double shift and looked wiped out.

Richard stood, took her coat and bag and led her to the sofa. 'Tea?' he offered.

'Ooh, I'd murder one, thanks,' she said, taking off a shoe and massaging her foot.

They all gave Pippa their tea ration. They hated the stuff, being American, and their father sent regular supplies of dried coffee, which was all right but not great.

Jacob paced the floor, his horn-rimmed spectacles shoved into his mess of hair. 'Didi said we could probably get to North Africa – they are allowing foreign journalists to shadow the Allies there – but Kirky won't hear of it. Says there are enough Associated Press and United Press there already, as well as William Randolph Hearst's outfit, and that our niche is ordinary people. But I'm so sick of this.'

'Well, Portugal or North Africa, possibly Switzerland, are the only places we could go,' Richard said, 'provided Kirky allowed it, which he categorically said he won't. And those cities are just full of refugees as well, so it would be more or less what we'd be doing here. We have to face it, Jacob – nobody is getting into Nazi-held territory unless it's behind the Allied army, so we'll just have to do our jobs and hope we get back to mainland Europe soon.'

He made Pippa a cup of tea and she took it gratefully, smelling it appreciatively before taking a sip.

He decided now was the time to tell Jacob the latest news. Kirky had telegrammed earlier when they were out. 'We're being sent to Belfast,' he announced.

'What? When?' Jacob demanded.

'Soon as possible, I think. The telegram came today. We're supposed to go and report on the arrival of US troops there, what life is like, that sort of thing.'

'Oh, for God's sake...' Jacob left the room, slamming the door. Pippa jumped at the sound.

Sarah just grinned. 'He'll be fine once he calms down.'

Pippa winced. 'He's not too happy, is he?'

'No, he sure is not. We did a whole piece on Jewish refugees, telling their stories, and he worked really hard on it, getting a cross-section of people, and the shots he took were incredible. It was some of our best work, but Kirky rejected it, saying everyone knows all they need to know about the Jews and that American readers are just interested in hearing how their boys are doing over here and don't want to read papers filled with stories of refugees who don't even speak English.'

'Oh, that's disappointing for him, and it's awful what's happening to the Jews. I was coming through Liverpool Street at the beginning of the war and saw all them little kiddies, little cards round their necks. It would break your heart,' Pippa said, moved at the memory. Then she turned to Richard. 'How come you're not as furious? You worked on that piece too.'

Richard shrugged. 'Kirky said from the off that he wasn't paying us to come over here and bring back stories of refugees, that he would tell us what he wanted and we'd supply it and that was the deal. I guess I'm just more accepting of the fact that he hasn't changed a bit.'

Richard glanced at the headline of the *New York Times* he'd picked up earlier. The US Navy was making great inroads into the Japanese fleet – they were calling it the Battle of Midway – and it was heartening to read. Seeing the effectiveness of the Japanese in Singapore, he didn't share his compatriots' view that overcoming them would be a walk in the park.

'I'm going to have a bath if nobody minds.' Pippa examined her fingernails, which were yellow and chipped. 'Soaking my hands is the only way to get the sulphur off them. I really hope the bullets and whatnot we're making do as much damage to the flippin' Germans as they do to us. Doris beside me swears her hair is going yellow an' all.'

'Off you go, and I won't tell if you put in more than the regulation five inches,' Sarah said with a wink.

'Nah, we all have to play by the rules. But I'll tell you somethin' – when this bloomin' war is over, I'm gonna fill myself a big deep bubble bath, with loads of salts and lovely smelling things, and I'm gonna lie in it for hours, and I'll top up the hot water with my toe when it gets even a tiny bit cold.' Pippa laughed, then groaned as she got to her feet again, putting her hands to her lower back. Being bent over a bench all day making bullets was no joke.

When she was gone to the bathroom, Sarah stood and walked over to Richard. 'You're going to see Grace, aren't you, when you go over to Ireland? That's why you're not as ticked off as Jacob?'

Richard knew lying to Sarah was pointless; she could read him like a book. 'I've written to tell her I'll be in Belfast, and I said I could be in Dublin on the twenty-fifth of July and she could meet me there…' He paused. 'Is that crazy?'

Sarah didn't answer and he knew why. Since they'd been living together, Sarah and Pippa had become very close, and Sarah didn't want her brother to break her friend's heart. Richard had no intention of breaking anyone's heart, but he did badly want to see Grace. He hadn't gone to see her when Declan died, choosing to stay with Pippa, which was the right thing to do but not the easy thing. Grace didn't feel about him the way he hoped she might, and he had to accept it. Was going to see her now just the action of a friend, or was he torturing himself even further?

He also wanted to discuss further the contents of the letter he'd received from Mrs McHale, the American Miss Marple, as he'd nicknamed her.

Sarah sighed and stuck her hands in her trouser pockets. She had taken to wearing pants all the time now, and Richard often smiled at what their mother would make of this latest in a long litany of rebellions. 'Not crazy, but...dangerous.'

'How could it be dangerous?' Richard asked. 'We're friends, and I'll be in her country. Surely the most natural thing in the world is for us to meet up? The letters we write are news-filled, not bubbling over with suppressed passion. Besides, she's mourning Declan and I'm with Pippa now so...'

'So...exactly. That's what worries me.' Sarah's dark eyes locked with his.

'Why?' He listened for the sound of the bath running; the pipes in this old house made a ferocious racket, so it was safe to speak. 'I told Grace how I felt last year. She didn't reply. I had asked that if she didn't feel the same about me that we should never mention it again, and we haven't, and now we never will.'

Sarah put her hand on his shoulder. 'Richard, you can lie to Pippa, you can lie to me, you can lie to Grace – hell, you can lie to yourself if you want. But deep down we both know what's going on here, and you seeing Grace can't lead to anything but heartache for her, for you and especially' – her head inclined towards the bathroom – 'for Pippa. And she doesn't deserve it, Richard, she really doesn't.'

'I'm not going to do anything. I just want to see her...' He heard the longing in his own voice. 'Anyway, she probably won't be able to come, so it's all a bit of a moot point.'

'But you have made a plan to meet her?'

'Well, I just sent a telegram to say I'd be in the Shelbourne hotel on the twenty-fifth at noon, because I didn't know if there would be time to get a letter to her and a response before we go. I might do a report from Dublin anyway, that was always a plan of mine, so I could take in seeing Grace too, but –'

'I'm not going to stop you if you're determined, but be careful, Richard. If you want to be reckless with your own heart, that's your choice, but don't be reckless with Pippa's, all right? Do you plan to marry Pippa? Seriously? Because you want to and not some made-up reason about her being under American protection?'

'I guess I do.'

'You guess?' She raised an eyebrow. 'You're not sure?'

'No, I am…I am sure. I love her and there's nothing between me and Grace…never can be.'

'Well then, promise me you'll propose, properly, when you get back from Ireland, OK?'

'I will, I promise.'

She nodded and kissed the top of his head before retreating to the room she shared with Jacob.

CHAPTER 25

'Sarah's right, you were lucky to get out of Sumatra alive, reading between the lines,' Pippa said as he got into bed.

'I know, we were,' he said quietly.

'Tell me about it,' she snuggled up to him. 'You never tell me anything about that time, but I know you can't sleep for thinking about it.'

He'd blocked out those days with the Japanese after he and Jacob had been found by the scouts while bathing in the sea.

'No, I…'

'Maybe if you talked about it, you might be able to let it go, 'cause, Richard, every night you wake up screaming. That's not good for you.'

He sighed. Revisiting that time while conscious seemed a horrible prospect, but perhaps she had the right idea. Exhaustion overwhelmed him, stemming from nightly interruptions. He also feared he might mention Grace during his nocturnal ravings. Nightmares never troubled him before, yet now they persisted without relief. He and Jacob avoided discussing it, but Richard recognized his friend felt equally haunted. He frequently pondered whether he would have confided in Grace. He believed he probably would have, though such matters proved impossible to convey in writing. Despite her worldly innocence and struggle with polio, Grace possessed remarkable resilience. She could handle the truth.

'It was… Are you sure?' he whispered into the night.

'I'm sure,' she whispered back.

'Jacob and I were marched out of the sea at gunpoint. They gathered our clothes – we were in our underwear. We couldn't understand them of course, but they told us to walk. We didn't know it, but the Japanese had invaded Sumatra in March. But they focussed on the south and the west. They wanted to hit the Dutch East Indies assets and cripple their resistance, so the part of the island we were on wasn't a priority for them.' He swallowed, allowing his mind to go to the place once more.

'For all of that night, barefoot and in wet underwear, we marched. They'd bound our wrists, and the ropes chafed and drew blood. Our feet were bleeding, and we were stung repeatedly by bugs. It's so hot and humid there. If Jacob and I spoke, they hit us with the butts of their rifles. Once I tried to say something and I got a blow to the temple. I think I collapsed, but I remember having water thrown on my face and being dragged up to keep walking. We eventually stopped, and they told us to drink from a stream. They had set up a camp of sorts in the jungle – I think there were ten or twelve Japanese there, no more. It was a few days, two or three maybe, I don't know. I was delirious, I think.'

Memories flooded into his brain, the fear, the pain, the hunger and thirst. He had been barely aware of Jacob.

'The commander, I don't know what his rank was, gave us some food and water and told us to lie down and sleep, which we did. They bound our feet then too. I woke up to sounds of laughing and gunshots. They were drunks, and they were all laughing and shouting and screaming and taking potshots into the jungle.' His voice shook. 'I remember looking around, thinking this was where I was going to die. A boy from Savannah, Georgia, is going to die in a jungle in Sumatra, no grave, nowhere for my family to visit – they'd never even know what happened to me.'

Pippa laid her hand on his chest and never said a word. She knew he needed just to get it out now; he'd come this far.

'They had a gallows – they'd built it out of timber and vines – and they told us to stand on the narrow bench beneath it. It was about two feet off the ground. With our hands and feet bound, we were helpless, and we were so weak and sick by that time too, even if we could have fought back, we had no strength. Some of the bites were infected, as well as the cuts on our feet and wrists, and I was running a fever. Jacob was too, I realised later. Then, and I think this was just for fun, they placed the ropes around our necks, tight enough to be uncomfortable but not so tight we couldn't breathe, all the time laughing and drinking more and more. The commander didn't take part, but he smoked and watched as his men did this.

'All that night, over and over, they made like they were going to knock the bench from under our feet. We stood there, exhausted, but I knew if I fell asleep, I'd hang myself, so I focussed on staying awake. They laughed and drank all that night. It felt like weeks…' He realised he was crying when Pippa wiped away his tears.

'How did you get away?' she asked.

'There was a raid, low-flying aircraft strafing the jungle. Maybe they saw the camp or maybe they didn't, but the Japanese ran for cover and left us standing there, bullets ricocheting off the camp, splintering trees. We had no option but just stand there. A bullet whizzed by my ear, but then it all stopped. The Japanese were still gone and we were alone, so I shuffled along the bench. I could just about reach Jacob even though the rope was tight around my neck, and I managed to slip the rope off his head. He was able to do the same for me, and we got down. We were bound, but the camp had tools and weapons. The Japs left in a hurry and we had no idea when they'd be back, but we managed to cut the ropes that tied us up and we just ran for it.'

'Oh, Richard, you poor duck, what an ordeal. How did you manage in the jungle, though, sick and everything?'

'A family took us in. I don't remember too much about how we got to their house, but there was a couple and their children and they took us in and cleaned us up and put something on our wounds – I don't know what, but it sure smelled strong. They fed us and let us sleep, and then when we were able to move again, the man and his sons took us to the north coast port where we got picked up.'

'God bless them. That was a big risk they took.'

Richard nodded. For the rest of his life, he would be able to see them, Arif and his wife, Zahira. They'd saved his life, and there was nothing in it for them – only severe punishment if they were captured by the Japanese. Arif spoke some English, and he explained that Indonesia was a colony of the Dutch and the people of the vast archipelago desperately wanted their independence. So if they had to face the Japanese, they wanted to do so as independent people, not the slaves of the Dutch. If the Allies won the war, he had hopes that Indonesia would be free, and so anything he could do to help win the war was worth doing.

'I'm so glad you survived, Richard,' she whispered. 'It scares me how close you came to death.'

Richard exhaled. She'd been right; it was good to talk about it.

CHAPTER 26

That night, as Pippa lay in an exhausted sleep beside him, he felt like such a cad. She was a wonderful girl. She cared so deeply about him, worried for him and knew him well. But as the night wore endlessly on, he couldn't sleep, so he lay there, thinking about Grace. Grace, who did not want him. Grace, who was in mourning for Declan. Sarah was right about one thing: Pippa did not deserve this. He'd chosen her after Declan died, sure he was making the right choice, but now he was conflicted. If Declan McKenna were still alive, he wouldn't be having these doubts, but Declan was gone.

The moonlight shone through the thin curtains and illuminated Pippa's face slightly. She was an endearing mix of fortitude and vulnerability, and his heart melted when he saw how brave and moral she was. There was no way Pippa would have a bath in more than five inches of water, though nobody would know; she would never use black-market food or flout any of the Emergency laws. She was as English as afternoon tea, he admired her dogged loyalty to her country, she was going to do her bit to win this war, no matter what the personal cost.

And she loved him, he knew. And he'd told her that he loved her too, which he did. Just not the way he loved Grace. *Grace doesn't want you, you idiot.* He forced the mantra to permeate his brain. Grace didn't want him, but Pippa, a beautiful, kind, brave girl, did. Why couldn't he just take that opportunity with both hands and grab it?

Pippa stirred and reached for him. Still half asleep she ran her hands over his chest and threw her leg over his, dropping kisses on his neck. She was passionate and ardent in her need for him, and he loved how unabashed she was. Girls in his world resisted men's advances until marriage, and once the deal was sealed, he got the distinct impression that women would just about tolerate the intimacies of the bedroom but a nice girl certainly wouldn't enjoy it. Pippa made no secret of the fact that she loved making love with him, that she found him irresistible and that she enjoyed their time alone together as much if not more than he did.

He leant up on his elbow and looked down into her sleeping face. Her eyes opened, then closed again. She murmured, 'What is it?'

'I know I asked you before, when I was sent to Singapore, and you refused, saying you'd wait for a more romantic proposal than you'd get the protection of the United States if we married.' Richard tucked a stray strand of hair behind her ear. 'But I wanted to marry you then and I want to marry you now. Not for a practical reason, or because it's the sensible thing to do. I want to marry you because I want you in my bed every night as my wife – and because I love you.'

She lay there, and for a long moment, he thought she might cry. She didn't answer him, but her eyes raked his face for something, he didn't know what.

'Do you love me?' he asked tentatively.

'You know I do.'

'So? What do you say? Will you marry me?'

Again a long silence as she considered it. 'What about Grace?' she said eventually, fully awake now.

'What about Grace?' he asked her in return.

'Are you telling me that you don't love her?'

Richard frowned. 'As a friend I do, yes, but not like this, not like what we have. Grace and I have never... We're not... We're just friends. Nothing more. And we never will be.'

'Because you don't want to, or you do want to but she won't?' Pippa asked in her matter-of-fact way.

'Because we are just friends, Pippa, I swear. Nothing has ever happened between Grace and me. I've only met her in person once, for less than an hour. You don't have to worry, I promise.'

She was thinking, he could see. She gazed at the ceiling, the moonlight illuminating her bare torso, and she had never looked more beautiful to him.

He smiled. 'Penny for them?' he said, repeating the phrase she used when he was deep in thought.

'I'm thinking that I'm giving you the power to really hurt me, Richard. Like, really, really shatter me into a million pieces, and I'm scared. I'm not sure that you don't love her, even if you won't admit it, and if I married you, I think I'd always be second best, the consolation prize. Sometimes I think I could cope with it, that having most of you would be enough, but I know it would eat away at me and break me in the end.'

The raw emotion of that admission cut Richard to the quick. What kind of a monster was he to treat this wonderful woman so shabbily? A wave of guilt and shame passed over him.

He got out of bed and pulled on his trousers before opening the box where he kept his watch and the gold ring with the ruby of his high school, Georgia Military College Preparatory School. He hadn't enjoyed it there, but the high school ring he'd received when he graduated had somehow found its way to Europe in his packed bags. It was all he had at this short notice. The gold wedding band he'd bought Pippa ages ago in Plymouth to pretend they were married was in her jewellery box.

He walked back to the bed where Pippa was sitting up now, the sheet drawn around her naked body, and knelt on one knee. 'Pippa Wills, I love you. And I want to marry you. Please, will you do me the great honour of becoming my wife?'

She swallowed and blinked, and she looked so adorable, he almost laughed. This was the right thing, he was sure of it. Grace was a pipe dream. Pippa was real, she was here, and she had given him everything. They would be happy together, he just knew it. It was to Pippa he confided his darkest memories, to her he told the daily frustrations of his job, with her he laughed at the movies or at one of her stupid corny jokes. They had more than most people who married. He would marry Pippa, and all thoughts of Grace Fitzgerald would fade away.

'I will,' she said as tears fell down her cheeks. He took her small hand, stained yellow from the sulphur of the munitions factory, and slid his large ruby ring on her finger.

'We'll get a proper one tomorrow, but for now…'

'Is this really happening?' she asked as he got back into bed beside her.

'It really is,' he replied. He felt her body respond to him, and before he could think any more about what he'd just done, he and Pippa gave themselves over to the insatiable need they had for each other, all thoughts of everyone and everything else forgotten.

CHAPTER 27

KNOCKNASHEE

JULY 1942

Nancy O'Flaherty gestured with her eyes for Grace to let Connie Collins, Neilus's brother, who was currently sporting a split lip and had grazes all over his knuckles, go ahead of her. It was almost closing time, and Nancy had already turned the sign to closed. Biddy O'Donoghue was just gone, having sent a parcel to someone, her daughter probably, who was over in England working in the typing pool of an RAF base, so only two customers remained.

Connie mumbled something to Nancy. He wrote to a woman in Chicago every month without fail, and he always looked sheepish posting it. Like everything in Knocknashee, it was a badly kept secret. Charlie said Connie was the least mad of all the Collins brothers, and had even been doing a line with a girl from Abbeydorney for donkey's years. She had been nice and normal, which knowing the Collinses was an achievement. Apparently her mother was fine with the romance – she liked Connie – until she met the rest of the brothers, and once that happened, she found a cousin in Chicago badly in need of someone to mind their children and the girl from Abbeydorney was whipped from under poor Connie's nose.

That was years ago. Rumour had it that she never married either, and they wrote to each other every month. It was a tragic story, and Grace wondered why Connie didn't just go over there and see if it would work. Surely it would be better than working a scrappy bit of a windy farm on the side of a mountain and getting into battering matches with his brothers every night of the week.

He paid for his stamp and nodded to Grace with another mumble as he passed.

Nancy came out from behind the counter. 'Something is going on, Grace, with himself above,' Nancy said quietly. She knew Grace had outmanoeuvred the canon by hiring Eleanor and was all for it, but like Grace, she was well aware how dangerous he could be.

'What?' Grace asked, her heart pounding.

'Look, in all my years, I've never once given information to anyone except the person it's intended for. I take this job seriously, and people trust me. But Grace, I tossed and turned all night, worrying and trying to decide what I should do. As the dawn broke, I decided I'd have to tell you something. It could get me dismissed, so I'm trusting you, but you have to know.'

Grace had never seen the normally unflappable Nancy in such a state. It was true that she was the soul of discretion, so this was something big.

'He telegrammed your man Francis Sheehan and said there had been a hiccup but for him to hold tough because there might be a headmaster's job going soon if he can be patient.'

'He wants rid of me.' Grace had always known it, but now it was confirmed. He cared nothing for the fact that her parents established the school, her sister ran it, and now she did. He saw her as a threat, and he didn't like anything not completely in his control.

'I'm so sorry, Grace' Nancy said, her face full of compassion.

'If he wants me to go, I have to.' The reality dawned on her. She'd lost just about everything – her parents, her sister, Declan, her mobility with the polio – and now her livelihood was going to be next to go. 'No doubt he'll give Eleanor the sack too.' She paused. 'Did he send that telegram from here?' she asked, surprised the canon would risk it, knowing she and Nancy were friends.

Nancy shook her head. 'From Ballyferriter. He drove out there in his fancy car.'

Grace understood. Jarlath O'Keeffe, the postmaster in the next parish over, must have tipped Nancy off.

The canon had been missing for weeks at a time, and the word was that he was travelling, though where to in the Emergency was anyone's guess. He had bought a new car and astonished the parish. It was a Bentley, no less, maroon in colour and by far the most extravagant vehicle anyone had ever seen. He swanned around in it and seemed to love the stares and naked jealousy on the people's faces as he drove by.

'What can I do, Nancy?' Grace asked.

'I don't know, love, I really don't. I'm sure he can argue that Sheehan is more qualified and more experienced, and what with him being a man...'

Grace felt the blood pound in her ears.

'And I just heard Kit Gallagher died a few days ago – who'd have thought her sister would outlive her – so...'

Grace knew she was right. Canon Rafferty would never forget a slight, and the fact that she had the audacity to confront him once, after Agnes died, and then to go behind his back and hire Eleanor, well, those were slights he would not forgive. Kit Gallagher, one of the few living witnesses to the canon's baby-selling business, was gone now. Not that she would ever have betrayed him anyway, but still.

'Thanks for letting me know, Nancy,' Grace said sadly. There might have been a time she would have tried to find a way, but now, with the weight of grief and loss threatening to smother her, she knew she hadn't the energy for the fight. The loss of the school, everything her parents had worked so hard to build, her life here in the only place she'd ever known apart from the hospital – it was all about to be taken from her, and she could do nothing to change it.

Nancy squeezed her hand.

She headed out onto the street in a daze. The children were all out playing as the day was sunny and they'd been released from their jobs. She waved as they called out their greetings. How could she leave them to that monster Sheehan and the strap? The thought brought tears to her eyes.

Glad to get home without being stopped by anyone, she went into the sitting room that overlooked the ocean, sat in her father's chair and begged for her parents help.

CHAPTER 28

Every day Grace lived in fear of the canon's arrival, knowing it was coming and also knowing there was nothing she could do to stop him.

Two days after her conversation with Nancy, as Grace screwed the lid on the big bottle of ink that she used to fill the inkwells in the desks, she was startled by a sound. The school was quiet; the children were still on holidays.

The door of her classroom opened, and the canon stood there. He didn't say a word at first, no apology for disturbing her, no word of greeting. He just stood there.

She swallowed. She would not show weakness. Maybe this wasn't it. But here he was, and this was not a social call; whatever else was happening, it wasn't that.

'Hello, Canon,' she said politely.

'Miss Fitzgerald.' He nodded coldly. Everyone called her Miss Fitz, but when he said her name, it was with the intonation on the 'miss', as if he didn't acknowledge her marriage to Declan. He had been most put out that they'd married outside of the parish and had given a sermon to that effect, about people being too proud and having notions of grandeur, that their own place and the place of their neighbours was beneath them. He also treated Declan as if he were some kind of criminal sent to borstal because he was badly behaved, not an innocent child who'd lost his mother. But nobody in Knocknashee thought either she or Declan was looking down on them; everyone knew why they didn't want the canon to marry them.

'How can I help you, Canon?' she asked, with a forced smile.

'I've come here today, Miss Fitzgerald, to raise once again the issue of the unruly behaviour of the pupils.' His sibilant tones made her skin crawl. 'I have brought this to your attention on a number of occasions, but it seems that nothing is done.' His rheumy dark-blue eyes fixed unblinkingly on hers.

'I don't really know what you mean, Canon. What behaviour specifically?'

His long hairy eyebrows shot up in surprise. 'Well, Miss Fitzgerald, if you are unaware of the obvious problems with your pupils' behaviour, then I feel it is not incumbent on me to enlighten you about what is essentially your job.' The words oozed disdain.

'Well, with all due respect, Canon, I can't deal with a problem if I don't know what it is? Nobody has mentioned anything to me about any of the children in the school –'

'That, and the fact that you enrolled students not of the Catholic faith without consultation, and hired an entirely inappropriate person who claims to be a teacher, though we have no evidence to support that claim…' He broke eye contact and gazed into the top corner of the room.

She waited for him to finish the sentence. Silence hung in the still air as dust motes danced in the shaft of sunlight.

'Mrs Worth submitted all her qualifications –' she began, but he cut across her like a hot knife through butter.

'So…I'm sure you can see…given your failure to do the job adequately, and some very poor management decisions on your part, that your employment here is no longer…tenable.'

Grace didn't reply. She would not make this easy for him.

'I have appointed a replacement, and Mr Francis Sheehan is

infinitely better able to maintain discipline. It's a job for a man anyway...' he examined his fingernails, refusing to meet her eye.

'What are you saying, Canon?' Grace forced herself to ask.

'I am saying that it is now time to have a man take over, for the reasons I've listed. I'm sure you understand. And he will need the parish-owned house that comes with the position, but I'm sure a woman of your...resourcefulness...will be fine. I understand you have associates in a variety of locations.' The way he said it made her sound like a woman of ill repute.

'You can't dismiss me. I haven't done anything wrong,' Grace said, more calmly than she felt.

His watery eyes were cold, and he didn't reply. They both knew he could do exactly that.

The standoff lasted several seconds. Grace's heart pounded so loudly in her chest, she was sure he could hear it. She had one chance to fight back. She had to. 'I know you sold babies in America, that you used my sister and then you used Kit Gallagher. Not just Siobhán McKenna, there were others.' She hoped it didn't sound blurted; she feared it did.

He smiled then, a horrible mirthless grimace. 'Are you threatening me, Miss Fitzgerald?'

'No, I'm telling you the truth. I know what you did, and I will go to the bishop and reveal what kind of...person...you are.'

'And Bishop McElroy will believe you over an ordained priest? A canon?' The contempt was naked now.

'He will when I tell him what I know...'

His laugh was a terrifying sound, something she'd never heard before. A kind of phlegmy hiss. 'You have nothing – you know it and I know it. Mrs Gallagher is now with God, as is your sister, and any person who claims some knowledge of me in the United States is a liar. So Miss Fitzgerald, let's not drag this out, shall we? You should know only a fool picks a battle they can't win, and you can't win against me. Both you and that godless Worth woman are now surplus to requirements, so please pack your bags and get off parish property.'

Grace swallowed. He was right. He'd won. She fought back tears.

'Remove your personal effects from the house by Sunday evening, Miss Fitzgerald. You are no longer required at Knocknashee National School.' He took several steps toward her then and she feared he might attack her, but he stopped a foot from her. 'I expect you to go quickly and quietly. If you challenge me, I will make your life very difficult. I will see to it that no school in Ireland will take you on, so do not test me on this. And if needs be, I can disrupt the life of that unnatural Tilly O'Hare too, not to mention that bastard child who I don't believe for one minute was born inside wedlock to Alfie O'Hare and some Frenchwoman.'

Grace felt dizzy. 'What do you mean, remove my things? That's my home! My parents –'

'Were given that house as part of their employment at the school, and it is owned by the parish. Your sister in her capacity as headmistress was allowed to continue there and subsequently yourself, but as you're no longer an employee, then you have no right to the house.'

'But that can't be right…' Grace's mouth was dry. She swallowed and hated to see the gleam of satisfaction in his dark eyes. 'It's my home, my things. I own –'

'Nothing but your personal effects. I have no desire to hear about your private business. They will need to be removed immediately. I'm sure the new incumbent has no interest in being surrounded with your' – he curled his lip –'things.' The inference always that she was somehow distasteful.

'What is wrong with you?' she heard herself ask, swallowing back tears. 'Why do you hate me so much? Is it because I know what you are? And you can't bear that? Is that why? I know that you took advantage of my sister when she was just a girl, that you stole my money, that you profited off the misery of poor Charlie McKenna, that you sent Declan to a place akin to hell for a child, and God knows how many other lives you've blighted. I can see you for what you really are, so are you afraid of me and that's why you're getting rid of me?'

She was burning her bridges now, she knew, but she would have her say. 'You pretend to be a man of God, a leader of the people of this place in the ways of righteousness, but you are nothing but a predator, a thief and a liar. And I may not be able to beat you this time, but one day, Canon, the day of reckoning will come, in this world or the next, and you'll have to answer for your deeds. And that is a day that should strike terror into your black heart, because nothing, absolutely nothing you do is in line with the teachings of Jesus Christ. You are the instrument of Satan, and I hope you enjoyed your ill-got gains, because there will be a price to be paid.'

Grace felt strangely calm. She'd never in her life spoken to anyone like this, but she had no regrets. She meant every word.

He raised his eyebrows once more as a ghost of a sneer played on his lips. 'I'll expect the keys of both the school and the house delivered to the parochial house by 6 p.m. on Sunday.' He turned then and slid out of the room, like the snake he was.

She would not give him the satisfaction of crying, however much the tears threatened. She had played her trump card and he'd laughed at her. What should she do now?

She saw Janie O'Shea, her trustworthy classroom monitor, pushing one of her small cousins on the swing that hung from the bough of the oak in the middle of the village green. She opened the window and called to her. Janie put another girl in charge of the toddler – she was so conscientious, that girl – and crossed to the schoolhouse.

'Janie, can you go and see if Charlie McKenna is at home?'

'He is, Miss Fitz. I saw him go in only a few minutes ago.'

'Can you ask him to come over please?'

'I will of course, Miss Fitz.' She paused. 'Is everything all right?'

'Fine, Janie, everything is grand,' she lied. 'I just need Charlie to help me lift something heavy.'

'I'll get him now.' She ran across the road and knocked on Charlie's door. Grace could see him there, his postman's jacket off, standing in his shirt and trousers. He nodded and looked over, saw her and made his way across. Within minutes he was in the school.

'What is it, Gracie?' he asked, leading her to the teacher's desk and sitting her down. 'You're as white as a sheet.'

'He's dismissed me, told me I'm to hand over the keys of the school and the house to him by six on Sunday. According to him the house is owned by the parish as well, so I have to leave. Francis Sheehan is coming as headmaster, and Eleanor is being sacked as well…' She swallowed. It felt like her entire life had just been upended.

'Right…' Charlie exhaled. Unlike Richard or even Declan, he knew what sort of power the canon had. He'd lost his children because of him, so he was one of the few people who didn't underestimate the man.

She'd confided in Charlie what Mrs McHale had written, so Grace told him what she'd threatened. 'I really let rip at him, called him a liar and a predator and a thief… Oh, Charlie, I've really done it now…'

'You didn't say one word that wasn't true, but what did he say to that?'

'He just laughed. He said Agnes and Kit Gallagher are both dead, and nobody would believe me.'

Charlie sighed. 'He's not wrong unfortunately. And the men of the cloth, they stick together, Gracie, you know they do. Father Iggy is nice, and there are plenty of good priests, but at the end of the day, they are all part of the same organisation and they back each other.'

'I can't win, can I?' she asked him, tears flowing down her cheeks.

Charlie sighed. 'I want to say you can. I want to borrow Dr Ryan's car this very minute and drive to Killarney and tell the bishop everything. But Gracie, I'd be steering you wrong. He might listen, he might even believe it, but he won't take your side over a canon – that's just not how it works.'

'So that's it, I lose everything?'

'Not everything, love. You have your friends, you have your qualifications, you have people who love you…'

It was then that Grace disintegrated. This was it, the end. She'd borne everything with as much strength as she could, the death of her beloved parents, her being struck with polio and having to spend years in hospital without even a person to visit her, the torture of living with Agnes, the constant put-downs and cruel treatment. She'd endured it all. She gave up the chance to go to America and see Richard and maybe have her polio treated so that she could care for her sister. Then when Agnes died, though she felt sadness and loss, and wished she'd known about the role Canon Rafferty played in making Agnes the way she was, she took over the school and did the right thing. And finally, she found love, and a group of friends, and for the first time since she was a child, she felt safe and happy. But fate wasn't going to let her enjoy it, no. God took Declan and now he was taking all she'd worked so hard to build. Maybe it was punishment for being untrue, for marrying Declan when she was in love with someone else, but that wasn't a terrible thing, was it? She did love Declan. Not like she loved Richard, but she did love him and she made him happy and he knew she loved him.

Charlie rubbed her back as she sobbed into his chest, shedding bitter tears for herself, for her parents, for Agnes, for Declan and for the whole sorry mess.

'Tilly will let you put your stuff above. We'll store it there until we figure out what to do. I'll come and help you to pack up. Don't worry, Gracie, it will all work out...and you're not on your own.'

* * *

People were so kind when they heard the news, and the parents and children were visibly upset. She had several offers of help, places to store her things and even accommodation from her neighbours, but the kindness just made the loss all the more unbearable.

Eleanor had taken the news stoically and said that she was at least grateful that she had experience in the Irish system now so might be able to get a job in another school. It would mean travelling, but she could drive; she learnt how when she did her ARP training, and there was an old jalopy that once belonged to old Mr Worth that she was going to try to get going. Her husband sent her the lion's share of his salary every month, so she would be fine.

'Please don't worry about me, Grace, you've enough to be thinking about. I'll be fine. I met Mr Jeffers who runs the Protestant school out towards Inch, and he might be able to think of some place I could get a job, or maybe even there. He's quite elderly now, so maybe he'd be happy to retire.'

'And if you do, take the girls with you. That Francis Sheehan is horrible.'

'I hate the thought of someone harsh coming into our lovely school,' Eleanor said sadly.

Grace could only nod; no words would come.

The next few days were a flurry of activity. She packed up all the kitchen and stored things in boxes that Tilly took on the trap to the farm. The O'Hares had a big byre that was no longer used and where everything would be safe and dry.

'I suppose the crockery and cutlery and pots and pans are technically his too…' Grace said as she and Tilly began.

'Canon Snakey and Francis Sheehan can go and jump in a lake. No, Grace, he wants it empty, then empty it shall be. We won't leave a stick of furniture or a spoon, and you may be sure that not one of your neighbours or friends will be offering Sheehan so much as a cup of tea when he lands. Let him see how he likes that.'

Tilly, with the help of Janie and Eleanor, worked methodically through the house, wrapping every single thing. Charlie led a team of men in dismantling beds and tables and chairs, stacking them all in a horsebox belonging to the Collins brothers and moving all of that to the farm too.

Dymphna assured them that folding sheets and towels was not too strenuous for her so late in her pregnancy, so she and Mary O'Hare emptied the bedrooms.

'Nancy is going to store all your linen in her spare room – I wouldn't trust the byre not to be damp,' Mary said as she folded the crocheted blankets and cushion covers Grace loved so much. Some had been made by her mother, more by herself.

'Are you all right, girleen?' Mary asked after Charlie had brought Dymphna home. Janie and Eleanor had left too, and Tilly was gone to the farm with another load of stuff in the trap. Grace and Mary were resting on the windowsill of the sitting room, which now, like the rest of the house, was completely empty.

'Not really. I can't help but think if I'd have just been less cheeky to the canon...'

'You told the truth, and that man is fearful of you, Grace You're a source of terror to him, like the strong red-headed women of our country, Máire Rua, Granuaile, Queen Meadhbh, St Brigid, the Morrigan, the goddess Clíodhna, the list goes on and on. And what do they all have in common?'

Grace smiled. She'd heard the stories of these women all her life from Mary O'Hare. 'They all got their way in the end?'

'Indeed they did.' Mary chuckled. 'Brigid got the king to give her the lands her cloak could cover for a monastery – he laughed and agreed, but she laid down her cloak and it covered acres. Máire Rua took on Cromwell's army and won. Granuaile, the pirate queen, bested Queen Elizabeth the First no less. Queen Meadhbh ruled all the men of Connaught, and even the men of the mighty Eamhain Mhacha were in mortal fear of her – not of her husband, Allil, but Meadhbh herself. The Morrigan struck fear into the hearts of her enemies, and Clíodhna was the Queen of the Banshees. So, Grace you're the next in a long line of powerful red-haired Irishwomen. Men fear ye, with good reason, because in the end, ye always triumph, and this time will be no different.'

'So Canon Rafferty is my enemy, is he? I had hoped not to have one.' She smiled ruefully.

Mary didn't laugh. 'Be in no doubt, Grace, he's an enemy of yours. People nowadays go on with all this old rubbish of not having enemies, but there is evil in this world and there is good, and there is manys the battle fought between them make no mistake about it. And Rafferty is a formidable one at that. But the blood of those women runs in your veins, and the love and good sense of your parents surrounds you night and day. And poor Declan, I can see him around you too. So don't ever doubt it, you're not on your own. And anyway' – she heaved her arthritic bent body off the sill, wincing as she did so – 'this is only round two. There'll be plenty more to come before this is over. He won this battle, but he won't win the war, I can promise you that.'

Grace knew Mary O'Hare well enough to know she didn't make predictions lightly and that whatever she said had an uncanny habit of coming true. She was a Bean Feasa, a wise woman, and a *seanchaí*, a storyteller, and people around here knew better than to dismiss what she said.

'Do you ever see Alfie?' Grace asked.

'Never. That's why I know he's still alive. If my boy was gone over, I'd know.' She said it with such certainty, it reassured Grace. Mary rarely mentioned seeing the dead, or communicating with them; she said no good came of such meddling, that the dead should be left to rest.

'And my parents, do they have anything to say to me?' She hated asking and knew there was a chance Mary would rebuff her, but she was feeling so lost and alone, she had to ask.

'Didn't I just tell you? This isn't over yet, they're with you, and in the end, you will prevail.' She walked slowly across the floor. 'Now I'll take a slip of your mother's cherry tree, and we'll plant it above for you, and I'll wait outside for Tilly. Say your goodbyes to the house for now, Grace'

Grace walked through the hallway and into the empty kitchen – so many meals here, with her parents, with Agnes, then with Declan – and then let herself out into the yard behind. She opened the door to her little whitewashed bath house and to her surprise found it empty. Charlie and Tilly must have disconnected the boiler Declan made and removed the old trough-turned-bath. All that was left were the connections on the wall. Some day she might have a home again, and she could put her bath house back together. She was glad it wasn't being left here for the canon to throw out; he'd enjoy doing that. She turned back to the house. Her mother's cherry blossom tree had bloomed earlier and was now in leaf. She remembered her daddy teasing her mother about what an unsuitable tree it was, such a short blossoming time, and in a place like Knocknashee, which was habitually windy, it was even shorter, but Mammy just said it was worth it.

Grace did as Mary told her and walked through her home, running her hand along a windowsill, touching the walls, feeling calmer than she had since that terrible conversation with the canon. This was just bricks and mortar, and yes, it was the only home she'd ever known, but it was the people who made a house a home and she had so many people who cared for her. She heard her heels echo on the floorboards as she walked through one last time. Memories of her parents, her sister and brother and Declan played like a film in her head.

'I'm not leaving you here,' she whispered to the silent empty house. 'I'm taking you all with me, and maybe Mary is right, maybe this isn't the end. Be with me now, all of you, stick close by – I need you like never before.'

CHAPTER 29

CORK, IRELAND

Grace assured Lizzie on the platform at Glanmire Road Station in Cork that not only did she have everything she could possibly need but that she would also be fine, and reminded her that she had travelled across the Atlantic and so a trip to Dublin was hardly life-threatening.

'And you have the address of the hotel?' Lizzie asked for the fourth time.

'I have, and I'll find it easily enough, I'm sure.' Grace smiled patiently. It was actually lovely to have someone fuss over her, Charlie and the Warringtons were as close to parents as she had now. She'd had a lovely few days with them, visiting the children in their care in the polio hospital and enjoying home-cooked meals at night. They'd been overwhelmed by the gifts from Tilly – so much food. She'd been right; cities were having a much harder time with the rationing than those in the country.

She'd told them about the canon, and Hugh had reiterated the offer he'd made long before Agnes got sick, that she come and be a teacher in the hospital and they would give her a home with them. The children liked her, were often patients for protracted periods of time and needed consistency of education so they didn't fall too far behind. While the offer was generous and tempting, she wasn't sure it was the right move.

'Are all of your things at Tilly's?' Lizzie had asked. 'We could store some things for you if you wanted.'

'Thanks, Lizzie, everything is at the farm.'

'I can't imagine having to leave your home... What a cruel thing.'

Grace swallowed.

'You must be excited to see Richard again,' Lizzie said, and Grace knew where this was going. Lizzie, as well as Tilly and Dymphna and even Eleanor, had all dropped fairly heavy hints that maybe she and Richard could be more than friends, and maybe now that things had gone so badly in Knocknashee, it might be the perfect time. But she'd pretended in each instance not to understand their meaning.

She refused to allow those thoughts in. He was with Pippa, and she was in mourning for Declan. And while all the grieving in the world wouldn't bring Declan back, it wasn't right to even be thinking about another man.

Richard wasn't coming to see her specifically. He was reporting from Belfast and doing a piece on Dublin in the Emergency, so she was a sidebar to the business trip.

Around every corner in Cork was a memory of Declan, and that, combined with the evidence of everyone else getting on with things, hurt her heart in ways she couldn't even express. Of course people must carry on – what else should they do? But she felt lost and alone. She could get a job in Cork, in the hospital, and she was grateful for it, but it had never been her plan. Her memories of Declan and her parents, and even Agnes, were in her home in Knocknashee, and she'd had to give all of that up. She knew she needed to make plans, decide what to do, but she was so battered and sad and it was too hard. She'd go to see Richard; a trip to Dublin to see her old friend was just the tonic she needed. She'd reserved a room in a hotel near Baggot Street Bridge that looked respectable while not being too expensive, and it was the only bright spot in an otherwise hard life.

'I am. He's been on such an adventure since we last saw each other, all the way to Singapore and Ceylon. He even sailed through the Suez Canal, can you imagine it? I can't wait to hear all about it.'

'Dublin train delayed!' the stationmaster bellowed to the groans of passengers as he marched along the platform.

'For how long?' someone called.

'No idea,' the stationmaster responded airily; clearly he couldn't care less.

Lizzie turned and smiled ruefully. 'Well, looks like I get you to myself for a while. Will we have a cup of tea in the café?'

'We might as well.' Grace linked her as they walked down the platform past the ladies' room to the café. There was a bar as well, and that was where the men headed, but she and Lizzie found a corner of the busy café and ordered two cups of tea. A few tiny dry scones sat sadly on a plate on the counter, but neither of them were tempted.

'Grace, I'm glad I got this opportunity, because Hugh and I are worried, and I couldn't find the right time, so…'

'What is it? Are you all right? Is Hugh?' She felt immediate panic. Could they be sick?

The older woman smiled. 'We're fine, it's nothing like that. No, we're worried about you. I know you're grieving, and of course you are, Declan was a special person, but you look like you have the weight of the world on your shoulders, and we want to help.'

'Please don't worry, I'm all right. I just feel so…'

'Tell me, Grace,' Lizzie said quietly.

And then, like someone had opened the floodgates, it all came out. The canon, the loss of her job and home, the fact that she felt so alone in the world, that everyone had someone, one person who was theirs, but she didn't and probably never would have. She even told Lizzie that Richard had a girlfriend. And she expressed how she was so grateful for their offer of giving her a job and a place to live, she really was, but it just all felt so overwhelming.

It was soon time for her train and Lizzie accompanied her to the platform.

'Take care Grace, please, we worry.' She hugged her. 'I know it all seems so dark now, but it will all work out, you just need to be patient, and in the meantime lean on the people who love you.'

Grace nodded, her eyes filling with tears once more at the kindness of this woman.

'Thank you Lizzie, I don't know what I'd do without you.'

'We'll always be here for you Grace, Hugh and I, you're never alone.'

A brief tight hug, and Grace boarded the train, her heart a bit lighter.

CHAPTER 30

DUBLIN, IRELAND

'Oh, Richard, it's wonderful to see you,' she said, her voice choked and her eyes bright with tears. It was overwhelming to see him again after all this time; so much had happened.

'Grace, I'm very sorry about Declan. I…' Richard stood and hugged her. He looked different, older, and his hair was cut very short, much shorter than she remembered.

'Thank you, and I know you are.' She shook her head and lowered her voice. 'Look at us here in this fancy place.' She grinned.

'It *is* fancy, but I thought we deserved a treat. I've booked us afternoon tea in the restaurant, if that's all right?'

She couldn't take her eyes off him as she sat down opposite him. 'Well, since I usually have brown bread and jam for lunch, and I doubt they'll have that, I suppose I'll have to put up with it.' She giggled and felt herself relax. It wasn't strange or awkward, it was just Richard, and she was at ease with him.

He ordered her a lemonade and one for himself, and they chatted easily until the waiter came and ushered them to the table. The snow-white linen tablecloths, shining silver and glittering crystal nearly took Grace's breath away.

The last time she'd set eyes on him was on the beach in Knocknashee; it felt like a lifetime ago. They just sat in easy silence drinking each other in.

'Are we really here?' she asked.

'It's so strange, isn't it? I know we've only met in person once before, but you know me better than...well, just about anyone else I've ever met.'

' I feel the same. I say things to you I would never say to anyone, not even Tilly. I can't believe me throwing that letter into the sea has led to all of this, and now we're here...'

'I'm sure glad you did.' Richard's gaze locked with hers.

'Richard, is this very dear?' she whispered as they were approached by a liveried waiter wanting to take their order.

'I'm on expenses,' he whispered back. 'I'm calling you a lead.'

'Kirky won't be happy with this. I'd better make up something very salacious,' she murmured as the waiter left with their order for the full afternoon tea, after having first opened Grace's napkin and placing it on her lap with a flourish.

'Miss Fitzgerald, what kind of a reporter do you think I am?' Richard joked, mock offended.

'A very good one,' she answered honestly.

'Well, thank you very much. I'm actually doing a story on a bunch of Jewish kids who got out of Berlin on the Kindertransport and somehow wound up in Northern Ireland. Jacob met the rabbi who came with them in Belfast at a synagogue there. He looks around a hundred years old, tiny wiry man, but he's a ball of energy and passionate about these children. He offered for us to come out to their farm in a place called Ballycreggan to meet him and a schoolteacher called Elizabeth Klein and talk to the kids. Apparently they have a whole thing going out there, a school, a place to live, even a synagogue. It's going to be a real feel-good story, as we say in the States, so Kirky won't care about my expenses. We're making him a fortune. Now forget me – how are you doing?'

'I can't really believe I'm here to be honest. Generally I'm sad, and a bit lonely and worried about the future, but at this exact moment, I'm fine, more than fine. Oh, Richard, it's so good to see you.'

On and on they talked about this and that, conversations tumbling over each other, hopping from one topic to the next.

All about how Declan died, and though it was hard for her to recount, she felt proud that she could tell him without crying. Then she went on to Tilly and Eloise and Odile. He gave her all the details he'd got from Didi in his letters, but they talked and speculated and hoped that Bernadette was still alive. He explained to her about the assignment in Belfast, how Sarah was doing, and he mentioned Pippa.

She told him about the canon, how he'd sacked her and made her homeless in one fell swoop.

'That bas…' He stopped himself swearing in front of her, but she could see he was furious.

She nibbled a tiny egg sandwich from the elaborate tray of sweet and savoury food the Shelbourne had managed to produce. Here, as in London, anything could be procured if you were willing to pay for it.

'He can't just do that, no way. You have to fight back, Grace, you just have to. Look, I've got something for you.'

He took a letter from his pocket and handed it to her. It was from Mrs McHale.

'Will I read it aloud?' Grace asked.

'If you'd like,' Richard replied. 'You remember who Mrs McHale is, don't you?'

'Of course. She was so helpful to you when you found Father Dempsey for us.'

Grace began to read the short letter. '"Dear Richard. I've decided to stop calling you Mr Lewis, since you're only a boy and I'm an old lady."' She smiled at that. '"I thought you might be interested to know I tracked down the man who complained to the bishop in New York about having to pay three thousand dollars to adopt an Irish baby, and he told me something you might consider useful."'

Grace sat up as she read on. '"The gentleman didn't want to talk to me at first. He'd never heard back from the bishop after he wrote, and naturally he and his wife didn't want to pursue it any further. But he since has had a change of heart. His daughter is now over eighteen and knows all about her adoption. Still, he wanted it kept quiet, and so I promised it would go no further. He agreed to meet me in a coffee shop in Manhattan. He brought a copy of the letter he wrote at the time and showed it to me. He sent one to the bishop and kept a copy for himself. Well, I don't drink coffee and they don't do proper tea in these places – it's desperate old slop they call tea – but at least we had a nice slice of lemon cake. I asked the waitress for the recipe, but she didn't know; apparently it's made somewhere else altogether."'

Grace smiled again. She could almost hear Mrs McHale's voice. '"I asked him did he remember the woman who brought the baby, and he did and said she was called Kit Gallagher and there had been an Irish priest with her. Was it Father Noel Dempsey, says I, and he says he didn't know but he wasn't American, he was Irish, and Father Dempsey is American. The man said he was never introduced to the priest but he remembered him as a tall, scrawny-looking man with long, straggling eyebrows, who had some kind of a speech impediment – he kind of hissed his s's – and he would never forget the gleam in his eyes as he counted out the money in hundred dollar bills.'"

Grace looked up at Richard, her eyes wide, but carried on. '"Now I don't know if this is any good to you, Richard, but I still thought you might be interested on behalf of your Irish friend. The man I spoke to told his daughter where she came from. It came out somehow – some busybody in the family let something slip, so they had no choice but tell her the truth. But thanks be to God, it all worked out fine, so maybe this man would talk to you or your friend if needs be."

'"I wear the lovely slippers you got me every day, and they do wonders for the rheumatism in my toes, and I say a prayer for you and your sister and your friend Jacob every evening, that God will keep you safe."

'"Don't forget to send my regards to your friend in Knocknashee, she sounds like a lovely girl altogether. And I will tell you here and now, Richard, the people from there are salt of the earth, you won't get better. Fondly, Mrs Patricia McHale."

'"PS – I just got word that unfortunately the man has changed his mind. He said he was worried that he would be in trouble because he had a minor criminal conviction when he was young and his wife is fearful that they could face problems if it got out. He just asked me to forget he told me anything. I said I'd already written to you, which was sort of true – I had but not posted it – so here we are. He seemed very nervous all of a sudden, almost as if someone had threatened him or something. I'm sorry about this, but at least you know the truth."'

Grace handed the letter back to him.

'She has great hopes that I'll be her way back to Dingle some day. I think that's why she's taken a shine to me,' Richard joked.

'Please tell her she'd be made very welcome if she ever wanted to visit, and I'm sure she'd be with Mary O'Hare or Nancy O'Flaherty five minutes before all manner of mutual cousins and relations would be unearthed.'

'I will. That's interesting about the canon, isn't it?'

'I suppose it is. We knew it anyway, but to have it confirmed...' Grace shrugged and sighed.

'But Grace, don't you see? It's proof, something to hold over him. This man was extorted by Canon Rafferty, and there's a letter in existence to the bishop of New York to prove it, so you can fight back. Even if the man has gotten cold feet, there is still proof.'

Grace didn't feel as enthusiastic as she knew he hoped she would be. It was as if all the fight had gone out of her. She was tired.

'Thanks, Richard, I mean it, but I don't think I can. I'm feeling kind of defeated by life at the moment, and I know that's selfish of me when so many people in the world have lost so much more than I have – I often think of Pippa and how she has nobody but you really – but I don't think I have the fight in me to take him on, not again.'

Richard leant across the table and took her hands in his. 'First, you don't have a selfish bone in your body, so don't say that. Of course you feel low. You lost the love of your life, and that's so tough. It doesn't matter more than a hill of beans, as my father might say, who else has lost what – you can only feel what you feel. So I don't blame you one little bit for thinking you can't face it.'

'I sense a "but" coming…' Grace gave him a weak smile.

He grinned. 'There is. Because however awful the timing, this matters, Grace. And I know you feel battered and broken down by life right now, but if you don't stand up to him and fight back, and you have the ammunition to do that now, then I fear you'd regret it for the rest of your life. That school, those kids, your community – they're your whole world, Grace, and if you let him bully you out of it…'

'They used to be,' she said quietly.

'But not any more?'

'I don't know. Lately I've been thinking that maybe there's nothing for me in Knocknashee any longer. Everyone else is getting on with life, and that's right, they should, but I feel like I'm just going through the motions…' She stopped herself then. 'I'm sorry, Richard, I'm being such a mope. You must regret offering to meet me.'

'Please, Grace, stop apologising. We're honest with each other, right? We tell each other the truth…we don't hide or pretend…'

She needed to change the subject. 'Now enough about me and my tale of woe. How about you? How are things? How's Pippa?'

Something in his face was unreadable, as if he was torn or something. 'Fine, she's fine.' Was he going to tell her that he and Pippa were together? Were they engaged even? It was obvious that they were in a relationship, but it wasn't her business, she supposed. If he didn't want to confide in her, that was his prerogative.

'And Sarah and Jacob?'

'Both well. Jacob is not too happy being sent to cover the kinds of stories Kirky wants, but things are good. I think they might get married actually. Neither of them would care about the ceremony – Sarah wouldn't give a hoot about dresses or a big do in a hotel or anything like that – but I think they'd like to.'

'Well, if this war has taught us anything it's that we don't know what the future holds, so we should just try to be happy when we can be. I'm sure their wedding would be perfect, even without any fancy dresses or hotels.'

'Was your wedding day perfect?' Richard asked.

The sadness washed over Grace as she considered the question. 'It was, you know. We got married in the church of the hospital. Peggy Donnelly made me a dress, and I can say, though it might sound vain, I looked lovely in it. All our family and friends were there, and it was a special day.'

'I'd love to see a photo – did you take one?'

'Yes. Eloise took some, but I never got to see them. She was going to develop the film back in Dublin – getting the chemicals you need to do that is very hard now, I think, because the governments use them up for military reasons – but then she got arrested.'

'You should ask her for them,' Richard said gently. 'To remember your perfect day. If she can't develop the film, let me know and Jacob will do it for you.'

'Are you coming to my rescue again, Mr Lewis?' Grace asked with a laugh.

Richard looked at her then and didn't return her laugh or make a joke. He simply said, 'I'd do anything for you, Grace, anything at all.'

CHAPTER 31

BELFAST, IRELAND

Richard sat on the train back to Belfast, his heart heavy. He could feel Grace's pain and sense of despair and longed to make it better. He was so disappointed that the evidence Mrs McHale had provided wouldn't work, that it was too late, and though it seemed damning to him, according to Grace, it wasn't going to be enough. He'd have to take her word for it. He knew nothing about how the Catholic Church worked and Grace was encyclopaedic in her knowledge of it, so if she thought it wouldn't be enough, then it wouldn't.

He and Jacob were staying at a lodging house off Donegall Square that was all right, but the landlady was stingy in the extreme. He didn't eat his boiled egg the first morning and suspected the second morning that he got the same egg back, so he made a small pencil mark on it, and sure enough, he got the same boiled egg each day. The scrape of margarine on the black bread and weak tea for breakfast weren't an encouraging start to the day, but he usually ate them.

People didn't grumble too much; there was no point. The war was the cause, and for as long as it raged, this was how people had to live. But Mrs Greenaway took the deprivations to a new level. The water was rarely warmer than tepid and the towels were paper thin, but given the extensive damage done by the Belfast Blitz, they were lucky to get any lodgings at all so didn't complain.

Belfast felt very different from Dublin, more like cities in the United Kingdom, everyone on a hair-trigger, waiting for the next blow.

He and Jacob had taken to skipping the evening meal and going to a pub on Union Street near the offices of the *Belfast Telegraph* called the Inkwell. The owner's wife was a nice lady and a great cook, and she provided dinners for the many foreign newspapermen in the city. It was simple fare, meat and potatoes mainly, but it was filling and tasty and better than Mrs Greenaway's miserable offerings.

They'd got to know lots of other reporters and photographers from various papers around the world there, and in general the group were generous in sharing information and leads.

He arrived into Belfast Central station and made his way to the lodging house. Mrs Greenaway was peeking out of the net curtain as he walked up the path, her pale-pink cardigan and her thin blond flyaway hair making her look almost translucent, he often thought.

'There's two letters for you, Mr Lewis,' she said, eyeing him beadily as if he was trying to do something underhanded. She was suspicious by nature, he realised, and made everyone feel guilty even if they'd done nothing wrong.

'Thank you, ma'am,' he said politely as he took the letters from the hall table.

She nodded, looking down her long nose. 'Your friend Mr Nunez is gone out.' She said it in the same tone that might have been reserved for 'he's gone out to throttle someone', and Richard suppressed a grin. 'I don't know where?' Her intonation suggested he might be withholding this information.

'Oh, he's a law unto himself, Mrs Greenaway, he could be anywhere Ma'am, but I sure do appreciate you taking such good care of us while we visit your beautiful city.' he said using his best Southern charm, which he knew was not the reply she wanted.

Before she had time for any more enquiries, he bounded up the stairs, and went into his sparse, stuffy room. The small window appeared to be painted shut so no fresh air got in.

The first letter was from Pippa, the other from his father. Her writing was nothing like Grace's neat cursive; it was more childish, big and loopy, and she put hearts over her i's instead of dots.

It was thick, and he settled down on the hard narrow bed to read it.

Dear Richard,

Greetings from sunny London. It's really hot here now, which makes the factory even more like a furnace. Me and the girls will be making bullets in our bras and pants soon if it doesn't cool down. Mr Aberforth, the supervisor, makes us cover our hair – he's got some awful stories about hair getting caught in machines and he loves telling them – so we have to be covered, but cor blimey, it's hot.

Life here is much the same, except me and Sarah miss you two a lot. We don't miss there never being any milk or the dirty dishes left in the sink to be seen to by the washing-up fairy, but we do miss you both.

She's writing for Glamour *magazine now, did she say? She's writing about wartime fashion and the things girls over here do to stay looking nice when there is literally nothing to buy in the shops. She gave the piece to me to read, and it was really good, really funny too. She wrote about how we use tea to tan our legs and how we draw lines down the backs with pencil to look like stockings. She even included how women are devils for using bits of parachute silk to make our unmentionables. It's true, though. A German crash-landed up near Coventry somewhere, and when he landed, the girls up there didn't want nothing to do with him but they fought like cats over his parachute.*

I was walking by the courthouse yesterday. Sarah and I were manning – or womanning, as she says – a bric-a-brac stall in the community hall to raise funds for refugees. It's a bit pointless 'cause nobody's got nothing they're giving away; everyone's lost so much already. It was mostly bits of old tat, but I suppose if you've got nothing left, a cushion cover or an ashtray with a pretty picture on it can mean the world. We go down to the refugee centre most evenings, just to help. Mostly people are trying to find out about their families back wherever they came from. News is almost nonexistent, and what we do hear is all bad. Poor buggers. One chap, his name is Wojtec but you say it like 'voy-tek', is from Poland. He was in the army. They were taken prisoner, but he managed to escape. He got shot and the wound got infected – it's a miracle he survived at all. I've been teaching him and a few others English, so there's gonna be a whole bunch of refugees with Cockney accents and terrible grammar roaming about London thanks to yours truly. Wojtec lost his entire family. His dad died defending their city from the Germans, his mother was hit by the butt of a rifle in the head when she objected to the German soldiers picking up boys to conscript them – some of them were only fourteen or fifteen years old – his brother was killed in action, and his little sister died of an infection in the first year of the war. I told him my story, so he and I get along. He knows I know what it feels like to have nobody. His English is getting better all the time, and it's nice to be able to help.

Anyway, as I was saying, I was walking by the courthouse and wondering if we should set a date? I don't mind, but it's not like we got any big preparing to do. I expect your mum and dad won't be best pleased to find out you got hitched to some English girl that they ain't never heard of, and that she's not got a brass farthing to her name neither. I'm worried what they'll say, to be honest. I tried talking to Sarah about it, but she says your dad is all right, that he'll be happy if you're happy, but your mum is difficult to please at the best of times and not to bother trying. I reckon she's gonna hate me.

Are you happy, Richard? I hope so. How long more will you be over there? Our bed is very big without you.

Love,

Your Pippa xxxxxxx

He sighed. What was wrong with him? Sarah was right – he was lying to himself and lying to Pippa, and it wasn't fair. But it wasn't like he didn't love her. He did. He'd been sure when he proposed, but after seeing Grace for that wonderful afternoon, sad as she was, all he wanted was to leave Belfast, go to Cork and wrap her up in his arms and care for her always. It was wrong and awful, he knew. It made him a horrible person, only using Pippa as a stopgap, someone to fill a void left by Grace. There was nothing for it; he had to call it all off. He knew this for sure now. Whether he and Grace ever worked out or not, Pippa deserved to be someone's number one. She should have all the happiness and security and love someone could give her, not him and his fickle ways. He felt like a heel, and rightly so.

He and Jacob were close to finishing their time here anyway; they just had to do the Ballycreggan interviews with Rabbi Frank and Mrs Klein, go out there and take a few photos, and that would be it. He'd go back to London, tell Pippa the truth, that she deserved so much better than him, and then...well, then he didn't know what he would do. One step at a time. He had to admit he was a tiny bit excited at the prospect of Grace breaking her ties with Knocknashee. It had always been a huge stumbling block in his mind. She was so much a part of the fabric there, and he couldn't imagine himself living there, or her ever leaving. Now that she no longer had a house or a job – though he hated that she was so upset – maybe it meant she was a bit more free? Did that make him a selfish pig? Probably.

He folded the letter and left it on his nightstand. Two girls. He loved them both but one far more than the other. One loved him and wanted to marry him, and the other... The other he had no idea what she felt about him beyond friendship.

He slid his finger under the flap of the second envelope, forwarded on from London. His father's letters were usually perfunctory and short, asking after his welfare, reminding him to look after Sarah, telling him some funny story from the yacht club.

This was longer than usual, and he wondered what his father wanted to say that took so long.

Dear Richard,

I hope this letter finds you well and still in one piece. I worry about you and your sister, and while I know it's not possible to avoid danger in these times we live in, I would urge you to be cautious. If it looks dangerous, and you have an option, don't be a hero, son.

Life here is fine. The bank is doing well. We grow year on year, acquiring new accounts all the time. I know you rejected the life of a banker, as did your brother. Hell, I'd almost give it to Sarah if I thought one of my offspring would follow in my footsteps. But you won't and don't want to, and that's fine. I'll try to leave it in as good a shape as I can. In fact I'm considering selling it. Several of the larger operations want to buy me out, and while that was never something I would have considered in the past, I think perhaps it's time now.

Richard felt a sharp pang of guilt. His father had worked so hard to have something substantial to leave his children, but he and Nathan and Sarah had rejected it. Arthur Lewis was a self-made man – he didn't inherit a red cent and built everything he had with his own sweat – and it felt spoiled and indulged to refuse to follow him.

Your mother was in the hospital recently, her heart, they say. I'm having a guy come from Orlando to look at her as I don't trust the guy here. She hasn't been well, Richard. Even though things are strained between us, I still will take care of her. Or at least arrange for others to do so—she doesn't want anything to do with me over supporting you and Sarah.

As I told you before, you are a man with your own path in the world, wherever it takes you, and I'm proud of you. Your mother, on the other hand, has not thawed, I'm sorry to say. I have tried to speak to her, but she refuses to discuss either you or Sarah. I used to pretend that she did, telling you both that she was asking about you and so forth, but she wasn't. I wish it was different.

You remember James Ginsbury—he was a year ahead of you at school? Well, I'm sorry to say he was killed in Hawaii when the Japanese attacked our base there. We met his parents recently at a civic function—I don't recall what the purpose of the dinner was, something charitable. Your mother and I both attended; she was anxious to save face, I think. You know how I despise those things. Anyway, seeing Mrs. Ginsbury's clear distress at the death of her boy was something I was sure would move your mother, but it did not.

I hate to tell you this by letter, Richard, but it looks like we are getting a divorce. You and Nathan and Sarah were the glue holding us together all these years, and now the time has come to admit it was a failure as an experiment. The truth is your mother never loved me. She's always felt I am beneath her; she's told me so on a number of occasions, so I believe her. When we met, her family were very well to do, I was a nobody from nowhere. The only reason she accepted me was I had a knack for making money, and your

Mama sure likes nice expensive things. She felt I could elevate her even higher financially and she could elevate me socially. In theory it might have worked—but in practice it didn't.

Marriage is hard when you truly love each other. The early days are fine, all romance and roses, but to make it last, first of all you need to be married to the right woman, and even then it takes guts and determination as well as a whole heap of patience and compassion. We just didn't have the right building blocks.

Your mother will keep the house in Savannah, and I will go live in Richmond Hill,—I've bought a place there. You, Sarah, and Nathan are welcome to visit any time you like, and to stay if you wish.

I know you are probably in shock, and for that, I'm sorry, but we only get one life, Richard, and we have a duty to ourselves to make it as happy as it can be. Your mother and I do not make each other happy, and that's the plain truth. I hope you don't think I'm being selfish. Maybe you do, but I pray you can understand, even slightly, as a man who has made his own decisions. If your mother could even come some of the way to meet me, if she wasn't so cold about her own children, maybe things could be different, but she refuses. In a way you inspired me, Richard, to take my life into my own hands.

I don't mean to upset you son, and I look forward to hearing from you.

Your loving father,

AJL

He was shocked in one way but in another not at all. His mother was cold, no doubt about it. He never remembered any hand-holding or joking or teasing between his parents. His father loved her, he was sure, but the most affection he ever saw between them was when his father would peck her chastely once a day on the cheek that she proffered almost absentmindedly. They'd had separate bedrooms for as long as he could remember; he'd just assumed it was what older people did. He spent no time whatsoever thinking about their sex life, but now that he was forced to confront it, the idea of his mother ever doing anything as primal as making love was a complete anathema to him. She would never lower herself.

Did he mind? He thought about it. It would be a scandal for sure, and he felt a bit sorry for his mother; the shame of divorce would be a bitter pill to swallow. But then she was also a bitter pill to swallow, so maybe it was natural justice.

He found he wished his father well. The sign-off of the letter, 'your loving father', was positively gushing by Arthur Joseph Lewis standards. He got the sense too that his father was worried and fearful of his son's reaction, which was touching.

It was just before five – he would make the post office if he hurried. He composed the telegram in his head on the short walk and paid for the message to be sent.

Got letter. Am happy for you. Will write tonight. Love, R.

He hoped it would put his father's mind at ease.

CHAPTER 32

KNOCKNASHEE

Grace was staying with Tilly and Mary while she figured out what to do. Moving to Cork to live with the Warringtons seemed to be one of her only realistic options, but she was loathe to leave her friends and her life in Knocknashee. On the other hand, seeing and witnessing the terror felt by her pupils under the new regime of Francis Sheehan would be torture.

She'd walked past the school and her old house just this morning imagining him yelling at someone, the sound of crying as he administered the strap. Eleanor had been sacked too, as Grace knew she would be, and an awful miserable-looking man called Anthony Nolan had arrived in in her place.

School hadn't started back yet, but it broke her heart to see how the children looked at her in Mass, or on the street, as if she'd somehow betrayed them.

She made herself useful at Tilly's by helping around the house and farm, but this wasn't a long-term solution. Eloise had arrived a few days ago. Tilly was convinced of her innocence and, to be fair, so were the authorities it seemed, but there were still so many unanswered questions.

Grace was deep in thought when Eloise came in the back door of the farmhouse, having been in the village. She looked up from peeling potatoes to see something was wrong; Eloise had been crying.

'Eloise? What's happened? Are you all right?' Grace wiped her hands and went over to the Swiss girl.

'I'm fine, Grace, I…' Her big blue eyes filled with tears.

'Sit down, tell me…' Tilly was up the yard – Rua was getting new shoes and the blacksmith needed help with him as he could be skittery – and Mary had taken Odile for a walk.

'I… It's stupid, but I thought it was over, this whole ordeal. But it's not. Nobody here believes I had nothing to do with that U-boat attack.'

'What happened?' Grace asked, half guessing.

'Pádraig O Sé was so horrible.' Her voice cracked, and she wiped her eyes with a handkerchief. 'He said that just because the police released me didn't mean I didn't have blood on my hands, and for all he knew, they might have let me go so I could lead them to whoever was telling me what to do. It was outside his shop, and Mrs O'Connor, the woman whose husband was in the boat with Declan, passed by and just said something about it being easy to shed crocodile tears but there had been no trouble here until I came and that I should clear off, that I'd done enough damage…'

Grace tried to soothe her. 'Ah, you know what he's like, and Margaret O'Connor blamed Declan too – she was sure his outboard engine had blown up and that was what happened. You don't want to be listening to them.'

'No, Grace, I can feel it since I came back – people don't want me here. I'm going to go back to Dublin, maybe even home to Switzerland, I don't know…'

'But you're innocent, and if you go now, you'll only give them what they want,' Grace said, but a question played on her mind. If she didn't ask it now, she might never again get an opportunity.

'Eloise, I did wonder, though, why did they release you all of a sudden? Did they not say why?'

The other girl looked at her, as if assessing whether Grace too was one of the people who didn't quite believe her. Grace kept her face neutral. She didn't want to hurt Eloise, but she did want to know.

'They never said. It was the morning of the twelfth of June. The day before had been the Mass for St Anthony of Padua in the prison – they have a special Mass for him or something. I'd been kept in solitary confinement up to then so going to mass never came up, but I said I didn't want to go and they asked why, and I told them that I wasn't Catholic, that I'd never even been to Mass before coming to Knocknashee. They questioned me again then. I'd not been questioned for around two weeks before this, and I was sure they were finished with me – I'd told them anything I could.' She sounded sincere.

'The questioning was different this time, asking me about my religious history in Switzerland. My parents were atheist, so I never had anything to do with any church – my father hated churches and clergy of all kinds. But still they went on, had I been baptised, communion, confirmation, had I ever been to confession. It was ridiculous, and I laughed at one point because it was so silly. I didn't know how else to explain that I had never been part of any religion in my life.' Her blue eyes were clear and innocent. 'I asked them why they wanted to know and what this had to do with anything, but as usual they didn't tell me. They asked me to say any prayers I know, which of course I didn't know any, and then they asked who the priest was in my home village. I didn't know who that was, as I explained, but I told them the name of the church and they sent me back to my cell. The next day I was released. No evidence to hold me any further was all they said.'

As she finished, Tilly came in the back door, a leather apron around her waist from shoeing. 'What's wrong?' she asked, seeing Eloise's tear-stained face.

'Nothing, Tilly, I'm fine.' Eloise was quick to reassure her.

'Well, you're clearly not, so someone better tell me what's happened.'

'Pádraig O Sé was horrible, Margaret O'Connor too…' Grace filled her in.

'Oh, for God's sake, that pair of old busybodies! 'Tis a shame to waste two houses between them. They're going to get a piece of my mind now, let me tell you…' Tilly jaw was set defiantly and her eyes narrowed as she headed for the door.

Eloise stood and followed Tilly to the door. 'No, Tilly, please don't, just leave it be. But…I am going to go back to Dublin, maybe back home…'

Grace hated to see her friend's stricken face.

'No, Eloise, please…don't go! I'll sort this out, I swear.' Tilly was fighting tears, and she never cried. 'I'll make sure nobody says –'

'Tilly, you can't, truly, you can't… The people here believe what they believe and we can't change their minds. It's best I just go.'

Grace knew this was between them, so she took her bag and slipped outside, not wanting to intrude. It was a beautiful day and the walk to the village was downhill, so she decided to go and see Dymphna and Charlie. The baby was due any day.

Her leg ached a bit these days, and she missed her little bath house, the components of which were in the byre along with her things. Tilly had set up a bath for her upstairs and insisted on dragging buckets of hot water up, and though it was so kind of her, it wasn't the same.

She'd written to Father Iggy just filling him in on her new situation; she'd post the letters when she got to the village.

People nodded sympathetically to her, and she could feel their palpable support. Nobody wanted that pair of monsters in the school, but there was nothing to be done. Like her, they were at the mercy of the canon.

She posted her letters, and as she went to knock on the McKennas' door, Paudie and Kate appeared, white-faced.

'Da's not here, Mammy told us to get Dr Ryan, she's having the baby…' Paudie blurted it all out in one sentence.

'She did a wee on the floor.' Kate giggled. Grace glanced around and to her relief saw Eleanor coming out of O'Donoghue's, a basket over her arm. Grace beckoned her over. Eleanor crossed the road and immediately took in what was going on.

'Now you two go to Mrs O'Flaherty in the post office, tell her that we're with your mammy and ask if you two can stay with her for a while, all right?' Grace tried to sound calm.

'Does Dr Ryan have a special shovel to dig the baby out?' Kate asked, her eyes wide.

'No, you silly,' Paudie admonished her. 'The baby comes out of Mammy's tummy through a special tunnel called the vagina that's between her legs. You have one too, but you don't need it for ages because you're only a child. Men don't have them, they have penises, and...'

Eleanor caught Grace's eye. Paudie was a voracious reader and a precocious child, so he would have found it out from a book, or he would have pestered Dymphna or Charlie to tell him, but maybe his little sister didn't need all the exact details just now. 'Right, you two, why don't you run over to Mrs O'Flaherty now, and I'm sure she'll have something interesting for you to do.'

'But I want to see Mammy and the new baby!' Kate protested.

'And you will,' Grace reassured her. 'But Dr Ryan will be looking after your Mammy for a while, so we'll let him do that. And then when the baby comes, we'll take you over to meet your new brother or sister, how does that sound?'

'Births can take ages. Humans gestate for 266 days, but a wolf only takes 64 days and an elephant takes around 640 days,' Paudie explained. 'And most monkeys are the same more or less as humans, which shows how that cycle predates humans as a species.'

'We're not going to see Mammy for 266 days?' Eight-year-old Kate looked devastated.

Paudie was kind, and he put his arm around her. 'No, Kate, the baby has already been gestated – that means growing in the mammy's tummy – so now it just has to come out, and that only takes a small while.'

'Like ten minutes?' She looked up at her brother who was,

according to Kate, the world's leading authority on absolutely everything.

For once he looked unsure, and one of his most endearing traits was that despite his undeniably vast knowledge, he never pretended to know things he didn't. 'I don't know. Mrs Worth, you had babies – how long does it take?' he asked.

'Well' – Eleanor smiled – 'it depends. Libby was born in two hours, but Joanne took sixteen hours, so it varies from baby to baby.'

'But the baby will be here by tomorrow?' Kate asked.

'I would think so,' Grace said. 'And in the meantime, you can both go to the post office, and maybe Mrs O'Flaherty will let you help her with the letters, won't that be fun?' She put her arms around them and hugged them. They trusted Grace so they did as she told them.

Eleanor murmured once they were out of earshot, 'Dr Ryan is gone to Tralee. There was a court case there today, and he was called as a witness – I met him this morning.'

'Oh God, look...let's go in and we'll see...' Grace said, pushing open the door. There had been a midwife in the parish for years, a lady known as Nurse Joan, but she'd retired and moved to live with her daughter in England.

Dymphna was upstairs at least, and on the bed. She seemed reasonably calm considering, though her voice did sound a little strained. 'Is Dr Ryan coming?' she asked.

'I'm afraid not, Dymphna, he's in Tralee, but Grace and I are here, and I've helped deliver babies twice before and I've had three of my own, so I think we can manage.' Eleanor sounded confident, which Grace was grateful for. 'How often are the pains coming, do you think?'

'Don't know...' Dymphna said through gritted teeth.

'Grace, could you time them so please? This is one now, and when that subsides, just count how long before another one starts up.' Eleanor, as she was in all things, the picture of calm efficiency. She gently moved the sheet that Dymphna was lying under and had a look between her legs, gently felt her abdomen and then took her pulse by holding her wrist and reading it off the time on her watch.

'I'd say you're doing really well, Dymphna. This is your third, so all the furniture has been moved around already. Baby's head is engaged, and your heart rate is fine' – she gave a little chuckle – 'so it all looks good to me.'

'How did you learn this?' the expectant mother asked as the pain subsided.

'During the Blitz I volunteered as a first-aid warden – it was necessary if anything happened during the schoolday – and delivering babies under emergency circumstances was part of the training. On two occasions it came in handy, so you're not my maiden voyage.' Eleanor chuckled and was so assured, Grace felt herself relax.

She counted the minutes between several pains and said, 'I think they are two minutes apart and last about ninety seconds each.'

'Excellent. It will be time to push now, so Dymphna' – Eleanor took the woman's hand – 'when you feel the urge to push, just bear down, put all your energy into it and push as hard as you can. These contractions now feel a little different to the earlier ones, don't they? That's because they're for pushing the baby out – your womb is fully open so the baby can come. Grace and I will be here, and everything is fine. You'll have your baby in your arms very soon.'

The next hour passed by in a blur. Dymphna's body seemed to take over, and her delivery of her child seemed to transcend her conscious decision-making. Grace was both fascinated and awed. It was the most powerful thing she'd ever witnessed. Eleanor stayed calm through it all, and Grace held Dymphna's hand and mopped her brow with cold water.

From between Dymphna's legs, Eleanor called, 'I can see the head, and a lovely head of dark hair they have too. One more big push now, Dymphna, for the head and then the shoulders, and the rest is easy…'

The sounds coming from Dymphna were primal, guttural, and the tendons stood out on her neck as the sheer force needed to push her child into the world gripped her entire body and mind. Grace's hand ached from being squeezed, but she was not going to let go.

'One more, Dymphna, just one more! The baby is almost here…' Eleanor said, and Dymphna bore down, her chin on her chest, pillows propped behind her, as she gave birth. All in an instant, the pain subsided, the baby slid out of her body, and Eleanor announced, 'It's a little boy, Dymphna. You have a beautiful little son. Well done – he's handsome.'

A lusty cry rent the air.

Eleanor laughed. 'Nothing wrong with his lungs anyway.'

She cut the cord, wrapped the baby in the cotton sheet and blanket she had ready and placed him in his mother's arms. The hair stuck to Dymphna's head and the tears ran down her cheeks as she accepted the baby, gazing down in astonishment at her son, a new life, a new person in the world. Grace didn't realise she was crying until Eleanor handed her a handkerchief.

'Oh, Dymphna, he's so beautiful. He's just perfect.' Grace gazed at him.

'Isn't he? Hello, little man, you're very welcome…' she whispered, kissing his forehead. 'Thank you, Grace and Eleanor. I don't know what I'd have done.' She looked up at the two women for the first time.

'Well, I did nothing. It was all Eleanor,' Grace said.

'Not at all, I think I might have broken your fingers.' Dymphna winced apologetically.

'I'm delighted to have been able to help in even a small way,' Grace said, unable to take her eyes off Declan's little brother. She turned to Eleanor, who was washing her hands in a basin of water. 'Is there nothing you can't do?'

'We're not done yet, we need to deliver the afterbirth, but don't you worry about that,' Eleanor said to Dymphna. 'It will come itself shortly.'

'Will I go and find Charlie?' Grace asked.

'Please do,' the new mother said, not taking her eyes off her son for a second.

Grace didn't need to look far. Charlie had arrived back to the post office after his afternoon rounds to find Paudie and Kate there, stamping an old book with a stamper and ink. Nancy had given him the news, and he was hurrying home when Grace opened the front door. Together they stood in the hallway.

'Is she all right?' he asked, his face white with worry.

'She's fine. They both are. Eleanor was with us, and she'd delivered babies before, so both mother and baby are doing really well, Charlie. There's nothing to worry about.' Grace smiled as his eyes filled with tears.

He choked out, 'The baby is born already?'

She nodded. 'I think you'd better go and see your son and his mammy, don't you?' She gently led him up the stairs and knocked at the door of the bedroom.

'Just one minute, we're just getting tidied up here,' Eleanor called.

'A boy?' he whispered.

She nodded. 'A beautiful, dark-haired little boy. He's gorgeous, Charlie. He looks like Declan.'

'Seámus Declan, that's what we're calling him. We agreed on that if the baby was a boy.'

'That's a beautiful name. Congratulations, Charlie. Declan would be so proud.'

Charlie pulled her in for a tight hug then, no words needed.

After a minute or two, Eleanor opened the door. Dymphna was sitting up in a freshly made bed, dressed in a clean nightie, her hair brushed and tied back with a ribbon, nursing the little baby. The beam she and Charlie shared said it all.

'I think we'll let this little family get to know each other. Let's make some tea,' Eleanor murmured, her hands full of used sheets.

As they backed out of the room, Dymphna looked up. 'Can you get Paudie and Kate for me, Grace?'

'Of course I will.'

'Grace and Eleanor were amazing, Charlie. I couldn't have done it without them.'

'Thank you both, I'm so grateful…' he said, his voice rough with emotion, never taking his eyes off his son.

'Our pleasure,' Eleanor said. 'Congratulations again – he's a smashing little chap.' She shut the door and followed Grace downstairs.

CHAPTER 33

BELFAST

AUGUST 1942

As he walked to the pub where all the journalists gathered in the evenings, his mind raced. He would tell Jacob tonight that he was going back to London in the morning. He had plenty of material now to run several articles for Kirky, both on the subject of Belfast and of life in the south of the country, which was neutral. He would do his best to explain the neutrality stance of Ireland to the American readership. He could let Jacob cover the Ballycreggan story alone; Richard would use Jacob's notes to write the article up afterwards.

The pub was crowded and a haze of cigarette smoke hung in the air. He hadn't taken up the habit – he found it disgusting – but he was in the minority. He looked around for Jacob, but he wasn't there.

'Richard, what'll you have?' asked Vincent Barrett of the *Irish*

Times, a man Richard didn't particularly like but who was a central figure in their world here in Belfast.

'A beer please, Vincent,' he said, deciding he might as well join the group at the bar, most of whom he knew. He was greeted and welcomed by five other newspapermen, three journalists, an editor and a photographer as he squeezed onto a stool. Ed Jordan from the *Guardian* was in the middle of a story, everyone listening as he spoke. Ed was a character from the English West Country who married a girl from Coleraine, County Derry; she made it a term of their marriage that she never live more than a mile from her mother or her five sisters. Ed was hilarious on the subject of the McIlhenny women and how they were like the Mob. His byline was always 'I'm running for re-election in my marriage, so I'm on my best behaviour.' Ed was average-looking at best, and his wife, Mila, was a beauty by any standards, so he always said he had to work hard to keep her. The funny thing was that Mila adored Ed, hung on his every word. Richard had been in their company several times, and the love they shared was heartwarming to behold.

Vincent passed the pint of warm British beer, and Richard tried not to grimace as he took a sip. Ed was mid-flight with his story; Richard listened to get caught up.

'So as far as I can gather, the police in the south intercepted a German spy and put him in the one cell they had in the rural garda station, somewhere in rural Cork. Apparently he said he was hungry, and the policeman told him to eat the cheese and bread he had in his knapsack, which he did, but when he fell asleep, they couldn't wake him, and would you believe this, he'd only taken a cyanide pill, stored in the cheese.'

'The south's rife with Nazis,' interjected a correspondent Richard recognised but couldn't name from the *Belfast Opinion*, a notoriously unionist-leaning paper. 'They're cosying up to the IRA. Germany are promising the papists all sorts in return for their help to win the war. And de Valera isn't doing half enough to clamp down on them – there's even a German legate in Dublin, for God's sake, operating under their bloody noses.'

Richard hated to hear the criticism of the Irish government when he knew the truth was the complete opposite. The south was very pro-Allies, but the *Opinion* was always looking for stories that showed the south in a poor light. The paper had printed a story only last week – in what Richard thought was unnecessarily salacious detail – about the hanging of a young Catholic man called Murphy. He was only nineteen and was executed for his involvement in the killing of a Royal Ulster Constabulary police officer. Everyone had run the story, but the *Opinion's* piece was almost gleeful in tone.

'I don't think that's fair,' Richard said quietly, and several eyes turned to him.

'Oh, you don't? Based on what, might I ask?' the Belfast man asked belligerently.

'Well, the authorities in the south are routinely returning any downed Allied airmen back to Britain and interning Germans. They've taken down all signage, they've stopped broadcasting the weather, the papers down there are very careful about what they print so as not to aid the enemy, they're giving detailed weather reports from the west coast to the British command to assist shipping and air warfare, they're providing food, and there are thousands of Irish people in the Allied armies. So it's not fair to say they're helping the Germans. If they're helping anyone – and let's not forget they are a neutral country – it's our side.'

'Hear, hear.' A slightly drunk Vincent Barrett clapped him on the shoulder.

'Well, I'm not so sure. I was speaking to a detective recently down there in Dublin,' Geoff Richards, a reporter for a paper in Manchester, added. 'I was sent down to cover the strikes and protests there after the Murphy hanging, and he told me about a priest, down in Kerry somewhere, who approached him after a U-boat attack off the coast – several people killed, merchant seamen and some locals who went out to try to rescue them. This clergyman told the detective that a German woman was hanging around, no reason to be there, taking photographs and all sorts, and that she was most likely a spy. The priest said she told him in confession that she was working for the

Nazis. He got a pang of conscience being Catholic or some blooming thing, and he tipped off the Irish police. They were delighted of course. They'd been flummoxed up to then, how the Germans knew the exact location of the merchant ship, and that wasn't the only one. The detective said there had been a spate of attacks along that part of the coast and it was too much of a coincidence that they got their target perfectly each time, so it was clear someone was giving them information. This priest broke the seal of the confessional and told the detective what he knew, which would have been a dilemma for him, but he said his conscience made him go forward with what he knew. They picked her up, the German bird, but of course she denied it all, and what's said in confession isn't admissible in court down there it would seem, and she'd covered her tracks well, and so she got away with it.'

Richard put his glass down. There couldn't be two incidents like that in Kerry. The story was too specific to be a coincidence. So it was the canon who pointed the finger at Eloise and got her and Tilly arrested. Were there no lengths to which that man wouldn't sink? There was no truth to the story, because he knew for a fact that Eloise wasn't Catholic. He and Grace had discussed it, how she'd never met a person with no religion whatsoever before and how she found it hard to understand.

So that story about her telling him of her guilt in confession was total nonsense. She would never have gone to confession, and she knew how everyone felt about the canon so she would never have confided in him. He remembered Grace saying how she wished Eloise and Tilly wouldn't go out of their way to antagonise the canon; the two of them thought it was funny, but Grace was afraid of what he might do.

Then came a dawning realisation. Why would the canon tell that to a detective? Just out of spite? Or was there something more? Was he trying to cover up the real culprit? He had a new car and was away a lot. Someone was giving information to the Germans, and it wasn't Eloise. Could it be him? Surely not?

But then, as Richard knew, the man was capable of anything.

He needed to think. He bade the group farewell, claiming he was going to track Jacob down, and started walking. His mind buzzed as thought after thought washed over him. Could Canon Rafferty be working for the Nazis? It was outlandish, but so many parts of the puzzle seemed to fit. The canon had lots of money, so he could be being bribed. Grace had mentioned how he'd condemned from the pulpit people from the parish who'd joined the British forces. He'd repeatedly said the war was not Ireland's business and they had no quarrel with Germany. And he was undoubtedly duplicitous enough. He was ideally positioned to give the enemy information. He had a car and travelled all over the place without anyone asking questions.

But would he go that far?

Rumours were rife of individual Catholic clergy operating against the Nazi regime in Catholic countries all over Europe. There was a Monsignor O'Flaherty in Rome running an escape line, according to a journalist Richard knew back in London, against the direct orders of the pope himself no less. Several more stories had emerged too. Didi had told him of a friar in Normandy who was hiding lots of people in his monastery. Even in Germany Catholic priests were being targeted and yet several of them were loud in their criticism of the Nazis. But those were individuals. The Catholic hierarchy as a whole were being conspicuous by their refusal to condemn the Nazis outright. Was the canon one of those Catholics who saw the eradication of Jews as a good thing? Could he be that evil? Richard's answer, based on what he knew of the man, was a resounding yes.

Anyone who could sell babies, try to destroy a man who'd lost his wife as he'd done with Charlie, incarcerate a child in a hellhole as he'd done with Declan, have an inappropriate relationship with a young girl as he'd done with Agnes, and try to have an innocent young woman tried for espionage was almost certainly capable of working for the most heinous regime to ever exist. Not to mention the way he treated Grace. Richard found he wanted that evil man to get what he deserved so badly, he had to do something to make it happen. This was too good an opportunity to miss.

He had enough to go to the Irish police. But would they believe him? He needed proof. And not just hearsay from a guy in a bar – he needed irrefutable proof. The canon had an uncanny knack of wriggling off the hook, and Richard was not going to let that happen this time. He needed something to tie the priest to the Germans that would be so damning, he couldn't get out of it. Because if he got away again, Richard feared the consequences for Grace. And Grace believed Rafferty when he said he would exact his revenge on Tilly, on Mary, and even on little Odile. Richard had to do something, and he had to make sure it worked this time.

On and on he walked, his mind whirring, Jacob and Pippa and his return to London forgotten.

Until he had a plan.

CHAPTER 34

KNOCKNASHEE

Tilly, Charlie, Dymphna and Grace stared at him as he entered the McKennas' small living room two days later. Richard had telegrammed Grace and asked her to trust him – he was coming to Knocknashee but nobody but the McKennas, Tilly and her could know.

'Richard, now you have us all here, and God knows we're delighted to see you, could you tell us what this is all about?' Charlie asked, perplexed. He was perched on the arm of one of the fireside chairs, Dymphna in the same chair beside him with baby Seámus sleeping peacefully in her arms. Tilly was perched on a stool she'd brought in from the kitchen behind.

Seámus was the sweetest baby, and Grace had told him as they walked to Charlie's from the bus-stop, how Odile adored him but her affection had to be curtailed because her hugs and squeezes were sometimes a bit too enthusiastic. Grace had been asked to be his godmother, which she said was an honour, and Hugh Warrington would stand as his godfather. Richard had wondered if being a godmother would be a bittersweet experience, since Grace would no doubt be thinking how she should be planning her own family with Declan. She sat in the other fireside chair, and he caught her eye and gave her what he hoped was a reassuring smile. His dash down the length of Ireland had been on a whim, and he hoped he hadn't made an enormous mistake.

He took a deep breath. 'I can, but please let me finish before you dismiss what I'm about to say. I know this is really crazy, and I'm sorry for all the cloak-and-dagger, but it has to be this way.'

Grace had the same gaunt look he'd seen in Dublin just last week, and knowing he could make the person who hurt her so badly pay for his crimes at long last spurred him on. Just being here would be so hard for her.

Slowly and in detail, he told them first about Mrs McHale and her discovery and then about the conversation he'd been a party to in the pub in Belfast. The group sat in stunned silence.

Tilly was the first to recover, her face dark with fury. 'And this journalist has it right, you think?' she asked.

Richard nodded. 'It was just newspapermen chat, fairly common among us, but he would have no reason to lie. And I know him – he's a decent guy.'

'So it was the canon who had us arrested? It was him working for the Germans all along?'

'Well, this guy said the priest said the woman confessed to him, and I knew Eloise wasn't religious, so…'

Tilly's hand flew to her mouth. 'It *is* true. They asked Eloise why she didn't want to go to Mass for this special feast day and she said she wasn't Christian or Catholic or anything and couldn't understand why they kept asking about her faith, or lack of it. They even contacted a church in her home town back in Switzerland, and once they were sure she was telling the truth, that she'd never had any sacraments, they just let her go. We couldn't understand why at the time, but now it all makes sense. They assumed he was telling the truth, being a priest and everything, but her never setting foot in a confessional box meant he was lying, and so they had nothing on her.'

'I think that's right, but I need to get more proof. *We* need to get more proof.' He glanced around the room. 'As Grace is always telling me, he's a formidable enemy, but if we are smart, we'll get something on him, and then we can go to the police. And once we have evidence, all the bishops in Rome won't be able to help him.'

'The car, the trips away all the time – he's definitely getting money from somewhere,' Charlie said slowly. 'They must be paying him for information.'

'But hold on a minute,' Dymphna's raised a finger in thought. 'I know he's not very nice and he's done some terrible things, but what on earth would the Germans want with him? How would they have even contacted him? I don't know…it all feels a bit far-fetched.'

'Maybe he's not working for the Germans,' Grace mused. 'It seems very outlandish, I agree, even for him. But even lying to the detectives, subverting the course of justice, that's a crime. But Richard's right, we need something. Either evidence of the baby-selling or the lying or something. I think we all know he's capable, and he does have a lot of money. But we need to be so careful. He hates us, as we know, all for different reasons, and me in particular. He's delighted that he's made me unemployed and homeless – he enjoys other people's misery.'

She stood up and stretched her aching leg.

'He would have known that the men here in Knocknashee would go out to find survivors of a U-boat attack, so while I'm not saying he got Declan killed, if what Richard suggests is true, then he is at least partially responsible. Giving information that would assist U-boats attacking in our waters when we're a neutral state, that's treason, isn't it?'

Richard had never seen Grace so determined or furious.

'I would think so,' Charlie said, his face unreadable.

'So the most obvious thing is we need to get into his house, see if there's anything incriminating there. Agreed?'

Silence fell. The parochial house was a large detached building at the end of the town, on its own grounds. Father Lehane and the canon shared it, along with their new housekeeper, a meek older lady called Mrs Coughlan.

'Agreed,' Tilly and Richard said in unison, but Charlie and Dymphna looked less sure.

'And what if you're wrong? And what if he catches you in his house?' Dymphna asked.

'He won't catch us – we'll just have to come up with a way,' Grace said calmly.

Charlie turned to his wife. 'Something is odd about all of this, love. We might have only one opportunity to get him out of our lives for good – we have to take it.'

'I know.' Dymphna sighed. 'I'm just wary of him…'

'We all are, but that's how he's got away with everything for so long.' Tilly threw her hands up in frustration. 'We have to stand up to him, Dymphna. If not now, then when?'

Dymphna sighed again, resigned. 'Well, Father Lehane always says both the eight and the ten o'clock Sunday Mass, and Mrs Coughlan always attends the ten.'

Charlie ran his hand over his stubbled chin, deep in thought. 'So tomorrow morning they'd both be out.'

'But the canon would still be in the house,' Grace said.

'The housekeeper serves his cooked breakfast at ten to ten, and he eats it while the curate says Mass.' Dymphna knew the workings of the parochial house from her days as housekeeper. 'He's a creature of habit, so he does the same thing every week. He does the midday Mass on Sundays and only does one or two during the week. Father Lehane has to do all the others.'

'Well, how about we ask someone to go and look for him to go on a sick call?' Tilly suggested.

'He wouldn't come when summoned,' Dymphna shook her head. 'When I worked there, he used to tell me that he was not ever available for sick calls. If the curates couldn't do it, then it didn't get done, unless it was someone very well-off or influential. Poor Father Iggy was different, dropped everything if someone needed him, and so does Father Lehane. The canon might visit a sick parishioner at some point, but only when it suits him.'

'And even if we could lure him out, how do we get in?' Tilly stood and tapped her fingers on the mantelpiece, her mind mulling it over.

This was for the locals of Knocknashee to figure out, so Richard stayed quiet. They were trying to speak in English for his benefit, but they lapsed into Irish more often than not, so he was at a complete loss. He liked hearing them speak in that language normally, when tensions were reduced. It was beautiful and melodic, and Grace often told him how it was so much easier to express oneself in Irish because there were so many words for the same thing, each one with a slightly different meaning. But even she conceded it was a difficult language to master. Eloise, the natural linguist, admitted defeat early on, so if she couldn't figure it out, there was little hope for him.

'The key is under the Infant of Prague beside the back door.' Dymphna slipped back into English after seeing his face and shot him an apologetic glance. 'At least Kit Gallagher told me where they kept it when I took over, and so I assume it's still there. He has a very ornate desk with drawers in the drawing room in the front, and there are a bunch of small keys in his bedside locker, which might be something to do with it. But I always wondered how it opened, because whenever I polished it, I could never see a keyhole. It must be there somewhere. He didn't like anyone in his study, so I was rarely in there.'

Tilly's eyes were bright. 'I have it.'

'Go on,' Grace urged.

'Well, the only thing he loves is that Bentley, so how about I go up, knock on the door and say someone must have scratched it accidentally, that I noticed it when passing with the pony and trap while delivering my vegetables to O'Donoghue's before Mass. That'll bring him quick enough.'

'That would draw him out,' Grace said, 'but when he finds no scratch, he'll just go back in, won't he?'

'Oh, it will be scratched all right...don't worry about that,' Tilly said with a wicked smile.

Grace frowned. 'He'll be apoplectic, Tilly.'

'And I'll say I saw a car driving through a few minutes earlier, so I'll suggest he go straight to Sergeant Keane to report it. It will be some tourist, no doubt, this time of year, and if he goes now, there's a chance the sergeant will catch them and they'll have to pay for the damage. A dark-blue Ford, I think it was, and the scratch will have some dark-blue paint…'

'I don't know, Tilly…' Grace was worried, Richard could tell.

'Have you a better idea? Revenge and retribution are the only things that move him, so let's use them to our advantage. Charlie and Dymphna can be on the way up to Mass as well and say they saw the car too.'

'That's no problem.' The postman nodded.

'So we're doing this?' Richard asked.

'Breaking and entering? Yes, we are,' Grace replied. 'Right, so Richard, can you do this with me?'

Silence descended once more. Richard knew what everyone was thinking. Grace would not be fast enough to get in and out of the house, but nobody wanted to say it.

'Grace, please don't get upset at what I'm about to say.' Charlie stood and took her hands in his. 'But I think Richard should do this alone, for two reasons. Firstly, searching the house will have to be quick, and secondly, I think you should be with Tilly outside so you can't be blamed afterwards if something goes wrong.'

Richard hated the look that crossed Grace's face. Defeat. 'I don't agree, Charlie,' he interjected. 'I need Grace with me, and she's as well able as anyone else. She knows the layout of the house, I don't, and I need her quick thinking as well. We won't have much time, and we can cover more with two of us. Besides, what else can the canon do to her at this stage?'

Grace shot him a grateful smile and his heart sang. Regardless of what happened next, they were a team.

'How will you know what to look for?' Tilly asked.

'We won't, I guess. We'll look for the key in his nightstand that Dymphna mentioned, and we'll try to open the locked desk – I guess that's the best idea? But we'll search as much as we can and hope. If we can't find anything, then we'll have to come up with another plan, but for now this is the best we've got.'

Grace nodded. 'He's right. Richard can go upstairs for the key, have a look around, and I'll search downstairs. We'll try to get into the desk. That's all we can do.'

'It might be best if I'm not seen,' Richard said, 'so it feels like a regular Sunday, everyone doing what they normally would.'

'Absolutely. The less things look out of the ordinary, the better. We can make up a bed for you, Richard – the children can sleep in with us,' Charlie offered.

'Eloise left a camera here, a spare one. I think it's fairly easy to use. Maybe you should take it in case you find something,' Tilly suggested. 'If you take a photograph, we'll have proof.'

'Good idea – can you bring it tomorrow?'

'We can.' Tilly looked at Grace, who nodded.

Richard tried to hide the look of disappointment on his face. He knew there was not much space in Charlie's cottage, but even to be under the same roof as Grace for one night would be something he could only dream of. But of course she would go back to Tilly's.

Seámus stirred. Dymphna put him to her breast, and he fed contentedly. Richard watched as Charlie gazed at them both with such love. He'd lost so much in his life, the poor man, and Richard was happy he was finally getting some peace.

Richard remembered his father's words: *First of all, marry the right person.* Maybe there was more than one right person? Charlie had loved his first wife dearly by all accounts, and now he was besotted with Dymphna and little Seámus. But for himself he knew the truth. There was only one woman for him, and she was sitting just a few feet away. But what to do about it? It was tempting just to blurt it all out. She looked so frail, beaten down by life's blows – would he be taking advantage of her despair to declare his feelings? And of course she was a moral person, so her first question would be 'What about Pippa?' And of course she'd be right. *No.* He'd thought long and hard while on the many modes of transport he'd had to take to get here. Before he could even think about talking to Grace, he needed to go to London, see Pippa, be honest and end that relationship gently and respectfully. One step at a time.

CHAPTER 35

The canon's face was like thunder the following morning, as he had to open his own front door because both Father Lehane and Mrs Coughlan were at Mass. His displeasure was compounded to see Tilly there.

'What do you want?' he asked rudely.

'Good morning, Canon, I was just on my way to drop some vegetables to O'Donoghue's before Mass and I saw a scratch on your car. I think I saw it happen actually. Mr and Mrs McKenna were walking up too, when a blue car, I think it was a Ford, came too close and it scraped yours.' Tilly's face was a picture of innocent concern.

'What?' The canon's brow furrowed and he barged past her, almost pinning her to the wall. He was so focussed on his precious car, he didn't bother to look up. Richard and Grace were waiting in the stand of trees beside the parochial house, just in earshot.

Charlie, Dymphna, and now Nancy and two of the young O'Sheas were examining the long scratch on the wing of the Bentley, which showed all the signs of being hit by a blue car.

'Who saw it?' The canon demanded. 'Apart from her?' He tipped his head in Tilly's direction.

'I did. I was outside our house – waiting for my wife. Canon, there was a man and woman in the car, not locals, they drove on – maybe they didn't know they hit you?' Charlie suggested mildly.

Tilly suggested they go for Sergeant Keane, because whoever did it should have to pay. She said she'd heard of a similar thing happening in Killarney to another car and it had cost five pounds to fix.

Sure everyone was preoccupied by the car, Grace and Richard ran across the lawn, found the key under the Infant of Prague statue, and let themselves in the back door of the parochial house. Richard had Eloise's camera in a case, the strap around his neck. He pointed to the staircase and she nodded. He climbed the stairs two at a time while she remained downstairs. The polished tiles of the hallway and dark wood panelling were as she remembered from her last visit. The door to the kitchen at the end of the hallway was open so she could see that it was neat and tidy and smelled of baking and washing-soda crystals. There was nothing untoward or odd there.

She could hear Richard moving upstairs and then his footsteps coming down as they met in the hallway. He dangled the small brass key on a ring on one finger. They could still hear the muffled carry-on outside over the scrape but they had to act fast. They entered the drawing room together, careful to stay away from the windows that looked down the street where everyone had gathered.

The desk was in the corner, and Grace recognised it as Gothic. It was made of a highly polished dark wood, almost black. Set on the desk, perhaps part of it, it was hard to tell, were a pair of cabinets at either end, and on top of them, forming an arch, was ornate woodwork with carved designs; it must have measured eight feet wide by two deep. Under the desk was one long drawer the full width of the piece, with a set of four drawers going to the floor on either side of where a person would sit. It was very ecclesiastical – she'd seen similar in sacristies, and another once when she took a school trip to the bishop's palace in Killarney. There were no visible handles on the drawers or doors. Dymphna was right – there didn't seem to be a keyhole.

'We have the key, but how do we open it?' Richard whispered as he gazed at it perplexed.

Grace racked her brain to remember what Paudie had said about desks like this. They should have consulted him before now; if only they'd thought of it. Poor Paudie had been so interested in telling her, but she'd only been half listening. She forced herself to focus.

'Paudie had a book about this sort of thing, and I think to access the side drawers, the long one below needs to be removed, then you reach into the cavity and there are concealed handles or latches or something inside?' she whispered back.

'But how do we open the long drawer?' Richard crouched on his hunkers, trying to see if there was a way to open it from under the desk.

His bulk seemed to take up the entire space, so she placed her hand on his arm. 'Let me try, I'm smaller.' He moved aside to let her get closer.

The cornice around the top of the desk was carved with a rope pattern, and Grace felt along the length of it, underside of the wood, something Paudie had said coming back to her. Sure enough, hidden in one of the carved embellishments on a corner, on the overhanging underside, was a small keyhole.

'Found it. Give me the key,' she said, holding out her hand. Richard gave it to her.

After fiddling for a moment to fit it in, she turned it. The lock clicked fully, and the whole drawer, eight feet long and about six inches high, opened and sprang forward enough that they could pull it out. There were several buff-coloured envelopes inside. The other drawers and the cupboards on top remained locked.

'There must be another locking mechanism,' she whispered, trying to remember all the clever tricks cabinetmakers of old had come up with. She wished Paudie was here now.

She couldn't kneel on account of her steel, so she beckoned Richard over from where he stood shielded by the wall. Glancing out the window through the net curtains she could see that the sergeant was on his way across the street, and more people had gathered, though Mass should have started by now.

'Pull the long drawer out, then reach into that space, feel with your fingers for anything, a knot or a joint or something, and press it.'

The conversation outside continued, and she could hear the indistinct muffle of voices. Her heart pounded. The canon was only twenty yards away – he could turn and be back in the house within a minute or two.

Richard did as she told him, placing the long drawer across the arms of a chair to the right of the desk. He knelt down and reached into the opening, his cheek pressed to the wood of the desk. Then he smiled as the drawers and the two cabinets clicked and opened slightly. 'There was a button or something at the very back,' he whispered.

Grace pulled the drawers on the right as he opened the ones on the left. But they were both struck dumb as the drawers revealed their contents.

On Grace's side there were rolls of bank notes, stacked neatly three rolls deep in each of the four drawers, and Richard's side held envelopes containing several sheets of paper, which he extracted. The heavy cream paper with a black border had an eagle insignia on the letterhead, wings outstretched, standing atop a swastika. In the last drawer on Richard's side, face down, was the framed photograph of Alfie O'Hare and Constance, stolen from Mary O'Hare's mantelpiece. Why would the canon take that if he wasn't up to something? Richard took Eloise's camera out of the case to take photos.

Grace turned towards the window. She could hear the voices outside still, the Canon was furious and gesticulating wildly to Sergeant Keane, but any moment he might storm back. 'We can't delay, we need to do this now.'

She went to the window, opened it and shouted at the top of her lungs. 'Sergeant Keane, come quickly, please, come now!'

Sergeant Keane was standing by the Bentley. By now almost everyone who had been on the way to Mass was gathered around the priest's damaged car.

The crowd turned, their faces registering astonishment at seeing Miss Fitz screaming out the window of the parochial house.

The canon turned then, his face ashen. 'Get out of my house this instant, you impertinent young woman!' he bellowed.

'Come quickly, Sergeant, please, just you...' she shouted, ignoring the priest who was making for the house but was stopped by Charlie, Nancy and several other parishioners.

The sergeant did as she asked, and Richard went to let him in the front door.

'I demand you stop this instantly, you have no right...' The canon was incandescent with fury, but the crowd stood firmly between him and the house, and every time he went to get around them, someone moved, making it impossible.

The sergeant entered the drawing room and stood for a moment, taking in the sight of all the money. In the buff folders that Richard had just opened were typed letters, several maps and some black-and-white photographs of the coastline.

'Canon Rafferty is the spy, Sergeant. It was never Tilly or Eloise. He was the one who told the detective from Dublin that Eloise confessed to him that she was working for the Germans. It was a lie – Eloise has never been to confession. It was him all along.' Grace was surprised at how clear and strong her voice was.

The sergeant, once he'd assessed that Grace was probably right, sprang to action. He shut the window, and gestured that they should leave ahead of him. 'Right, let's all get out and lock the door. The Dublin team will want to search this room, so we'll leave it as we found it. We don't need the whole parish traipsing through for a nose around.' Grace and Richard followed him out as he secured the windows and turned the key that was in the lock, dropping it into his pocket.

The crowd were gathered, all facing the parochial house in astonishment. Grace, Richard and the Sergeant standing on the front step when from behind the gathered crowd came the sound of several failed attempts at ignition of the Bentley. The canon had taken the opportunity while everyone was watching the goings-on at his house to try to get away. The engine was not cooperating, however, and Sergeant Keane walked back to the car and opened the driver's door.

Grace and Richard joined the people of Knocknashee, all agog.

'Please come with me now, Canon,' he said quietly. You could hear a pin drop.

'How dare you? I'll do no such thing…' His sibilant hiss was even more pronounced with his indignation.

'It would be better if you came of your own accord, Canon,' the guard said reasonably, 'but if I have to forcibly take you into custody, I will.'

The canon weighed up his options, and realising he had none, got out of the car and walked, with as much dignity as he could muster, across the street to the barracks, one step ahead of the sergeant.

Nobody spoke. Sergeant Keane must have placed him in the only cell there was, because a minute later, he was back.

'If everyone could disperse now, that would be best. I'll be notifying my superiors, and this matter will be dealt with in due course.'

Realising the normally friendly and avuncular guard meant business, and that whatever had just happened was not a trivial matter, the crowd began to move. Outside the church Father Lehane had appeared to see what on earth was keeping his congregation – Mass should have started ten minutes ago.

Everyone walked up to the church, struck dumb by the shock of what they'd just witnessed, and Grace smiled as she saw Charlie take a spark plug out of Seámus's pram and slip it in his pocket. No wonder the Bentley didn't start.

CHAPTER 36

They both gave individual detailed statements. Grace included everything about Agnes and the babies in America and the canon's threats to her. She didn't mention what he said about Tilly or Odile. Sergeant Keane wrote their words verbatim.

He'd called on Eloise to translate the German documents, which she did willingly, and without him going into any detail, it would seem that they were damning in the extreme. There was no way the canon was going to wriggle out of this one. Grace knew the sergeant could have waited for the Dublin detectives to come and have the letters translated then, but Grace suspected he wanted to show that the powers of authority trusted Eloise and that she was on their side. He was fond of Tilly and it had been a kind thing to do, and Grace felt a wave of affection for him. Once everyone knew Eloise had helped in the investigation, any remaining clouds of doubt would surely dissipate.

Grace was at ease with him. The sergeant was a decent man who showed remarkable astuteness in when to apply the law and when to turn a blind eye. The whole peninsula was full of illegal poitín stills, for example, but so long as it was for personal use and people didn't get rowdy or start fights when drunk, he let well enough alone. But a man raising his hand to another, or worse, to a woman or child, or a person stealing from another, or trading on the black market to dodge the rationing, well, that person would feel the full force of the law.

'It's hard to believe, isn't it, Sergeant?' Grace asked when he closed the book and they were alone.

'Do you know what, Grace it is and it isn't,' the sergeant, a man she'd known since she was born, replied. 'At the time Miss Meier was arrested, the gang up in Dublin were convinced that someone was giving information – the attacks on our waters are just too precise to be flukes. The coastline here is treacherous, as we know, but they're able to navigate it. That would be impossible without detailed local information. They have other evidence too, intercepted incriminating correspondence and so on, so he's just the last piece of the puzzle. The commissioner knew someone here was working for Hitler, and they were right. They just got the wrong person last time. The fact that the canon identified Eloise Meier and hid it by using his position as a priest won't work for him either.'

'Will he get away with it, do you think? I know I made a big scene by screaming – maybe I should have been more discreet – but so often I thought I had him and he got away. I didn't want to risk it. And if he'd have come back and found us there in his house...'

The sergeant shook his head and lowered his voice to a murmur. 'Between you, me and the wall, you did exactly the right thing. It's public now too, happened in full view of everyone, so there's no hushing it up – you know the way stories spread. He's slippery, but there's no getting away from this, it's too serious. Watch now what will happen. The whole Church, from the bishop up, will wash their hands of him. They won't go down with him.'

'I hope so.'

'And I'd be getting ready to get back into your school too if I was you.' The sergeant smiled broadly. 'My Mairead will be leaping around the kitchen if that happens. She hates your man Sheehan, and that other fella Nolan is as bad.'

'Well, I don't know about that. Francis Sheehan is officially the headmaster now, I presume. He and the Nolan man were installed by the Department of Education, so I don't know how easy it would be.'

The look on the sergeant's face was enigmatic, but he said nothing.

'I'm staying with Tilly, but Richard will probably have to leave – he needs to get back to London.'

'That's fine, I have all I need, but he left an address so we can contact him if needs be.'

He accompanied her out to the public area where Richard was waiting. 'Good man yourself, Richard. You did a good thing today.' Sergeant Keane shook his hand.

'Thank you, Sergeant,' Richard said as they made to leave.

''Tis we should be thanking you, Mr Lewis. You've potentially saved lives by doing what you did. Yourself and Miss Fitz here make a right good pair of detectives.' He smiled.

Grace and Richard walked back to Charlie and Dymphna's. Tilly was gone to the farm to get Odile and Mary, who would be disgusted she missed the comeuppance of the canon, no doubt.

Knocknashee was buzzing. Nobody liked the canon, but to have him exposed as some kind of criminal… The details were sketchy, and in the vacuum, Grace just knew rumours and gossip were flourishing. She also knew that nothing they made up or surmised could be as damning as the truth.

Grace and Richard had assured the sergeant that only they, Charlie, Dymphna and Tilly knew the full truth and that they wouldn't say a word. He was relieved, because a full investigation, or indeed a reopening of the original investigation, would be underway within hours and the authorities from Dublin would not be pleased to discover when they arrived in Knocknashee that the dogs on the street had all the details, public as the event was.

They had lunch with the McKennas, speaking in a kind of code so the children wouldn't understand.

'It's a lovely day,' Dymphna said as they finished their dessert of stewed apples and cream. 'Why don't we leave Charlie and Paudie to the wash-up and yourself and Richard go for a stroll?'

Grace was glad of an opportunity to spend some time alone with him.

'If you're sure, then we will, I think. Grace? What do you say?'

'I'll just get my cardigan.' As she went to the hallstand, she could hear Richard complimenting Dymphna on the meal and telling Paudie that he'd been to a lot of places and had never met a kid as smart as him. Kate was already smitten because she'd shown him how to knit before lunch and now he could do it. She spent most of the meal sitting on his lap, gazing at him in adoration. She kept asking him to say things because she loved listening to his accent. Grace smiled. Richard had that effect on people – they opened up to him because he was so warm and kind. It wasn't put-on or fake; he was genuinely interested in people.

He offered her his arm, and they made their way along the main street. She often forgot how tall and bulky he was. She felt like a leprechaun beside him and told him so; he laughed and said she was too pretty to be a leprechaun.

As they approached the school, several cars had arrived and were parked outside the new garda station. Before the war, the guard's house served as the local station, but the Emergency saw the hasty construction of a barracks on the main street. The detectives and senior officers from Killarney initially, she assumed, and soon the top brass from Dublin would be there too.

As they walked they tried to absorb what had happened.

'Can we go to the beach?' Richard asked.

'Of course, if you like.' Grace looked up at him. 'I can't wait to tell Paudie that his information about locks and furniture was so helpful.'

'I know. Without that information we would have had no idea how to even start to break into that desk.'

'Paudie doesn't do things by half measures. If he learns something, he learns it thoroughly. We have a professor on our hands with that boy, that's for sure,' Grace said with a chuckle.

'Was his father really smart?' Richard asked, and then blushed. 'Not that Dymphna isn't, I didn't mean that…'

Grace pealed with laughter. 'Don't worry, I won't tell her you said that. And anyway she's always marvelling where he got it. Tommy was a lovely man and Dymphna is well able, but I wouldn't say they were exceptionally clever, just normal level, you know?'

Richard shook his head in wonderment. 'This morning as I was shaving, Paudie was sitting on the toilet. He asked me if I knew about honey bees, and I said I knew they made honey but not much else, and he went on to explain how they're known for being interesting insects due to the fact that they live in social colonies with a strict hierarchy.'

He grinned and went on. 'Apparently, they can communicate with each other, so when a worker bee locates flowers that are a plentiful source of pollen that they process to make honey, she alerts her fellow workers to the location using what's called a waggle dance. This dance tells other bees everything from how far away the flower is, to which direction the bees need to fly in order to reach the flower, to the bee's relationship to the sun.' Richard laughed. 'The kid's a genius, and he's so interesting. I could listen to him all day, with his cute Irish accent. And English isn't even his first language.'

'Well, I don't know about that – you're the one with the accent,' Grace teased, feeling lighter than she had for weeks.

'Oh, faith and begorrah, sure 'tis a fine soft day we do be havin'.' Richard did a terrible version of an Irish brogue.

'Never, ever, ever try that again…' Grace rolled her eyes in mock horror. 'And we don't sound like that.'

'Ya'll sure do to me,' he replied with a wink.

'Would you go on out of that. I'm the one with the accent, and you here with your "y'alls" and "ma'am this" and "ma'am that"…' She nudged him playfully. 'You know, the first time I heard you speak, I thought you were putting it on – you sounded like a cowboy in the films – and I was going to giggle until I realised that was how you really spoke.'

He pretended to be horrified. 'Don't let my mother hear you say that. We were sent to elocution lessons so we'd sound cultured – when you come to Georgia, you'll see what I mean. My father is from Texas originally, and he sounds much more Southern than my mother likes, and she never allowed us to use Southernisms. We always did –

our housekeeper Esme is so funny with all her Southern sayings – but never in Mother's earshot.' He grimaced, and Grace wondered what kind of woman could treat her wonderful son so coldly.

'But when I came here last time, I was the same – I was sure you were playing with me. When I read your letters, I guess I read them in an American accent, so it was a shock to hear you speak. But at least I can understand you, because to be honest, I only understand about half of what Charlie says and almost nothing of Mrs O'Hare.'

'Really, why?' Grace stopped and looked up at him, shielding her eyes from the sun with her hand.

'Because what you hear and what my Georgian ears hear are two different things. We don't move too fast in the South. We like the shade and lazy days, and we talk slow. But over here it's like you are all against the clock. You need to get the words out as fast as you can, and when you all speak Irish normally, and only English to me, it can be a bit…'

'I know. We don't really like speaking English and so we make little effort to learn it properly. We all can converse of course, it's unavoidable, but I know what you mean. People here speak English carelessly, peppering their speech with Irish words and syntax that must be hard to follow. I suppose when we were occupied, it was a way of communicating that kept the British in the dark, so it's not entirely accidental.'

They walked in companionable silence for a while. The children were playing in the green, several of them up the tree, more playing in the sandbox Declan had made for them two years ago. She knew she and Richard were being observed, but people were letting them have some time alone and she appreciated it.

'So you reckon you can get your job back?' Richard asked eventually. 'You were just replaced, but you can write to the education office or whatever it's called and explain, right?'

Grace sighed. 'I don't know. I doubt it, but I haven't ever got any correspondence from them. It's normally the chairman of the board, which is the canon, or whoever is parish priest, who does the hiring and firing.'

Unlike the others who were keeping their distance, Biddy O'Donoghue was dying to talk to Grace, she could tell. The woman had spotted them out the window of her shop and was making a beeline for them.

'Grace, what in the name of God...' said Biddy as she came out of her shop and stood beside them, watching the cars from Dublin drive past.

Grace smiled, ignoring the question. 'Mrs O'Donoghue, this is my friend Richard Lewis. He's from America.'

'Very pleased to meet you, Mr Lewis.' Biddy looked Richard up and down, clearly liking what she saw. Her husband wasn't the only one with a roving eye, it would seem.

'It's very nice to meet you too, ma'am,' Richard replied, and Grace could tell his accent was melting the shopkeeper.

'We're just going to the strand for a walk, so we better keep going.' Grace squeezed Richard's arm so he would know she didn't want to get stuck in conversation. The town would talk of nothing else for years, but today she just wanted to spend some time with Richard.

'Oh, I was just wondering what the sergeant said about the carry-on in the parochial house?' Biddy said, bold as brass.

'Oh, that's top secret, I'm afraid, ma'am, highly classified. To quote Sherlock Holmes, we could tell you but then we'd have to kill you.'

Grace stifled a giggle.

Biddy opened her mouth to reply but closed it again, nonplussed. Richard and Grace walked on.

They crossed the strand as the evening sun was still high in the sky. It was warm, and they clambered over the rocks right beside where she'd thrown in the bottle all those years ago. The tide was out, and the honey-sweet scent of furze mingled with salty sea air as Grace turned her face to the sun, feeling its warmth.

'Well, Miss Fitzgerald, here we are again.' Richard sat beside her on the big flat rock where she and Tilly usually had their picnics, and where she and Richard had sat last time. The cerulean blue of the sky was reflected on the calm sea, and small puffball clouds scudded overhead. A pair of otters watched from just a few yards off the shore, their big brown eyes doleful. High up on the cliff, cute chubby puffins were industrious.

'We are indeed, Mr Lewis.' Grace smiled. 'We'll have to stop meeting like this.'

They sat in silence for a long moment, watching the tiny waves ripple on the sand. Overhead, gulls wheeled, waiting for the fishermen to come home and gut the catch, and the pink *rabhán* was blooming in the rocks all along the coast.

'So finally we nailed him?' Richard said.

'Seems so, thanks to you. You saved me, again. I don't know what angel was smiling on me the day I threw that letter into the sea, but I'm so grateful for it.' She paused. 'You've become very important to me.'

'You're very important to me too,' he said quietly. 'I can't talk to anyone the way I can talk to you.'

'You better not let Pippa hear you say that.' She gave a small laugh.

'Even Pippa,' he said. He picked at a piece of lichen on the rock.

He'd written about personal things before, his parents, Sarah and Jacob, Miranda his old girlfriend, and just a week or two ago, he'd written a bit about what happened to him in Indonesia. But she assumed he told Pippa everything also.

'My parents are getting divorced. My father wrote to tell me.'

Grace was shocked but tried not to show it. Marriage was for life here, no matter what. There was no such thing as divorce.

'Oh, Richard, I'm sorry to hear that. Are you upset about it?'

He inhaled and then exhaled through pursed lips. 'Not really. It sounds bad, but if you met my mother… Well, you know, I told you about her. She's kind of cold.'

'Well, I'm sure they know what's best,' Grace heard herself say lamely. In Ireland; marriage was for life, and that was all there was to it.

'I guess. My father wrote and told me things he would never say to me in person. We don't really have a close relationship, but since I came over here, he writes a lot and…I've gotten to know him better than in all the years I lived in the same house.'

'How have Sarah and Nathan taken it?' she asked.

He shrugged. 'No idea. I haven't discussed it with them. You're the only person I've told.'

She looked at him then, and he held her gaze. Neither of them spoke. There was too much to say; it was hard to know where to even begin.

'I need to go back to London, Grace,' he said eventually.

'Of course you do. Pippa will be waiting and...'

Something crossed his face, a hesitation, a doubt. It was fleeting and gone before she could decide for sure. It was as if he was going to say something and then thought better of it.

'The sergeant offered to get me a ride to Cork with one of the other officers. He said they'd be going at four or so, and I'll catch a boat from there.'

'So it's goodbye again.' Grace couldn't keep the sadness from her voice. 'I wish we had more time.'

'So do I. But it's just for now – there are some things I need to see to. But I'll write very soon and we'll see each other again, I know we will.'

Grace just nodded, blinking back tears. She should ask about Pippa, be enthusiastic and happy for him, but she couldn't do it. She should be elated – Canon Rafferty was finally gone, and if Sergeant Keane was right, they wouldn't see him for a very long time, if ever.

She loved this place. It was her home, and she had wonderful friends around her. She loved her job, and maybe somehow she could get it back, though it was unlikely. If she was to return, it would be a source of great happiness to her pupils and their families, but what if she wanted something else? She knew what it was, who it was, but she couldn't say. Unbelievably, this man, who she loved with all of her heart, was right beside her, real and breathing. The temptation to speak was enormous, but if she did, how foolish would she feel when he told her that he was in love with Pippa? He was leaving, back to his life and his future, and she should send him on his way with a friendly face. It was the right thing to do.

She glanced at her wristwatch, a present from the Warringtons for her twenty-first birthday. ' If he said four, we'd better get a move on.'

'Sure. I guess we should.' He stood and offered her his hand. She took it, savouring the feel of her hand in his. As they walked across the sand, he kept holding it, not offering his arm as he always did. It was probably wrong to walk hand in hand with another girl's boyfriend, but it might well be the very last time she would ever get to do it and so she didn't pull away.

He'd probably be a married man next time she saw him, and she had her pride. She would not be the poor spinster cripple hanging out of some other woman's husband. The thought made her cheeks burn in shame. No, that would not be her. She didn't need or want anyone's pity.

'Grace, are you OK? You've gone very quiet.'

'Yes, fine.' She smiled brightly. 'It's been a long day, and I'm not used to so much excitement.'

'Are you tired?' he asked.

'I didn't sleep well last night, worried about today, so yes, I suppose I am.'

'I think every kid in Knocknashee is going to be praying tonight that Miss Fitz comes back, and Mrs Worth too.'

'It won't be that simple, unfortunately. Will you write about all of this?'

Richard thought. 'It's a fascinating story, but I wouldn't be allowed to until there was a trial, and I doubt it will be held in public – under the emergency powers act, they won't have to – so probably not.'

'Am I wrong to be a little relieved?' she asked.

'No, but even if I could write about it, I would only do it with your permission, so if you don't want me to even mention it to anyone, then of course I won't. I understand – you have to live here, so it would be difficult...'

'And you get to go off and have adventures,' she heard herself say; she'd assumed it would remain a thought.

'You could too, if you wanted to,' Richard said quietly.

'In a war, a woman with polio, no resources and no family? I doubt it, Richard.' She sighed.

'I don't know about that, it all depends on how you look at it. The war has changed things. It allowed me to leave Savannah, to travel to places I could never have imagined, even in a million years, and look how your life too has changed. So anything is possible, Grace.'

She smiled. She didn't want to disagree, but the truth was that, yes, life could change, and hers had by the death of her sister and her friendship with him and her marriage to Declan. But unlike him she had no money, and anyway the polio was stopping her.

No matter what Hugh or Richard or Tilly said, she knew her options were limited. She had fewer choices. So she would wait for the letter that said the man she loved was married to someone else, someone with two working legs.

The town was bathed in buttery sunlight, the breeze warm on their skin and the church bells rang out the time of 4 p.m. all over the bay. In every house for miles around tonight, the conversation would be about the events of this morning before Mass and speculation as to what would happen next.

'Will Tilly come to collect you?' Richard asked as they reached the station. The detectives from Cork were chatting to the sergeant inside, probably waiting for Richard.

'She will. I'll wait at Charlie's until she's ready.'

'Would you like me to go in with you?' Richard offered.

Yes, yes, I would. And I want you to never leave again. I want you to take my hand, I want you to kiss me, and then I want to sleep in your arms and never, ever let you go, because never in my entire life have I loved anyone as much as I love you.

She forced the thoughts away for fear her mouth would betray her. 'No, I'll be fine, and you'd better get going. They look like they're ready to get on the road, away from this mad place.' She forced a smile. 'Say hello to Sarah and Jacob and of course Pippa for me, and thank you again, Richard. The words seem so inadequate, but...'

He turned to face her, but then gave a glance to the right, where a cluster of locals, Neilus Collins, Biddy O'Donoghue, Pádraig O Sé,

Bridie Keohane – who had never really forgiven Grace for marrying Declan – and a few others had suddenly found the corner of the schoolyard fascinating. They were under surveillance.

'I'll write from the boat. And I'll mail it when we dock.' He looked suddenly very sad. 'I hate to leave you again.'

'Ready when you are, Mr Lewis,' a detective said as he got into the driver's seat, his partner sitting in beside him.

'I'll be fine, especially now.' She took his hand to shake it formally. 'Take care, Richard, it was wonderful to see you. And I'll write tonight too. There's too much to discuss now, especially with the audience,' she said quietly.

He let go of her hand and gave her a hug then, brief but tight. She stood and waved as he got into the back seat of the waiting car and drove out of her life again.

CHAPTER 37

Two days later Grace lay in bed in the farmhouse. She could hear Tilly downstairs with Odile, who was screaming about something. The little girl was adorable but strong-willed, as was Tilly, and often it was a right set-to between the two of them. Grace would normally smile at the battle of wills, but today she felt so flat and low, she could hardly face the idea of getting out of bed.

Richard had returned to London. Yes, the canon was in custody, but that didn't give her any joy. The man was gone for now, but something told her he'd be back – he always was. Richard was probably in Pippa's arms now. Back to his life. And while he said they would see each other again, how could they? The war was raging, and if he had an opportunity to go anywhere, it would be either home to America or somewhere else to report on the war. He'd made such a huge effort to come here, to get rid of the canon for her, and she would be eternally grateful, but he had no further reason to ever come to Knocknashee again and she had no cause to go to him.

Maybe it was time for her to move on. Go to Cork, take the job in the hospital. Everyone assumed that she'd get her job back here, but that wasn't how it worked. Francis Sheehan was a man, and he was more qualified than she was, and there was no reason to dismiss him.

He and Nolan were perfect on paper, even if they were horrible to the children; there was no reason for the Department of Education to want a change.

She turned over, her leg still aching after Sunday's long walk.

'Grace.' Tilly's voice carried up the stairs.

She groaned. She didn't feel like talking, even to Tilly.

'Grace!' Louder now.

'Yes?' she called down.

'Can you come down please? You have a visitor!'

She felt vexed. Tilly should know she had no interest in anyone coming to poke their nose into the business in the parochial house. She didn't want to see anyone. It was too late, though. She could hear voices downstairs, so she had to go down. She dressed as quickly as she could, her mop of red curls unruly as she had no brush to hand. She didn't care anyway. Let whoever it was take her as they found her.

She strapped her calliper on and hobbled downstairs, opening the kitchen door. To her surprise Father Lehane was standing there.

He was puce-red and staring at his shoes as Tilly tried to get Odile to get dressed. The toddler was naked, and the poor priest didn't know where to look. He was nice if very innocent, and he worked so hard for the parish, taking on all of the slack left by the canon's laziness.

'Hello, Father Lehane,' she said, casting a quick quizzical glance at Tilly, who shrugged as she trapped Odile under the table and dragged her, roaring, up the stairs to get dressed.

'Hello, Miss Fitz,' the priest said, and blushed even redder. 'I hope I'm not disturbing you, but I wondered if I might have a word?'

'Of course,' she said, over the sound of Tilly negotiating loudly with Odile upstairs. Mary was gone down to Dr Ryan to see if he could do anything for the pain in her ankle. She was a healer and people came to her for all sorts of remedies, but she was a big believer in Dr Ryan too. They often consulted each other, and sometimes Dr Ryan would send patients to Mary and vice versa. 'How can I help you, Father?'

'Well' – he looked at his shoes again – 'I...ah...I went to see the bbishop this morning, and I explained the situation as best I understood it, about Sunday and everything…'

Grace failed to see what this had to do with her. 'I told Sergeant Keane all I know, Father…'

'Oh, yes, and I… Well, that will be dealt with in due course, I'm sure, but I…well, I went to him to ask him if I had his permission to reinstate you in the school and in your home.'

Grace swallowed, and tried to form a response, her mind racing. Father Lehane was nice, but he'd never shown any kind of initiative in all the time he'd been there. He'd been bullied by the canon, of course, but she genuinely never thought he had it in him.

'You see, in the absence of Canon Rafferty, I'm the stand-in parish priest, and the bishop gave me his blessing to do just that, so I went to Mr Sheehan and Mr Nolan an hour ago and relieved them of their duties. School hasn't started back yet so there's no disruption. They'll be gone by the end of the week, so if you're willing, Miss Fitz, and Mrs Worth too of course, to come back to the school, the parish would very much welcome that.'

Grace tried to process this. 'And Francis Sheehan and the other man are willing to go? Just like that?' She raised a sceptical eyebrow.

'Well, not really, but they have no choice. They were preparing for the school year but I told him to drop the keys of your house to the parochial house by 5 p.m. on Saturday coming, and if there is any issue, I will speak to Sergeant Keane, because after that time they would be trespassing.'

Grace was astonished. This was fighting talk from the normally timid-as-a-mouse curate. 'But what about the Department of Education?'

'I checked. They never processed the change of personnel, so as far as they're concerned, you are still the headmistress.' He made eye contact with her then for the first time. 'That's if you're still willing to be?'

Grace blinked back a tear. 'I am, thank you, Father.'

'No, it's we should be thanking you. The children love you, Miss Fitz, and the parents and everyone only ever sing your praises. I…I had a teacher like Francis Sheehan all through my early school years, and…well, it wasn't nice. I…I wanted something different for the children here, and I know they'll all be so relieved.' Grace could see how hard it was for him to get those words out, and how sincere he was. She felt a wave of affection for him. It was no small thing to do what he did.

'I'll move back home on Sunday, and Mrs Worth and I will be delighted to take up our posts when school starts again,' she said, relief flooding her body.

He nodded and gave her a shy smile. 'This is good news, very good news indeed.' He made for the door. 'I'm very glad to have you back, Miss Fitz.'

EPILOGUE

Her house when she went back reminded her of the way it was when Agnes was alive, austere, cold, unadorned. But with the help of her friends, she put all her throws and cushions and knick-knacks back, and soon it felt like home again. She had luxuriated in a hot bath – Charlie had plumbed it all back for her – and as she lay in the hot water she cried tears of relief, of grief, of loss and of pain. It felt good to let it all out. This was her life now, and while it didn't have Richard Lewis in it in any way but a distant friendship, she had her school and her home and that was important.

The children squealed with delight when the word got out after Father Lehane's visit and Sheehan and Nolan were booed by some of the braver children as they drove out of the village. Their return had been a horrible prospect for everyone, but now it was over. Grace longed to erase the fear for them, and she knew time and love and fun would do it. She and Eleanor had made a start by filling both classrooms with artwork, Sheehan had removed all the colour and joy from the school, and tonight there was to be an impromptu concert for all the parents and people of Knocknashee to see the children perform some songs. There was going to be tea afterwards and even a few biscuits donated by Biddy O'Donoghue and some sweets courtesy of Bríd. Everyone was looking forward to it.

There had been no word from the authorities on the situation with Canon Rafferty, but Eloise had come down from Dublin and had been warmly welcomed.

Even Pádraig O Sé had been his version of friendly. 'So you got away with it, did you, Fraulein?' he called from the door of his shop as she got off the bus.

Eloise just rolled her eyes as Tilly took her bag and put it on the trap pulled by Rua.

'Era, nobody thought you were a Nazi girl, you're too good-looking, and they're a desperate shower of knuckle draggers altogether…' He laughed.

'I suppose that's a compliment?' she replied.

'As close as you'll get to one from me anyway.' He'd waved and went back into his shop.

Charlie cycled up and rested his bike on the school wall, then walked into the playground with a bundle of letters, mostly for the school. She and Eleanor were sitting in the sun, taking a break from preparing the school for the concert.

'There's an old one in there. I'd say it went missing a good while back – that happens sometimes,' he said as he handed Grace the bundle. 'Yesterday, the McNamaras out Coiscéim got about seven letters at the same time from their daughter, you know the nun who's out on the missions, all posted ages ago.'

Grace leafed through them until she came to the old battered envelope. She recognised the writing as Richard's, but the stamps were American. Richard had been in England for almost two years now, so it really was an old one. She smiled. It would be nice to read what they were talking about back then. She slipped it in her pocket and carried on chatting to Charlie. 'You look tired, Charlie,' she said, concerned.

'Seámus has gone from sleeping all the time to not sleeping at all, the little rogue, so myself and Dymphna are worn out from him. Paudie asked us if we could make him a muzzle this morning as he was yawning over his breakfast, nobody is sleeping in our house if Lord Seámus isn't sleeping.' Charlie yawned himself. 'I'm getting too old for this caper, let me tell you.'

'Ah now, Charlie, if you can't do the time, don't do the crime.' Eleanor winked and they laughed. She was as local now as anyone, and even though she missed her husband terribly, life was so much easier for her and her daughters, especially now that she was reinstated.

''Tis too late now, Eleanor. I should have listened to your advice last year.' He chuckled. 'Come here, did you see there's a new fella over the Americans in Europe now, Roosevelt is after appointing him – Eisenhower his name is. They seem to think he's the right lad for the job, will take no more messing off that little runt Hitler.'

'Let's hope so. I know they say the tide is turning, but it could turn a bit faster, couldn't it?' Grace sighed. 'I know I should be praying for all the soldiers but I dreamt of a fruit cake last night, with icing and cherries and fruit and everything...'

'Oh, I'd love that, or a big creamy trifle, remember them, with fruit and sponge cake and jelly and cream...' He licked his lips. 'Maggie used to make beautiful trifle, God rest her.'

'Oh, I would just love a really strong cup of tea and a big – and I mean the size of a side plate – slab of chocolate...and a Sweet Afton gasper...' Eleanor said wistfully.

'I didn't know you smoked!' Grace said, shocked at her very proper friend.

Eleanor laughed. 'Oh, Grace, I wasn't always this sensible middle-aged mother of three. I had a wild side a hundred years ago.'

Charlie walked back to his bike. 'Myself and Dymphna will be asleep in the front row tonight at this rate,' he grumbled good-naturedly.

After a busy few hours of preparation, moving benches and setting up a little stage, the evening went off beautifully. Everyone enjoyed the refreshments and Biddy O'Donoghue was uncharacteristically generous, providing a plate of brack as well as two boxes of biscuits and three ounces of tea. Tilly dropped down some milk from the farm. Bríd spent the whole day making toffee apples. Admittedly each apple only had a small blob of caramel, as sugar was so hard to come by but nobody minded.

Father Lehane made a speech, to everyone's surprise, about how wonderful the children were, what lovely singing, and how proud he was of them all. As the parents all filed out of the largest classroom at the end of the evening, their children in tow, everyone looking forward to being back at school in a few weeks now the threat of Sheehan was gone. Life wasn't what she wanted it to be, but it wasn't that bad. She would be alone most likely for the rest of her life, but she had a good community and good friends. It was time to count her blessings and stop moping.

She locked up the school and crossed to her house, letting herself in. She stood and inhaled, the familiar smell steadying her. Dotted all over the house were her things, this was her home, where she belonged.

It was too late to have a bath, so she just went straight to bed, but as she undressed, she remembered the letter from Richard in her pocket. The day had been so busy, she'd forgotten about it.

She got into her nightie and pulled back the covers, settling down to read the old letter.

August 13, 1940

She realised it must be from just after he visited for the first time, bringing little Odile from France.

St. Simons Island, Georgia

Dear Grace,

I've written this and rewritten it around fifty times, so this time I'm just going to say what I feel and hope you don't run screaming.

Meeting you was wonderful. I loved it. You are everything I've dreamed and more, and I curse that bus for pulling me away so soon after I arrived in magical Knocknashee. I wish I'd had the guts to tell you that I love you and that meeting you in person was the best thing that ever happened to me.

I don't know how close you and Declan are—maybe you're only good friends. Or maybe I have no right to say these things, but I must. I love you, Grace. I've never felt about anyone in my whole life the way I do about you, and if you'd have me, I'd move heaven and earth for us to be together.

If you don't want that, I'll accept it and never mention it again, but please don't cut off our friendship. Just write back something cheerful, like you never got this letter at all.

Yours with all my love,

Richard

Over and over she read the words. How could this be? Of the dozens of letters they'd written, this was the one to go missing? This letter would have changed everything. She would never have married Declan. The realisation hit her like an icy wave, followed by a gut-churning sense of shame. How could that have been her first thought?

Richard loved her. Well, back two years ago he did. But so much had happened. She'd married Declan, and he died. And Richard was with Pippa now. They weren't engaged or anything, but they were living together. She tried not to be shocked by that, but she was really. American and British people had a different attitude to such matters, clearly.

What was she to do now? Should she mention it? What must he think? That she never replied because she didn't feel the same, so she was doing as he asked and not referring to it? Would it just be awkward and embarrassing to say anything at this stage?

Richard loved her. Romantically. He loved her. Two years ago. How could this be happening?

She couldn't tell him it arrived now. She would have to pretend she'd never seen the letter. There was no way she could admit she'd got it now, not now that he was with Pippa. He would write, tell her how he and Pippa were so happy and all of that, and she'd have to reply and say she was so glad for him. Just as he'd done when she told him about Declan.

She would have to hold the knowledge that they'd had a chance but never got to take it. And now they never would.

The End.

I really hope you enjoyed this latest visit to Knocknashee, and are looking forward to returning. The fifth book, Folded Corners, is available for pre-order and will be released in the summer of 2025.

IN THE MEANTIME, If you would like a sneak preview, read on!

* * *

Folded Corners
Knocknashee Story – Book 5

Chapter 1
London, England
August 1942

Richard suppressed a smile. Jacob could be very funny when he was furious, unintentionally of course, and Kirky had a way of winding him up that no other person had.

They were sitting in their apartment on a sunny Saturday morning. Richard had arrived back from Ireland three days ago. To his frustration and admittedly a bit of relief, he'd discovered Pippa had gone to Manchester. The munitions factory she worked at had another one up north, and the management had asked her to go up and train new recruits in a bullet-making process they'd recently adopted. She was an expert, it seemed.

He'd considered writing to her, but that was not a decent way to break off an engagement, and there was no way he could go up there right now.

Sarah read the telegram out loud again. 'Come to NYC. Be here by August 20. You're getting award. K.' She grinned. 'He's a piece of work, huh?'

'I wonder what award?' Richard mused. It was exciting, even if

Kirky's telegram was short on detail and even shorter on praise or congratulations.

'I think it's the Bustemer Award. I heard that anyway,' Jacob said.

'No way?' Richard almost spurted his coffee. 'The Bustemer? Are you serious?'

'That's what I heard from some of the guys from the AP. The piece we did on the Fall of Singapore was syndicated so often, apparently FDR even read it and called it important work in making the American people understand how critical our response is.'

'No kidding?' Richard beamed. Such recognition was sought-after by much more seasoned newspapermen than he or Jacob, so to win, if it was the Bustemer, would be amazing.

'No, but Kirky couldn't even say well done, or tell us what award. He couldn't stand for us to feel even a tiny bit proud of ourselves.' Jacob was pacing, his face in a scowl.

'It's just his way, you know what he's like. Not worth getting your knickers in a twist, as Pippa would say.' Sarah laughed as she made another big pot of coffee, which was in fact not coffee at all but roasted chicory and so disgusting he couldn't stand it.

'Sarah's right, Jacob. He was smirking as he sent it, you know he was. He's determined to not let us get too full of ourselves.' It didn't bother Richard as much that Kirky never praised them or gave them any credit, though a small bit of recognition would have been nice.

'We got the tickets sent to the UP office, only three unfortunately,' Sarah said. 'Ernie handed them to me as I was leaving. Not that Pippa could have come anyway with her work, but it would have been nice to show her New York City.' She sounded a bit disappointed that her friend wasn't to be included in the trip, but getting passage was extremely difficult. All non-essential travel was curtailed, but their press passes allowed them to move around far more than the civilian population. 'I suppose I should consider myself lucky to be included, considering it's you two getting the award.'

'Yeah, it's a pity about Pippa,' Richard heard himself say, and cringed inwardly at the lie. He was relieved. He would have to speak to her before he left, though. 'And as for you, you know Kirky has a soft spot for you. When do we sail?'

'Here's the thing, we need to go the day after tomorrow.' Sarah showed him the tickets. Sure enough, their passage was booked on a troop ship leaving Southampton in two days' time.

'But Pippa won't be back before we go, will she?'

Sarah shot him a look of sympathy, and another wave of guilt passed over him.

'She won't. She's there for another two weeks at least, and we'll be gone. You could send a telegram?'

'I guess.' He tried to figure this out. Going home at this point wasn't something he'd even considered; he needed to sort his life out. Much as he loved his home country, he wanted to get to the point where he could do the right thing with Pippa, face her and tell her the truth, and then...well, then he'd try to see Grace again. The very thought filled him with dread, and if he wound up alone, it was probably what he deserved, but he knew that he could no longer go on living a lie, that was for sure.

'Hey, Richard, I had an idea. How about we tell Daddy about it, and he might come up to see you getting the award? It would have to be something that big to get him to set foot across the Mason-Dixon Line, but he'd do it for you. It would be nice to see him, wouldn't it?'

'It would, especially now. Sure, let him know, tell him we'd both love to see him.'

Richard and Sarah walked the next morning to the post office, the man there eyeing them greedily now that he knew they were 'Yanks' and had access to all sorts of goodies denied the locals.

'My missus loved those chocolates you gave me...' he said ingratiatingly.

'Good. It's a shame we don't have any more. Things are getting tough over there as well now,' Richard said, shutting him down before he could ask for another handout.

Sarah sent a message to their father, and he sent one to Pippa, just saying he was going to New York and would write from there. He should send one to Grace too, he knew, but he didn't because he didn't want to elicit another lecture from Sarah. He'd write from the States.

The flurry of organisation meant there was no time for conversations, but they managed to embark on the SS Valiant at Southampton at the appointed time. The ship had been full to capacity with troops and supplies coming over, but like the last time they went home, it was empty, and they had a very comfortable crossing. Richard worked on his novel and tried to relax. All he could think about was Grace, though. He wondered how she was getting on. Had she gotten her job and house back? One part of him hoped she had, but a small part of him was relieved her ties to Knocknashee were not as bound fast as they had once been.

To their delight, their father sent a car to pick them up from the port, and the driver had instructions to take the three of them to the St Regis, where he'd reserved three rooms. Jacob normally would have complained about the price and waste, but he had the good sense and manners to just accept the generosity. That night, they and their father had dinner in the elaborate dining room, with the impeccably clad waiters. They'd invited Kirky, who hadn't changed a bit.

'You know they have their finger on the pulse, right?' Sarah admonished the editor gently. 'You tell them not to write this or not to cover that, but the thing is, they get what people want to hear. Ordinary people don't care about troop movements or political speeches – they want to know about the common man or woman on the street. So you're much better off letting them write what they like. They have an instinct for it.'

Richard caught his father's eye and shared a secret smile. Sarah Lewis was no Southern belle, there to look pretty and not have an opinion. She had many opinions, most firmly held, and she'd argue the dickens out of any man, regardless of who he was.

Kirky was exactly as he had been when Richard last met him, still short and bald, with blue eyes and saggy skin on his face. He wore a crumpled suit that looked like he might have slept in it, and his large, soft body seemed to spill over the sides of his chair. He was a tough New Yorker with an accent to match. He sat next to Richard's father, and the contrast was undeniable. Arthur Lewis stood over six feet and was as hard and athletic now as he'd been when Richard was a child. He held himself ramrod straight and exuded confidence and money. He'd shaved off his moustache, which made him look a bit more approachable, Richard thought.

'I actually agree with you,' Kirky said, to their amazement. 'Richard here knows how to reach people. He has an instinct for what they want and gives it to them.' Then he nodded at Jacob. 'And you take the pictures.' He allowed a slight wink at Sarah, which made her laugh.

'You know perfectly well he's a genius. Would it kill you to say so?' she challenged.

'I pay him, don't I?' Kirky replied, helping himself to more French fries.

'I think all three of you are marvellous, and I've even started reading your Yankee rag, Mr Falkirk,' Arthur said, with a smile to bely his words. Sarah glowed under their father's praise.

'Kirky please. The last person to call me Mr Falkirk was Sister Josephine in the fourth grade when she pulled me up by the ears.' He wheezed when he laughed, and Richard thought the man might be the unhealthiest person he'd ever met. He smoked incessantly, drank in the office as well as after work and only ate fried food. He was smart as a whip and married to the long-suffering Lottie, who they'd heard about but never met. 'But yeah, my Yankee rag is doing quite well down in your neck of the woods. I guess war don't care if you're a Yankee or a redneck, huh?'

'I think you're right.' Arthur tucked into his Cobb salad. 'But I'm mighty proud of these young people doing what they're doing to bring the real story to us at home. Without the valuable work they do, I don't think we'd really have much of an understanding of why it's so necessary.'

Kirky shrugged, which Richard took to be agreement, as Jacob seethed.

'So this award, Kirky, tell me about it?' Arthur asked.

'It's the Bustemer Award for Journalistic Excellence in Foreign Affairs. They got it for the piece they did in Singapore, though how they managed to get their sorry asses captured by the Japanese when that part of the jungle they were in only had a handful of Japs remains a mystery. It would take these guys…' He rolled his eyes.

'Ah, Kirky, you were worried sick, admit it,' Sarah ribbed. 'You telegrammed me every day wondering if I'd heard from them, and when they turned up, you were very emotional, you know you were.'

'I was trying to figure out how to get them out of there – bad for the image to lose two staff. Besides, I'd just paid for his new camera. I wanted my money's worth.' He gave that wheezy laugh again.

The dinner went on in a happy vein, Sarah able to tease and admonish Kirky in a way Richard and Jacob wouldn't dare. He asked them in great detail about the events after the Fall of Singapore, and Richard and Jacob gave him plenty of information on other newspapermen in London, for which he had a voracious appetite. He knew absolutely everyone.

'So you guys are booked back on Saturday, right?' he said as he raised his hand for the check. Though Arthur had offered, Kirky insisted on paying.

'But you're coming to the awards ceremony?' Richard asked.

'Nah, I've got plans. Lottie wants to go to some thing in Brooklyn. I mean, I said to her, Lottie, I said, Brooklyn might as well be Bangladesh as far as I'm concerned. I hate to leave the island of Manhattan, but her girlfriend is in a play or some crap like that. It's gonna be torture, but I'm facing worse torture if I don't go, so…' He shrugged, resigned to this fate worse than death.

Richard found he was disappointed; he would have liked to have had Kirky there to see their work acknowledged. It was a very prestigious award, and he was proud not just of himself and Jacob but of Kirky for taking a chance on two kids with not much experience.

'About that…' Jacob began. Richard knew he and Sarah really wanted to spend some time in the States, maybe even get down to Savannah, see their old friends; it had been so long. 'We were wondering if we could extend the trip a bit…'

'What? Are you nuts? There's a war on, kid, if you didn't notice. I need you back there filing copy and taking pictures. As it is we're down a lot of stuff because of the travelling. No way. Back on that boat with you three the second this dumb shindig is over.'

'Well, come now, Kirky,' Arthur interjected. 'My children and Mr Nunez here have been working very hard for you and your newspaper, and I think a little vacation is justified. I know the war is still on, but who knows how long that's going to be the case, so I feel it's really time they took a break, don't you?'

Kirke signed for the food and stood, heaving his heavy body up. It was sweltering outside, and Kirky was sweating profusely. 'One week, that's it. Now try to stay out of trouble, OK?' He patted Sarah's shoulder as he walked away.

'Did we just get a week's vacation?' Jacob asked with a grin.

'We sure did.' Sarah was giddy with the excitement. 'Let's go home right away after the ceremony, what do you say, Richard? See Esme, and maybe go to the King and Prince one night, catch up with everyone...'

'I sure would love to have you home for a spell,' their father said. 'Y'all need feeding for a start. You've gotten so thin, Sarah. If you stood sideways and stuck out your tongue, you'd look like a zipper.' He laughed, and Richard noticed he'd slipped into his old Southern accent now that Kirky was gone.

'Now then, Mr Nunez, tell me about yourself, since we haven't met before?'

'Well, sir, I'm a Jewish communist who loves your daughter,' Jacob said, with a hint of belligerence. He was not going to grovel.

'Well, I'm only interested in the last part of that sentence, son. So long as you treat her right, we won't have a problem.' Arthur drained his glass of red wine.

'I certainly will, sir. We take care of each other, and Richard too,' Jacob answered, softening.

'I'm like their baby.' Richard chuckled as he wiped his mouth with the napkin and swallowed the last sip of beer in his glass.

'Well, I have a quick meeting to attend to since I'm here, so how about you young folks have some fun this evening and I'll see you all tomorrow?' Arthur said as they walked out of the restaurant. He had the doorman hail a cab.

'Are you happy to go home?' Sarah asked, linking Richard's arm as they crossed the lobby.

'Sure, sounds good.' He desperately wanted to get back, but he could see what this would mean to his sister. 'I'm sure looking forward to Esme's cooking and a little bit of heat.'

'We're going to head out to hear some music – you coming?' Jacob asked.

But Richard wanted to get back to his room, write to Grace and try to figure out his next move. 'No, I'm beat, I'm going to bed'

Sarah headed for the door. 'OK, Grandpa, catch you in the morning…'

'You go on, I'll catch up,' Jacob said, falling into step with Richard as he made for the elevator. 'I forgot my wallet in the bedroom.'

As they entered the gilded, mirrored space, Jacob shuffled from foot to foot, casting sidelong glances at Richard.

'What?' Richard asked. They knew each other so well now, they were tuned to each other.

Jacob reached into his pants pocket, pulled out a small box and flipped it open to reveal a diamond solitaire. 'I got it from my uncle's shop this morning. I'm going to propose to Sarah. I should probably have asked your old man for permission, but I thought that Sarah would hate that, like she was a possession or something, going from one man to another. She'll most likely turn me down I know, but I'm going to try. What do you think?'

Richard smiled. 'I think she'd be a very foolish girl if she did. But she might. Not because she doesn't love you, she does, but you know how she is about marriage and all of that. But I wish you luck, my friend.' He clapped him on the shoulder.

As he walked to his own room, he wondered what kind of engagement ring he would buy if he was proposing to Grace. Pippa had said she didn't want one; she wasn't able to wear it at work and she wasn't a big ring kind of girl.

He remembered Grace telling him ages ago in a letter about the

Claddagh ring, a special Irish ring with a crown and a heart being held up by a pair of hands, and how if you wore it one way, it meant you were spoken for, but if you wore it another way, you were 'on the lookout'.

A warm feeling washed over him. Only thoughts of Grace could do that.

Chapter 2

St Regis Hotel, New York, USA

August 19, 1942

Dear Grace,

Greetings from the Big Apple. I think you told me before why it's called that, but I forget. I'm here because Jacob and I are getting an award for journalism for the piece we did on the Fall of Singapore. It's all very exciting, and Sarah and Jacob have even managed to get an extra week's vacation out of Kirky, so we're going to the ceremony tomorrow night and then down to Savannah. She "flailed him to flitters," as you said once, which I remember because it's such a great phrase, as so many of your Irish phrases are. Anyway, she gave it to him hot and heavy about how we should not be directed, that we had an innate sense of what people want and how he should be much nicer to us. He won't be of course, he's sour by nature, but it was good to watch Sarah in full flight. She's as fearless as you are, blessed am I amongst women!

Our father came up to New York and went to bat for us to get some time off too, and eventually Kirky had to back down. I'm looking forward to seeing Esme and having some home-cooked Southern food. I guess I should go and see my mother, but to be honest, the thought doesn't fill me with delight. She'll probably just reject me again, and though I tell myself I don't care, I guess I do really. While I was in London, I could kind of switch that off, but now that I'm back, I guess I have to face her. Or maybe I don't. What would you do? She hasn't written or made any contact, and she's allowed my father to leave her rather than support us, though to be honest, her grievance is mostly with Sarah and Jacob. But still, I don't know. Go there and be a dutiful son to get another emotional kicking? Or don't bother? Any advice welcome.

Hey, guess what? Jacob is going to propose to Sarah. He just showed me the ring. His uncle is a jeweller here in NYC. It reminded me of the time you told me about Claddagh rings. He'd asked my father, who said "I wish you luck, but I don't think she'll go for it." She's no demure Southern belle, my sister, and being a happy little wife at home with babies and the help is never going to fly, but Jacob doesn't want her to be like that anyway. I hope she accepts, but like my father, I'm doubtful.

I'll be back in London in two weeks' time, so I'll write again then, or I might send you a postcard from Savannah—I think I've sent you a few over the years. I'd love for you to come and see my city. It's really beautiful and full of character and stories; I think you'd love it. I hope we can do that someday.

Did you get your job and house back now that the canon is gone? Write and tell me everything.

Lots of love,

Richard

He folded the letter and stamped and addressed it. He knew he should write to Pippa as well, but everything he'd say would sound like a lie. He couldn't tell her the truth about what he wanted, and he couldn't pretend everything was fine either. Maybe he'd send her a postcard from Savannah, a nice view of River Street or Forsyth Park or something.

He wrote a quick note to Esme to say he couldn't wait to see her; he hoped it would get there before they did.

The next day and a half flew by. Richard spent time with his father and told him about his life and his experiences in the Far East and a bit about Grace. They walked around Central Park, his father every inch the Southern gentleman, with cane, cashmere overcoat and trilby despite the heat, smelling of old leather, it was the most conversation they'd ever had.

'Sounds like you were lucky to get out alive. I'm sure glad you did, Richard. I know the times we live in and all of that, but can you please try to be more careful?' his father pleaded. 'I was out of my mind with worry. I telegrammed Sarah every day for news.'

Richard smiled, unused to this new version of his father. 'She said.'

'I think I was driving her crazy, but I…' He paused. 'Look, son, I know I haven't been the most…well…hell, I don't know what the word is, but not the best kind of father for you children. I should have been there more. I should have communicated more when I was at home, but I guess I just didn't know how to. Children, where I came from, were women's work – men provided and women nurtured. But your mother is not the nurturing kind, we both know that. I should have stepped up, but I didn't, and I want to apologise.'

'There's no need –'

His father held up his hand for silence. 'There is. I failed, and maybe I can't ever make it up to you at this late stage, but I'd like to try.' He stopped then and faced Richard.

'You don't need to try, it's happened already.' Emotion made his voice crack.

His father just nodded, but Richard could see he was choked up. That little speech would have been hard for him.

Pulling himself together, Arthur changed the subject. 'So you reckon our Sarah is going to marry Nunez? 'Cause I sure don't.'

Richard didn't think he knew of the impending proposal but he was astute so nothing would surprise him about his father.

'I don't know, probably not. But not because she doesn't love him – she really does and he loves her. They are a great team, and I think they'd go the distance actually. But she's against the way marriage ties women down, and maybe she got it from Mama, but she hasn't a maternal bone in her body.'

Arthur shook his head and chuckled. 'She's something, isn't she?'

Richard smiled. 'She sure is.'

In the afternoon he gave Sarah some time alone with their father while he paid a surprise visit to Mrs McHale, who he took for a drink at the sports bar Toots Shor's. He thought the St Regis or somewhere fancy would have been more to her taste, but she said she was dying to go to the bar across from Radio City Music Hall, where all the celebrities were known to frequent. She needed a young man to take her because it wouldn't be the done thing for an old lady to go to a sports bar alone.

They had a wonderful two hours. He told her all about Grace and the canon, and she'd clapped and hooted with delight when he told her of his final denouement. She was a hoot. She drank gin and tonic and was ecstatic when she saw Joe DiMaggio deep in conversation with some other men. Richard loved baseball and missed it since he'd been away, so he shared her enthusiasm but did dissuade her from approaching him.

He invited her to attend the awards ceremony, and she accepted as if he'd offered her the crown jewels. His father would probably not thank him for having to escort an old Catholic lady, but he'd get over it.

When he got back from his outing with Mrs McHale, it was time to dress. He'd had a rented black tux delivered to the hotel – he had no need of evening wear in this new life. After dressing, he met Sarah, who was wearing a midnight-blue silk trouser suit with a men's shaped jacket and heels that looked like she would break her ankle if she walked even a step. She'd had her hair done, which was so badly needed, and wore a little make-up. She was really very pretty, he thought, but he didn't tell her because she would not react well to such a remark and would ask him if that was all men thought about when they saw a woman, was she pretty or not. It was safer not to bother.

She whistled when she saw him. 'Looking sharp, little brother,' she said as she gave him a nudge.

'You clean up well yourself.'

'I do, don't I?' She winked. 'Daddy is in the bar. He's ordered cocktails, so let's go in. Jacob is still getting ready.'

'In his own room?' Richard murmured, with a wink.

'If he had his way, he'd sublet his bedroom and give the money to the communists, but yes, for the purposes of getting dressed, he's in his own room.' Sarah shot him a wicked grin. Richard knew there was no way they were going to be separated.

She wore nothing on her left hand, so he assumed either Jacob had proposed and she'd turned him down or he'd not asked her yet.

Their father was reading the paper in a corner of the bar, with a bottle of Taittinger on ice and three glasses beside him. He put it down as they entered.

People here grumbled about the war, how certain things were now hard to get and how labour was in short supply as so many men had joined the forces, but Richard knew they had no real concept of it. He hoped it never came to it, that American cities, like London, would be flattened by bombs, citizens hungry, bereaved, maimed, medical supplies perfunctory at best. He realised he'd been changed fundamentally, that the war-hardened man who came back was not the wealthy entitled boy who left.

'Well, well, well, don't you two look as fine as a frog's hair split four ways?' Arthur grinned as he poured them a drink. 'Now, I want to raise a toast to you both and say how proud I am of you. I wish Nathan was here – I called him, but he's deep in training army medics so can't be spared. I'm very proud of my children.'

'Thanks, Daddy. I'm so happy to be home again, even if just for a while. We love London, and it's good to feel like we're doing something worthwhile, but it sure is nice to be home too.'

Arthur waggled his finger and looked at her in mock disapproval. 'This is New York, Sarah Elizabeth Frances Lewis. This is not home.'

'Well, back in the United States then and going home tomorrow. Though the rail journey isn't what I'm looking forward to...'

'Well, funny you should say that, because today I went and bought myself a little toy.' Arthur sat back with a self-satisfied smirk.

'What kind of toy?' Richard took a sip of the cold champagne.

'Well, over the last few months, I've been taking flying lessons. I passed the test for my pilot's licence three weeks ago, and today I bought an Aeronca five-seater touring aircraft, so if you'll risk it, I'll fly us home tomorrow.'

Something about the enthusiasm, the boyishness of his father, touched Richard. He'd wanted to surprise them, and he had.

'I'm in,' Richard said. 'If you say you can fly, I believe you.' He meant it. His father did nothing by half measures.

'I've never been in a plane in my life,' Sarah said. 'I'll be terrified, but I trust you, Daddy.'

'Well, that's two votes of confidence.' Their father grinned again, topping up their glasses.

'Aren't you having one?' Richard asked.

'No, I'll be keeping all my wits about me for tomorrow.' As he spoke, Jacob appeared in a tuxedo. He looked very handsome, his chestnut hair oiled back, his green eyes shining. Arthur poured him a glass as Richard and Sarah teased him playfully and told him about the plan to fly.

'Amazing, I'd love it, thanks,' Jacob said, accepting a glass.

The bar was almost empty – it was early yet. And as Richard settled deeper into his seat he saw, to his surprise, Jacob get down on one knee. Was he going to do it now?

Sarah looked confused then shocked as he opened the box and showed her the ring.

'I know I should pick someplace more romantic, and probably we should be alone, but I can't wait another second. This box is burning a hole in my pocket. Sarah, if I promise that you'll never have to do anything I say, that I will never want a baby, or drapes and comforters in matching chintz, or a house to put them in come to that, that I'll never say "my wife does that" about any domestic chore, that I won't expect you to change your name or anything else about your perfect, lovely, beautiful, kind, brave, strong, terrifying self, would you please, please, please marry me?'

Richard and his father shared a smile. It was a genuine plea, and they were both rooting for him.

'But why? We never talked about –' Sarah began.

'Because if I die, or if you die, I want to be your next of kin and I want you to be mine. I love you, Sarah, you know that. You are perfect in every way. And I know you think marriage is outdated and only a method of enslaving women and taking their rights away, but if I swear here in front of your brother and father that I would never dare even think about doing that, will you please let me be your husband? Hell…I'll change my name to Jacob Lewis to prove it if you want. You can wear the pants, I promise.' He laughed then. It was a running joke since some man told Jacob that he should put his foot down about his wife smoking and drinking and wearing trousers. Jacob had said he would, just as soon as he'd done the ironing.

Sarah thought for a moment and then looked down at Jacob Nunez, the great love of her life, on his knees before her. 'OK, but I'm going to make you stick to every one of those promises, and if you even try…' She was beaming, though, and her eyes were bright with tears.

Jacob slipped the ring on her finger and stood, took her in his arms and kissed her. Richard and his father clapped, and the barman sent another bottle of champagne to their table.

Chapter 3

Cork City, County Cork, Ireland

August 1942

Grace looked around the cavernous church as everyone gathered for Mass. The walk to the front door had been a wet one. It felt like it would never stop raining, despite it being summer, but she was determined to be here, to hear Father Iggy celebrate Mass. School wasn't back for another two weeks so she was visiting the Warringtons, mainly to reassure them that she was alright after everything that had happened.

Hugh and Lizzie had invited Father Iggy to share in their Sunday dinner, which was so kind of them. People always assumed priests were inundated with invitations, but Father Iggy had let slip the day before yesterday when they had tea that he would be alone in the parochial house once he'd said the noon Mass.

Another of the priests was on call, but his sister lived close by so he'd be at her house and everyone knew where to find him in the case of an emergency, and the other two priests in the parish were going home to their families out in the countryside somewhere.

Father Iggy had family, but they were up the country, so once Grace knew he'd be alone, she asked Lizzie if they wouldn't mind inviting him, and of course they obliged.

She'd always enjoyed the Saturday evening Mass. The canon had put a stop to it in Knocknashee, claiming people came after the pub and it was blasphemous, but that wasn't true, not really – it was more that he didn't like to leave his warm fire and his bottle of brandy. Poor Father Lehane was run off his feet since the canon was arrested as no replacement had yet been sent, so nobody liked to ask him to do more than he was doing already.

As Father Iggy came onto the altar in his brightly coloured vestments, Grace felt a wave of affection for the small chubby priest with the jam-jar-thick glasses. They had an unlikely friendship, she supposed, but friends they were, and she knew he valued her highly.

To his left, an enormous beautiful flower arrangement had been placed on the altar, the sweet aroma filling the church and mingling with the fragrance of the incense and beeswax. The smell brought her back to earlier years, and she felt a pang of sadness. When she was a little girl, her mother would always take her shopping on the first of October, the feast of St Thérèse of Lisieux, known to everyone as the Little Flower, to whom her mother had great devotion. Part of their day out, which always involved getting tea and a cream bun in the Imperial Hotel, was to visit the Holy Cross Priory, the Church of the Immaculate Conception and finally St John's, to say a prayer to the saint. They would light a candle at each one for Mamó and Daidó, her grandparents – most churches had a special altar to St Thérèse set up – and it was a lovely time.

She thought she would light some candles after Mass; there were so many souls for her to pray for now, so many people she had lost.

The choir sang 'Veni Creator Spiritus', and though the Mass was in Latin and Father Iggy had his back turned to the congregation, there was a beautiful sense of peace and community. The church was filled to capacity, mostly adults as the children were tucked up in bed. People here looked hungry and cold, even more so than in Knocknashee. She knew from personal experience and from the children in school how everything was hard to come by now as the war dragged on and on and on. Even the basic requirements for living were stretched to the breaking point, and luxuries were really a thing of the past. Parents in Knocknashee tried their hardest with little in the way of resources, but up here it was a different story. This was a poor parish, and before the Emergency ever happened, things were tight, but now hunger and cold and lack of access to medicine or even proper sanitation was a real issue. Father Iggy did his best, but the parish wasn't in much of a position to help. She knew it broke his heart to see the people hungry, children especially, but there was little he could do.

He intoned the words of the familiar Tridentine Mass, and soon it was over. The choir sang 'Tantum Ergo', and everyone filed out into the dark, still night. The sky was cloudless now that the rain had finally stopped, and the stars twinkled overhead. Hugh had said he would drive over to collect her; he was working late in the hospital, so he would be out anyway. She waited for him on the steps of the church as the crowd dispersed.

As the congregation thinned, she heard Father Iggy's voice behind her. 'Warm enough for you, Grace?' He grinned, and she saw his black clerical coat was thin and frayed and his shoes were the worse for wear too. 'God never got the reminder that it's supposed to be summer in Ireland.'

'It could be warmer but it's lovely. Aren't the stars so bright tonight?' She looked up. 'That was a beautiful Mass, Father.'

'Well, if you wouldn't have bright stars at the moment, when could you have them? God knows we need cheering up.' He gazed upwards beside her.

'Come hungry tomorrow.' Grace smiled as she turned to him. 'Lizzie is cooking like she's feeding fifty, not four.'

'Indeed I will, but where is she getting it, or should I not ask?' Father Iggy chuckled. 'People are saying stuff can't be got for love nor money.'

'Well, one grateful parent keeps chickens, and so one of them... Well, less said about it, the better.' She laughed. 'And another of the parents of one of the children in the hospital sent a big ham – they keep pigs apparently – and Lizzie and Hugh just got an allotment, so she's forever growing things from seeds, and Tilly sent up some stuff with me. So there'll be a fine feast for us tomorrow.'

'Are you sure I'm not imposing, Grace? I'm fearful I am.' His brow furrowed.

'Not in the slightest, we are delighted to have you. Please, Lizzie is really looking forward to it and so am I. We'll have a lovely day. There'll be music on the wireless and a roaring fire despite it being August, and wait till you smell the apple crumble – my mouth is watering at the thought.' Grace groaned as the rain started again.

'Will we step in? At least we won't get soaked inside,' he suggested with a rueful smile. 'We can see out the window if Hugh comes.'

'Good idea, but you don't need to wait with me, Father. I'm sure you've other things to do.'

'Grace, having you come to Cork is the nicest thing to happen for a long time, so of course I'm not going to let you stand outside in the rain on your own.'

They stood into the porch and watched the rain coming down in sheets.

'Do you like it here?' she asked.

He paused before answering. 'It's not really a matter of liking it or not liking it. We go where we're sent, and we do the best we can.'

Something about his demeanour worried her. He seemed to have lost his sparkle or something. In Knocknashee he was always jolly and cheerful, always ready with a kind word or a trick or a joke for the children; here, he seemed to be more serious or something.

They had a close bond from the time he'd spent in her parish, so she felt she could ask. 'Is something in particular bothering you, though? You seem a bit…I don't know…sad?'

He looked down at his shoes, sighed and plunged his hands in his trouser pockets. She knew priests were supposed to be removed from their flock; they were not really allowed to have normal human feelings.

'You can tell me, if it would help, and I promise it won't go any further,' she said softly.

'Oh, Grace…' He sighed. 'I…I shouldn't complain. I've it much easier than so many others have, but…'

'But what?' she asked, but before he could answer, Hugh's car drew up outside.

'Ara, I'm fine. Don't mind me and my moaning, big pity about me.'

On impulse she reached over and hugged him. He wasn't much taller than her and she was tiny, but he was twice as wide as she was. To her surprise, he hugged her back. She smiled at him and went out to Hugh.

If you would like to preorder this book and have it delivered on publication day just click:

Folded Corners - The Knocknashee Story - Book 5

If you would like to join my readers club, just pop over to www.jeangrainger.com and sign up. It's 100% free and always will be and I'll send you free ebook as a welcome gift.

GLOSSARY

An fear marbh – the dead man

Naomhóg – a small canoe like boat

A stór – my love

A leanbh – dear child

Sliotar – a small ball made of leather used in the national sport of hurling.

Cuiosach – alright – but only just alright – (some words are hard to translate!)

A pheata – my pet

Subh – jam

Druid – the pagan doctor/wise man

Gardai – Irish police force

Sutha talún – strawberries

Beal scoilte – literally means mouth escaping – but means indiscreet or gossipy

Cailín – girl

A chroi – my heart _an endearment

Garsún – young lad

Tory tops – pine cones

Aoife – pron. EE-fah

Cigire – the inspector (usually a school inpector)
'An bhfuil fonn snaimhe oiribh? – have ye an interest in swimming?
aghaidh linn – off we go
A Mhuire mathair – Mary our mother – an Irish hymn
Seámus – shay-muss (Irish version of James)
Rabhán – sea thrift - a pink hardy flower found on the coast
Poitín – in illegal alcoholic spirit made from potatoes

ABOUT THE AUTHOR

Jean Grainger is a USA Today bestselling Irish author. She writes historical and contemporary Irish fiction and her work has very flatteringly been compared to the late great Maeve Binchy.

She lives in a stone cottage in Cork with her lovely husband Diarmuid and the youngest two of her four children. The older two come home for a break when adulting gets too exhausting. There are a variety of animals there too, all led by two cute but clueless microdogs called Scrappy and Scoobi.

ALSO BY JEAN GRAINGER

The Tour Series

The Tour

Safe at the Edge of the World

The Story of Grenville King

The Homecoming of Bubbles O'Leary

Finding Billie Romano

Kayla's Trick

The Carmel Sheehan Story

Letters of Freedom

The Future's Not Ours To See

What Will Be

The Robinswood Story

What Once Was True

Return To Robinswood

Trials and Tribulations

The Star and the Shamrock Series

The Star and the Shamrock

The Emerald Horizon

The Hard Way Home

The World Starts Anew

The Queenstown Series

Last Port of Call

The West's Awake

The Harp and the Rose

Roaring Liberty

Standalone Books

So Much Owed

Shadow of a Century

Under Heaven's Shining Stars

Catriona's War

Sisters of the Southern Cross

The Kilteegan Bridge Series

The Trouble with Secrets

What Divides Us

More Harm Than Good

When Irish Eyes Are Lying

A Silent Understanding

The Mags Munroe Story

The Existential Worries of Mags Munroe

Growing Wild in the Shade

Each to their Own

Closer Than You Think

Chance your Arm

The Aisling Series

For All The World

A Beautiful Ferocity

Rivers of Wrath

The Gem of Ireland's Crown

The Knocknashee Series

Lilac Ink

Yesterday's Paper

History's Pages

www.ingramcontent.com/pod-product-compliance
Lightning Source LLC
Chambersburg PA
CBHW030355310726
48979CB00001B/316

* 9 7 8 1 9 1 7 7 3 2 0 3 1 *